Eva's Promise

Risen Halo Publishing
Eva's Promise

Author's Note: This is a work of fiction. Names, characters, places, and incidents are a product of the author's imagination. Locales and public names are sometimes used for atmospheric purposes. Any resemblance to actual people, living or dead, businesses, companies, events, institutions, or locales is completely coincidental.

Eva's Promise/ M. L. Bull
ISBN: 978-1-7333248-2-3 (Paperback), 978-1-7333248-3-0 (Hardback), 978-1-7333248-4-7 (E-book)

Cover Designed by M.L. Bull
Cover Image from istockphotos.com
Keychain of back cover design handcrafted by Regina Boger, owner of small business Regina Lynn Design in Fort Wayne, IN.
Edited by M. L. Bull and HugeOrange from Ephrata, PA
Printed in the United States of America

DEDICATION

For Family & Friends

Eva's Promise

M. L. BULL

EPIGRAPH

"Charity suffereth long, and is kind; charity envieth not; charity vaunteth not itself, is not puffed up, doth not behave itself unseemly, seeketh not her own, is not easily provoked, thinketh no evil; rejoiceth not in iniquity, but rejoiceth in truth; beareth all things, believeth all things, hopeth all things, endureth all things."

1 Corinthians 13: 4-7

. PROLOGUE .

Twenty-six-year-old Eva Rose Conway braced herself for the new beginning of her life. It was a cool afternoon, feeling more like early October instead of late August. Bright green oak leaves rattled the gentle breeze, suitable to the present ceremony. She drew a deep breath and exchanged glances with her fiancé's grandfather, holding a colorful flower bouquet tied with a blue ribbon.

Her bouquet stuck out of the white rose scenery like a sore thumb, but it was all she could get before the outdoor wedding. Grandpa Ricardo Felipe Morales was the only father Eva had, never knowing her biological father in Rome. He gave her a lopsided grin, wearing his gray cowboy hat, which matched his thick, western mustache, double-breast suit, and leather boots.

"You look beautiful," he whispered as the hired male pianist played "Canon in D" by Pachelbel.

Eva smiled shyly. "Thank you, Papa." Growing up, she had been self-conscious of her appearance, worried her peers would notice something misplaced. Or worse, not notice her at all. But today differed from her high school days. As all eyes set upon her, Eva realized she was the guest of honor—and for good reason.

Her wedding dress was a white silk bodice and flowing skirt, sewn with lace embroidery, sheer-and-lace sleeves, and pearl buttons. Her raven-black hair with wavy end curls rested on her shoulders, draped with a hair net veil.

Grandpa Ricardo held her arm and sauntered with her down the mossy lawn aisle scattered with white rose petals. Emily Witherspoon—her daycare student—was her flower girl.

Before Eva's big reveal, she overheard the oohs and ahhs of the guests seated on the black folding chairs. She presumed the little girl had captivated them with her big, blue eyes and angelic smile as she walked the aisle with her mother.

Eva gave a timid wave to a few attendees and co-workers from her job. She locked eyes with her husband-to-be at the decorated altar. He looked so handsome, strong, and confident, towering over the shorter, bald Pastor Joe Tyson. He smiled and watched her every step as she approached him. Her fiancé—Andre Lucas—wore a navy-blue tuxedo with black lapels, a white dress shirt, a navy-blue bow tie, black pants, and navy-blue Stacy Adams.

Though he was a skinny kid of a measly five-foot-four, he had changed much after puberty. Now he was a six -foot, one hundred and eighty-five pounds muscular giant. His small haircut of lustrous black curls glistened in the sun, his reddish-brown eyes glinting with tears.

For eight years they waited to marry.

They got engaged right after high school, but Pastor Tyson advised they hold off tying the knot until after finishing college. Eva and Andre agreed, but it wasn't easy. They struggled to keep focus on their studies instead of each other, making small talk on campus whenever they traced each other's paths. Eva finished her education first. As advised by her mother, she earned her associate degree in Early Childhood Ed, deserting the ambition of her true passion.

Though she enjoyed working with kids, sometimes within she kicked herself. But in a single-parent, low-income home, it always seemed her mom knew best. It took longer for Andre to earn his degree, majoring to become a veterinarian. But when he crossed the graduation stage and received his Doctorate in Veterinary Medicine, the gaze he and Eva shared said it all.

Their long wait was finally over.

Eva stood beside Andre and handed her bridal bouquet to her mother, who acted as her maid of honor. She lifted her face to her fiancé, her married name echoing in her mind. *Mrs. Lucas . . . Mrs. Eva Lucas.* Her last name would take getting used to; she'd been a Conway since the day she was born.

Goosebumps rose on her smooth olive skin, her heart

thumping anxiously in her chest. She released a slow exhale and felt her pulse relax as they held hands, but it appeared her fiancé was more of a bundle of nerves than herself.

Andre's forehead beaded with sweat, and his hands were moist and cold as ice. He dropped his shoulders as the soft piano music ended.

Pastor Tyson cleared his throat. "Dearly beloved, we're gathered here today in the sight of God to join this man and woman in holy matrimony. Who gives this woman to join to his man?" He glanced around the outside assembly.

"I do," her mom said, sniffling with a hankie.

Eva glanced at her mother with teary eyes and whispered, "Thanks, Mom."

Her mother having a tight rein on her, she knew witnessing her only child leave the nest formed a pit of loneliness. Ever since her mom was a teenager, she had been under her mother's wings and kept her company after her parents' long-distance breakup.

She faced the pastor as he inquired about her fiancé's consent to their wedding vows.

"I do," Andre said, gazing into her eyes.

The pastor turned toward Eva. "And do you, Eva Rose Conway, take Andre to be your lawfully wedded husband and live together in the estate of holy matrimony? Do you also promise to love, comfort, honor, and keep him, in sickness and in health, for richer or poorer; for better or worse . . . as long as you both shall live?"

"I do." Eva wore a dreamy smile.

Pastor Tyson grinned. He opened his bible to a page he bookmarked with his forefinger. "As stated in Mark chapter ten verse nine, 'What God hath joined together, let not man put asunder.' By the power vested in me, I now pronounce you husband and wife. You may kiss the bride."

Andre and Eva faced each other with nervous expressions, hoping they don't embarrass themselves in front of everybody. Neither of them had dated or kissed before—not even while engaged. Now that they could was both scary and alluring. Being six inches taller than her, Andre bent his back to reach her. He gulped and closed his eyes.

"I love you, Eva Rose," Andre whispered, leaning his forehead against hers.

"I love you too, Andre," Eva whispered back.

She closed her eyes and felt Andre's lips touch hers for the first time.

Regardless of the celebrative whistles and applause, to them, time had stopped. They were in their own palace, taken away to a faraway land. They had to exit, but they hated for their first kiss to end.

Pastor Tyson cleared his throat, giving them a cue.

Eva and Andre broke their smooch and blushed.

"Oh, sorry," Andre said with a chuckle, "I guess we got

carried away there." He shrugged and wore a wry grin.

Eva giggled. She brushed a wisp of her dark hair from her face and embraced Andre's bicep.

They faced the gathering and waved at them, strolling the aisle as the people congratulated them. Their wedding was the start of a lifetime of adventures. While the pages in their book of marriage filled with memories, there would also be hardships along the way.

Life was unpredictable, a journey down a bumpy road of many twists and turns. But no matter what tests their future held, Eva would keep her word and believed Andre would do the same.

As the crowd followed them to the limo, she looked above at the partly cloudy sky.

She prayed their marriage would survive.

• CHAPTER 1 •

Andre

Seven Years Later

Thirty-four-year-old Dr. Andre Lucas glanced at the wall clock in his clinic every two minutes. He hoped he'd finish treating his animal patients in time to meet his wife at The Redfish Grill, their favorite restaurant. Eva hated him being late for special occasions, and this year he wanted their wedding anniversary to be a moment neither of them would forget.

As he was in previous years, today he aimed to leave work earlier. Besides, after not being there during Eva's agony of childbirth, he owed it to her—big-time. He rushed into the hospital from the showering rain, worried sick about her and their child's health and well-being. Heavy bleeding and shortness of breath were major concerns. Her physician diagnosed her with amniotic fluid embolism, a rare pregnancy complication. During her contractions, amniotic fluid entered her bloodstream, causing a life-threatening reaction. With only minutes to spare, doctors and nurses worked promptly to save his wife's life and the baby. Thankfully, the delivery worked out, and a year and four months ago, she bore him one incredible, little boy.

Andrew was an angel, always smiling and ready to give a hug to anyone. Their son was one of the best things he'd ever received, and he made it his mission to be the father he'd never had. His father—Derek Lucas, was African American, and his mother—Marie Morales, was Latina. But sometimes he wondered if they adopted him. He acted so much different from them.

His parents were drug addicts and shared a toxic relationship, which resulted in heated arguments and petty apologies. When he was five, his grandfather took custody of him, moving him from Philadelphia to his corn and livestock farm in Garden Ridge, North Carolina. Grandpa Ricardo told him he and Andre's mom were from a northwestern Mexican city called Chihuahua, like the small dog.

Andre and Eva visited the place for their honeymoon, but he wasn't thrilled about boarding a plane. Since he was a little boy, he had a fear of flying. His wife held his sweaty hand the whole two-hour flight there, comforting him when they flew against turbulence. It was easier for

Eva though, who had flown with her mother to Garden Ridge from Seattle, Washington at the start of their freshmen year of high school.

This was when they met and became friends.

But their love hadn't happened instantly, at least, not for Eva. For a while, she had been drawn to a stellar point guard of the basketball team. His name was Caleb Williams, an attractive jock who was one of the most popular boys of Garden Ridge High School.

It wasn't until their senior year Andre told her how he felt about her. Neither with a date to the prom, they watched *The Grapes of Wrath*, played rounds of UNO, and ate dinner with his grandfather. Outside on the porch that night, Andre had talked to Eva about building a relationship with Jesus Christ.

He'd also told her she shouldn't feel like she had to be popular to be important because she already meant an awful lot to God and him. His kind words had made her cry, overwhelmed since ninth grade, the *one* guy who accepted her was under her nose the entire time.

Andre shuffled a stack of patient records, placed them in his folder, and put the folder into his leather briefcase. He glanced at the ticking wall clock above the wooden cabinets again. *Tick-tock . . .tick-tock . . . tick-tock . . .* It was six-thirty in the evening, and this morning at breakfast he said he'd meet Eva no later than seven tonight. He fastened the latches of his briefcase and toted it along his side, hustling toward the exit door.

A small knock on the front door froze him.

Andre sighed and glanced over his shoulder at the entrance. *Oh, no. Not again.* He flared his nostrils and opened the door. "Yes?" His tone was flat and weary.

"I'm sorry, Dr. Lucas," Mrs. Witherspoon said with an embarrassed look, holding her two-year-old son Tyler on her hip. "Emily wouldn't stop crying until I brought her here again."

Andre gritted his teeth and scratched his temple. With Eva on his case about managing his time and working late, he wasn't in the mood for a last-minute checkup. He looked at the nine-year-old girl in a lavender T-shirt and jean jumper dress, standing in front of her mother. Except for her two ponytails and bulky eyeglasses, Emily was the spitting image of her mom.

He imagined her in her puffy, flower girl dress and white rose crown when she was two and couldn't help but smile. In her arms, she cradled Halo—an orange, seven-weeks-old tabby kitten.

Emily raised her head, her rosy cheeks stained with fresh tears. After three times in a row, Andre understood her obsessed checkups. Her former cat Mittens died in a roadkill accident.

Since she was six, Mittens was Emily's best friend, and her death to a taxi broke the little girl's heart for weeks. Recently, her mom bought her a new kitten for acing her fourth-grade spelling test in school. Emily named it Halo because the fur on top of the kitten's head glows in the sunlight.

Andre thought the name suited the endearing little tiger, and being as sensitive about animals as she was, he couldn't turn the child away. At the same time, he wanted to relieve Emily of her anxiety and save her the trouble of making unnecessary doctor visits.

Emily sniffled. "Dr. Lucas, Halo is sick."

Andre angled his head and sighed. "Okay. Bring him to my exam table."

Emily and her mom entered the air-conditioned office.

"Thanks for letting us in, doctor." Mrs. Witherspoon sat in a chair and adjusted her sleepy toddler son from her hip to her lap. Her daughter Emily placed her kitten on the exam table in the center of the small room.

Andre released the heavy door and let it close itself. "So, what's the problem?" He walked over to the feline and stood across the table from Emily.

"Umm . . ." Emily nibbled her lip, trying to think of another excuse.

"How about I give Halo a complete exam?" Andre glanced at her mother, and they shared an amused smile, each knowing there was more than likely nothing wrong with Halo again. But if it would ease a little girl's nerves and help her feel better, Andre figured another checkup before his next annual couldn't hurt.

Emily's face brightened. "Okay."

Andre stroked Halo's head and the back of his fur coat, inspecting for fleas. "Hey, Halo. It's nice to see you again. Your coat looks clean and beautiful. Do you mind if I check your eyes and ears, buddy?" He opened a side drawer of his counter behind him and pulled out his exam instruments.

Emily watched as Andre checked Halo's eyes and ears.

Halo meowed when Andre removed an otoscope from his right ear.

"Looks like his eyes and ears are healthy," Andre said. "No retinal damage, and no ear mites or signs of infection."

"What about his heartbeat, Dr. Lucas?" Emily asked.

Andre smiled. "All right, let me have a listen here." He unclipped his stethoscope from his hip holder and plugged the earpieces in his ears. Andre held the metal diaphragm over Halo's chest, listening to the kitten's heart and lungs. "Halo's heart sounds like a steady beating drum. And I heard no sign of congestion." He linked the earpieces around his neck.

"That's good," Mrs. Witherspoon said. "Emily complained about Halo's breathing before at home. I caught her sleeping by his kennel in the kitchen yesterday morning."

"Hmmm . . ." Andre arched his brow and snapped on

latex gloves. "Well, let's check Halo's mouth, shall we?"

"Okay," Emily said with a half-shrug.

Andre opened Halo's mouth and examined the kitten's tiny white teeth, tongue, and tonsils. "Nope. No signs of cleft palates or inflammation. Everything looks good."

Halo meowed again as Andre picked up the squirmy critter and felt around the kitten's abdomen. "No signs of umbilical hernia. I guess there's one thing left to check." Andre put Halo on the table, raised his tail, and coated the kitten's rectum with Vaseline. Finally, he inserted a baby thermometer to check Halo's temperature.

The thermometer chirped.

Andre removed it from Halo and read the digital degrees. "His temperature is . . . a hundred and one point five, which is normal for kittens—unlike humans. Halo's healthy as a horse and caught up with his vaccinations according to my records. No worries here."

"I told her, doctor." Mrs. Witherspoon wrapped a lock of her straight, blonde hair behind an ear and rocked Tyler in her arms.

"Here, you go." Andre smiled and handed Halo back to the little girl, who held him in her arms.

"Thank you, Dr. Lucas." Emily grinned hard, revealing her missing front tooth. She scratched her fingers behind Halo's pointed ears, making him purr.

"You're welcome, sweetheart," Andre replied, smiling, "but try not to worry yourself. Sometimes we can think something is wrong to the point we expect to find something. I know you're scared something bad will happen to Halo. But if you take good care of your kitten—which you clearly have been doing—Halo should be fine, okay?"

Emily nodded and wiggled her glasses up her nose. "Yes, Dr. Lucas."

Her mom stood with Tyler in her arms, who was still fast asleep, sucking his thumb. She smiled and held out a hand. "Thank you, Dr. Lucas, for your patience."

Andre grinned and shook her hand. "No, problem, Mrs. Witherspoon."

Mrs. Witherspoon watched Emily walk a distance away toward the entrance door and whispered, "I'm sorry we bothered you. I know you have special plans tonight."

Andre waved a hand and smiled. "That's okay. I understand Emily well. I was close to animals as a kid too. It's why I became a veterinarian."

"You know," Mrs. Witherspoon said, "it's her dad. He gave her Mittens on her sixth birthday, and she misses him, but she isn't alone. I can't wait until Neal can visit home. Every day I hope and pray he's safe." She sighed wistfully. "You're lucky to have the one you love close to home."

"No, Mrs. Witherspoon . . . I'm blessed," Andre corrected. "I hope everything goes well with Neal's visit."

"Thank you," Mrs. Witherspoon said, smiling, "and happy anniversary to you and Eva."

Andre's expression glowed. "Thanks. Have a good evening."

"You too." Mrs. Witherspoon turned her attention to her daughter. "Let's go, Emily. I need to get groceries at the store." She walked toward Emily and exited the office.

Andre pulled his cell phone out of his lab coat pocket. He dialed the number of the flower shop he ordered roses from for Eva. They were to arrive at their home in the afternoon, and he hoped his wife didn't go shopping or anywhere else after leaving work at the daycare. It would be terrible if the flowers got stolen.

They cost fifty bucks.

Someone answered his call.

"Hello, my name is Andre Lucas. I ordered a bouquet of white roses to one-forty-three Pasture Road. Have they delivered? . . . They have? . . . Great, thank you."

Andre ended the call and glanced at the ceiling. "God, please let Eva get them. I work so hard for my money." He checked the wall clock for one last time.

6:38 p.m.

Meeting deadlines had always been a struggle for him, especially when it came to spending private time with his wife. Somehow, he had to keep his promise. He needed to prove to Eva he meant those vows to love, comfort, and honor her always, and he had faith in God's sovereign power of wondrous miracles.

Anything was possible to those that believed, even if one doesn't know how the result will turn out. Andre grabbed his briefcase and rushed out of his office, striving to fulfill his wife's expectations.

Not showing up could break Eva's heart forever.

• CHAPTER 2 •

Eva

Same Evening

Thirty-three-year-old Eva Lucas sniffed the fresh-cut, white roses in the vase and placed them on the dresser in their bedroom. A gentle smile inched up her face and traveled to the deep walls of her heart as she read the small, greeting card:

Whether near or apart, you'll be the only girl who holds the key to my heart. Happy Anniversary to the most beautiful woman I know!

Love you forever,
Andre

Her husband was always sweet and kind to her since they first met in high school. She could still picture the teenaged boy he was. Buried in a gray, oversized, 76ers sweatshirt with knee-grass-stained, denim jeans, he helped her open her locker. After she moved from Seattle, being a new, shy student in a different school was difficult. But meeting Andre on her way to Mrs. Chapman's ninth-grade English class was one of the best times of her life. Since then, it began a friendship that grew stronger each summer vacation they had spent together.

They shared many similarities the more they knew each other. They both were biracial, caught in the middle of failed relationships, and moved away from the city to North Carolina. She didn't know he did chores early in the morning on a farm before school. But based on his clothes, she presumed he was careless of his appearance or wore his older brothers' hand-me-downs.

When her mother Melanie was seventeen, she met Andrew Martello, a young, Italian landscape artist during a college summer trip to Rome. Their relationship started through their artwork, but they quickly fell in love with each other. Holding strong traditions, Andrew's mama disapproved of him getting involved with a black woman.

After the breakup, her mom returned to the States a broke, pregnant art student who had no clue where neither she nor her baby's life was going. Eva grew up living on welfare, but her mother's skilled hand and artistic talent also helped them through poverty. Eva walked over to the front of the queen-sized bed, wrapped in her lilac, downy robe. Piles of fashionable dresses on hangers lay across, covering the bed's comforter. Although Eva was a shopaholic, tonight finding the right outfit was like trying to pull a stubborn tooth. She tucked her left forearm under her right elbow and nibbled her index fingernail, scanning her row of best outfits.

"Hmm . . ." Eva shifted her eyes from her black, maxi dress to her peach wrap dress her co-worker Louise bought for her birthday. Either of these would be perfect, but she couldn't choose between them.

"Mrs. Flowers! Can you come here, please?" Eva called.

Mrs. Violet Flowers was their next-door neighbor across the street from them. She was a heavyset woman who embraced her African heritage. Her gray hair stayed in a braided crown bun. Being a widow, she appreciated getting company from the Lucas family.

"Yes?" The elderly woman waddled through the door in a long, silky, purple-and-yellow kaftan dress and strap sandals.

Eva sighed and rounded her shoulders. "I can't decide what to wear."

Mrs. Flowers jerked her head back and chuckled. "What? You have enough clothes to open a store. You ought to be able to find something nice." She tilted her head and studied Eva, as if she were scrutinizing her inner soul. "It's nerves, honey. You and Andre ain't been out to dinner in a while."

Eva slumped her shoulders with an exhale and glanced

at Mrs. Flowers with a wry smile.

This was true.

Aside from a light goodnight kiss, there wasn't much time for her and Andre to do anything special together after their busy schedules. Since their son was born, they were always tired, rushing to get shuteye before Andrew awoke them for a bottle-feeding or changing.

"I guess I'm a bit nervous." Eva raked a hand through her wet, shoulder-length tendrils. She sighed again. "I thought to wear my black or peach dress. What do you think?" She held each dress by its hanger and placed them against her average height, petite frame, switching between them.

"Well . . ." Mrs. Flowers curled her upper lip. "I like the peach better, but the material's kinda thin and you may be chilly without a light sweater. The weatherman said it's supposed to be cool with clear skies tonight." She shrugged. "How about you wear your wedding dress?"

"My wedding dress?" Eva raised her brow and chuckled. "It's been seven years, Mrs. Flowers. I'm not sure if I can fit it anymore."

Mrs. Flowers sucked her teeth and waved a hand. "Oh, please, honey girl. You don't look like you've gained a pound since Andy was born."

A light bulb lit above Eva's head. "Andy! He's by himself. We're in here talking and he—"

"Don't worry," Mrs. Flowers said, raising her hands

and interrupting Eva's nervous jabbering, "that little fellow ain't wandering anywhere. He's in his playpen busy as a little bee."

Relief suffused Eva's features. "Oh, good."

"Now, you get dressed while I go downstairs and warm Andy some mini ravioli."

Eva smiled. "All right, but don't do the dishes. I'll get them when we come back!"

Mrs. Flowers exited and closed the door.

Eva walked to the large closet and slid hanging clothes on the rack bar. She found her old wedding dress in the back covered in plastic. Eva pulled it out and studied it for a moment, teary-eyed. Through the years, she marveled how their life had fit together like a jigsaw puzzle.

With her husband's well-paying job, they never worried about providing their daily needs or keeping up with bills. They were also fortunate to have their beautiful home, and Grandpa Ricardo, a caring patriarch who was always there if they needed him. Finally, they had their adorable son Andrew who was a special gift and the latest chapter in their lives.

She removed the wrinkled plastic and stroked her hand on the shiny, smooth material. The last time she touched it was after she and Andre returned home from their honeymoon, and she washed and hung it in the closet. Feeling her dress brought back good memories, memories she was sure she and her husband would never forget. For a whole week, she and Andre vacationed in Chihuahua, Mexico, staying in the Wingate hotel. They played golf at the San Francisco Country Club and ate fine dining at the 'Època restaurant. But Eva's favorite spot was touring the breathtaking Copper Canyon. She smiled and giggled, remembering the first night of their honeymoon.

Excited about their married life, Andre had hurried their luggage like a silly klutz into their room. With an amused smile, Eva propped her head with a hand and waited for him on the luxurious, king-sized bed. As the last tote bag slid off Andre's shoulder, he caught his breath, holding her gaze. His lopsided grin was priceless, closing the door behind him with his foot for their privacy.

Finally alone, their wedding day had struck home, and they took the golden opportunity given them. It was already dark by the time they flew into Mexico, and they couldn't think of a better time to carry out their romance. Eva had melted in Andre's affection. The second his arms embraced her; she knew she had a gem.

When their bodies joined, their hearts sang in perfect harmony. Eva closed her eyes and sighed, brushing her dress against her cheek. Because neither of them had experienced it before, she had cherished their first time most of all. Eva's iPhone on the dresser rang, interrupting her muse. "Oh, hello?"

"Hey, it's me, Andre. I'm calling to let you know I've closed my clinic and I'm about to get to the parking lot."

Eva grinned and played with her damp, wavy, long hair. "Okay. So, how was work?"

"Perfect." Andre sighed and paused before making his next comment. "Emily came with her new kitten again."

Eva angled her head and turned down her mouth. "Aww . . . poor little girl."

"Yeah," Andre said, "but hopefully it'll be for the last time until necessary. I talked with her to resolve her problem. So, did you get the roses I ordered you?"

"Yes—" Eva handled one of the roses and sniffed it—"and I got the note you sent with them. It was thoughtful, considering the fact the delivery man sent me the wrong bouquet on our wedding day. They're beautiful. Thank you."

"You're welcome," Andre said. "You know, I've got another gift for you too."

Eva beamed. "Really? What is it?"

Andre laughed. "Do you think I'm gonna tell you over the phone? It's a surprise. I'll show you at dinner."

"But—"

"Eva," Andre interrupted sternly, "you'll get it at the restaurant."

Eva giggled. "Okay, I'll wait." She untied the strap of her robe. "Well, I've freshened up, and I'm about to get dressed. Mrs. Flowers is already here to babysit Andy."

"Okey-dokey. I'll see you soon."

Eva sulked and cleared her throat. "Humph, I hope so, *Dr. Lucas.*"

"Honey, please, don't talk like that. I'll be there, okay? No more excuses."

Eva sighed over the line and made a half-shrug. "Sure, okay."

Her husband broke the silence between them. "*Bebe, te amo . . . tanto.*"

Eva found another smile and blushed. She always liked when he spoke in Spanish to her. "I love you too . . . but please, don't be late again. It's so embarrassing."

Andre chuckled over the phone line. "I won't I promise. Goodbye."

"Bye. Love you!" Eva pressed the end-call button. She exited the master bedroom and skipped down the hallway into the bathroom. Born with her father's good hair, Eva blow-dried and styled hers in a matter of minutes. When she finished, she returned to the bedroom. Her wedding dress fit her like a glove, so Mrs. Flowers was right about her not gaining much weight.

Of course, it wasn't a surprise. Eva had always been thin as Olive Oyl since she was a small child. Her mother worried she wasn't eating enough and always packed her two bologna sandwiches in her school lunch instead of one. Times were tough back then and made her more appreciate what she had now.

Ironically, she had a big appetite for a person so little, and especially for pasta and seafood. Eva dropped her cell phone in her leopard clutch purse and snapped it. She took a last look at herself in the dresser's oval mirror and fingered a couple of loose strands of her hair into place.

Then she trotted downstairs to the first floor of the house. In the living room, an episode of *Barefoot Contessa* was on the flat screen above the electric brick fireplace. Mrs. Flowers enjoyed watching her cooking shows on Food Network whenever she was over at their home.

"I'm ready," Eva announced, strolling into the kitchen. She found Mrs. Flowers standing in front of the double-basin sink.

Andrew was sitting in his blue highchair, eating his small plastic bowl of Chef Boyardee's ravioli. Tomato sauce stained his cheeks and '*Daddy Loves Me*' bib, but after many failed tactics and tantrums, Eva was just glad he wasn't using his hands. She gasped with enthusiasm, her hand over her heart. "Is my little Andy using a spoon?"

"Mm-hmm," Mrs. Flowers said over her shoulder, washing out one of Andy's sippy cups with a scrub brush. "Andy and I had a little one-on-one talk about using good table manners."

"You're growing into a big boy," Eva said, smiling at her son.

"Raa-vee! Raa-vee!" Andrew grinned and tapped his saucy spoon on the tray of his highchair.

"Yes, I see," Eva said with a grin, nodding. "Is it good?"

Andrew ate another spoonful and jiggled like he'd gotten an electric shock. "Mmm, Mommy . . ."

Eva and Mrs. Flowers laughed at the little boy's wit. Although he couldn't speak too many words, he was an intelligent toddler who understood what others were saying to him. Eva glanced away from Andrew, realizing Mrs. Flowers was washing the dishes.

She frowned and walked to the old woman, her hands on her hips. "Oh, Mrs. Flowers . . . I told you I'll get them when Andre and I come back home."

"It's all right, Eva," Mrs. Flowers said, focused on her scrubbing, "staying busy helps me forget."

Eva dropped her shoulders, sighing. She knew what Mrs. Flowers meant by her remark. She was talking about her husband Clyde, the one and only lover in her lifetime. Two years ago, he was called home after a lost battle with Alzheimer's disease. He was a veteran of the Korean War who enlisted after high school.

Clyde sent money to Mrs. Flowers and her family to help save their farm. Often Mrs. Flowers told Eva long past stories of their young courtship and how she never stopped waiting for her war hero's return. Eva wrapped an arm around the old woman's shoulders. "I'm sorry. Mr. Clyde was a good man. I know his loss is tough for you."

"Yes, very. I still miss him," Mrs. Flowers said. "You

know, true love never dies. One might try to replace it with other things or people, but it never dies." She felt tears form in her eyes and blinked them back. "Well, I don't want to spoil your happy day. You and Andre enjoy yourselves." She patted Eva's arm around her.

"Thank you, Mrs. Flowers. I appreciate your kind help. Good night." Eva turned her attention to Andrew. "Good night, baby. Be good for Mommy, okay?" She kissed the top of her son's curly black hair and added, "Oh, make sure you call if you need me for anything. My cell number's on the refrigerator."

"Girl, if you don't get outta here—you know I always do," Mrs. Flowers said, smiling.

Eva giggled. "Okay, take care." She exited the house. Outside gripping the gold knob, she placed her other hand to her stomach. A bad, queasy feeling caught her off guard, like a foul smell down a country road, making her feel like throwing up.

She took a deep breath of the cool air and locked the front door. *Don't embarrass me, Andre. Please, be on time.*

• CHAPTER 3 •

Andre

Andre barged through the swing exit door of Pet Friends Veterinary Clinic and felt a drizzle tap his forehead. Thunder crackled and rolled in the distance. He paused in his tracks and frowned at the sky. Giant, thick clouds smothered the fiery sunset, casting a shadowy, gloom over the wide parking lot.

A thunderstorm? Though a forty-percent chance was in effect, the weatherman was wrong this time. Andre took a long breath of the damp, earthy air. His heart skipped a beat. He had to get to the restaurant before it rained. He left his umbrella home, and the last thing he wanted was to arrive with his navy tuxedo soaked, not to mention double pneumonia.

Andre jogged toward his 2017 blue velvet Chevy Impala and unlocked the doors with his keychain remote. He plopped in the driver's seat and shut the door. Andre let out a sigh, slipped his cell phone out of his hip holster, and placed it in the car holder clipped to an air vent. More thunder clashed, startling him as he pressed the six-speed engine button. Lightning flashed twice behind the monstrous clouds, giving a quick illusion of a bright summer morning. Andre buckled his seatbelt and glanced at the clock on the panel screen of his car.

6:43 p.m.

Time was always a key factor, wondering and questioning if he trusted God enough to have another child. Would he finally take a leap of faith? He couldn't disappoint his wife again, and he wouldn't. He hadn't told her all his romantic plans for them, but after dinner, she would find out in the hotel suite he booked for them. There were seven minutes to spare. Maybe he wouldn't be late. Andre shifted the gearstick in reverse, speeding out the parking space.

But he was too late.

Steady rain pitter-pattered the windshield and sunroof of his car, blurring his view. Andre turned on the wipers and stared hopelessly, clutching the steering wheel. Ever since he got his license at eighteen, he never liked driving in the rain, but within seconds, the dry road across from him became a slick, black stream. *Please, God, not again.* From his wedding anniversary to his son's baby milestones, his number of tardies was ridiculous.

He hoped Eva and Andrew knew how much he loved

them, and how important they were to him.

Andre bit his lip and shifted into drive, cruising down the sloped, paved entrance to the clinic. He glanced up Lime Street, his attention caught by a long line of several cars and blowing horns.

Traffic was jam-packed.

Just great. Andre gritted his teeth. With the weather against him and traffic crowded, going the longer route was the only option. He turned onto Colonel Highway, taking a backcountry road. He rode past his grandfather's farmhouse and nearby cornfields. As he made a sharp, smooth turn onto Pasture Road, he flicked on his high beams to better see the flooded street.

Andre drove by a yellow deer sign and the Old Thomas family's place, the rugged remains of a small, wooden shack. Fifty years ago, it caught fire after a lightning bolt struck the rooster wind vane during a thunderstorm. Its roof had collapsed from the burning flames, but the ancient house was still standing despite the tragic disaster.

Andre's mobile phone in the holder vibrated. He stole a glance at his cell while steering his wheel.

Eva sent a text message: *Please hurry. I'm hungry. Waiting @ The Redfish Grill.*

Andre replied via Bluetooth, keeping his hand on the wheel: *On my way. Love you!*

He peeked at the clock.

Five minutes to seven.

Andre's smile dropped as he looked up from his phone again. In the burst of lightning, a deer leaped in front of his vehicle in the middle of the street. He gasped and stomped on his brake, his heart pounding against his ribcage. His tires squealed, sliding into the white-tailed animal.

"Aaaah!" Andre closed his eyes tightly, gripped the wheel, and braced himself for the collision. There was a hefty thump of an impact. The deer smashed through the windshield and knocked Andre in his head. Shattered glass flew inside the car's interior. He slumped over in his seat and lost control of the wheel. The car swerved and scraped against the metal guardrail.

Sparks sputtered from the railing as the car screeched off the road and crashed into a neighbor's front yard tree. Thick, gray smoke spewed from the crushed car like carbonated fizz down a shaken-up soda can. Andre's eyes were open, nothing more than slits.

His vision blurred at the lifeless touchscreen between the front air vents. Andre's body was stiff and ached with excruciating pain, leaning against the passenger seat. He squirmed and attempted to straighten himself, but the deer's weight on his lap pinned him down.

Andre winced and exhaled shallow breaths in a panic. He reached a cut, bleeding hand to his crown and felt a deep gash on his head. Andre studied his hand and nearly fainted from the sight of his blood.

"Help . . . somebody . . . help me," he said breathlessly. No one could hear him. Except for the thunder and rain pelting his car, he heard nothing. It seemed all hope was lost. After waiting for what felt like infinity, someone knocked and shined a flashlight on his face inside the car.

"Hold on, sir! We're gonna get you out!" a policeman said, his voice muffled against the passenger window. The officer spoke to his colleagues and walked off from the car wreckage. Fire truck and ambulance sirens rang and approached the accident scene. Motor equipment zoomed off, and metal bent and broke apart as personnel of firefighters rescued him.

Breathing heavily, Andre moaned and fluttered his eyes at the bright lights of the emergency vehicles, raising his bloody hand to his face.

In an instant, his whole life flashed before him: *his drug addict parents arguing over him in their rundown apartment, his five-year-old self playing on the tire swing at his grandpa's farm, his school and college graduations, he and Eva's first kiss on their wedding day and flight to Mexico, and Andrew's birth when he first held his son.* Tears fell from the corners of his eyes, silently mouthing his lips.

Words had become harder to grasp. He was a fish without water. He wanted to speak again—to call for help, his thoughts and memories slipping away like sand flowing through an hourglass.

But as gentle as wind, darkness settled in and would remain for weeks.

• CHAPTER 4 •

Eva

For thirty minutes Eva waited for her husband, sitting at their reserved, two-seat table. She grinned as a tall man of cinnamon-brown complexion in a dark-colored suit entered the golden revolving door with a black umbrella. Her heart leaped. *Andre?*

She craned her neck above the artificial potted plants on the shelf for a better look. When the man closed his wet umbrella and sat at a table with another woman, her smile faded. Awaiting his arrival was becoming more unbearable. She frowned and lowered herself into her chair. *Where could he be?*

Andre was late many times, but he was never *this* late. He should've come by now with his surprise gift. But at the restaurant, he wasn't anywhere. Though it was raining, The Redfish Grill was a five-minute drive from the clinic. She couldn't think of what's more important now than celebrating their anniversary.

They had endured a lot together, especially during the birth of their son. Eva thought she'd die, that she'd never get to hold the baby she carried for nine months. With every shallow breath behind her oxygen mask, her fear was intense, but she felt Mrs. Flowers' prayers from the waiting room.

Because Andrew was born healthy and she lived for another day, an angel must've watched over them that afternoon. Hearing Andrew's tiny piercing cry for the first time brought tears to her eyes and a sigh of relief. Since then, it mattered little to Andre if they had another baby. He was just grateful she and their son survived the delivery.

Eva pulled her iPhone out of her clutch purse and pressed the side button, lighting her touchscreen. She glanced at the time displayed in big, white skinny numbers.

7:20 p.m.

She willed herself to keep calm as Stefano approached her table in his stylish uniform: a white dress shirt, a black bow tie, a gold vest, black pants, and polished dress shoes.

"Mrs. Lucas, are you ready to order?" he asked.

Eva sniffled and picked up her Redfish Grill menu.

Her vision blurred with angry tears, staring at the

restaurant's slogan above the red rockfish logo: *Elegant Seafood at Its Best.* "I guess I should. There's no telling when my husband will come."

Stefano sighed. "I'm sorry he hasn't shown again. I know this meant a lot to you, but you mustn't doubt yourself. Andre loves you a great deal. You must believe that." He shrugged. "He probably got caught in the storm. I'm sure he intended to be here."

Eva swiped a tear from her cheek and hung her head. "He did, and he promised he'd come, but he always gets tied up in work." She leaned back with an exhale. "I feel so stupid. I should've expected nothing different from him. Andre's always late. It's . . . just the way he is." She opened her menu and skimmed the entrée selections. "I'll have the grilled salmon with—"

"Broccoli slaw and iced water with lemon, right?" Stefano grinned and jotted on his notepad.

"You know me well," Eva said with a blushing smile.

The muscular, six-foot-three, Italian waiter scribbled again. "Would you like any of our appetizers while you wait? We have some tasty new crab cakes I think you'd love."

"No thanks," Eva replied dispiritedly, "the breadsticks on the table will do for now."

Stefano tucked his notepad in the back pocket of his pants. "All right, I'll be right back with your drink." He placed a hand on her shoulder. "Cheer up, Eva. I'm sure

Andre's dorky self will come here soaked from head to toe in no time."

Eva glanced at the waiter and chuckled. "Thanks." She watched as Stefano left and disappeared through the French doors to the kitchen. Eva closed her menu and placed it and her phone aside on the table. While waiting, she texted her husband four times, but he responded once. She pinched the bridge of her nose and shook her head. *How could you do this, Andre?*

Six times was a world record. If he was running late, the least he could've done was tell her when he called earlier or send a message ahead of time. Instead, he left her hoping like many times before. Perhaps Stefano was right. Maybe the weather held up Andre, or his lateness had to do with her surprise gift. She hadn't a clue of what it was, but thinking like a man, she imagined one thing.

Lingerie.

Ever since Andrew was born, she and Andre hadn't been too intimate for a long time. They'd only talked about giving their son a sibling to play with, a thoughtful picture never put into focus. Andre's anxiety hindered their venture.

Whenever Eva snuggled him and attempted to grasp his attention, he claimed he wasn't ready, panicked, and pushed her away when things got too steamy. But Andre's sad, yearning eyes and returned kisses told her differently. It hurt to watch her husband struggling with his desire because of fear of losing her in childbirth.

But maybe—maybe he'd finally overcome his cold feet. Although the outcome was unknown, Eva had told him God could work everything out and allow her to have a healthy delivery. Where was Andre's faith? Seemingly, her near-death experience scared him more than her. And if the worse unfolded, she imagined Andre would never forgive himself.

Eva averted her eyes from the empty chair in front of her. She surveyed the other happy customers talking and eating with family and friends. Eva listened to the clinking of silverware and relaxing jazz music sifting through the ceiling speakers. She sighed, grabbed a breadstick from the straw basket on the table, and gnawed on it.

On her right, a family of eight was having a dinner party. The birthday boy who sat in the center of attention wore a polka-dotted party hat. Based on his blue number helium balloon, he had turned twelve. To Eva's left, she saw a young couple who looked like they had come from a formal dance. The man opened a small black box and proposed to the woman, who smiled, said yes, and gave him a light kiss.

Disappointment wilted Eva's shoulders, crossing her arms. When she finishes her meal and goes home, she would have a word with Andre tonight about breaking promises.

"Here you go, Mrs. Lucas." Stefano placed a glass goblet

of iced water with a lemon slice on the sugared brim of the cup in front of her.

She gave a weak smile. "Oh, thank you."

"You're welcome. Your meal will be ready in about ten minutes."

Eva nodded. "Okay. Thanks."

The waiter left again.

Eva took the lemon slice off her brim, squirted juice into her water, and rattled the ice cubes in her glass. She took a sip to wash down the breadstick she'd eaten and put her cup down.

Her cell phone vibrated to life.

Eva's ears grew warm, answering without checking her caller ID. "Where are you? I've waited like an hour!"

"Excuse me?" an older gentleman said.

Eva frowned at the unfamiliar man's voice. "Wait . . . who is this?"

"Ma'am, this is Captain Victor Pierce of Garden Ridge Police Department."

"Is something wrong?" Eva's heart skipped a beat.

The captain sighed. "Yes, ma'am. I'm so sorry . . . but your husband's been in an accident."

Fear clawed through Eva and ripped her resentment to shreds. Now she'd wait a century if it meant seeing Andre alive and well. Her body tensed up, pondering the mild to severe endless possibilities of her husband's condition.

"Uh, thank you for informing me," she said. "Is . . . is he all right?" Panic skittered through her chest.

"I'm not sure, ma'am," the captain said. "It appears he suffered a deer-vehicle collision. He lost control of his car after the impact and crashed into a tree. Paramedics took him to Garden Ridge Hospital about ten minutes ago. I'm really sorry this happened."

"Thank you," Eva said and forced down a swallow. She ended the call and sat mutely amid the energetic commotion in the restaurant. She felt like she'd been transported through a fantasy portal—that her life wasn't real anymore. In ten words, her world had turned upside down, and nothing mattered but her husband's life. Was he dead? Or had he survived the car accident?

Eva took a pen from her clutch purse and wrote a note on a paper napkin: *I had to leave for an emergency. Thank you for your service.* She took a couple of dollars from her wallet, hid it and the note under her goblet cup and hurried out the revolving door.

• CHAPTER 5 •

Eva

She barged through the hospital and paused at the reception counter. Brushing her damp, crimped hair from her face, she caught her breath amidst the nurses' ringing telephones and light chatter. "Excuse me, I'm Eva Lucas. My husband, Andre, arrived about ten minutes ago. He was in a car accident."

"Yes, ma'am," a blonde nurse in blue scrubs said, "the doctor took him into surgery. If you'd sit in the waiting room, he'll speak with you later."

"Okay, thank you." Eva sat in the waiting room. She tied her hair in a ponytail, clasped her hands in her lap, and took a few deep breaths. Hearing about her husband in surgery upset her stomach again. Had she sensed something would happen to Andre before she left home? Was her nausea a warning sign? Questions about Andre swam through her mind. *What if he doesn't look the same? What if I don't recognize him? What if he's in a coma? Oh, no . . . what if he dies under the knife?* Though she wished for the best, she wasn't prepared for the worst. Eva leaned back in her chair and bounced her leg. She glanced anxious eyes at the CNN news blasting from the flat screen mounted on the ceiling above a vending machine.

Eight other people occupied the sitting area, but Eva felt alone. She bowed her head as tears stung her eyes. "God, please, don't take my husband. *Please* . . ." What would she do if Andre died? He was an important member of her and Andrew's lives, and they needed him. As time passed and visitors left, Eva fell asleep.

An hour later, she finally received an update. Someone tapped on her shoulder, and she opened her weary eyes. Two doctors in white lab coats stood before her. One, an older African American with a bald spot, looked at her over thick eyeglasses. The other, a lanky redhead in teal scrubs and a surgeon cap, tugged down a surgical mask from his face. Based on the men's solemn expressions, Eva could tell she was in for heavy news.

The bald doctor cleared his throat. "Mrs. Lucas?"

"Yes?" Eva rose from her chair.

"Hi. I'm Dr. Edwin Brown, Andre's critical care physician." The bald doctor gestured to the redhead physician beside him. "This is Dr. Alex Larrabee, the neurosurgeon who performed Andre's surgery."

Eva shook each of the doctors' hands. "Nice to meet you both." She folded her arms and swayed to keep her composure. Her legs were as fragile as toothpicks as if they could barely hold her weight. "How's my husband? Is he okay?" Her eyes welled up and her heart punched in her chest, longing for good news.

Dr. Brown licked his full lips, raising his thick hands. "Mrs. Lucas, I don't want to drag this out. Andre's in critical condition. He's . . . he's in a coma. I'm sorry."

A tear spilled from Eva's eye. Her chin quivered as she lowered her head. The moment the doctor said *coma,* her life was sucked into a black hole—she was trapped in darkness, filled with uncertainty.

"We did CT and MRI scans on your husband, which showed serious damage to the left frontal and parietal lobes of his brain," Dr. Brown added. "It appears he has a common injury called Diffuse Axonal Injury or DAI. We also found a few cerebral contusions, caused by bleeding on the external tissue from his brain striking the skull in his accident."

"Oh, God . . ." Eva stifled a sob with her hand. *No! The doctor's lying. It can't be true—it can't! How can this be happening?* Andre was a tall, strong man and stayed physically active. From what she could remember, he had never been severely sick or hurt a day in his life.

Dr. Brown continued. "An Officer Greg McKee found this on the interior floor of the damaged car. He dug his hand in a side pocket of his lab coat.

Greg McKee? Eva recognized the name as the father of her daycare student Autumn McKee, who was a policeman.

The doctor fished out a small black box and handed it to Eva. "Here, ma'am . . . this belongs to you."

"What?" Eva frowned and took the box from him. She unfastened the gold latch and opened it. Before her eyes embedded in gray velvet was a personalized keychain. It was made of shiny pennies and a stainless-steel tag linked with key rings to a swivel clip. Each penny was engraved with a tiny heart and a name.

One penny was etched with her name and the other with her husband's name. The tag was carved with the numbers *08.28.10*—Eva and Andre's wedding date. Now she understood this was the surprise gift her husband intended to give her during their anniversary dinner. It was the most unique, beautiful keychain she ever saw, designed as a reminder for them.

She whimpered and licked her tears, tracing her forefinger over the penny etched with Andre's name. "Thank you," she whispered and sniffled. "I love it."

"You're welcome. We know he wanted you to have this." Dr. Brown sighed and changed the subject back to Andre's medical condition. "Miraculously, he suffered no spinal cord injury. If it wasn't for the weight of the deer pinning down his body, police believe the forceful impact would've ejected him from his car."

"So, he'll be able to walk?"

"I don't know," Dr. Brown said. "Unfortunately, it's too early to tell for sure. For now, he's been transferred to ICU where his trauma team will monitor him. Some of the staff is waiting to meet you."

Eva closed the box and dabbed her knuckle at a tear. "What happened in his surgery?" She turned her attention to the neurosurgeon.

"I performed an external ventricular drain placement," Dr. Larrabee said.

Eva grimaced and darted her eyes. "What's that?"

"I inserted a catheter through a hole in Andre's skull into the ventricle of his brain. It's a procedure that will help us track his intracranial pressure. Brain swelling increases pressure in the brain. But the sooner we drain your husband's cerebrospinal fluid, the sooner we can prevent further damage," Dr. Larrabee added.

Eva swallowed a lump in her throat. "What happens if his brain pressure gets too high?"

"Andre would need a decompressive craniotomy," Dr. Larrabee answered. He sighed and elaborated on the medical procedure. "The surgery involves removing a large area of his skull. This is so his brain has more room to swell. After his swelling subsides, I would replace it in a second surgery called a cranioplasty, but we're hoping Andre won't need these procedures."

Eva glanced at each doctor. "Can I see him?"

Dr. Brown nodded. "Of course, but don't remove his cloth restraints or tubing. All the medical equipment is there for Andre's safety as hard as it may be to watch. Be careful also to keep noise and physical contact to a minimum. Talking to him and holding Andre's hand will be enough for him to know you're there."

"Please, clean your hands before you enter the room," Dr. Larrabee added. "Your husband's stationed in room I-7. We'll take you there."

"Thank you, doctors." Eva followed the physicians down the hall toward the double doors to the ICU unit. As she passed other distraught patients, she braced herself for the flood of emotions that would overwhelm her the second she stepped into Andre's room. She released a slow breath and relaxed her shoulders as she turned a corner with the doctors.

Above their heads, a large sign labeled the wing section of the hospital: Intensive Care Unit. *Intensive.* She didn't like the sound of the word. Standing in a circle outside the labeled door were two female nurses and a male nurse in colored scrubs and a middle-aged woman in a dress suit and high heels. She observed as they whispered and watched her approaching them.

From a tinted window she saw a shadow of a man in bed in the ICU ward. She placed a hand on the cold pane and peered at the darkness. *Andre . . .honey, is that you?*

"Mrs. Lucas, these are some of the members of Andre's healthcare team to support you and your husband," Dr. Brown said, making her look away from the window.

A young, Chinese-American woman in light blue scrubs smiled and extended a hand. "Hi, I'm Jia Li, Andre's practitioner. I'll be keeping track of your husband's intracranial pressure and the recovery of his level of consciousness."

"Hello." Eva shook the practitioner's hand.

A brunette nurse in pink scrubs introduced herself to Eva. "Hi, I'm Nurse Daphne, one of Andre's bedside nurses. I'll assist in Andre's IV medications, nutrition, and other daily needs."

Eva nodded timidly. "Hi, nice to meet you too." She looked at the dirty-blond male nurse standing beside Daphne. "And you are?"

"Hayden Rivers, ma'am. I'm another bedside nurse of Andre's healthcare team," the male nurse said, shaking her hand. "I know you're facing a difficult time, but I give my full support. Dr. Barbara Washburn's a social worker and here if you need extra help too."

"That's right, Mrs. Lucas," the social worker said in a Caribbean accent. "We want you to know we're here for you. My office is open every day from 7:00 a.m. to 5:00 p.m. I can help guide you toward the best treatment for your husband and answer questions you may have." She offered her business card. "You can call me whenever you're ready. No pressure."

"Uh, thank you." Eva allowed a smile and hid the card in her clutch purse. She scanned the group of people around her and felt their love and concern, as overwhelming as the whole situation was for her. "Thank you . . . thank you all very much."

"We have Andre ready for you to visit," Nurse Daphne said, opening the door of Andre's room.

Eva faced Dr. Brown, her eyes filled with worry.

The physician gave a nod, giving his reassurance for her entrance.

Eva squirted sanitizer from a wall dispenser in her palm and rubbed her hands together. She took another deep breath and entered the room, closing the lightweight door with her elbow. As she approached Andre's motionless body, she felt like she stepped in Dr. Victor Frankenstein's laboratory—that her husband was a human experiment.

Wires and plastic tubes from beeping machines, monitor screens, and plastic bags were attached to his body everywhere, except his hands and feet. He wore a plastic cervical collar for neck support, and his wrists were tied on the side rails of his bed.

Eva hid her nose and mouth in her hands and stifled a gasping sob. Her heart broke at the sight of him, her eyes pooling with unshed tears. She sat in a lounge chair at the left of his bedside. "Andre? Andre, I'm right here. Honey, please . . . please don't leave me." She leaned forward and got a closer look at his face.

His curly, black hair had been cut for his operation, but other than a few nicks and bruises, he looked normal. Eva held Andre's cold, bandaged hand. She longed for a word, a gesture, or a moan, but he made no sound or move. He was as still as a wooden log lying on the ground, and she doubted he'd ever wake again.

"Andre, I'm so sorry." Eva placed a hand to her mouth and sobbed again. "If I hadn't urged you to come on time for dinner, you might've not gotten in a car accident. I'm sorry I doubted you were coming as you promised. Now I know you were . . . you just didn't make it." She stroked her fingers over Andre's shaved head. "Please, forgive me . . . I love you." She stifled another sob, willing herself to be strong.

"Now, you listen good, Andre Miguel Lucas, you fight to get better, you hear me? Your son needs you . . . I need you." She bowed her head in prayer. "God, please help my husband. Heal his mind and body in Jesus Christ's name. Amen."

Someone opened the door.

"Mrs. Lucas, I'm afraid visiting hours are over," Dr. Brown said.

Eva sniffled and lifted her tear-stained face to the doctor. Her eyes darted from him to Nurse Daphne.

"I'm not leaving him." She gulped a hard lump.

"Ma'am, I'm sorry but—"

"Doctor, please," Eva interrupted, "it's our seventh wedding anniversary."

The doctor set his mouth in a tight line, sighing. "All right, but only for tonight." He faced his nursing assistant. "Daphne, give her Andre's privacy code number. I'm sure she'd want it."

"Of course, doctor," Daphne said.

Dr. Brown smiled and marveled over Eva's determined attitude. "You know, I can see why Andre loves you. He's a very lucky man. Good night, Mrs. Lucas."

"Good night, doctor," Eva replied as he left the room.

Nurse Daphne walked to the bedside near her. "Mrs. Lucas, I have Andre's privacy code number for you."

"Privacy code number?"

"Mm-hmm," the nurse replied, "it'll help you keep in contact with the trauma team and how Andre's condition is progressing. By using our HIPAA system, we can grant your request to help you feel you're involved in Andre's care, despite your absence. It helps us to respect patient privacy and meet the needs of loved ones."

"Oh, all right." Eva found a smile, drying her wet cheek.

The nurse jotted on a sticky note and gave it to Eva. "Here you go, Mrs. Lucas. The ICU unit is open from 8:30 a.m. to 8:30 p.m. When you call, make sure you state your relationship to Andre and give his privacy code number over the phone."

"Thank you," Eva said.

"Would you like a blanket?"

Eva nodded. "Yes, please."

"Okay. I'll be back." The brown-haired nurse smiled and exited the room.

Eva let out a slow breath and leaned back in her chair. With her husband hanging between life and death, she hoped everything was fine with Andrew and Mrs. Flowers at home. She should check on them, but she was so concerned about Andre, she decided to wait until morning. Besides, she had record proof she could trust Mrs. Flowers since the day her son was born, and the elderly woman always said Andrew was like a grandson to her.

She turned her attention back to Andre and lightly kissed the stitches on his head. "Happy Anniversary, Andre. I received your gift from the doctor. It's beautiful." Eva released his hand wrapped in gauze and turned over to her side in the chair, trying to get comfortable. "Good night. Sweet dreams."

Her eyes grew heavy in a matter of seconds. She didn't realize she drifted out until a wool blanket was draped over her and the single ceiling light switched off.

Eva squinted at the nurse in pink in the well-lit doorway.

"Goodbye, Mrs. Lucas," Daphne whispered. "See you

in the morning."

Eva shut her eyes, repositioned her body, and waited to doze back off.

• CHAPTER 6 •

Eva

The Next Day

Sun rays pierced through the thin hospital curtain and beamed on Eva's face. She fluttered her eyelids open to the glare of a brand-new day, hearing the beeps and pings of Andre's life support machines. Eva pulled down the tan, wool blanket and straightened in the upholstered guest chair. She placed her feet on the ice-cold linoleum floor, startled by its freezing touch.

Her body was sluggish and stiff. For the whole livelong night, she had slept in a fetal position, hugging her legs to her chest to keep warm in the cool ICU ward. Eva massaged and rotated her neck to loosen a tight kink. She leaned forward and checked on her husband. Several hours had passed, but nothing changed. He still rested peacefully—as quiet as a feather fluttering in the wind.

Can he hear me when I talk to him? Is he listening to me? She spoke again. "Good morning, Andre."

Eva yawned. "How did you sleep? I slept terribly." She slumped her back and brushed a lock of messy hair from her tired face. Looking at her husband, she chuckled, imagining his witty joke.

"Pretty good, but my eyes can't decide when to open," he'd say.

Eva held her husband's hand and wore a wistful smile. "Oh, Andre, I wish you'd wake up. I miss hearing your voice."

Seconds after her remark, Nurse Jia entered the room, dressed in her blue scrubs and black Crocs, her jet-black hair tied in a sleek ponytail. She smiled at Eva and kicked a wedge under the door to prop it open. "Good morning, I'm here to check Andre's level of consciousness. I'll be examining him using our hospital's Glasgow Coma Scale."

Jia grabbed a three-ring binder from a slot at the footboard of Andre's hospital bed, unfolded it, and clicked a pen. "The Glasgow Coma Scale is an assessment method to test how well a patient responds to external stimuli. Each day I'll observe Andre's eye, verbal, and motor responses, and rate him based on his physical reactions. The higher the total score, the better his brain's recovery."

The nurse practitioner sighed. "However, a low score can mean he's stagnant or getting worse. The good news is Andre's intracranial pressure monitor can alert us of an emergency."

"Yes," Eva said, "but Dr. Larrabee warned Andre could need another operation."

Jia nodded. "That's right. Bleeding or high brain swelling is serious and can be fatal. Typically, a score of fifteen means a patient is fully conscious, but a score of three means the patient is in a deep coma."

She walked to the bedside. "Good morning, Andre. Can you open your eyes for me?" She gently stroked Andre's shoulder and observed him, but his eyes stayed closed. With her ink pen, she applied pressure to Andre's middle finger of his left hand, quietly counting for ten seconds while watching him.

Nothing again.

Jia scribbled on a sheet in the notebook. She placed the binder down and held Andre's hand. "Hey, Andre. Can you try to squeeze my hand, please?"

Eva gulped and studied Andre's stone-still face. In the past few hours, his appearance looked older, tired, and worn.

"Come on, now. Squeeze my hand, Andre," Jia said again, but Andre's hand remained limp in hers. She sighed and jotted another note. Then she took a penlight from her shirt pocket and shined it in each of Andre's eyes, checking if his pupils' contract. She shook her head and wrote in her notebook again.

Eva shifted her eyes nervously and licked her lips. "What's his score?" From Jia's downhearted expressions she sensed in her gut it was below fifteen.

"Three," Jia said with a sigh, "same as yesterday in the emergency room, but it's expected. He's had a severe brain injury. The impact of the deer plus the head-on collision is like a double whammy."

Eva lowered her head with a hopeless exhale.

Dr. Brown strolled into the room with his hands in the pockets of his white lab coat. "How's Andre this morning?"

"No change, doctor," Jia replied. "He's still in a coma."

"Well, that's typical," Dr. Brown said. "Only a small percentage of patients wake the first day after a traumatic accident."

Eva angled her head, inquisitive. "When did he lose consciousness?"

The doctor fidgeted with his eyeglasses. "We don't know for sure exactly, but he was unconscious while paramedics rushed him to the hospital. The important thing is to make sure Andre's brain pressure remains under control."

Eva slipped on her white-silk cameo heels and stood with her clutch purse. Tears stung her eyes, staring at the catheter inserted in Andre's head and the trachea tube lodged and hanging from his neck. "Doctor, how long . . . how long will he . . ."

"Unfortunately, we can't say," Dr. Brown answered. "Every patient is different. He could be in a coma for a few days to a couple of weeks. Usually, it doesn't last longer than two weeks, but if it exceeds that . . . there's a sad possibility he won't recover. I know it's hard leaving him behind, but your husband will be taken care of."

He tucked his hands in his lab coat's pockets and continued. "We'll keep you informed if there are significant changes, and don't forget you can call or visit within our ICU hours for updates too. For now, you should stay calm and take care of yourself."

Eva wiped beneath her eyes. "You're right. I should go. I need to make some calls and look after our son. Our neighbor's watching him right now. Uh . . . thanks for helping Andre."

Dr. Brown smiled. "No need to thank us. It's our job."

"Take care, Mrs. Lucas, and try to get some proper rest," Jia added.

"I'll try." Eva wore a weak smile and looked back at Andre again. She planted a soft kiss on her husband's cheek. "I love you," she whispered in his ear. "Hold on for me, honey, okay? I'll visit you tomorrow." She tilted her head and watched him a couple of seconds more as his ventilator whooshed and paused in the middle of the quiet, sterile room. She drew a long breath and exited. Now outside in the hospital corridor, she felt like she left one world and entered another. She rubbed her hands with sanitizer, turned the corner, and strode the hall toward the automatic entrance doors.

Eva plopped in the driver's seat of her Tungsten silver Volkswagen Golf and held her steering wheel, resting her forehead on her hands. Her shoulders bobbed as buckets of hot tears rolled down her cheeks. Feeling hungry and cranky she was a perfect replica of a two-year-old having a tantrum. She couldn't wait to eat breakfast, take a warm shower, and cuddle in her bed.

Last night had been a wrestling match between dreadful anxiety and hopeful desire. She sniffled and peered at the dazzling sunrise behind the hospital building complex. Eva bit back a whimper, soaking in her sorrow.

Heartbreaking thoughts beguiled her, weighing her heart with guilt. *It's your fault! You shouldn't have texted him. You distracted him from the road. It was you! All your fault!* Her mind reflected on her conversations and everything that happened. Certain words stood out from the others. *Police. Car accident. Surgery. Diagnosis. Brain injury. And coma*—yes, especially *coma.* She hoped it was a bad dream, but after waking in the hospital room, she realized it was a living nightmare. She took her cell phone out of her purse and pressed the on-button.

Eva checked her text messages and missed calls. For a

second, she stared at the last text Andre sent her before his accident: *On my way. Love you!* Although he was late from work often, Eva knew he intended to meet her last night. Stefano was right. Andre loved her more than words could say. In fact, so much, he was willing to selflessly sacrifice his desire for the safety of her life.

"Oh, Andre . . ." Eva thought and sniffled. Her cellphone chirped off and bubble notifications popped on the screen. She swiped her finger and found three missed calls. One of them was from Mrs. Flowers, and the other two were from Mrs. Gracie Higgins, her director at the Sunrise Christian Daycare.

Each morning she began work at 6:30 a.m., but it was well after seven. Now was a good time to inform them about her whereabouts and Andre's car accident. She dialed the number of her workplace and pinned her phone to her ear.

The dial tone rang.

"Sunrise Christian Daycare, how can I direct your call?" the receptionist asked in her thick, Southern accent.

"Oh, hi, Janet. It's me, Eva. Is Mrs. Higgins there?"

"Yes, she is. I'll transfer you to the classroom."

Eva smiled. "Thanks."

There was a long pause over the phone line.

"Hello, how can I help you?" an older woman said and coughed. Her low voice was raspy from her past years of smoking but filled with a heartfelt welcome.

"Hello, Mrs. Higgins. It's Eva."

"Eva? Eva Lucas? Well, where are you for Pete's sake? What happened? I thought you checked in. Louise was climbing the walls trying to handle ten kids alone in the two-year-old classroom. I left the office to help her. It's against regulations to have an unequal teacher-child ratio, and you know this! I allowed their parents to drop off their kids expecting you'd be here!" Her tone was sharp, unmerciful.

Eva felt like she was being lectured by her bossy, toxic mother. She grabbed a napkin from her glove compartment and slammed it, overhearing children screaming and crying in the background of the call. "Well, I'm sorry, okay! My husband Andre had a car accident last night." She sniffled and wiped her runny nose.

Her director gasped. "Oh, no . . . I'm *so* sorry. Forgive me, I didn't mean to go off the deep end. I've been under a lot of stress this morning."

Eva sighed wearily. "I understand, and I don't blame you for being upset. I should've called or sent a message sooner, but I wasn't thinking about it."

"It's okay, Eva. I wouldn't either," Mrs. Higgins said. "I hope you don't mind me asking, but how bad was his accident?"

"Well, right now, he's in a coma," Eva answered, "the doctor said he has a brain injury. Diffuse something. I don't remember the name of it. It's been a long night." She closed her eyes and rubbed her forehead. "I need . . . I need time to cope, Mrs. Higgins."

"Of course, dear," Mrs. Higgins said, "I reckon' I can limit the scheduling. I'll give you a week, but I'm afraid it's all I can spare."

Eva found a smile. "Thank you, Mrs. Higgins. Tell Louise I said sorry and hello. I'll be back after next week."

"Good, and I'll be praying for Andre," her director said.

"Thank you. Goodbye." Eva exhaled and ended the call. She scrolled through her contacts list and started to redial her home number, but her ringtone jingled off, notifying her of an incoming call.

Eva grinned and answered. "Mrs. Flowers?"

"Hey, morning, Eva. I was calling to find out if you and Andre were all right. How was your anniversary dinner?" Mrs. Flowers said blissfully. She snickered. "Did y'all sneak into a hotel?"

Eva stared into space and hesitated to speak up, startled by Mrs. Flower's question. *Why had she asked that?* Her eyes welled up again. Had Andre planned a secret romantic evening with her alone? Maybe he had after all, but he wanted to surprise her.

"Eva? You still there?"

"Oh, yes, ma'am. I'm here," Eva said with a sigh. "We didn't have dinner, Mrs. Flowers."

"You didn't?"

Eva dabbed her eyes with her crumpled napkin. "No, ma'am."

"Don't tell me that Andre didn't show up again," Mrs. Flowers said.

"He didn't, but it wasn't his fault. Mrs. Flowers, Andre had a car accident."

Heavy breaths filtered through her receiving end and Eva thought the elderly woman was having a heart attack. She frowned. "Mrs. Flowers? Are you okay?"

"Yes, honey—Mrs. Flowers swallowed hard— "I'm . . . I'm just shocked, that's all."

Eva sighed and explained the details of her husband's medical condition to Mrs. Flowers. "He's in ICU where his healthcare team is monitoring him."

"Oh, dear lord. I'm sorry, Eva. Is there anything I can do?"

Eva shook her head. "No, ma'am. You've done plenty already. Thanks for watching Andy for me. My mom rarely visits, and when she does, it's always at the wrong time. I don't know what I'd do without you."

"You're welcome. It's my pleasure. Your little boy lights up my life." Mrs. Flowers chuckled.

Eva found a giggle. "What's he doing anyway?"

"He's peeking at me from his playpen," Mrs. Flowers said. "I've already given him his breakfast and bath, so you don't have to worry about it when you get home."

Eva rolled up her eyes and mouthed a "thank you" heavenward. Though inside she was a mourning widow, this old lady was a true saint. She giggled and cocked her head. "Can you put Andy on, please?"

"Sure, hon. Let me put it on speaker."

Eva waited with a smile stretched across her face. Her heart danced with joy, listening to her little boy's small voice. "Hi, baby! Have you been a good boy?"

"Yeeaaa!" Andrew replied on the phone. He babbled excited baby talk Eva wished she could understand. She gasped with enthusiasm as if she knew her son's every word. "Is that so? You did? Really?"

Eva chuckled. "Was he a good boy, Mrs. Flowers?"

The old woman answered, taking back the phone. "Mm-hmm. You should've seen him last night. He was trying to show me how to read 'The Cat in the Hat.' He kept interrupting me during his story time, pointing his little finger at the words in the book."

Eva laughed. "Aww, he'll get it after a while. Hold tight with the little man. I'll be home soon."

"Okay, hon. See you then," Mrs. Flowers said.

Eva ended the call and informed Grandpa Ricardo and Pastor Tyson of the incident. Both of them were surprised, and the pastor said he'd start a prayer chain for Andre's recovery.

"Thank you, pastor. It means so much to me," Eva said toward the end of the call.

"No, problem, sister. It's the least I could do," Pastor Tyson replied.

"All right, bye now." Eva pressed the hang-up button and scrolled through her contact list again. She stared at her mother's cell number, biting her lip. Calling her mom didn't seem like a good idea. Even after seven years, she still struggled to accept the fact her daughter was married with a child of her own.

With aversion and worry, Eva glanced in hesitation from the passenger seat to her iPhone in her hand. She filtered a breath through clenched teeth and tossed her cell on the empty seat like it was a contagious disease, hoping her mom doesn't call her. It could ring any minute—any second.

For some odd reason, she always knew when something bad happened in Eva's life like she had a crystal ball that told her daughter's misfortune. After the tragic news she's gotten, the last thing she needed to tolerate was her mother's berating, obnoxious behavior.

It was the main reason there had been friction between them since she was a little girl, hardly ever able to get along with her. They favored in height and body figure, but were as different as salt and sugar.

Eva rolled her eyes and turned her key in the ignition, praying in her mind. *God, help Andre get well soon. Amen.*

• CHAPTER 7 •

Eva

Wednesday, Sept. 6th

Eva leaned her forehead against the yellow-tiled wall and thought she would puke. Her tears mixed with the sprinkling, hot water trickling down her naked, slender body. Since the devastating call from the police, she had cried for an eternity, pondering how she'll adjust to her new situation. Life as she knew it would never be the same; and if faced with the worst, she wondered how she could live without Andre's presence.

After coming home from her overnight stay in the hospital, her week off flew by fast, but Andre was still in a coma. His Glasgow Coma Scale remained at three, and though he wasn't getting worse, it seemed he would never get better. She bowed her head and took a series of deep breaths, trying to keep from losing her mind.

Eva closed her eyes and banged her fists on the tiles. She wanted to scream and question God why he had let something so terrible happen to her husband.

But all she mustered was a weak whimper. She turned off the squeaky knob and stood there a moment longer, recalling her past week. Yesterday, she discussed with Mrs. Flowers Andre's frequent unresponsiveness and her concern he won't wake up.

Their conversation had shifted into another long story about Mr. Clyde and his Alzheimer's diagnosis. It was good to have someone to relate to her emotional pain, but a part of Mrs. Flowers would never know how she feels. Andre was an independent, young man who was a hard worker at the top of his career. He had big plans and ambitions for her and their son, dreams that now may never come true.

Last Friday wasn't easier.

For the first time, the electricity and water were cut off. Eva had made visits to the utility companies and requested bill transfers. Aside from her checking account, she didn't know the first thing about paying bills, as Andre had always handled the math of them for her.

Her mother's credit score wasn't the best, so she never taught her, much less discuss about her grandparents. Getting counsel from a bank teller helped answer her few questions.

Eva sniffled and opened her eyes, returning to present

time. At breakfast, Mrs. Higgins had called her, and she reassured her she was clocking in for work. She imagined her daycare kids missed her playful energy and fun-loving attitude. But now, being happy felt like rock climbing without a safety line.

She fought to reach the summit of joy in her life. Each passing day brought her closer to making a harsh decision, a decision she'd never be able to forgive herself for making. Now she understood how Andre felt if she bore another child and died. Though Eva didn't want to concentrate on the *'what ifs,'* life had a way of showing one up when least expected, and she had to accept it.

Eva grabbed her towel draped over the shower curtain rail. She muffled a frustrated groan that echoed in her ears. As hard as it was, it was time to leave her wrecked emotions behind and pull herself together, especially for her son. Andrew was unaware of his father's accident, but he was also bright and alert. Sooner or later, he'd notice something different, if he didn't already.

Looking at his little, innocent face, a whisper spoke from his maple brown eyes as he surveyed the rooms in the house and didn't see his father: *Where's Daddy?* Eva pulled back the shower curtain and stepped out of the bathtub, wrapped in her towel. She rolled on her deodorant, rubbed lotion on her body, brushed her teeth, and put her contact lens back into her eyes. Then she styled her shoulder-length hair with her comb and blow dryer and left the bathroom. Eva walked into the master bedroom and paused. Her eyes flooded, staring at Andre's sage green terry robe hanging on a hook beside the dresser.

She wore a wistful smile and imagined her tall husband wearing it after taking a shower. He looked so real before her, leaning on the wall with his arms crossed, giving her his charming, lopsided smile. *Andre?* Her heart stopped beating at his presence. She scuttled over and handled the collar of the empty robe.

Eva closed her eyes and sniffed. It still held the fragrance of his rainforest soap mixed with his cologne. Andre smelled so fresh and enticing. He always used bars of soap whenever he took baths as his grandfather raised him to do. Once he told her Grandpa Ricardo jokingly said scrubbing with bar soap created more suds and a cleaner bod, and that's what Andre grew up believing.

A tear rolled down Eva's cheek, stroking her hands around the collar and soft interior of the robe. She appreciated the clothes and gifts he bought her over the years, but all she cared for was his undivided attention, even if they sat in silence.

She sighed at Andre's side of the queen-sized bed. The daycare uniform she wore to work lay over the blanket. Each day she and the other teachers wore a yellow T-shirt painted with an orange sunrise, a khaki skirt, and white tennis shoes. Eva got dressed in her clothes and looped the strap of her teacher ID around her neck. She looked in the oval mirror of the dresser and tied her hair in a side ponytail.

Just 6:00 a.m., it was still dark outside, but the sun was peeking through thick, cumulus clouds huddled in the deep plum and gold sky. Today's sunrise reminded her of one of her mother's landscape paintings. Although her mom was a handful, she had a lovely talent Eva admired and thought should get more recognition than she received.

She glanced out the window and whispered a prayer, asking for God's strength and a sunny day. Rain would add to the gloominess hovering over her head. She had grieved for what used to be—now she had to move on toward her future.

"Hey, Eva! Andy's all set! Are you ready, hon?" Mrs. Flowers called from the living room.

"Yes, ma'am! I'm coming!" Eva took her clutch purse from the dresser and headed downstairs to join the others.

"Surprise!" the kids shouted as Eva entered the door.

She gawked with a hand over her racing heart and scanned the two-year-old classroom. Unlike a typical day of chaos, everything was neat and tidy. All art supplies were in the tin cans on the back shelf, the kids' coats and backpacks were in their cubbies, and the toys were in their labeled plastic bins.

Eva read the white banner hanging across the ceiling the daycare kids made for her: *Welcome Back, Mrs. Lucas! We Love U!*

A bright red heart replaced the word 'love.' Painted around the welcome greeting were colorful childlike handprints. Each pair of small hands had the name of one of the ten children underneath: *Tyler, Autumn, Reggie, Brianna, Dinah, Juan, Sidney, Garrett, Isabelle, and Chase.*

Tyler Witherspoon was the quietest student in the class, but he was also a stubborn thumb sucker, a baby habit Eva and his mother strove to get him to stop.

Autumn McKee was an auburn-haired princess. She was also Mrs. Higgins' granddaughter and a soon-to-be big sister to a new baby brother. Reggie Gibson was a little gentleman, always doing nice favors for his teachers and female classmates. Brianna Luiz was shy and liked to play by herself, but she had one of the most contagious giggles Eva ever heard.

Dinah Welch was the main student to watch. She was a little troublemaker who picked on other kids, but she was also the only child in class who could already write her first name. Juan Diaz was an artist in the making, preferring to color and draw more than play with toys.

Sidney Webb was a motor mouth. She enjoyed talking about her family, which included her parents, her aunt, her grandma, two older brothers, an older sister, and three dogs. Her stories were always funny and entertaining, but sometimes she talked too much, like during naptime.

Garrett Fisher obsessed over superhero action figures, his favorite being Batman. Isabelle Holt was a tender heart, who Dinah called a crybaby. Close to her mommy, she cried every time her mother had to leave for work. Chase Daniels was a lovable teddy bear and being big for his age, the tallest kid in the class.

Eva looked from the banner. Below on the fine motor table were containers of banana nut and blueberry muffins, a bowl of fruit cocktail, a bag of Styrofoam plates, plastic spoons, and small cartons of milk.

Happy tears filled Eva's eyes. "Wow. Thank you. I . . . I don't know what else to say."

"Well, the kids wanted to throw you a welcome back party," Louise said. "So, I asked permission from Mrs. Higgins, and she gave the OK."

Louise Burnett was Eva's co-worker in her classroom. After a disappointing breakup, she raised her daughters alone. Her sense of humor and good nature helped relieve Eva's stress load during their workdays. She and Eva supervised five kids each, but they had all the children take part in their circle time together.

"Thanks," Eva told Louise.

"You're welcome." Louise smiled and clapped for the toddlers to get in order. "All right, class! Let's get seated!" She raised an open hand and counted down her fingers. "Five . . . four . . . three . . ."

Little boys and girls scampered around the table and plopped in the colored plastic chairs. Reggie and Autumn raced after the same chair beside Eva as she took her seat. Both were close to her and always fought over getting her attention.

"I wanna sit here," Autumn whined.

"No, it's mine!" Reggie frowned, tugging the chair toward him.

Louise stopped counting. "Reggie, Autumn, it doesn't matter where you sit."

"But I touched it first." Autumn sulked and looked up at Louise, peeking through her curled bangs. Her yellow bowknot headband held back her wavy, auburn hair and matched cute with her bumble bee sweater.

Eva wore a wry smile and lifted her shoulder as Louise rolled her eyes and sighed wearily. She eyed the long-faced, black boy beside Autumn. "Reggie, can you be nice and let Autumn sit beside me, please?"

"Okay," Reggie muttered. He crossed his arms and plopped in a chair next to Juan.

"Thank you." Eva smiled at Reggie and revived his wide, dimpled grin.

Come on, class, bow your heads," Eva instructed.

The toddlers wove their hands and bowed their heads. Before every meal, they said their grace together, which Eva and Louise had taught them. With their daycare teachers, the kids recited the blessing over the food:

God is great and God is good,
Now we thank Him for our food,
By His hand, we all are fed,
Give us Lord our daily bread,
Amen, thanks, God.

Some of the children tried opening their milk cartons themselves.

Louise opened the containers of muffins and gave the kids one based on what flavor he or she wanted, while Eva served them fruit cocktail from the bowl.

"Yes, Jesus loves me! For the Bible tells me so," Eva sang, plucking a ukulele.

All the toddlers sat on the round, blue alphabet rug during circle time. Sidney and Isabelle played tambourines, Chase beat on a bongo drum, and the other kids clapped to the song.

Louise sat opposite from Eva and sang the verse with her, rattling a pair of Mexican wood maracas. *"Jesus loves me! This I know, for the Bible tells me so. Little ones to Him belong, they are weak, but He is strong. Yes, Jesus loves me! Yes,*

Jesus loves me! Yes, Jesus loves me! For the Bible tells me so . . ."

"Yay!" the children said after the song ended.

"Okay, class, it's nap-time!" Eva took the tambourines from the two girls and the drum from Chase. She and Louise placed the instruments in the clear bin as the children scattered to their blue cots. Across from the quiet reading area were two rows of five little beds.

Eva and Louise tucked the kids in with their blankets from each of their wooden, name-tagged cubbies.

Louise draped Chase with his Bob the Builder fleece blanket. "Y'all know the rules. Go to sleep and no—"

"Playing!" the kids interrupted in unison. Some of them giggled while snuggling under their blankets.

Eva chuckled and covered Sidney with her pink, Barbie blanket. "Make sure you stay quiet and take a nap, sweetie, okay? You can talk about your birthday party later."

"Yes, Mrs. Lucas." Sidney held her teddy bear underarm and shut her eyes.

Louise stood from her knees. "Phew, finally I can relax."

Eva chuckled beside her co-worker and watched the children. Louise wasn't exaggerating. From six-thirty in the morning to twelve-thirty in the afternoon a lot happened in a daycare. The kids' naptime was their only chance of freedom to take a break.

Louise left for the Teacher's Lounge and returned with

a Styrofoam plate of food and a paper cup. Then Eva took her turn and likewise came back to the classroom. The teachers sat at the same fine motor table and ate their lunches, whispering over their food.

"So, how's it going?" Louise asked, pouring ranch dressing on her Caesar salad. She placed her sauce cup down. "Mrs. Higgins said you suffered a family tragedy."

"My husband had an accident," Eva said, rolling a rotten grape tomato on her plate with her fork.

Louise's jaw dropped. "What? Is Andre okay?"

"He's in a coma." Eva hung her head, staring at her plate of salad. "I can't bear looking at him anymore. Seeing him . . . the tubes and wires on his body. It makes me sick to my stomach. It's already been a week, Louise. I'm not confident he'll recover."

Louise touched Eva's hand. "You can't lose heart. Andre's a strong man. He'll bounce back from this."

"But when?" Eva's vision blurred, her chin quivering. "I've waited for days, praying and reading him scriptures from the Bible . . . hoping he'll open those gentle, brown eyes of his. Nothing's changed." She blinked and a tear fell onto a leaf of lettuce on her plate. "And if matters couldn't get worse, Andre made most of our income. By myself, I can barely keep up with our household bills."

Eva cupped a hand over her mouth and stifled a sob. "I grew up on welfare. There were times my mom didn't know if she'd be able to keep me. I don't wanna be on assistance, but I also don't want anyone to take Andy away from me."

"Don't worry, Eva. God can work it out," Louise said, trying to raise Eva's spirits. "You might not feel like it, but He's right by your side, girl. He sees your pain and knows your struggles. He might not act in *our* timing, but God's got your back."

Eva gave a half-shrug. "Perhaps, but I'm still scared. Yesterday, Dr. Brown warned me about the effects of brain injury in his office. Andre . . . he may never be the same again." She took a fast breath, regaining her composure. "I try to be happy for the kids, but I'm so burned out, and things will get tougher before they get better. I know they will."

"Well, I'm willing to help wherever I can. You know me." Louise sipped from her cup.

Eva frowned and shook her head. "Oh, no. I can't allow that. You're a mother of four and your daughter Kenya is still so young. How are you supposed to help me *and* take care of your own family?"

"I guess you have a point there." Louise twitched her mouth, thinking. "But I'll at least be praying for you and Andre. Y'all are good people and two of my best friends."

"Thank you, Louise. Thanks a lot." Eva found a smile and dried her cheek with a napkin. She drank from her cup of iced water and bit a Ritz cracker with a slice of cheddar cheese. Although she was heartbroken over Andre's accident, it taught her not to jump to conclusions.

One night had changed her life forever, and there was no telling what numbers would add to the equation. How will she solve the dilemma that beset her? As bill collectors harassed her with calls, her family expenses piled up like dirty laundry. Time was moving quicker than she could believe, and Andrew was a growing boy eager to interact with other kids and learn new things.

In a couple more months, she would need to move him into her own classroom—which meant paying more for his daycare stay. She needed a miracle, and negotiation from the president of the daycare couldn't hurt. At the same time, she understood her director had to keep strict regulations. Equality was their policy, and that meant treating all parents with the same respect and financial payment, even if a parent's an employee.

"Have you heard from your mother?" Louise asked, pulling Eva out of her trance.

Eva darted her gaze from a side window to Louise. "Not lately. We aren't too close." She ate a spoonful of strawberry yogurt from a container.

Louise knitted her brows. "How come? I'm sure she'll help you."

"You don't know my mother." Eva leaned back and pursed her lips with a look of disapproval. "She doesn't just *help* out. She tries to take over everything, including how I take care of my son. She's been nitpicking me since I was a little girl. After coming home from dealing with stuck-up cheerleaders in high school, I literally used to feel like my mom was bullying me too. She made me feel like nothing I did was good enough, or I was incapable of thinking for myself."

"Set her boundaries," Louise suggested, shrugging. "You might still be her child, but she has to respect your wishes as an adult married woman too."

Eva folded her arms and sighed. "I'm afraid she'll get offended. She can be fussy and irrational, which makes matters worse. She's an artist and always traveling places like a nomad. I don't have the slightest clue when she'll visit again."

"You mean, your mom . . . pops up unannounced?" Louise wrinkled her nose.

"Yep," Eva said, "and it hasn't been the first time either." She blushed and glanced around, ensuring nobody but her co-worker heard what she whispered next. "One time, Andre and I were right in the middle of attempting a *lovemaking* moment and the doorbell rang. We wondered who would come to our house at midnight, and lo and behold, it was my mom, standing with luggage in each hand for two weeks visit."

Louise snickered. "Wow. I know Andre didn't like that interruption."

"Actually, it didn't faze him," Eva said, "I mean we've

agreed to have another child, but it never worked out. Andre was always scared ever since . . ."

"Since what?"

"Ever since Andy was born." Eva lowered her head, fidgeting with the hem of her yellow T-shirt." I had contracted a rare complication infection in my bloodstream called amniotic fluid embolism. It has to do with the fluid that surrounds a baby in a mother's womb. A small percentage of women experience it at least once. I couldn't breathe . . . I was so scared I thought I would die."

Louise gawked. "Oh, wow. I didn't know that."

Eva sniffled and lifted her sad eyes to her co-worker. "I don't blame Andy for it though. We were both victims in a crazy ordeal, but the doctor said many women who experience this have safe, full-term deliveries afterward." She ate another scoop and stuck her spoon in the yogurt container. "Somehow Andre thought if I get pregnant, it'll happen again. He was afraid he'd lose me. My mom's arrival had completely turned off his mood. But he was polite and treated my mother with the highest respect."

She sighed. "He's only complained once I need to have a serious talk with her about respecting our privacy and our home. Truth is, my mom's lonely. She raised me by herself, you know, and suffered a broken heart, which I don't believe ever healed."

Eva leaned back again. "I never knew my father, but

she loved him dearly. I can only imagine how she felt, his parents rejecting her for the color of her skin."

"Why didn't your father marry her?" Louise asked.

Eva held out her hands and shrugged. "Mom said he was loyal . . . too loyal to his mother and Italian roots."

"That's too bad." Louise shook her head. "I can understand your mother's pain. I've got four girls of my own and love them to death, but it's hard being a single mother." She sniffled and held back her tears. "It's harder when . . . the father of your kids wants nothing to do with them."

Eva placed her hand over Louise's, feeling empathy for her co-worker. By God's grace, she had a good husband who played the role of fatherhood in their son's life. But after Andre's car accident, she got a bitter taste of the struggle of single parenthood, a struggle that could last the rest of her life.

• CHAPTER 8 •

Eva

Two Weeks & One Day Later

Please wake up, Andre. I miss you . . .

Eva opened her tightened eyes as the thought echoed through her mind and stirred under the palm leaf comforter. She hugged her husband's pillow, peering at the young couple in the silver-framed, wedding photo on her nightstand. A photographer took the picture during the outdoor reception. There was an awesome turnout on the cool, summer afternoon.

Guests and loved ones surrounded them in a lively crowd. Neighbors, co-workers, family, and friends answered their invitations and came to show their love and support. It made Eva feel special, as often she felt unwanted by anyone, even her mother sometimes. But she and Andre were on cloud nine.

They were happy and perfect together, slicing their four-tiered cake. It was made with a vanilla bean fondant and designed with tiny roses around it in cream-white frosting.

Moisture surfaced Eva's eyes, studying the photo.

Regret was something she didn't want to feel, but she wondered if she should've married Andre. Falling in love wasn't completely pleasant. Pain and hurt also came with it when things went wrong. She didn't think about it then, but she surely focused on it now.

Eva stared at the vase of flowers on the dresser she got the night of their wedding anniversary. The white roses were wilted, and the leaves were dried to crisp, a couple of petals sprinkled on top of the dresser. Like their marriage, they were falling apart, their beautiful newness wearing away. She rolled over and looked up.

Her heart quaked in her chest at the eerie shadow hovering from the sunlight across the ceiling. It looked like a beast reaching out a clawed hand. But then she remembered the oak tree nearby the driveway. She sat up and glanced out the window beside the bed, relieved to see a naked branch, rattling in the light, morning breeze. All the bright, yellow leaves had fallen off it as the first day of autumn began.

Andrew whined out his sleep.

"I'm coming, Andy!" Eva got out of bed and tied on her lilac robe. She tucked her bare feet in her soft, matching slippers, left the master bedroom, and rushed down the narrow hallway to her son's room.

Andrew's bedroom was styled with a sailor boy theme. The wallpaper was navy blue and white striped with an anchor and lifebuoy pattern design. Above his white crib was a navy-blue ship helm engraved with his name. Mr. Clyde had made it before he was born. Aside from being a war veteran, he had an extraordinary talent for wood-carving objects.

Close to a single window in the room, a white, boat-shaped bookcase held Andrew's favorite Dr. Seuss books and nursery rhymes. Framed baby photos of his early months of life rested on the middle shelf. Below the window was a treasure chest for his toys.

Eva poked out her lip and approached the crib. "Aww . . . what's wrong baby?"

Andrew was standing with his small hands gripping the edge railing. His pudgy cheeks were wet and glistened in the sunlight. Not seeing "Mookie" in his crib—as her son called him—Eva discovered what troubled his little soul. Mookie was his stuffed, brown plush monkey with Velcro hands and feet.

Andre had bought it for their son for his first birthday. Andrew loved *Curious George* and attached to his monkey instantly, taking him everywhere. But last night was the first time he slept without it. For him not to realize until morning, her son must've been exhausted from crying last night. Having his daddy in the hospital, he wouldn't let her go to save her life.

Eva gasped and knitted her eyebrows. "Uh-oh, looks like Mommy forgot to tuck in Mookie. I'm sorry, honey." She lifted Andrew into her arms, kissed his cheek, and toted him on her hip. "Come on, let's find him. I'm sure he's around here somewhere."

She unfastened the anchor latch of his treasure chest and peeked inside. Lego blocks, shape puzzles, electronic learning systems, and a few other stuffed animal friends filled the base of the chest. "Nope, he's not in there."

Andrew wrinkled his face and started whining in disappointment.

"Shh . . .we'll find him, Andy." Eva exited her son's room and journeyed downstairs to the living room. Mookie with his stitched smile across his face was lying sideways on the gray carpet floor near Andre's tan recliner. The stuffed monkey must've fallen from her lap when she stood from it to sneak Andrew in his crib.

Eva bent down, picked up Mookie, and handed him to her son with a smile. "Here you go, Andy."

Andy sniffled and cuddled the soft monkey to his face. "Mookie . . . mine." Approaching the terrible twos, "no" and "mine" were becoming some of his favorite words.

Eva chuckled, rolling her eyes. "Yes, he's yours, baby. Now, let's get breakfast." She carried her son into the kitchen and sat him and his monkey in his highchair.

The digital phone on the counter rang.

"Hello, Lucas's residence?" Eva held the phone in the lock of her shoulder and took a carton of eggs from the refrigerator.

"Hello, Mrs. Lucas, this is Dr. Brown." His voice was thick and raspy.

Eva pushed the speaker button and put the phone on the counter. "Hi, doctor." She frowned. "Are you feeling, okay?" She placed a frying pan on the electric stove.

Dr. Brown cleared his throat. "Well, I'm a little under the weather, but I can't complain."

Andrew babbled and drummed his hands on his food tray, tuning out the adult conversation.

"Shh, be quiet, Andy." Eva glanced at her son with her forefinger to her lips. She rolled her eyes again and focused back on the call. "Sorry, doctor. My son wants to be gabby. You were saying?"

The doctor hesitated.

"Dr. Brown? You still there?" Eva grabbed a bowl from the dish rack and cracked an egg in it.

"Oh, yes, Mrs. Lucas. I'm here. It's just . . . I'm trying to find the right words . . ."

Eva frowned, whisking. "The right words for what?"

"Mrs. Lucas . . . it's going on four weeks." Dr. Brown sighed. "For the sake of you and your son, it's time you think ahead about your husband. Can you meet me in my office, please?"

Fear plunged in Eva's stomach. She paused. "Okay, sure. I'll be there after work today."

"Good. I'll meet you later, Mrs. Lucas."

"Bye, doctor." Eva gulped and ended the call. Nobody had to say anything. Yesterday afternoon she received an important letter about Andre's health coverage, but she buried it under junk mail. There was no need to read it. She already suspected matters took a turn for the worse, and she hoped she'd have the strength to go through whatever was coming next.

Silence suffocated Eva with every passing minute. For some odd reason, she was taken to another waiting room from the main crowded one where Mrs. Flowers kept a watch of Andrew for her.

Wrestling with her apprehension, she fiddled with the metal clip of her clutch purse and scanned the lifeless waiting room. Dr. Larrabee and another male specialist she didn't recognize from Andre's trauma team were performing a serious exam on her husband. Although Dr. Brown hadn't gotten into detail of everything, she sensed something about it differed from a normal Glasgow Coma Scale test. She closed her eyes tightly and wove her hands under her chin. *God, please let me get good news from this exam. Please . . .*

Andre had to be okay. He had to get better and come home again. For some time, she had prayed faithfully and believed God would work a miracle, and she refused to let her hope die. Before she left Andre's bedside, she kissed his cheek every visit and it was always warm to the touch. His black, curly hair had also grown back over his head stitches the past few weeks, and that couldn't happen to a dead person, could it?

"Mrs. Lucas, the exam is finished. Dr. Brown is waiting for you," Nurse Jia called.

Eva left and walked to the doctor's office.

"Please, come in," Dr. Brown said, sitting behind his wide desk.

Eva sat in a chair in front of the doctor. She observed as he stood and closed the door of his office for their private discussion.

Her heart pounded. "Please, tell me. How is he?"

Dr. Brown filled his seat and laced his large hands on his desk. "Dr. Larrabee and his assistant performed a brainstem exam on Andre and your husband passed the test."

Eva grinned. "Really?"

"That's not a good thing, Mrs. Lucas," Dr. Brown said.

Eva's smile faded. "Oh, it isn't?"

Dr. Brown's wide forehead creased with three lines of wrinkles. "No. We were hoping his result would be negative. But based on the fact his Glasgow Coma Scale test hasn't improved for the past three weeks, it makes perfect sense." He pulled off his eyeglasses and placed them on his desk, leaning back in his chair. He fluttered his eyes and hung open his mouth a second without words. "Mrs. Lucas, were you contacted by your health insurance company?"

"Yes," Eva said, "they sent me a letter, but I never read it yet." She glanced at the floor, ashamed.

"Why not?"

Eva gritted her back teeth and massaged tension from her neck. "I-I haven't had the time."

"Well, your health insurance company knows you've been struggling to pay your husband's medical bills," Dr. Brown said. "Life support is expensive, and I'm aware you have a toddler son at home. The funds you use to sustain Andre's well-being can help you with other things like food and utilities. Therefore, they set a maximum day limit."

"No! They can't do that. I mean, it still hasn't been a month since Andre's accident," Eva replied.

"That's true," Dr. Brown said, "but supplying him with life support is clinically unprofitable." He picked up his glasses and licked his lips, bracing himself for his next words. "Mrs. Lucas, I'm afraid Andre's suffered brain death."

Brain death? What's that mean? The words were like a whirl of vertigo after getting off a merry-go-round.

Eva inclined her head with a confused look, leaning forward. "Brain death? Can . . . can you fix it?"

"No," Dr. Brown said, fidgeting with his glasses, "his brain will likely begin liquefying within the fourth week. Even if he wakes, he'd be no better than a vegetable. I wish I could do something else, but the trauma team and I have done everything we can for him."

Eva's eyes swarm with tears, her chin quivering. "So . . .what are you saying?"

Dr. Brown drew a long breath and exhaled slowly. "I'm so sorry, Mrs. Lucas, but your husband . . . your husband's dead."

Adrenaline rushed through Eva's veins. "No!" She jumped from her chair and paced the floor with her hands on her hips. She jabbed her forefinger on the doctor's desk, debating her claim like a lawyer in the courtroom. "Andre's not dead! He's still breathing . . . his heart is beating—"

"Mrs. Lucas, your husband's connected to a ventilator, which artificially supplies oxygen to his heart. They've tested him and all his vital signs. Without it, he can't breathe, and his heart would stop beating in a few hours or so. The only things worthwhile you can do is . . . donate Andre's organs and let him rest in peace."

"You'd like that wouldn't you, doctor," Eva scolded, crossing her arms. "My husband sliced open like a game of Operation—his eyes, heart, and lungs taken from his body!"

Dr. Brown flared his nostrils and willed himself to stay calm. He sighed again. "Please, don't take it personally. It's not about money. There are just a lot of suffering people waiting for transplants. Your husband could save someone else's life. In Andre's case, no paperwork is necessary. Your consent to remove Andre from life support will help to proceed with transplantation."

"Is that so?" Eva said, peering at the afternoon sunshine from the window blinds of the office. She glared over her shoulder at the doctor. "Well, I'm not giving it!"

"Listen to me, I know you're upset," Dr. Brown said, "you have every right to be, but Andre registered as a donor. This already gives authorized consent to the Organ Donor Foundation. The fair thing to do would be what he would've wanted, and not yourself."

Eva stepped over and plopped in the client chair. She stared at the doctor. "All right, fine . . . I'll consider it, but I'm not making any promises."

"That's fine," Dr. Brown said. "Whatever you choose, I'll support it one hundred percent. Andre will remain on life support for three more days. Just take your time and think about your decision. However, the transplant team *can* continue transplantation without your permission. It'll be less painful if you give your blessing."

Eva took a deep inhale and sighed.

When Dr. Brown told her Andre was dead, a part of her had also died—her hope and faith the impossible was possible. Though it was her choice to make, she couldn't imagine ending Andre's life. Since the day they said, "I do," they had become one, and pulling the plug to her would be like suicide. But one question reigned above her final decision of Andre's fate.

How could she live without her husband?"

• CHAPTER 9 •

Eva

Three Days Later

Before church service, Eva called Mrs. Flowers to watch Andy again and visited the empty sanctuary to think things over. She dragged up the middle aisle, walking like a zombie in a graveyard. Eva fell on her knees in front of the altar, crouched over, and sobbed with her face to the floor. She made a thundering cry throughout the massive church, releasing her bitter anguish and frustration.

Deciding what to do about Andre was hard, but knowing she'd have to let her husband go was harder. Her mind had gone blank, and all she could do was allow her river of heartache to overflow.

Seven years wasn't a complete decade. Her marriage with Andre was fun, sweet, and adventurous, but much too short. Together they were supposed to see Andrew have his first day of pre-K, graduate from college, and grow old to witness the next generation. Her sobs echoed in the vacant, spacious room. Footsteps came from behind her. Pastor Tyson must've overheard and come to check out the matter.

A thick hand with stubby fingers touched her shoulder.

She raised her tear-streaked face to him.

Pastor Tyson knelt near her, his expression filled with great concern. "Sister Lucas, what's wrong? Is it Andre?"

"Yes." Eva sniffled and wiped beneath her eyes. "The doctor said there's nothing else he or the staff can do. He wants me to donate my husband's organs for recipients on the National Transplant Waiting List."

The pastor sighed. "Well, what do you want to do?"

Eva shrugged. "I don't know, pastor, but I have to decide today. Why would a loving God want my husband dead?" She studied the pastor's face. "Why did this have to happen?"

"Sister, I can't answer that," Pastor Tyson said, "but I know there is always a reason for everything. You'll know in due time. You believe and trust God for guidance." He patted her shoulder, stood, and started leaving to his office.

"Wait!" Eva called.

The bald pastor paused and glanced back. "Yes?"

"Can you pray for me?" Eva said.

Pastor Tyson smiled. "Sure, sister." He joined Eva on the floor. "You ready?"

Eva nodded and closed her eyes, her hands in prayer pose. "Yes, pastor." She relaxed her shoulders and waited for the pastor to begin.

Pastor Tyson bowed his head. "Father God, I ask you to help this young sister. Give her the strength to accept whatever Your will is for her husband. Please, guide her in her decision-making that she does the right thing. Comfort her through her grief and provide for her and her son whatever they need. Protect them and bless them, in Jesus Christ's name. Amen."

"Amen," Eva echoed, stifling a sob.

"Be encouraged, sister, and never forget the Lord has the last say," Pastor Tyson said.

Eva nodded and bit her lower lip.

The pastor entered back into his side office. Since his prayer, Eva felt better, but her husband's departure was still around the corner. She exited the sanctuary and returned home again.

After Eva stepped out of the shower and tied on her robe, she sat on Andre's side of the bed. She picked up the framed picture of her husband on his nightstand and stared at the photo of him in his white lab coat and name tag, crossing his arms. Since her talk with Dr. Brown in his office, she had come to terms with the chance her husband would never come home.

What should I do, Andre? Eva sighed at his picture. Out of nowhere, his kind voice spoke to her mind as clear as day, "Do what you know is right." She gulped and fought back her tears. It was a hard pill to swallow, but it was the truth. As much as she hated to admit, Andre was a proud, registered donor, and after death, he wanted others to remember him for giving the gift of life to someone else.

Her vision blurred, talking to Andre's photo. "Okay, honey. I'll do it . . . I'll give my consent for you." It was a picture, but it was more than an object to see and hold. The photo held Andre's witty character and his spirit, his optimistic attitude of seeing the bright side of dark situations.

The longer she stared at his picture, the more her sad frown turned upward to a smile. She was glad she had an entire collection of photos of him. When the surgery was over and his casket buried off, she wanted to cherish his handsome face, to keep it locked in her heart forever like a treasure in a safe.

She wondered who would get Andre's organs after the operation. No matter who, she hoped it to be people who would take care of them and not take her husband's sacrifice for granted. Her sixteen-month-old son was about to lose his daddy without a word in it edgewise, and the thought of it broke Eva's heart. Truth is, it was the main reason she had a hard time choosing what to do. Raised without a father in her life, she had wanted for it not to be the case of her child or children. Eva placed Andre's photograph back on the nightstand. She cracked open the door of the master bedroom and poked her head in the outside hall.

Aromas of maple sausage and fresh brewing coffee wafted through the air. Mrs. Flowers insisted on cooking a big breakfast to uplift Eva's spirits. Eva tiptoed down the narrow aisle and peeked in Andrew's bedroom. The little boy was still asleep. He was so peaceful, so she didn't bother him.

She came downstairs and entered the kitchen. "Good morning."

With a spatula, Mrs. Flowers added one last pancake to a stack of them on a plate. She glanced over her shoulder with a half-smile. "Good morning, hon. How are you feeling?"

"I'm hanging in there." Eva wore a weak look. "I'm taking Andre off life support."

Mrs. Flowers paused and sighed. "You finally decided, huh? I know it was difficult."

"Yeah," Eva said, "but it's what Andre would've wanted me to do. It doesn't make me happy, but I love him too much not to respect his last wishes."

She dragged a chair from the kitchen table and sat down. "Thanks for making breakfast."

"You're welcome, hon," Mrs. Flowers said. "You've had a lot on your shoulders since Andre's accident. Having to make a tough decision, I thought the least I could do was give you one less thing to worry about."

"Well, I appreciate it," Eva said with a smile.

"Is Andy up?" Mrs. Flowers offered Eva coffee.

Eva cupped the warm mug. "Nope. He's knocked out. Andre's absence has been hard on him. Andy's been antsier lately. He's a bright kid and knows when I'm sad or something's wrong. I told him his daddy was in a *deep sleep*, but I'm sure he doesn't understand what I mean. It's getting tougher for him to fall asleep at night." She blew off the steam and took a sip.

"Poor child." Mrs. Flowers sucked her teeth.

"How am I supposed to tell him his daddy died?" Eva said. "I can't—I just can't do that. Someplace inside won't let me say goodbye." She stared in her mug, on the verge of crying again.

Mrs. Flowers wiped her hands on a towel and joined her at the table. "I understand what you mean. When you're used to someone always there, it's hard to imagine them ever leaving, especially when it's someone you love. But unfortunately, life happens. People are born and die every day. That's why time is so precious to us."

Eva raised her head and looked into Mrs. Flowers'

eyes. If she could turn back the clock, she would in a heartbeat, and had Andre known ahead of time about his accident, she knew he would too. She took another sip and glanced at her brown leather wristwatch. "Well, it's getting late. I'd better wake Andy for church." She sighed and forced herself from the table. "He's gonna be cranky, but he'll likely fall asleep on the ride there."

"Yes, probably." Mrs. Flowers chuckled.

Eva headed back upstairs to her son.

The church grew quiet as Eva arrived and sat on a pew with her son, but she wasn't looking forward to the many bawling faces of the congregation. What she needed was encouragement through her bereavement and not a load of tears and pity.

Pastor Tyson stood behind the pulpit and began his Sunday sermon. He opened his bible and smiled. "Good morning, church!"

"Morning!" a few members said.

"Today in my office I thought to myself about the story of Job," Pastor Tyson said. "His experiences are a great lesson for us and showed how quickly turning points can change one's life. But through the storm and the rain, the heartache and pain Job suffered, he refused to curse God. You know, we look to God for good things to happen, but the minute trouble comes, we sometimes forget He exists."

Eva squirmed and wrapped her arms around Andy in her lap. She was feeling attacked by the pastor, but rather than tiptoeing to the ladies' room, she listened to the entire message. It turned out it was what she needed to hear, a wake-up call to the beneficial effect of hardships. That though we had no control over life, the struggles we go through make us and the relationships we share with others stronger.

She hadn't thought about her situation that way. But since becoming "the breadwinner," using her smarts she'd learned how to manage money in ways she never would've if Andre hadn't gotten injured. She also conceded how much she missed her mom, and her desire to strengthen their mother-daughter relationship.

After several years of friction, toxicity, and manipulation, it wouldn't be easy, but with the Lord involved in the matter, it was possible. The closing of the service ended with the church choir singing the gospel song, "My Help (Cometh From The Lord)" by Brooklyn Tabernacle Choir.

Eva closed her eyes and waved her hand in her seat, allowing each note the lead alto singer and the choir sang to soothe her afflicted soul. Their harmonies were magnificent, during the triumph finish, and she nearly thought she would fly to the clouds. The congregation crowded on the pews rejoiced and applauded after the

the song ended. Some stood, while others bounced happily and waved their hands and paper fans, chanting hallelujahs and amens.

A tear dripped from Eva's chin.

Regardless of what happened, she believed the Lord would carry her through. After a few uplifting remarks, Pastor Tyson said the benediction.

Eva greeted and hugged a couple of people. Even despite some of their doses of compassion, she could tell some of the young women weren't sorry for her. Having wanted Andre for themselves, some of them were pleased for her misfortune, but Eva ignored their sarcastic comments.

Vengeance belonged to God, and in due time, He'd likely handle them His way. Besides, there were more important things to think about, such as giving her consent tomorrow. It would be the last time she sees her husband in the hospital on the machines.

Before she leaves, she would ensure she told him five simple words. *Goodbye, I'll love you forever.*

• CHAPTER 10 •

Eva

Monday, Sept. 25th

The pit of Eva's stomach fell as Dr. Brown and a middle-aged man in teal scrubs stepped into the hospital conference room. She looked up as the critical care physician introduced a lean, suntanned man.

"Mrs. Lucas, this is Peter Sullivan. He's the family care coordinator of the Organ Procurement Organization," Dr. Brown said.

Eva allowed a smile and shook the coordinator's hand. "Nice to meet you, sir."

"Likewise, Mrs. Lucas. I give my *deepest* condolences for your loss," Peter said, as empathetically as he could.

Eva gulped. *Condolences?* She felt like the coordinator spoke a word of a foreign language. Was she about to end her husband's life? Forever? She leaned back in her chair and wove her clammy hands on the table.

"I'll leave you two alone to discuss matters." Dr. Brown left as the coordinator sat in a black swivel chair beside Eva and placed a manila folder on the long, polished table. "I'm here to discuss your husband's social history. Do you feel ready to answer a couple of questions for me, Mrs. Lucas?"

Eva took a long inhale and nodded. "Sure."

"Great." Peter opened his folder. "I also have paperwork for you to fill out."

"Paperwork?" Eva frowned. "I thought all you needed was my consent."

Peter pulled a pen from the chest pocket of his shirt. "Yes, it's true, but this is to protect us in the court of law. You don't know how many lawsuits have been about families who claimed doctors stole their loved ones' organs without permission."

"Okay, I understand," Eva said.

Peter nodded. "Good. We'll begin with a short questionnaire." He slipped a form and a packet of paperwork from the folder and clicked his pen.

Eva answered the coordinator as he slashed X marks in the boxes of Yes or No questions. The man also jotted notes on the form from Andre's blood type to medications he took while alive, to illegal drug use. She knew her husband's info like her social security number, so the interview was a breeze.

"Andre's parents were drug addicts," Eva said, "but he never took drugs or drank alcohol himself."

Peter scribbled on the form. "Okay, this ends Andre's social history information." He yanked up a quick smile that reminded Eva of a ventriloquist puppet. "I guess I can explain the donation process." He read from the Organ Donor Foundation paperwork. The closer he got to the end of the packet; the faster Eva's heart pounded in her chest.

"If you'll sign here, we can confirm the donation today." Peter handed her his pen.

"Thanks." Eva took it in her trembling hand and stared at the blank dotted line. Unshed tears formed in her eyes as she scratched her cursive signature and gave the coordinator back his pen.

"Thank you, Mrs. Lucas." Peter caught a glimpse of Eva's sad eyes as she looked away from him. He lowered his head in a moment of silence. "I know it's hard for you, but organ donation can make the grieving process much easier for families."

"We'll remember your husband, Mrs. Lucas," he added. "I'll get you in contact with the recipients of Andre's organs."

"Mm-hmm," Eva muttered with a nod.

Peter gave a half-smile. "You can go sit with Andre after our discussion."

"Thank you." Eva snatched a tissue from the Kleenex

box on the table and dabbed her eyes and flushed nose.

"Do you mind telling me things about him I can share with his recipients?"

"All right," Eva said, "well, he worked as a veterinarian. Since he was a boy, he loved animals. He was kind, handsome, and enjoyed making people happy, especially kids. He was a good father and husband and liked helping those in need." She chuckled, reminiscing about him. "He wasn't always on time, but he tried. His job tied him up a lot, but he loved me and our son so much."

"That's wonderful," Peter said, smiling. "Well, I've gotten the information I needed, Mrs. Lucas. Thanks for your generous offer."

"Don't thank me," Eva said, "thank Andre." She stood, pushed in her chair, and exited the conference room. Eva drew a long breath and marched to her husband's ICU room for the last time.

When she got there, Hayden stood along Andre's bedside, filling a specimen cup from a syringe. He turned around and gasped at Eva's presence after the door shut. "Oh, hello, Mrs. Lucas."

From the distance, Eva saw Andre's bare thigh and stepped backward. She blushed and clutched the strap of her sunflower tote bag. "Sorry, if I startled you."

"That's okay. I was just getting a sample for a urinalysis test. Dr. Brown wants to ensure Andre's kidneys are healthy for successful transplantation." He capped the tube and stuck a written label on it. "I'm sorry about your husband. So, how are you holding up?"

"How would you feel?" Eva berated, gritting her teeth.

Hayden wore a hangdog expression and turned aside.

"I'm sorry." Eva closed her eyes and shook her head. "I didn't mean to be rude."

"You've been through a lot, Mrs. Lucas. You have the right to be angry." The male nurse straightened kinks in the tubing of Andre's Foley catheter and pulled the hospital blanket back over Andre's lap. He peeled off his rubber gloves and threw them in a flip trashcan. "If I were you, I'd feel the same way."

"Are you finished with him?" Eva glanced from Andre in bed to the male nurse. "I can wait outside." She turned aside toward the door, still feeling a little embarrassed.

"Nonsense, I'm done with him." Hayden's sneakers squeaked as he walked up to Eva. He touched her shoulder. "I'll leave you with Andre until Dr. Brown arrives to take him for chest x-rays."

Eva found a smile. "Thanks."

"Let me take this sample to the lab." Hayden left.

Eva approached Andre's bedside as the ventilator hissed in the dreadful silence. She sat in the upholstered chair next to him, the same chair she had been praying and reading Bible scriptures to her husband in for the past three weeks.

Today marked the fourth week since Andre went in

his coma, and the week his remains would get removed for other awaiting patients. She leaned forward and watched Andre with a pensive smile. Over time, his skin had changed from a healthy cinnamon brown to a sallow beige. He had also lost weight, and his stubble beard cast a five o'clock shadow around his chin and square jawline.

"Andre . . . it's me, Eva." She held his cold hand and wove her fingers with his. "I told Andy about you, but I know I'll have more explaining to do later when he gets older. He misses you—*so much*." She sobbed and shook her head in bafflement of the whole situation. "I don't know what it is. Part of me still refuses to believe you're dead—that you're gonna open your big, brown eyes, get up, and say hello!"

She made a sad little laugh and regained her composure. "But . . . I know I must move on. I'll miss you." She stroked her hand over Andre's glossy, dark curls and softly kissed a corner of his lips. "Goodbye, honey. No matter what, I'll love you forever." She walked to the door.

Shortly after, Dr. Brown came into the ICU ward.

Eva sniffled and dried her tears.

"Hello, Mrs. Lucas. Is there anything I can do to help ease your pain?" Dr. Brown said.

"No, I'll be fine." Eva's stomach revolted. "Excuse me . . ." She slapped a hand over her mouth and barged past the doctor, rushing to the nearest Women's room.

Eva hurried into a stall and hovered over a toilet. For a moment, she fought the violent jerks and tried to keep from puking, but the reverse motion made her sicker. Soon, she had coughed up the morning breakfast she'd eaten. She stayed in the stall a good ten minutes, struggling to gather herself together.

"Mrs. Lucas! Mrs. Lucas, hurry quick!" Nurse Daphne called into the restroom.

Tremors shook Eva's body. She exited and wiped her mouth with a wad of toilet paper. Eva frowned at the elated face of the brunette nurse in purple scrubs, poking her head from behind the entrance swing door. "What is it?"

Daphne grinned. "It's your husband! He's awake!"

Eva widened her eyes. "He is?" She thought she would faint. Was it a joke, or was the nurse telling the truth? She wasn't in the mood for anyone playing games with her emotions.

"Dr. Brown listened if Andre's heart was still beating, and out of nowhere, he moaned and opened his eyes. It's a miracle!" Daphne said, smiling.

Eva blinked and felt breathless. "Oh, my goodness." She placed her hand over her mouth and broke down as what Pastor Tyson said in the sanctuary echoed through her mind. *The Lord has the last say . . . the Lord has the last say . . .* She couldn't contain the joy bubbling up inside her, much less stand straight. Her legs were flimsy as cooked spaghetti, leaning against the opening of the stall.

Daphne ran over and squeezed Eva in a hug. "I knew it! Your husband's still alive. He's alive!"

Eva stared in disbelief. "Are you serious? I . . . I can't believe it."

"Come on, you can wait for the results. Nurse Jia will call you when he's ready." Daphne looped an arm around Eva and walked her out of the restroom.

"Mrs. Lucas?" Peter strode into the waiting room with the paperwork.

"Yes?" Eva rose from her seat with her sleeping son in her arms. Since her husband awoke from his coma, what would the coordinator say now?

Peter tilted his head and folded in his mouth. "Uh . . . I heard about your husband's recovered consciousness, and in the conference room, I got the impression you didn't want to donate Andre's organs."

"No, I didn't," Eva confessed. "I'm sorry."

The coordinator held the organ donation packet horizontally in his hands and tore it in half and the halves into two more halves. "I've talked with Dr. Brown about the dead donor policy of my Organ Procurement Organization. It forbids our transplant team to remove organs from non-deceased patients. Therefore, your husband's organ donation has been canceled, Mrs. Lucas."

"Thank you," Eva said humbly, "but if things ever change again, I'll make sure Andre helps to save others' lives."

"Have a nice day, Mrs. Lucas," Peter said.

Eva offered a smile. "You too."

The family coordinator left the waiting room.

Eva filled her chair and contemplated the patients Andre would've saved whose lives were still on the line. As much as she was happy her husband had a second chance at life, she prayed God would make another way to spare those people on the waiting list too.

"Mrs. Lucas, you can come in," Nurse Jia said, catching her attention.

With a timid smile, Eva handed over her son and his stuffed monkey to Mrs. Flowers. "It's best for Andy to stay here. We don't want to overwhelm Andre."

Mrs. Flowers sat the little boy in her lap. "I was thinking the same thing. Best wishes."

"Thanks." Eva stood and wiped her sweaty palms on her ruby wrap dress printed with big white flowers and followed Jia through the hospital corridor. They turned the corner and arrived at the same door labeled I-7 of her husband's ICU ward.

Eva clipped her tinted aviators on her collar. Her heart was in her throat as the nurse practitioner insisted she walks in first. For weeks she waited and prayed for this moment, and now that it was here, she found herself afraid. Why was she scared to see her husband?

Jia read the worry in Eva's nervous eyes and placed an arm around her. "It's okay. The doctor and I will be right beside you."

Eva found a calm smile and relaxed. "Thank you." She and the nurse shared a side hug, and then she rubbed on sanitizer and entered the ICU ward. It was very quiet inside the room. The life support machines were shut off and pushed against the wall as Andre could miraculously breathe on his own.

She sheepishly watched him lying in bed and huddled near the doctor. Her husband hadn't spoken to her, but his drowsy eyes followed her cautious movement, suspicious of her presence. Staring at his face, she felt her eyes get wet and instantly identified a harsh reality. Although Andre was alive, he was a long way from a full recovery.

• CHAPTER 11 •

Andre

His heavy-lidded, brown eyes fluttered and stared at the African American man wearing glasses in a long, white coat and the young woman in a red gown beside him. Their faces were close to his and stretched with enthusiastic smiles as if fascinated by his existence. *Why are they looking at me? Where am I? What happened to me?* His whole body was numb, feeling nothing, except the turning of his neck and the motions of his face.

Andre inhaled deeply and felt cool air seep through the back of his throat. Before the lady in red came, the man in the coat removed a strange, uncomfortable tube that punctured his neck.

He glanced downward and found his wrists tied to the side metal railing of the bed. His heart raced, panicking. *Why am I tied up? What did they do to me?*

The man in white asked him a question and pointed at his tongue to ensure Andre understood him.

Exhaling wheezy breaths, Andre mimicked the man's demonstration, sticking out his tongue too. The man and the young woman exchanged smiles, thrilled by his physical response. At the foot of his hospital bed was another woman with a jet-black ponytail in blue clothes, recording notes in a binder. She glanced up from her notebook with a smile, and he tried to smile back.

The young woman in a red gown with white splotches on it moved closer to his bedside, looking over him. Awe transformed Andre's face as he studied her. His lower lip drooped, slowly breathing. *Who are you?*

He hadn't seen many people since he first opened his eyes, but she was the most gorgeous person he saw, like looking at night and day simultaneously. Her long, wavy hair was black as shadows, her olive face bright and beautiful like the shining sun. Her pretty, straight smile helped him remain calm with his medical condition, ensuring him everything would be okay.

As the man in glasses had, she said something to him, offering a kind greeting, grateful he's awakened.

Andre moaned and faltered, speaking in a slow monotone drawl, "W-who -a-a-are y-y-you?"

The woman in red frowned, and he got the impression he was mistaken. She shook her head and spoke again, informing him who he and she was. *Andre? Eva? Wife? What's a wife?*

The woman searched his eyes and talked to him again, asking if he knew her. Remembering her was as hard as solving a Rubik's Cube blindfolded. Did they know each other? Had he seen her before?

Andre sighed and wore another blank stare, unable to answer her confidently.

Her face fell and she fled away from him, the doctor chasing after her. *Wait, come back! Where are you going?* His cloudy eyes followed them as they exited the room. Fear gripped hold of him. He wanted her to stay by his bedside. But within he'd gotten an eerie sense he made a terrible mistake—an unpleasant incident to her and himself.

Forgetting who she was.

• CHAPTER 12 •

Eva

"Mrs. Lucas! Mrs. Lucas, please!" Dr. Brown said, trailing her down the hospital corridor.

Eva squeezed her eyes shut and sobbed, leaning her head against the cool wall. "He doesn't know who I am. I prayed so much for him to be made whole. He's supposed to be in better condition than this. And what's up with his speech? He talks as if he's unsure of himself."

"Broca's aphasia," Dr. Brown said. "It's a speech disorder that makes it difficult for one to express language. It's caused by damage to Broca's area in the frontal lobe. Reading, writing, and comprehending can also be a challenge, but his intelligence has remained intact. Speech therapy can improve it to some extent. However, his speech will likely remain impaired." He sighed and continued. "You should be reasonable, Mrs. Lucas. Andre suffered from head trauma. It's common for patients to suffer amnesia and not recognize loved ones after severe car accidents."

"What am I supposed to do?" Eva said, frustrated.

"Be patient with him. He can emerge from his present state. His memory loss may be temporary. You of all people should be grateful. Brainstem death is an irreversible and fatal condition. There's no explanation other than God for him waking up again, especially with his lack of breathing problems."

"I am grateful, Dr. Brown but—" Eva inhaled a breath and craned her neck, crossing her arms— "what if he never remembers me again?"

"Let's not worry about that now," Dr. Brown said. "You must have faith Andre's memory will progress, among other things."

Eva grimaced and inclined her head. "What do you mean?"

Dr. Brown tucked a hand in a pocket of his lab coat and sighed again. "Mrs. Lucas, Andre's . . . a quadriplegic. I performed different exams shortly before you came in, and he showed no signs of sensation in any of his limbs."

Eva's shoulders felt leaden as if a ton of bricks fell on her. Her husband didn't know her, he could barely talk, and he was paralyzed below his neck. Though thankful he awoke, she was also unsettled.

How was a five-foot-six and 129-pound woman supposed to care for a six-foot disabled man by herself? It was a lot different from aiding him through a common cold. Andre needed twenty-four-hour, around-the-clock care. She wasn't confident she had the body strength and time to tend to his needs with her full-time job.

Her eyebrows furrowed. "But . . . how can he be paralyzed if he has no spinal cord injury?"

"Paralysis can happen in many ways," Dr. Brown said. "In Andre's case, it's his closed head injury. There's a loss of messages traveling from his brainstem to the motor cortex in his frontal lobe."

The doctor slipped off his glasses and cleaned them with a hankie from his chest pocket. "A brainstem injury is as severe as a spinal cord injury. The brainstem is a small part of the brain but controls heart rate, blood pressure, body temperature, and breathing. It's why Andre had been on life support."

Eva cocked her head. "Oh, I see. It's like someone cutting a plug in an outlet with scissors, right?"

"That's correct." Dr. Brown adjusted his glasses back on. "The motor cortex is a crucial part of the frontal lobe and involves the execution of voluntary movements, such as lifting a pencil or walking. With physical therapy and lots of practice, your husband *can* recover his mobility again. I've witnessed it happen to many. Brain tissue has a remarkable way of repairing itself over time, which is another key factor of him regaining consciousness."

"So, now what?"

"Now since Andre's stabilized, we'll move him to the Acute Care unit to ensure he's oriented with his new situation," Dr. Brown replied. "Even though he can breathe on his own, he'll also remain on a feeding tube for now. With his present condition, it's a good idea for you to speak with Barbara Washburn."

The physician put a hand on Eva's shoulder. "We can discuss more in my office. Please, join me?"

Eva responded with a nod and followed the doctor.

Dr. Brown swiped his ID card dangling around his neck over a security scanner. He held open the door for Eva and then sat at his desk. The doctor pulled two caregiver brochures from a drawer of his desk and handed them to Eva. "These brochures explain the steps of caring for someone like Andre, such as bathing and eating."

"Thank you, doctor." Eva took the colored brochures and skimmed over them.

"Your husband's condition is sensitive, and after his discharge will require a conscientious caregiver. As a quadriplegic, he'll need to be rotated every so often in his sleep to prevent other complications, such as bedsores, blood clots, and muscle atrophy. The less he moves, the stiffer his muscles can become, which can be painful. He must stay active, and he'll still need a urinary catheter and to be on a bowel program."

Eva stopped reading a section about transferring a paralyzed patient from a wheelchair to a bed of one of the tri-fold brochures. She looked up with a frown. "What's a bowel program?"

Dr. Brown reclined back and laced his hands over his potbelly. "A bowel program is a method to help quadriplegics and paraplegics train their bodies on a schedule who suffer from neurogenic bowels. Drinking plenty of water and eating fiber and protein foods are ways to help make it easier for the disabled too."

The doctor cleared his throat. "Andre also has a neurogenic bladder. It means his brain doesn't signal to his bladder, causing him to suffer episodes of accidental leakage or retention. I'm sure you know while comatose he was on a Foley catheter. Your husband can continue using this type, but I recommend he catheterize in ways that put him at lesser risk of urinary infection."

He spoke on. "Using clean intermittent catheterization is one of the most common. However, in Andre's case, he'll need help until possibly regaining strength in his arms and hands. The directions for this are explained under the Bladder Health category in the *In-Home Personal Care* brochure."

Eva unfolded the rest of the brochure she was reading and caught a glimpse of one of the male instruction diagrams. Her cheeks burned and her heart quivered as she closed the brochure.

She felt like a scared, nervous teenager taking a sex education class. Eva gulped a hard lump, willing herself to stay calm.

Dr. Brown wore a wry smile. "Because of his memory loss, Andre may be uncomfortable with you at first, not to mention the fact you're his wife. I suggest you hire a skilled caregiver to tend to his personal needs. From him or her, you can also learn how to build Andre's trust and care for him yourself."

Eva bit her forefinger nail. "How much will that cost?"

"I'm afraid the prices vary." The doctor took a slow breath. "Most caregivers request a payment range of nine to fourteen dollars per hour."

"I don't think I can afford it," Eva said with a weak look. "Plus, I work in the daytime."

"Well, there are part-time caregivers. Perhaps you could hire one while you're at work during the day, and care for Andre yourself at night."

"I suppose," Eva said with a shrug.

"I'm sure Barbara Washburn will help you," Dr. Brown said.

Eva twisted her mouth. *Barbara Washburn . . . why does he keep mentioning her?* The doctor was trying to give friendly advice, but she refused to resort to monthly financial handouts as her mother did. How can she go back on her word?

"Barbara's a kind, understanding person," the doctor

added, "who I promise will do whatever she can for you. Try calling her."

Eva nodded but didn't make another comment.

"I'm deeply sorry for Andre's disabilities, but don't forget there's still hope," Dr. Brown said. "If he can wake after several weeks in a coma, it must be possible, right? For amnesic patients, it's crucial not to pressure them into remembering the past. Showing old pictures has been a better, proven way to stimulate their memory. You should try it with Andre."

"All right, I'll try it. Thank you, doctor." Eva exhaled a breath and offered a handshake.

Dr. Brown shook Eva's hand. "You're welcome. And remember, take your time, relax, and learn the processes. I know this whole situation feels awkward to you, especially with your husband's memory loss. I wish Andre the best recovery."

Eva exited his office and headed back to the waiting room. The next week would be harder on everyone, but especially for Andre. Although he arose from his oblivious cocoon, he became a different man.

Confusion swirled around him like a biting wind, and she wished she could help him—to comfort him in his new, misplaced world. But their marriage changed the moment she looked into his hollow eyes, and it will take a while before he trusts and loves her again.

• CHAPTER 13 •

Eva

Tuesday Afternoon

Against her will, Eva swallowed her pride and visited Dr. Washburn's office. After ignoring her phone calls, she didn't know whether the social worker would invite her in or not. But she finally acknowledged working extra hours at her job wasn't bringing home enough bacon to cover her and Andre's expenses.

She straightened and knocked on the clear glass window of the door.

"Come in! Come in!" Dr. Washburn chirped in her Caribbean accent.

Eva entered and studied her surroundings. Her nose tingled from the pungent scent of perfume mixed with burnt coffee. She found the ebony-skinned woman behind a wooden desk, dressed in a lavender blouse. Her flared collar draped over the top of a white blazer, and her thick, salt-and-pepper hair was styled in a stiff bouffant.

Dr. Washburn smiled, her gold front tooth sparkling in the sunshine. "Oh, Mrs. Lucas! Please, have a seat, my dear."

Eva wore a weak smile and sat in a leather chair in front of the social worker. She gripped her clutch purse in her lap, hoping she wouldn't fall into a trap. Welfare had its gains and losses. As a working recipient, the second she got a raise, benefits given to her could be taken away. And after confiding her confidence for her family's sake, she didn't want to end up hanging on a thread.

The social worker made a steeple with her hands. "I'm glad you finally came and hope you can excuse the smell in here. I forgot to turn off my coffee maker and my office is still *airing out*. Anyway, I express my sincere sympathy for what happened to your husband. I know you've been having a hard time. How have you been since Andre's brain injury?"

Eva glanced upward at the soft-humming ceiling fan and exhaled slowly. "Well, I've cried a lot, but I'm trying to stay strong for our son."

Dr. Washburn nodded. "That's good. How did Andre's accident happen?"

Eva gulped and studied her lap. "He collided with a deer and suffered a head-on collision with a tree in someone's yard. When I got the bad news, I felt like someone ripped my heart out of my chest." Tears clouded her vision. "It happened on our wedding anniversary."

The social worker pulled a tissue from a Kleenex box on her desk and handed it to Eva.

"Thank you." Eva stifled a sob and swiped beneath her eyes.

"It's typical for us to blame ourselves," Dr. Washburn said, "but know none of what happened is your fault. The good news is, your husband's on the road to recovery." She tilted her head, curious about Andre's life. "What was he like before his accident? It's useful to the trauma team to rebuild the original life your husband had."

Eva sniffled again. "Andre was an outdoorsman and grew up on his grandfather's farm. He liked fishing, hiking, and horseback riding. One time he taught me how to ride a horse when we were teenagers." Her lips curved in a warm smile. "He was always caring and loved nature. We used to take long walks through the forest and climb the mountains where we'd sit and talk until sunset." She gazed outside the open window to her right, longing for the past to rewind and somehow become the present.

"He sounds like a well-rounded man," Dr. Washburn said. "And I'm sure he still is, despite his accident. Having therapy will improve Andre's disabled condition. He must relearn many everyday tasks, which means he will need physical, occupational, and speech therapy. Would you be okay with that, Mrs. Lucas?"

Eva sighed and let her guard down. "Yes, ma'am."

"Good. Because of your husband's disability, I'm sure you and Andre qualify for benefits." Dr. Washburn rolled her desk chair toward her computer. She typed on her keyboard and surfed up the Social Security Administration website. "There are two key government programs that can be beneficial to you and your family. One of them is Supplemental Security Income or SSI, and the other is Social Security Disability Insurance or SSDI."

She faced Eva. "Supplemental Security Income is a welfare program. If you and Andre are eligible, the SSA gives you money each month to help pay for things, such as food and utilities. Along with SSI, most people also get Medicaid, which can help pay the expenses of Andre's therapy and other daily supplies he'll need."

"I guess I have no choice," Eva muttered under her breath, fidgeting with the clamp of her clutch purse.

Dr. Washburn bit her lip and looked away from her computer screen. "Mrs. Lucas, after you've rejected my calls, I know you've been against welfare for whatever reason. But if you're struggling, there's no shame in asking for help. It's the best thing you can do for your family. However, to qualify, there are strings attached."

Eva frowned. "Such as?"

"Well, aside from disability, one must also have low assets and low income. For married couples, you must have below three thousand dollars of assets. Now this is for money in the bank and doesn't include your house or car."

"I got paid from my job last week," Eva said. "With the deductibles, it was seven hundred and ten dollars, and Andre has nine hundred left in his bank account."

"Do you have any proof of documentation?" the social worker asked.

"Yes, ma'am." Eva unclipped her purse and handed Dr. Washburn two folded paper forms. "Here's my latest pay stub and Andre's bank account summary."

Dr. Washburn put on her square reading glasses and unfolded the slips of paper, examining them. "Okay, let me add the total." She tapped on her calculator. "With your and Andre's assets, it makes one thousand six hundred ten dollars, which is below three thousand. Now since Andre isn't working, I imagine your monthly income is below the federal benefit rate."

"Are we eligible? I work nine hours per day at the daycare and make eight dollars per hour," Eva said. "Andre's grandpa tries to give us money, but we never accept it from him. He's already done enough helping us pay off the rest of our house mortgage."

"Let me calculate your wages." Dr. Washburn added another total. "Excellent! I divided your monthly wages by two, and it's approximately seven hundred twenty dollars, which is below the federal benefit rate for married couples in 2017. Do you know if Andre's receiving social security disability insurance?"

"I'm not sure," Eva said, tapping her chin, "but I imagine so. His employer took a premium from his paycheck every month while he worked at Pet Friends Veterinary Clinic."

Dr. Washburn angled her head, twirling her pen between her skinny fingers. "How long has Andre worked there?"

"Eight years." Eva crumpled her tissue in a ball and held it in her lap.

"That's great. It looks like you and your husband qualify for both insurance benefits," the social worker said. "I'll need your consent to ask some interview questions so I can fill these applications online for you."

"You have my permission," Eva said.

Dr. Washburn turned her attention back to her computer. She typed the information for both applications as Eva answered her questions. After their long discussion, she said, "If your SSDI case gets denied, you must request a reconsideration. It means sending your case back to the people who rejected you. However, if you show legitimate proof of your husband's disability by medical records, you should be fine."

"What about the Supplemental Security Income?"

Dr. Washburn sipped from her mug and frowned at the nasty taste. "Well, if everything goes fine, you'll get benefit checks mailed to you within the next sixty days."

Eva allowed a smile. "All right, thank you."

"You're welcome. I'm always here to help. If you have questions, don't hesitate to call me."

Eva shook the social worker's hand. "Trust me, I will. Goodbye."

Dr. Washburn brightened, placing her mug on her coaster. "Bye, Mrs. Lucas. I hope Andre gets well enough to go home soon."

Eva stood and exited the office.

Knowing they had a good chance for insurance benefits helped her breathe a little easier, but her sigh of relief could change fast. Sometimes life had a way of stealing happiness when one thinks things are getting better. Regardless, Eva was never one to give an easy fight. If her claim was refused, she had in mind to write an appeal before Dr. Washburn mentioned the possible drawback.

Andre needed a lot of expensive equipment and supplies, and she would do whatever she could to ensure her husband gets well. She cared about Andre, and despite his handicaps, she loved him. Though he became more distant and withdrawn, her faith Andre still loved her too hadn't stopped. Maybe she was fooling herself, or she felt obligated for Andrew's sake, but she believed in striving to keep their marriage afloat.

On their wedding day, she promised to stay by his side through sickness and in health, and that was exactly what she was determined to do.

• CHAPTER 14 •

Eva

Saturday, Sept. 30th

"Mr. Lucas, I'm holding the tube for you, okay?" Hayden said from an Acute Care room.

Eva strode the linoleum hallway, carrying her son on her hip. Having others tend to Andre's needs wasn't easy. His caregivers were compassionate and helpful to him, but sometimes Eva was irritated by them. Though they meant well, the nurses were aiding Andre with everyday tasks—which as his wife—she felt and knew she should be doing. From sinus allergies to a sprained ankle, she'd always been the one to nurse her husband back to health, but now was a different story.

"Good morning! How's my favorite patient?" an unfamiliar woman said over the blaring television.

Suspicion dawned on Eva's face. She couldn't identify

the nurse's voice, but it wasn't Daphne, her husband's primary bedside nurse.

Andre groaned.

"Uh-oh, that doesn't sound too good, Mr. Lucas," the woman said. "I'm about to check your other vital signs, okay?"

"Okay," Andre said in a monotone.

Eva started to stroll in, but found the cubicle curtain pulled across the hospital room. Either Andre was in the middle of something personal or exposed, so she shied away and waited in the outside hall. Since the day he awoke with retrograde amnesia, their relationship was in a tight corner, and she didn't want him more uncomfortable than he was.

"Looks like your blood pressure's normal, Mr. Lucas. One twenty-seven over eighty-two. You're doing well," the woman said.

Eva glanced below the curtain and saw men's sneakers along her husband's bedside.

"All righty, you're all done, Mr. Lucas," Hayden said. "I'm gonna take out the catheter and clean you off. Can you dump out his...? Yeah, thanks."

Eva blushed and stepped back from the curtain. She wondered if it was a bad time to bother Andre with a hospital visit, but she needed to bond Andre with their son again. For an entire month, Andrew had never visited his father, and he deserved to see his daddy like anyone else.

Andrew whined as Eva shushed him and swayed with him in her arms.

The curtain slid back, staggering her with a gasp.

A young, African American nurse stood before her. Her small frame and thin bone structure made her look like a college intern in her early twenties. A claw clip held her soft black hair, and her deep brown skin glowed without a blemish. She wore purple Minnie Mouse scrubs and a stethoscope looped around her neck.

The nurse revealed her pearly smile. "Hello, you must be Mrs. Lucas. I'm Dr. Sasha Joyner, Andre's acute care practitioner. I check on my floor staff from time to time." She glanced at Andrew, her grin still on her face. "Aww. . . and who do we have here?"

"This is Andy, Andre's and my son," Eva said.

Sasha waved at the little boy. "Hi, Andy. You're *so* cute. I'm pleased to meet you."

Andrew stared at her and leaned his curly head against his mommy, holding his stuffed monkey underarm.

"How is he?" Eva asked.

Hayden left the hospital room and stood beside Sasha in his blue scrubs clipped with his name tag.

"Andre's doing fine," Sasha said. "He's a miracle and appears to comprehend better than when first waking, but his speech is still impaired. His vital signs are also remaining strong and healthy." She put her hands in her shirt's pockets. "I'll remove his feeding tube next Monday which is also good news."

"He'll be in Acute Care for one more week to make sure he's aware of himself and his name, the time and date, and so forth," Sasha added.

Eva looked at the male nurse. "Is Andre off the—?"

"Yes, ma'am," Hayden said. "I took out his Foley catheter yesterday, as you requested, and started training him on a straight intermittent catheter in a urinal on the bed. But it's easier doing it from his wheelchair at the toilet."

The male nurse continued, folding his arms. "Either way, he should go four to six times per day to ensure his bladder stays empty, as Andre can't feel when it's full. It's important to protect him from infections and kidney failure. I've also trained him on an enema to help begin his bowel program."

Eva knitted her brows. "What's an enema?"

"It's a liquid injection used to stimulate the disposing of . . . well, stools," Hayden explained. "Has someone given you a caregiver brochure?"

"Yes," Eva said, "Dr. Brown gave me two, but I haven't finished reading them."

"Well, you should," Sasha said, "it'll help you feel less embarrassed and calmer while caring for Andre at home, and make him more at ease too."

"I know. I will, I promise." Eva closed her eyes and tucked her hair behind an ear. She readjusted Andrew in her arms. "So, how will I know when Andre has to . . . you know?"

"We've discovered he gets a sick taste in his mouth and gets lower back muscle spasms," Sasha added. "You can also check if his bladder feels distended. If you notice one or all these signs, he needs to go, even if he's too ashamed to say so."

Eva wore a weak look. "Can I visit him again?"

"Certainly," Sasha said, "but make sure you stay patient with him. He's mentally troubled and disoriented. We'll be nearby if you need us. Try not to take what he might say or do too personally, okay?"

"I'll try." Eva took a deep breath and walked into the hospital room with Andrew. Her husband was sitting up in bed in a thin, teal gown, his hands resting at his sides.

He stared at an episode of *The Price Is Right* on the flat screen mounted on the ceiling. To his left were a manual wheelchair and a nightstand with an empty plastic urinal on top. On the right side were an adjustable overbed table, the gym bag of his hygiene products she brought from home, and a commode toilet for easy transfer.

Eva smiled at her husband. "Hi, Andre. It's me, Eva, your wife again. How are you?"

"Fine." Andre glanced at her and focused back on the contestants spinning the money wheel on the screen.

Eva dropped her shoulder bag on the floor, adjusted Andrew to her lap, and sat in a leather chair next to the bedside. "Phew, this little boy's heavy. He can walk, but he's been kinda clingy lately." She looked at Andre, and for the first time in what felt like ages, her husband inched up a little smile.

"Uh, b-b-boy . . . cute. Who . . . baby?" Andre faltered, eyeing Andrew.

Eva's heart danced with joy. "He's our son." Her eyes pooled as her husband contorted his face and looked away, mortified. "Andre, it's okay . . . it's okay if you don't remember him." She stroked his right hand on the hospital bed. "His name is Andrew, but we call him Andy. He misses you."

"Daddy . . ." Andrew whined and squirmed in Eva's hold. He leaned over sideways and dropped his stuffed monkey on the floor, gripping his tiny hand on Andre's right thumb. It pained Eva to have to keep their son in her lap, her husband being unable to hold their child.

Andre squeezed his eyes and bit his lower lip, fighting back tears. "Why . . . h-h-here? Go a-a-away."

"But I brought more pictures to show you." Eva took out a rectangular, brown leather album from her tote bag and opened it before her husband. "These are a couple of photos of me, you, and Andy. That's you at the end of the aisle in the navy-blue tuxedo. I'm the woman in the white dress. Your Grandpa Ricardo is the old man beside me in the gray cowboy hat. He walked me down the aisle to you." Her smile fell. "I never met my father."

Andre studied the Kodak photo vaguely.

Eva caught his muddled expression. To him, it didn't differ from looking at a royalty stock image of strangers in a store-bought picture frame. She sighed and flipped to the next picture, hoping he'd recognize the snapshot of their newlywed photo shoot. In the photo, Andre stood behind Eva with his chin nestled on her shoulder and an arm hugging her waist. The photographer took the picture right when they were in the middle of a hearty laugh.

"Here we are again," Eva said, chuckling. "After we got married, we took many pictures together. I'm camera-shy, but you were so excited. You wanted the whole world to know it was our wedding day. I can't remember what but, you said something funny to make me smile."

Andre blinked and remained silent, emotionless.

Eva turned past newlywed photos of them making silly faces and stopped at a picture of Andrew when he was a newborn in his hospital bassinet. "This is Andy a little after he was born. It was a cold, rainy spring afternoon. You were trying to get to the hospital in time, but there was a multi-vehicle accident caused by a traffic jam. I told you I named him after my father."

Andre drew a breath and turned his face again. "No . . . more."

Their son whined and squirmed again.

Eva gazed at Andre sadly and wilted her shoulders, yearning for him to remember. "Look, maybe if you see more old pictures, your memory will—"

"Get . . . out! No more!" Her husband closed his eyes shut and struck his head wildly on his stack of pillows, fighting to speak and having a fit. "G-G-Get out! Get out! Get out! G-G-Get out!"

Sasha and Hayden scampered to Andre's room.

"Hey, what's going on in here?" Hayden said with a frown.

"L-L-Leave . . . me . . . a-a-alone," Andre said, weeping and looking away.

Sasha sighed and turned to Eva. "Mrs. Lucas, we'll keep you posted about your husband's condition. You can try visiting him again later, but it's best you leave at this time. I'm sorry."

Anger crashed through Eva like stormy waves striking a rocky shoreline. Her face burned. She closed the photo album, loosened Andrew's grip on Andre's thumb, and stood with her son. Andrew squealed and broke into a deafening tantrum that shook Eva's soul with devastation and embarrassment.

Sasha grabbed the shoulder bag and hoisted it on Eva's shoulder for her. "Sorry . . ." she mouthed softly, her heart breaking for the crying little boy. She rubbed Andrew's back and baby-talked him, hoping to make him feel better. "I know, honey. Hang in there. Your daddy will be home soon, okay?" She picked up and tried to give Andrew his monkey, but he was too upset to hold him.

Eva took the toy monkey from the nurse and packed him in her shoulder bag. She glanced at her husband with tearful eyes as Hayden calmed him during the commotion. "Forgive me, Andre. I didn't mean to upset you. It's just . . . I just—goodbye." She scattered before she cried in front of him, toting their hollering son, his ear-piercing screams echoing down the long hallway.

"I feel like I'm in quicksand," Eva said in Mrs. Flowers' living room. "No matter how many times I try to stand, I keep sinking deeper in a pit of misery." She raked a hand through her hair, stifling a sob.

Mrs. Flowers placed a tray of floral porcelain teacups and sugar cookies on the table. She joined Eva on her white loveseat sofa draped with a blue knitted throw and looked at the framed, black-and-white photograph of her husband in his Army dress uniform on the hearth of her fireplace. "I know the feeling, hon. It was difficult seeing Clyde's memory fading away too."

The old woman smacked her lips. "You never think a thing could happen after knowing someone for so long. But you gotta have faith and believe God's gonna work everything out."

"No offense, Mrs. Flowers, but I don't wanna hear about God right now. I don't mean to belittle you, but it's different between my husband and me. I mean, you and Mr. Clyde had decades together before his dementia took effect. But Andre's young. He's a father to a precious little boy he doesn't even remember." Eva eyed Andrew with a weak smile, her eyes brimming with tears of love and sorrow.

He was sitting on the carpet floor in front of her and Mrs. Flowers, rocking to nursery rhyme songs as he played on his zebra-shaped, VTech piano. His smiles and giggles warmed her heart and always brightened her mood. How can Andre not love this kid? How can he not care about their son? He was their flesh and blood, a special gift that had been given to them.

Eva folded her arms and sat backward. "One night completely wiped his memory, including his childhood. Wednesday, I showed him a picture of himself riding the tire swing on his grandpa's farm and he asked me who the kid was. I don't know if he'll ever remember his past again." She sighed hopelessly. "Dr. Brown suggested I show him pictures to stimulate his mind, but nothing's familiar, which bothers him."

She glanced at the old woman and hung her head. "I pushed him a little too hard this time. Maybe because Andrew was with me. Today was awful. I don't think he wants me around anymore."

Mrs. Flowers sipped from her teacup. She frowned

and set her cup on her saucer. "Don't you start doubting, Eva. Andre loves you."

"How can he love me when he doesn't remember who I am or everything we were together?" Eva faced the old woman with a heartbroken expression. "I love Andre . . . *so* much, but we no longer have chemistry, and it's never coming back again."

Mrs. Flowers took another sip. "Give it time. Take your troubles to the Lord in prayer. Ask God to direct you in what to do. People have their own interpretations of love these days, but rarely does anyone think about where love comes from."

She looked aside, thinking deeply. "Love . . . is a divine affection. First John 4:8 tells us God is love. It comes from the Lord, Eva. And nobody can love your husband better than Him. If you want Andre to love you and Andy back, you must first show unconditional love to him. Ask God to place *His love* in you . . . for Him to let you see Andre through *His eyes*, and I guarantee you'll miraculously witness Andre return the same feelings."

"That'll be the day," Eva said, rolling her eyes. "He's suffered a hard blow. He hesitates and falters in his speech often, and sometimes I'm afraid of him."

Mrs. Flowers frowned. "Well, you shouldn't be. He's your husband. Stay open to him, and let him know you're there for him, even if he acts like he doesn't want you near him. It's how God treats us. Sometimes we want nothing to do with Him either, but He's still faithful and shows mercy toward us day in and night out."

Eva felt a pang of guilt.

Mrs. Flowers was on point. Although she didn't always take advantage of the opportunity, God was still there watching and waiting for her to come and talk to Him any time of the day. She couldn't help listening, absorbing whatever wisdom the old woman could offer to help her marriage, family, and wellbeing.

"How much longer will Andre be in Acute Care?" Mrs. Flowers asked, changing the subject.

Eva sighed again. "One more week. Afterward, he'll begin therapy. His nurses are ensuring he's aware of himself and the basics, his car accident, and so forth." She wrinkled her eyebrows. "But I'm not too comfortable with those female nurses seeing and touching Andre. I mean, I'm glad he has a male nurse who also helps with his toileting and bathing, but it still makes me feel weird like . . ."

"Like you're incompetent, right?" Mrs. Flowers said, finishing her statement.

Eva grabbed a sugar cookie. "Yeah. Plus, Hayden isn't always there, so half the time it's a female nurse who assists him. If anyone tends to Andre's personal needs, it should be me. But, I'm scared I'll do something wrong, even despite reading the brochures and researching his conditions." She nibbled her cookie. "If I ever gain his love and trust, I don't wanna lost it from hurting him or making a stupid mistake."

"I understand what you mean, but at least Andre will be out soon. Whatcha gonna do after he gets discharged? He'll need supervision each day." Mrs. Flowers slurped another drink.

Eva took another bite. "Dr. Brown advised I hire a caregiver while I'm at work. I'll have to find the cheapest I can get. Someone of quality, but who doesn't mind getting paid on a biweekly salary."

"How about you place an ad in the daily paper?"

Eva finished her cookie and considered Mrs. Flowers' suggestion. "Okay, I'll try that then. Hopefully, someone would be kind enough to volunteer and help me. Let me jot a notice." She unsnapped her clutch purse and took out a pen and a receipt. She tapped her pen on her chin, thought a split second, and scribbled a quick, detailed ad.

"How's this?" Eva asked, holding out the paper.

Mrs. Flowers leaned over and read her newspaper ad:

CAREGIVER NEEDED FOR DISABLED HUSBAND!

Paralyzed husband with TBI (Traumatic Brain Injury)

Workdays: Monday-Friday. Weekends off.

Hours: 6:30 a.m.—3:30 p.m. (Sometimes 4 p.m. or

later if I have staff meeting/ shopping, or
somewhere else I need to go)

Pay: Biweekly—Open for compromise.
Male caregiver preferred. Must have professional
experience.

Please bring a resume for review.

Contact:
For more information visit, 143 Pasture Road,
Garden Ridge, NC.

"It looks good to me," Mrs. Flowers said, giving her approval.

Eva smiled and put the note in her purse. "Great, I'll submit it for the classifieds tomorrow."

Finding a responsible caregiver was a big deal and would be a major help for Andre and her. She desired it to be a man though, one who was strong enough to move and rotate Andre until he got a patient lift through his medical insurance.

She also wanted it to be someone who would push Andre to stick with his leg exercises, instead of letting him stay in a wheelchair all day. As Dr. Brown said, the more Andre sits in the same position for too long, the stiffer he'll become, and he didn't need additional health issues.

Later at night, Eva bought fast-food from McDonald's for dinner and drove home. She wasn't in the mood to cook, and wanted to fall asleep and forget the horrible day's visit. From her marriage to Andrew's emotional neglect and Andre's discharge, so much had consumed her thoughts. But the sun sunk behind the horizon, and she was ready to lie back and rest. She tucked her son and his toy monkey under his Cookie Monster blanket in the crib.

Eva kissed her son's forehead and stroked his hair as he slipped into sleep. "Good night, baby. Mommy loves you." She left her son's bedroom and went to bed in the master room. Sometimes nights were harder than others without Andre. Having him with her always made her feel safer in the house. She tossed and turned, struggling to relax. She always knew the side he stirred in his sleep, groping his vacant bedside for his athletic, lengthy body.

She moaned and opened her weary eyes with a sigh, staring at the pitch-black ceiling. Car headlights from outside glided across the plain white surface, keeping her awake. She thought about what Mrs. Flowers said about

God's abundant love. *Was it possible after a TBI tragedy? A loving, compatible marriage again? Could they ever get along?*

She needed help, comfort, and strength to continue for her son and disabled husband.

Many hours passed as she faded in and out of sleep. By dawn, she built the courage to pray again. She climbed out of bed in her silk, peach nightie, knelt, and laced her hands. "Dear God, help me. Guide me. I'm scared and don't know what else to do. Send a blessing—a miracle for Andre and me. Please, help my husband's memory restore, even just a little. God . . . you *are* love. And as Mrs. Flowers said, 'True love never dies.'"

Eva sighed and continued praying. "God, you know how impatient I can be. Guide me to be the sensitive, patient wife I need to be for Andre. I place our marriage in your hands. Let your love shine through me and on Andre, and that someday, he'll learn to love me and Andy too. Please, let him remember us again . . . in Jesus Christ's name, I pray. Amen."

She crawled back under the blanket of the queen-sized bed and hugged Andre's pillow, attempting to fall back to sleep. A tear spilled down her cheek and in her ear. One tear became two, and then several more, her shoulders bobbing with her quiet sobs.

Dealing with her husband's situation was the toughest dilemma she ever had in her life. It hadn't been an easy road, and especially after her latest visit. Andre was never a hostile man, even over disagreements, but now he had changed for the worse. Simply speaking to her husband became a dangerous undertaking, unable to predict his impulsive mood swings.

Knowing his brain injury caused his behavior, she didn't want to hold him accountable for his words or actions. After all, nothing was his fault. He was a victim of a terrible accident, and she understood his resentment toward a life he couldn't call to mind. But after Andre's frequent aloofness and violent outbursts, how and when would they ever get along again?

• CHAPTER 15 •

Andre

Monday, Oct. 2nd

Andre stared at his reflection in the bathroom mirror and marveled at the hole in his neck. For weeks he breathed through a plastic tube without a hint of his existence, and today he would eat his first solid meal. After eating from a bag through his arm, he lost fifteen pounds, and the muscles of his arms and legs had worn down like deflated balloons. He was thankful to be alive, but he wished he could get back the brain he once had.

His mind felt like an old, dusty book filled with cobwebs. Names of objects were harder to recall, and the slightest syllable was labor. He knew what he wanted to say, but he omitted the smallest of words. He watched Hayden rinse his toothbrush and squirt an amount of paste on the bristles.

As Hayden brushed his teeth, he tried to piece together the delightful memories of the photos Eva showed him last Saturday morning. From an intellectual perspective, he knew the couple in the pictures were them at younger ages, but he didn't remember *how* he felt then. He was only told about what happened, unable to relive the excitement he was feeling on their wedding day.

"Can you say aah for me, buddy?" Hayden said.

Andre opened his mouth wide. "Aaah!" He let Hayden brush his tongue and back teeth. The foamy toothpaste made him look like he had a horrific case of rabies, but he liked the minty taste.

Hayden filled a paper cup with cold water from the sink. "Now, take a sip and rinse out your mouth for me, but don't swallow." He held the cup to Andre's lips.

Andre carefully sucked a sip and swooshed it around in his mouth.

Hayden watched him, ensuring he doesn't gag or choke himself. "Great job, man. Okay, that's enough."

Andre spit it out into another empty paper cup held to his lips, and then Hayden wiped his mouth with a paper towel.

The male nurse smiled. "So, are you ready for breakfast?"

"Yes . . . h-h-hungry," Andre answered.

Hayden chuckled. "That's good. Mrs. Dorothy Jackson

is your speech therapist. She'll help you practice swallowing different foods."

Sasha poked her head around the corner in the doorway and smiled. "Well, good morning! I like your blue cardigan, Mr. Lucas."

"Thanks," Andre replied with a half-smile.

Sasha looked at Hayden. "Make sure you change his bedding."

"Yes, ma'am, I'm about to after I send him over to Mrs. Jackson."

Sasha gave a thumb's up and left.

Hayden flicked off the light switch and rolled Andre in his wheelchair to the large cafeteria in the hospital. An old woman dressed in a comfy alphabet sweater and vintage button-down skirt was sitting at a square table. Her thin, cottony, snow-white hair was like a cauliflower, and her sagging, blotched skin revealed she was at least in her seventies.

On the table were two Styrofoam cups and a food tray of Andre's breakfast—sliced banana, cream of wheat, and a carton of milk. Beside the old lady on the floor was a tan tote bag filled with a Scrabble board game and other supplies with the phrase SPEAK YOUR MIND in thick black letters printed on the front.

She grinned as Hayden pushed Andre up to his breakfast. "Well, hello, Andre. I'm Mrs. Jackson."

"Hi." Andre exhaled a few wheezy breaths and looked

over his food tray and then back at her.

"I've brought activities to improve your speech and memory skills, but first you need energy," Mrs. Jackson added.

Hayden smiled. "I'll leave him alone with you. Have fun, Andre." He patted his shoulder and exited the room, his Nike sneakers chirping on the newly waxed floor.

"Okay," Andre said, glancing over his shoulder.

"First, we'll try a few swallowing exercises. Are you ready?"

"Yes." Andre observed his therapist as she showed him different tongue exercises, mimicking her actions. He used one Styrofoam cup to sip water to rinse his mouth, and the other cup to spit it out. After his warm-up exercises, Mrs. Jackson took a VitalStim—an electric device to assist swallowing—out of her bag. She stuck the wired patches on Andre's neck. Then she picked up a spoon on the tray and fed him small morsels at a time, training his throat muscles used for swallowing.

"Can you guess the flavor?" she asked, spooning him a scoop of cream of wheat.

Andre savored the taste in his mouth and frowned. "Can't tell . . . d-d-don't know." He swallowed and licked the excess from his lips.

"It's peaches and cream. Can you say peaches?"

Andre tried to form the word with his lips. "Pou . . . pee . . . p-p-peaches."

"Very good." Mrs. Jackson spooned him the last of his cream of wheat and praised him for eating most of his meal. The only thing he didn't finish was his banana, which was a little too difficult for him to swallow.

Felicia—a tall, African American cafeteria worker in lime green scrubs, pushed a steel cart of cafeteria trays over to them. "What's up, Mr. Lucas? Did you enjoy your breakfast?"

"Yeah," Andre said, smiling.

"He did a great job," Mrs. Jackson chimed in.

"I'll take this for you, sir." Felicia grabbed Andre's tray and stacked it on the cart, wheeling it to the kitchen. "Have a good day, all right?"

"You t-too," Andre said.

Mrs. Jackson took out a stack of picture flashcards. "Okay, Andre. Let's practice some words to strengthen your vocabulary." She pulled the rubber band off the cartoon cards and held them before Andre. After she went over the cards with him, she flipped through them again, seeing how many names of the cards he memorized.

"And what animal is this?" Mrs. Jackson held up a card.

Andre's eyes darted from the picture on the card. He spotted the same young woman with dark hair behind his therapist, pushing the curly-haired, little boy in a black and white umbrella stroller toward them. His expression closed up, and his heart stopped by her sudden presence.

Uh-oh. What's she doing here?

"Come on, Andre, I know you can do it," Mrs. Jackson said.

Andre tried to focus and ignore the young woman, chewing on his bottom lip. "Uhh . . ."

"Hi," the dark-haired woman greeted with a smile, interrupting his speech lesson.

Mrs. Jackson grinned and extended a hand. "Oh, hi. You're a relative of Andre?"

"Yes, ma'am. I'm Eva, Andre's wife." Eva shook Mrs. Jackson's hand.

"How do you do, Mrs. Lucas?"

"I'm well." Eva glanced at the little boy under the canopy of the stroller. "Andy and I came from the daycare where I work, and I asked to take a brief visit. Dr. Brown advised I be present in some of Andre's therapy sessions."

"How nice! Please, join us," Mrs. Jackson said. "Andre and I were going over word cards. These will help him identify with everyday people, places, and things and build his language skills. You can go over them with him at home."

"Okay, great." Eva unstrapped a Cookie Monster backpack from her shoulders and placed it on the floor.

Andre cringed inwardly as she sat beside his wheelchair at the table, hunching like a turtle hiding in a shell.

Elation suffused Eva's countenance, but all he could think about was how much he wanted to disappear.

"You look dashing, Andre," Eva said, smiling.

Andre shyly glanced at her. "Uh, thanks."

Eva dug a sippy cup of apple juice from a drink holder on the backpack and gave it to their son.

Andrew took the cup and chugged down the juice like a thirsty traveler.

"All right, Andre, back to your exercise," Mrs. Jackson said.

Andre studied the cartoon image on the card again. "Um . . ."

His speech therapist offered a hint. "It's called man's best friend and likes—"

"Dog!" Andre interjected with a grin.

"Correct!" Mrs. Jackson showed him another card. "How about this one?"

Andre narrowed his eyes, brooding. He saw it before, the name of the animal on the tip of his tongue. "Uh . . . c-c-cow?"

"Not quite. It meows and many of them like milk," Eva hinted.

"Oh, cat," Andre said.

"Excellent!" Mrs. Jackson showed him one last card. "Try this one."

Andre peered at the drawing image and blinked. "Ha . . . house?"

"Brilliant! You're a fast learner." Mrs. Jackson gathered and shuffled the activity picture cards.

Eva grinned and placed her hand over Andre's. "Nice job. I'm proud of you."

Heat crept up in Andre's cheeks from her touch. "Uh, thanks." He hung his head, barely looking at her face. *Why do I feel weird? Why is she acting so nice? I don't want her here. How could she want anything to do with me?* Eva was a lovely, young woman with her whole life in front of her, and he felt she didn't deserve to have to put up with the likes of him.

Eva faced the speech therapist. "So, how long will you be teaching him?"

"Until his discharge, but I can continue with him in outpatient therapy. It depends on you and your preferences. Playing Scrabble is also a great way to help Andre's speech disorder and improve his memory," Mrs. Jackson said.

As his speech therapist and Eva continued socializing, Andre stared at the table with downcast eyes and let their chatter sink in his mind. Being ignorant of easy things was embarrassing, and now in his present condition, he felt incapable of advancing Eva and Andy's lives. Unless he gets help, he was trapped in bed, and the last thing he wanted was to be a burden to Eva. His trauma team of nurses and doctors was good to him and made moving on with life easier. The only world he knew was in the hospital and leaving it behind was a scary thing. To him, love was a mystery, while marriage and fatherhood were duties, he didn't remember he had.

Maybe he should stay where he felt safe and comfortable. Maybe it was best for him. His wife had wanted him to live with her, but perhaps he could change her mind. Besides, already having her day job, how much stress of caretaking can she endure?"

• CHAPTER 16 •

Andre

Saturday, Oct. 7th

"You'll get an electric wheelchair to supply you a sense of independence," Sasha said, pushing Andre's manual wheelchair. His second week in Acute Care had ended, and Dr. Brown said he was ready to transfer and begin physical and occupational therapy. While Sasha wheeled Andre to his new room, Daphne toted his gym bag.

After turning off the Acute Care wing of the hospital corridor, they took him in a homey, motel-like room. A cozy bed draped with a navy-and-gold, moon-and star quilt blanket centered the bedroom. Facing the front end of the bed was a double-door cabinet with drawers for storage space. Kitty-cornered on the right side of the cabinet was a dresser with a rectangular mirror. A 20-inch plasma TV was on a shelf of the cabinet, and a bathroom through a door was close to the visitor's chair.

Andre widened his eyes and inspected the different environment as if it was planet Mars. "Room . . . nice."

The nurses giggled.

"We're glad you like it," Sasha said. "This will be your room until you get discharged home."

Andre wore a wry smile and glanced down at his size eleven-and-a-half Air Jordon sneakers. *What was home?* He couldn't remember where he lived, the house address, or what he and Eva's house looked like, but he hoped it was as warm and welcoming as his new patient room.

"You should have him meet Dylan. I'm sure he'd appreciate it," Daphne said, placing Andre's gym bag on the dresser.

Sasha nodded. "I agree." She leaned over Andre, gripping the push handles of his wheelchair. "I'm taking you to meet your physical therapist, Mr. Lucas. Would you like that?"

"Sure," Andre said.

Sasha rolled Andre from his room to the exercise gym. Echoes of voices and clanking metal equipment met him as the nurse took him into the fitness center. For a long time, he thought he was the only one who had a traumatic brain injury, but as he surveyed the gym, he realized others faced similar challenges as him. Men, women, boys, and girls of different ethnics and ages trained with their therapists, striving to adjust to a more fulfilling life.

Some patients were amputees, some were paralyzed, and others suffered mental disorders. Inside were three rows of parallel bars and blue gym mats spread on the tables and sections of the floor. There was also a rack of dumbbells, kettlebells, and exercise balls, and sets of lift machinery to support disabled patients like him.

“Hey, Sasha!” Dylan Phillips, Andre’s physical therapist, walked through the back door of the gym in the nick of time. He waved and strode toward Dr. Sasha Joyner, sporting his gray T-shirt tucked in black sweatpants with white piping and white Skechers.

“Hi, Dylan,” Sasha said. “I wanted you to meet your latest patient, Mr. Andre Lucas. He’s a quadriplegic, but it could be temporary. He’s been in Acute Care for two weeks and is stable despite his brain injury.”

“Cool!” Dylan raised his dark shades in his blond, spiked haircut and placed his hands on his hips. “Hey, man. It’s nice to meet you.”

“Hi.” Andre found a smile. After seeing mostly women around him, he was glad to get in contact with another male friend again.

“Well, he’s about to have breakfast and speech therapy, but afterward I’ll bring him right over,” Sasha said.

“Great, I’ll look forward to it,” Dylan replied.

Sasha dragged Andre’s wheelchair and rotated it in the opposite direction, pushing it toward the gym’s entrance.

"Okay, Andre, it's your turn." Mrs. Jackson smiled and watched him whisper in Eva's ear.

"I think he's got a good one for you." Eva shuffled the wooden letters of Andre's tile holder. She paused and listened attentively to Andre's word again.

Eva giggled and looked at Mrs. Jackson with a playful smirk. She placed his letters on the crossword game board, horizontally spelling BUBBLEBATH linked to Mrs. Jackson's double-scored BUBBLE.

"Way to go, Andre!" Mrs. Jackson laughed and clapped for him. "That gives you—" she counted the letters and added up his score— "Twenty-eight points! Looks like you've taken the lead."

"Good job," Eva said, smiling and glancing at him.

Andre blushed and grinned. He liked playing Scrabble. It was his favorite activity because he always had fun while learning at the same time. Although his speech still needed some work, his vocabulary and spelling skills were improving. He was excited to learn, and wanted to fill his dull mind with as many words as he could.

Mrs. Jackson tried to steal the lead with a vertically-spelled, triple-scored FLOATS connected to BUBBLEBATH, but Andre had stolen the game with his last word.

Eva listened to Andre's whispered suggestion and horizontally spelled FATHER attached to FLOATS over two triple-score blocks.

"Awesome pick!" Mrs. Jackson said. "Let's see, that gives you—" she counted the letters with her pen again. "Twenty-one points! You win, Andre!"

"Yay!" Eva cheered and giggled, clapping.

Andre smiled and felt a burst of confidence and admiration boost his spirits, proud of himself for winning the game. He wanted to play another round, but Mrs. Jackson cleared the wooden tiles back in the plastic bag and closed the board.

"You're doing a super job, Andre," Mrs. Jackson said.

"Play . . . again?" Andre said with a sad frown.

"Don't worry," Mrs. Jackson said, "we will tomorrow, okay?"

"Okay," Andre said, smiling.

Sasha entered Andre's room. "Well, what's going on in here?"

"Andre won Scrabble," Eva blurted.

"Did he?" Sasha smiled. "Well, congratulations! I suppose you're getting better at the game. It's time for your physical therapy. Are you ready to go?"

"Yeah . . . I guess," Andre said.

Sasha gripped the handles of his wheelchair. "Great, let's head to the gym." She pushed him while Eva walked beside her down the hall, carrying her black camera case on her shoulder.

Andre drew a long breath. Nervousness settled in his chest. Being a paralyzed man, he knew there would be some pain in his joints, but he didn't know how bad it would hurt. Neither did he know what kind of muscle exercises he would do during his physical therapy.

He could only hope everything would go well.

• CHAPTER 17 •

Andre

Oct.07. 2017, 9:15 a.m.

Andre rested on the cool mat and watched the gleaming fluorescent lights above on the ceiling. He remained motionless as Dylan helped him perform a range of motion exercises and Eva video-recorded his first day of physical therapy. He wasn't in the mood for a camera beaming in his face, but he assumed Eva was taping for a reason.

Dylan placed one hand under Andre's left elbow and the other on his wrist. "All right, I'm going to flex and extend your arm to renovate movement of your elbow." He slowly bent and extended Andre's arm a series of times, counting to ten. Then he flexed and extended Andre's wrist, hand, and fingers. Dylan positioned Andre's arm flat on the mat. "Now, I'm moving to your legs."

"Okay." Andre observed Dylan leave his side and Eva

inch forward, filming him.

"How are you?" Eva asked. "Do you feel like your joints are getting looser?"

Andre gave a half-smile. "Fine. A little . . . maybe."

Dylan walked further at the end of the mat table. The physical therapist lifted Andre's left leg, having one hand under Andre's knee and the other holding Andre's ankle. He gently bent and extended Andre's leg, moving his hand on top of the knee during every flexion of his leg.

Eva panned her Sony camcorder to Dylan. "What's this exercise called?"

"Oh, this is Hip Passive Range of Motion. It helps increase flexibility and build his leg muscles." Dylan placed Andre's left leg down on the mat.

Andre peeked below his waist and couldn't hold his burst of laughter.

Eva giggled and spun the camera back to him. "What's so funny?"

Andre's voice trembled, struggling to keep a straight face. "Leg . . . my leg . . . aaahhh."

Eva rotated and zoomed the camcorder to Andre's left leg, which was shaking uncontrollably. She and his physical therapist laughed with him.

"Muscle spasms," Dylan hinted to Eva. "It's a common effect of paralyzed people when they're stretching their muscles, but it can also be a sign of pressure sores."

"Oh." Eva chuckled and smiled.

"How long . . . before . . . walk again?" Andre asked.

"It can take from six months to a couple of years," Dylan answered.

Andre sighed dispiritedly. Two years sounded like a long time.

"But be encouraged," Dylan added, "with hard work and practice you *can* walk again."

Andre hoped his physical therapist was right. If he gets walking, he could work and support Eva and their son. He stayed on the table as Dylan climbed over him and performed a few lower extremity stretches with his legs to improve his blood circulation. Afterward, Eva shut off the camcorder and along with Dylan helped Andre sit upright on the table for core exercises.

"I want you to try to pull your body toward me, hold it a couple of seconds, and then lean back," Dylan said. He glanced at Eva, cupped his hands under Andre's elbows, and leaned a short distance away from Andre. "Eva, guard his back."

"Right," she said with a nod.

Andre took a breath and bowed his head, attempting to push himself forward. His limp, numb body leaned back before he could reach Dylan or hold the position.

Eva caught Andre in her hands, keeping him from falling over the mat table.

"Try again," Dylan said. "You can do it."

Andre focused hard and licked his tongue on the corner of his mouth, struggling to inch toward Dylan. He fell back against Eva's hands again, dispirited. "I can't . . ."

"Try," Dylan urged.

"I can't," Andre slurred again with frustration.

"Don't give up," Dylan coached.

Andre tried three more times. The third time he gradually inched closer to Dylan, ignoring the burning pain in his lower back and closing the gap of distance between them.

"That's it," Dylan said, grinning. "You're doing good, man. Just a little more."

Andre inched a tad closer and held the forward position for a few seconds.

"Three . . . two . . . one . . . and relax," Dylan said.

Andre leaned back against his wife and let out a slow breath.

Eva embraced him from behind with her arms around his waist and planted a kiss on his cheek. "Yes, you did it! Good job, honey."

Andre inched up a smile as Dylan commended him with a pat on his shoulder, realizing his torso was still strong despite his paralysis. Although he needed help for many tasks, his chance to regain mobility was showing some promise. He wondered how he would progress the next weeks ahead.

Not having a spinal cord injury, he imagined he'd be

out of his wheelchair quickly. Yet, Andre understood the charismatic, intelligent man he was had transformed into a naive, dependent patient. And even if his walking ability was restored, with a weaker mind, he wasn't too confident he could pick up life where he left off.

• CHAPTER 18 •

Eva

Three Weeks Later

Hearing Andre's laugh was pleasant music to Eva's ears, but lately, his visits weren't amusing anymore. His mood changed like the phases of the moon. October was nearing its end, but Andre remained a complete quadriplegic. With his gradual recovery process, there were more dark eclipses than full moons. She was feeling her composure slip from under her like a trapdoor, and she hoped his spirits would rise by the time his discharge came.

Eva entered the rehab fitness gym, pushing Andrew in his stroller. As soon as she walked in, she saw her six-foot husband standing with the help of Nurse Hayden and his physical therapist. A sling hooked to a hydraulic lift that to Eva resembled Andrew's old baby jumper was also strapped on him. Dylan sat on a stool with wheels and guided his feet from the back. Hayden rolled the lift at the front as her husband took slow, wobbly steps across the hardwood floor. Regardless of how bad Andre felt, Eva was so proud of the progress he made, and she prayed his faith for walking alone someday would come back again.

Hope fluttered through Eva. It was always good seeing him out of his wheelchair and on his feet. Until the first time his trauma team worked with him in a standing position, she'd almost forgotten how tall he was.

Her smile slipped, noticing his impassive expression. As much as she missed him, his face told her he wasn't looking forward to a home or church visit. Things had changed. Dead silence was growing between them like thorns and thistles, threatening to split them apart. No longer did they play fun games together. No longer could she make him smile or laugh again.

Nothing she tried to help him feel better worked. Old pictures of memories collided with his pessimistic attitude until she quit showing them to him altogether. She was failing to rekindle the spark in their relationship. Now his trauma team was the only ones who could boost his mood.

"He's progressing well, Mrs. Lucas," Dylan said, "but he still has a long journey ahead of him."

Eva stole a glance at her husband.

Andre grimaced and bit his lower lip as if holding back an outburst. *Am I crowding him? Do I expect too much from his recovery?* She wanted Andre to understand she supported and cared about him, but she also didn't want to intrude his space to heal.

"Well, at least he's getting better. I should be on my way." Eva plastered a smile and wheeled the umbrella stroller backward a couple of inches.

"Hey, wait a minute. Aren't you taking Andre?" Hayden said, reminding her. "You called and requested to have him attend church today."

Eva paused and gulped. "I uh . . . changed my mind. I think he'd rather stay here until his discharge, right Andre?"

Her husband responded with a nod.

"Besides, I have many things to settle before he comes home," Eva added, massaging her neck.

Hayden frowned with concern. "Okay, well, you and Andy take care."

Eva gave a weak smile and peeked at Andrew under the canopy. "Come on, let's go, baby."

Andrew giggled and babbled what sounded like an asked question.

Eva sighed and exited the gym as another nurse entered inside. She flinched when the door slammed shut behind her. Her heartbeat banged in her chest like a boxer hitting a speed bag. *Why is Andre so quiet toward me? Is he angry? Is he depressed? Had I done something wrong?* Lately, he had the demeanor of a prehistoric caveman, at least whenever she was around.

Eva fled to the women's room. When she came out of the stall, she gripped the edge of a sink and speculated how Andre would adjust at home and his treatment while she's away. She heard of disgusting cases of disabled patients abused by their caretakers. She hoped and prayed nothing like that ever happened to him, especially with their marriage already on the rocks. Eva raised her head and studied her sad reflection in the wide mirror.

Heavy bags drooped under her cocoa brown eyes from waking early for work and lack of sleep at night. She was exhausted, and Andre wasn't discharged yet. It was the twenty-ninth of the month—a little over a month since Andre's arousal from his coma, but he still had a week and four days before his release date. She turned on the faucet, splashed water on her face, and dabbed it dry with a few paper towels.

Crying wouldn't resolve anything, and neither would worrying herself. She filled her lungs with a brave breath and straightened her posture. She had cried her last tear over her husband's attitude. If Andre pitied himself, she wouldn't join him. And if he was determined to remain a hard shell, two can play at that game. No matter how much he tested her, she refused to let her compassion to make her crack under pressure. Eva checked her brown leather wristwatch. It was eight o'clock—almost time for church service. She strode to the swing door and pushed

Andrew in his stroller out of the bathroom.

A car horn blew outside.

Eva hurried to a front window in the living room and peeked out the curtained blinds. A 1956 mint green and white Chevy Bel Air was rumbling on the paved driveway of the house. Mrs. Flowers volunteered to take Eva and her son to church this morning. Eva took her clutch purse from the dark brown sofa, strapped Andrew's Cookie Monster backpack on one shoulder, and lifted her son out of his playpen.

When she exited, Mrs. Flowers turned off the engine and got out of her car. The old woman stepped out of her comfort zone of African attire, arrayed in her Sunday best. Wearing a marigold skirt suit with a black print design, a black, wide-brimmed hat, and gold heels, she looked like a cut-out photo from *Ashro* magazine.

"Mrs. Flowers? Is that you?" Eva joked and closed the front door.

"Yep, it's getting colder," Mrs. Flowers said. "I gotta dress warmly. I can't be wearing my thin housecoats or day dresses with the weather changing. Winter will be here before you know it, honey."

"You got that right." Eva walked to the driveway.

Mrs. Flowers cackled and opened the back car door.

"Thank you," Eva said.

"You're welcome. I'll never forget my motherhood days. It *sure* keeps your hands tied," Mrs. Flowers replied, as Eva buckled Andrew in his car seat. Since she rode with Mrs. Flowers sometimes during the week, there was already a booster chair on the back seat for him.

Eva joined Mrs. Flowers in the car's front, taking the passenger seat.

Mrs. Flowers turned on the radio and scanned the static stations. The Mighty Clouds of Joy's 60s' rendition of "Amazing Grace" blared through the speakers, singing the first chorus of the song. Some singers sang backup while another one of them took a loud, screeching lead. The music comprised of a waltz drumbeat, an organ, and electric guitars. *"A-maa-zing grace! How sweet the sound. That saved a wretch like meee! I once was lost, but now am found, was blind, but now I see . . ."*

Mrs. Flowers hummed to the melody and pulled her car out the driveway, tapping her thick fingers on the silvery steering wheel. She glanced at Eva. "So, have you received news about your SSI benefits yet?"

Eva sighed. "Nope. All the waiting is driving me nuts, but I guess I should hear soon next month. Since Andre gets discharged in November, it'll be perfect timing."

"How's he doing emotionally?" Mrs. Flowers said.

Eva crossed her arms and studied the blurry view of red-orange maple trees outside her foggy window. "Who knows? He won't talk to me."

"He's going through," Mrs. Flowers said, "I'm sure he'll open up when he comes home again."

"That's the problem, Mrs. Flowers." Eva sighed. "He acts like he doesn't *want* to come home. It's how much quieter he is, the way he looks at me . . . I'm trying to keep it together, but he's getting under my skin."

Mrs. Flowers focused on the country highway and took a deep inhale of sweet sap in the breeze. "Do you love Andre?"

Eva was startled by her question but assumed the old woman was making a point. "Of course," she answered without hesitation.

"Then stay patient with the man," Mrs. Flowers said, giving her a look. "Eva, honey, I know you've been dealing with a hard time juggling responsibilities, but you can't always look at things from your perspective. Patience is the key to a lasting marriage—to any relationship."

"I know," Eva said, "it's why I changed my mind about taking him to church today. I might've invaded his space too much. Andre's always been a strong person, but he needs time to grieve the past and release his emotions. As far as I know, he hasn't cried since he learned he had a car accident."

Mrs. Flowers sucked her teeth and maneuvered into the left lane from behind a man driving a red Jaguar XF. "It's hard to grieve for a life you don't remember."

Eva's shoulders sagged. "That does make sense." She arched her brow. "Do you think his memory will come back?"

"Maybe," Mrs. Flowers said. "Somehow, I believe the old Andre we know is still inside him; and in due time, he's gonna show himself a man again."

Eva sighed. If only she had Mrs. Flowers' confidence, but the reality of Andre's mental state and condition had kicked into gear. She looked back out her window at old farmers harvesting and selling pumpkins and squash to members of the community. One of them was giving a group of people a hayride in a cart connected to a John Deere tractor, riding them through the dirt grooves of the orange, ripe patches.

Before Andrew was born, one autumn she and Andre had taken a ride with neighboring friends. They had so much fun together, laughing and talking among their neighbors in town about thanksgiving plans and the year's Super Bowl season.

The San Francisco 49ers weren't the most popular and hadn't won an NFL championship since the mid-1990s, but they were Andre's favorite team. Their hayride felt like it happened yesterday. But after several weeks passed, she had concluded her husband would never remember their past again.

Pastor Tyson read in Genesis chapter thirty-two. He preached when Jacob wrestled until daybreak with his thigh out of joint and how God blessed him, granting him the brand-new name of Israel. From this, he advised the congregation to never give up and to fight through their prayers to receive God's blessings.

Help me, Jesus. I need you. Eva bowed and closed her eyes in meditation. It was easier said than done, but she believed God could do anything but lie and fail. Getting through to Andre was becoming more difficult, but with the Lord's help, nothing was impossible, right? The choir rose from the balcony chairs in their royal blue robes and sang "Tis So Sweet to Trust in Jesus." After their song, the pastor ended the service with a closing prayer.

Eva held her son's hand and walked him through the crowd toward the lobby doors. She wanted to escape or hide, but the pastor called her name.

"Sister Lucas!" he said, waving over a sea of bobbing heads.

Eva turned around and gave a timid smile. "Hello, pastor."

Pastor Tyson grinned and shook her hand. "Greetings, sister. How's your husband doing in his therapy?"

Eva opened her mouth. "He's . . . um . . ." She fluttered

her eyes and paused like her tongue was snatched out, her mind going blank. Fallen in defeat and fatigue, she had no words to express Andre or herself.

"How about we talk in my office?" Pastor Tyson said.

Eva nodded silently and followed the pastor, walking her son beside her.

"Hi there, Andy." Pastor Tyson smiled at her son and patted her little boy's head as they walked back up the carpet aisle.

"Hiya," Andrew said with a big grin, waddling next to his mommy. He licked his tongue across his bottom lip.

Eva found a smile as the pastor laughed. She couldn't help herself. Andrew was her ray of hope. Regardless of how unhappy she felt, he always cheered her up, and she loved those rare moments of hearing his tiny voice, especially when she understood him.

Pastor Tyson opened the door to his office, and Eva took a breath and entered to exchange words with him. Now was a better time than never to consult her religious leader on behalf of her marriage.

She needed all the support she could get.

• CHAPTER 19 •

Eva

Sunday Afternoon

"Sorry, I kept you waiting, Mrs. Flowers," Eva said, sitting in the passenger seat of the car. She mentioned she talked with Pastor Tyson in his office, and he likewise suggested she be open-minded about Andre's feelings. Then she finished saying the pastor prayed on behalf of her and Andre's marriage and her husband's recovery.

Mrs. Flowers waved it off and turned her key in the ignition. "That's okay, honey. I understand. It's good to get help and guidance from a higher source of advice." She switched her gear in reverse and pulled out of the parking lot. From the church, the drive back to Eva and Andre's home on Pasture Road was a fifteen-minute ride.

"Goodbye, Eva!" Mrs. Flowers said out of the driver's window.

"Bye, Mrs. Flowers! And thanks again!" Eva waved and watched the mint green automobile careen in the one-door garage of a small blue and white ranch house across the street. She looked at her son, holding him on her hip again. "What do you say, Andy? You hungry?"

Andrew stuck a Velcro hand of his stuffed monkey in his mouth.

"I guess that means a yes." Eva chuckled and stepped through the door.

Her eyes enlarged at the quiet, messy house.

It looked like a tornado had struck the living room. The house was a disarray, an emblem of how chaotic her life had been for the past month. Little boy clothes dangled over Andrew's playpen and jumbo Lego blocks were scattered on the floor.

Countless mail and newspapers buried the side tables, and a stack of library books covered one side of the couch. On the center table of the room were her silver Dell laptop, an empty Domino's pizza box filled with half-eaten crust, and a Canada Dry soda can. If her mother saw her house, she'd never hear the end of it.

Eva dropped her jaw, blinking in shock. "Whoa, looks like Mommy has lots of cleaning to do." She sighed tiredly, sat Andrew on the book-free end of the couch, took off his puffer jacket, and hung it on the coat hanger. "Now, you stay here and keep your little hands off those books. I'll be right back, okay?"

She trotted from the kitchen to the utility room and grabbed a round, laundry basket. Then she returned and found her son in the same spot, laughing hysterically.

Eva knelt and wore an amused smile, tossing her son's clothes in the basket. "Hey, baby. Whatcha laughing at, huh?"

Andrew caught his breath, regaining his composure for a short moment. Then he snapped his monkey's feet together and pulled them apart, cackling again.

Eva guffawed at her son, aware for some odd reason the sound of Velcro ripping tickled him to death. There wasn't a doubt in her mind his infectious laugh couldn't lift anyone's mood, even if Andre heard it himself. After all, he had his father's sense of humor. She thanked God for the special little boy she was blessed to have, and for the joy and comfort he provided during such a tough time.

Someone rang the doorbell.

Eva's heart skittered, shutting off her laughter. *Who's that?* She gulped and wore a perplexed expression as she answered the door, peeking through the crack.

A young, Caucasian man who looked in his twenties was outside on the brick-paved walkway. He held a manila folder with a document hidden in it and a friendly, chipped-tooth smile was spread across his face. His eyes were kind and irresistible—orbs as blue as glacier ice. Clouds of frosty breath spewed from his lips. "Hi, I'm

Skye Garrison." He pulled something gray and rolled up from a back pocket of his Levi jeans, and for a split second, Eva's breath hitched.

"I read your ad in the paper?" Skye raised a brow, holding a folded newspaper.

"Oh, yes, of course." Eva released a sigh, thankful he didn't pull out a gun. She listened as Skye spoke on.

"I thought to stop by, and say I'm interested in working for you," he added. "I have experience in caregiving. Would you like to read my resume?"

Eva smiled. "Sure, come in." She motioned for his entrance.

Skye wiped off his suede hiking boots and came into the toasty-warm house, taking off an orange toboggan hat. Wisps of chestnut brown locks covered his head. He had more hair than Eva had expected under a small knit cap, styled in a wavy haircut that made him resemble Shaggy from *Scooby-Doo*.

He gawked at the living room.

Eva blushed as she closed the door behind her. "You'll have to excuse our messy home. I've been too tired and drained to keep up with housecleaning, but it's not usually like this. You can have a seat in the tan recliner."

"Thank you, ma'am." Skye unzipped his red, bubble jacket and sat in the recliner. "I typed it last night." He opened his folder and handed his resume to Eva.

She took a seat on the couch crammed next to Andrew

and skimmed the document. "You worked in a nursing home for five years? You look so young."

"I know. I'm twenty-four. It started as volunteer work for community service during high school. I interacted with the residents and assisted in bingo nights, but then I got hired for a paying job at the same facility when I was nineteen. I got trained by nurses to improve my skills, but I'm fairly capable of caring for your husband."

"I see. So, why do you want to work for me?" Eva said, curious.

Skye laced his hands and sighed. "Well, I enjoy helping the old and disabled, which is rare for young people today, but my maternal grandmother's one of my best friends. I can do a lot of good in caring for your husband and being his friend. I was in his shoes, Mrs. Lucas."

He licked his lips and continued. "Six years ago, I had an accident while riding my bike. I had the right of way at a pedestrian crosswalk, but a man in a garbage truck fell asleep at the wheel. He struck me head-on. In a flash, I was lying on the ground. I remember nothing after that, except being in the hospital with my mom. I found out later I suffered a brain injury."

Eva marveled at Skye, discovering a part of her prayer had been answered. Before her in her husband's favorite chair was a living, breathing miracle she believed God had sent to her for Andre's sake. From first meeting Skye, he looked like any normal, young man. She didn't have a clue he suffered a brain dysfunction, and witnessing his healthy presence helped increase her hope Andre would recover too.

"The doctor told my mom I had a subdural hematoma. It's a pool of clotted blood from a ruptured vessel between my brain and skull," Skye added. "I was paralyzed on one side of my body and suffered many life-threatening seizures. Doctors didn't think I'd survive, but my mom refused to lose heart. It might be a long journey, but your husband can get better, Mrs. Lucas."

"Thanks," Eva said, "I'm sorry about your accident. How old were you when it happened?"

Skye took his resume from her. "Eighteen, a little after I graduated high school." He slipped the document back into his folder.

"Well," Eva said, smiling, "you're the only person who visited me, and having been where he is, I can't think of a better candidate to help my husband than you." She leaned back and laced her hands. "However, there are some things about Andre's condition that might change your mind."

"Like what?"

Eva darted her eyes, nibbling her upper lip. She reminded Skye Andre's quadriplegic and informed him he has a neurogenic bladder, has a bowel program, and uses catheters. "Are you comfortable performing these procedures?" she asked after her statements.

"Yes, ma'am," Skye replied and cleared his throat, "I've done them before on other bedridden patients in the nursing home. These daily tasks can be uncomfortable. The important things are to make sure you use good sanitation and keep the patient calm."

Eva let out another sigh of relief. "Oh, well, that settles it. How does seven twenty-five per hour sound?"

Skye rubbed his chin. "Make it eight twenty-five and we've got a deal."

Eva tugged her earlobe. She wasn't sure she could give that much, but she was too desperate to complain, and beggars couldn't be choosers, right? She gave a lopsided grin. "Eight twenty-five it is. I'll give you the information you'll need about Andre's daily schedule later. I hope you don't mind, but I prefer to wait to tour you around the house. My husband suffers from amnesia, and I don't want him to feel like he's the only one new to our home."

"That's fine, Mrs. Lucas," Skye said.

Eva brightened. "Great! You can start on November ninth. That's when Andre gets discharged from the hospital." She tittered and wrung her hands. "I'd also appreciate it if you come by and give me a couple of pointers ahead of time too. I've been studying for Andre's sake, but I'm new at caring for a disabled husband, and I want to make sure I do things right."

"Of course," Skye said," and I'll look forward to meeting your husband." He glanced at Andrew crawling in his mommy's lap and smiled. "I'm guessing he's your son."

Eva wrapped her arms around Andrew. "Yes, this is Andy."

"Hi, Andy," Skye said, waving childlike at him.

Andrew leaned back against his mommy and avoided eye contact, playing with her fingers. Lately, he had become as withdrawn as his father, whining and clinging to her like a tick on a dog's back.

"Don't you wanna say hi?" Eva glanced down at her son.

Andrew blinked and remained quiet, staring.

"That's okay." Skye chuckled. "I'm sure he'll get used to me the more he sees me around." He stood and stretched out his arms. "Guess I'll show myself out. When do you want me to start giving you tips?"

"Is tomorrow afternoon good? Maybe around four?" Eva suggested.

"Cool, I'll be here. Thanks for the job."

"No, thank you for accepting it," Eva said with emphasis, giving him a long look. "Even though I don't like to admit it, I need some help. I'm sure you noticed that the minute you walked in. I imagine it will be harder when Andre comes home."

"Don't worry—" Skye walked to the front door— "I'll be glad to help, and I'm sure you'll get the hang of things too with practice, so just relax, okay? I'll see you later."

"Bye, Skye. Thanks again," Eva replied.

Skye gave a soldier's salute with a dopey grin and exited the house.

What a nice guy. Eva chuckled and shut the door. With Skye's help, it would relieve her from some strain of taking care of Andre, at least during the daytime. At night, she would have to be her husband's caregiver and monitor him when he sleeps, making sure he's rotated to avoid him getting bedsores.

She was glad she was a bookworm. Eva had checked out books from the public library, perusing about quadriplegia and the health risks of inactivity for these types of people. Online articles she found while surfing the web were helpful in broadening her knowledge of Andre's brain injury and speech disorder.

Eva rose from the couch with her son. "I'll finish cleaning later. Come on, let's get something to eat, Andy." She carried her son to the kitchen and sat him in his highchair. For lunch, Eva heated a bowl of Chef Boyardee mac and cheese and four chicken nuggets for Andrew. For herself, she ate a turkey club sandwich and finished a half bag of Lays potato chips. Later, she played Legos with Andrew again in the living room before cleaning them up in the plastic bag.

Unlike her, he hadn't developed a building strategy, and instead observed their pretty colors and rattled them around the floor. Lastly, Eva and Andrew watched the movie *Curious George 3: Back to the Jungle.* By the time the end credits scrolled, her son was fast asleep, cradled in her lap. She put him to bed for an afternoon nap.

"Sleep tight, Andy. I love you." Eva pulled a baby blue fleece blanket over him and his monkey and kissed him. She tiptoed out of Andrew's room and entered the master bedroom. It was so silent in the house she could hear her shadow's footsteps. She missed those secret whispers she and her husband shared during Andrew's naptime, peeking at him in his crib and admiring how much their son had grown.

Knowing Andre had become reticent toward her, she understood she'd have to endure a long wait for friendly relations with him again. The next months would be trial by fire, but now with an experienced, relatable guy like Skye by her side, she had faith everything would work out fine.

• CHAPTER 20 •

Eva

One Week & Four Days Later

Can a man fall in love with his wife twice?

Eva stared behind Dr. Brown at Andre and sighed hopelessly as the physician offered her last-minute advice. Her disabled husband was sitting in his ruby-and-gray electric wheelchair nearby the front entrance. He was trapped in his own universe, admiring the hazy, autumn morning through the automatic slide doors.

November had arrived, and it was time for Eva to bring Andre home. His natural life had endured, but she questioned if their relationship would too. Though Mrs. Flowers said it depended on her to reignite the flame, a happy marriage wasn't one-sided. It involved the shared exchange of good communication and affection from both spouses—important qualities Eva doubted Andre would ever give to her or their son. Since completing his physical therapy, Andre made little to no recovery. Aside from his face and neck, his thumbs were the only parts of his body he could feel, but his depressed mood concerned Eva the most.

"Have you considered placing him on an antidepressant?" Dr. Brown asked, catching her off guard.

Eva shifted her eyes back to the doctor. "Oh, no, doctor. To be honest, I'm kind of skeptical of medications." She glanced at her husband from behind again. "Andre's already been through a lot. I don't wanna risk him suffering from side effects through curing his depression. I've gotten him to smile and loosen up before during his therapy. I wanna try to pull him out of his low mood myself."

"Fine," Dr. Brown said, "but if all fails, consider getting him a prescription. Many TBI victims suffer major depression, especially those paralyzed from their injuries. If left untreated, he may develop suicidal thoughts or attempt to kill himself. Keep a close eye on him while he's in your care." The physician turned and looked at Andre, tucking his hands in his lab coat pockets. "Did you hire a daytime caregiver?"

"Yes," Eva said, "he and my husband's grandfather will be here soon. Grandpa Ricardo's bringing his Ford truck to load up the electric wheelchair."

"Good," Dr. Brown said, nodding, "well, I guess this is goodbye."

He offered his chubby hand. "Please, call if you have more questions."

Eva shook the doctor's hand. "Absolutely, and thanks for everything."

Dr. Brown walked over to her husband. He smiled and patted a hand on Andre's shoulder. "Take it easy, Mr. Lucas. One day at a time, okay?"

"Okay, doctor," Andre slurred, not making eye contact.

"Farewell, man." Dr. Brown strode down the hospital corridor.

Eva gulped and watched the doctor, holding her husband's gym bag. Until Grandpa Ricardo and Skye come, she was left alone with Andre, a tricky situation that resulted in flare-ups or dead silence. She inhaled a long breath and approached him. *God, help, Andre. Please, let him speak to me.* Eva stood beside his electric wheelchair and gripped the strap of the gym bag in her sweaty hands, joining her husband in the outside view. "It's . . . a pretty foggy day, huh?"

Andre made no comment.

Eva's teeth chattered. She glanced from him to the doors again. "Listen, we have to live together. We have a little boy who needs us . . . so we should try to make this work, right?"

"Whatever . . ." Andre muttered.

Eva's eyes watered, but she held back her tears. She

pursed her lips and sighed. There was no telling when Andre's distant attitude would change, but at least he spoke to her. It was the first time he had in two weeks. Eva hadn't visited him in quite some time since the day she changed her mind about taking him to church with her. Being unwanted and treated like she was invisible, there wasn't a point to anymore.

A holly green 1967 Ford pickup and an orange Jeep Wrangler crawled up and parked beside each other in front of the hospital. Red and brown fall leaves around the outside flower garden swirled and danced in the wind across the concrete walkway to the automatic doors.

Her face lifted as an old Hispanic man with a gray mustache and a young, white man with a shaggy haircut talked casually and walked toward the entrance. The automatic doors slid open with a buzz and clamped behind them.

"Hey! *¡Buenos Dias, Eva!*" Grandpa Ricardo spread his arms wide.

Eva giggled. "*¡Buenos Dias, Papa!*" She hugged her husband's grandfather and closed her eyes shut to dissipate the tears she felt slipping. She released a sad, but relieved laugh. "Oh, I'm *so* glad you're here." Eva stepped back and wiped her cheek dry. She looked at her hired caregiver. "And you too, Skye."

Skye buried a hand in his jeans pocket and waved the other. "Nice to see you, Mrs. Lucas."

"Andre, this is Skye Garrison. He'll be your daytime caregiver at home," Eva said.

Skye grinned. "Hi, Mr. Lucas. It's a pleasure to meet you. We have more in common than you realize."

"Uh . . . hey," Andre replied lowly.

Grandpa Ricardo pulled a pack of Big Red chewing gum from his checkered, western shirt and frowned at Andre, slightly tilting his head. "What's the matter, *nieto*? *¿Eres infeliz?*"

Eva's smile faded. "Um, I'm afraid he doesn't remember how to speak Spanish."

"Oh . . ." Grandpa Ricardo sighed. "Well, no matter. Maybe I'll teach him. I did before, you know. He couldn't speak a word as a boy, but he became pro speaker by the time he was ten, eh?" He folded a stick of cinnamon gum in his mouth, chewed, and put the pack back in his chest pouch.

"Yes, I'm sure he could—" Eva glanced at Andre— "if he tries." She dropped her shoulders with a heavy exhale. "I don't wanna be late for work. We better go home."

"Okay," Skye said, "we'll help him get in your car outside."

"Thanks." Eva turned her attention to her husband. "You can lead the way, Andre."

With his right thumb, Andre pushed the joystick knob of his wheelchair forward, riding himself through the automatic doors.

Eva, Grandpa Ricardo, and Skye followed behind him.

As Grandpa Ricardo backed his pickup near Eva's car, Eva and Skye stood with Andre on the sloped sidewalk. In the flatbed were a traditional manual style lift and a sling mesh, and connected to the back was a scooter carrier.

Grandpa Ricardo climbed out of his truck and rubbed his bronze, weather-beaten face. "All right, *muchacho*. Help me with my grandson."

"Yes, sir," Skye said.

Eva opened the passenger door and stepped out of the way as Grandpa Ricardo and Skye helped Andre transfer from his wheelchair into her car. It took a while before they found a solution as they struggled to get Andre's long legs inside her compact vehicle.

"You may need to get a wheelchair van with transfer features, Mrs. Lucas," Skye said, buckling the seatbelt around Andre's lap. "It'll make it a lot easier." He placed his hands on his hips, catching his breath.

Eva nibbled her lip. "Yeah, I've considered doing that, but they're so expensive."

Grandpa Ricardo rolled the manual lift from the passenger car opening and closed the door. "Do you want me to help? I'll get it for you."

"No, it's okay, Papa," Eva said, shaking her head and raising her hands. "We'll manage. The lift alone works wonders."

Ever since they married, Grandpa Ricardo was always ready to sacrifice for them. And though able-bodied for his old age, he was soon to retire, and she worried his money contributions would run deep in his future pension checks.

Besides, he had done enough by taking Andre in from his irresponsible parents, being a strong male influence in their lives, and helping pay off their house mortgage.

Grandpa Ricardo chomped his gum. "Suit yourself. We'll meet you at the house."

"Okay." Eva ran around her car and sat in the driver's seat. She flicked out her switchblade key and put it in the ignition.

"What . . . that?" Andre asked.

Eva faced him and studied the curious look etched on his face. She followed his gaze to the custom keychain dangling from her car key. "It's a gift you got me for our seventh wedding anniversary. Before your accident, you were going to give it to me." Her hopes rose. "Do you remember it?"

Andre drew his eyebrows together and angled his head, rummaging through his memory.

Longing whispered through Eva as he scrutinized the shiny pennies and steel tag glittering in the sunlight. *Come on, Andre. How can you not remember this?*

"No," Andre said finally, "but it's pew . . . beautiful."

Eva swallowed a lump, disappointed. "Yeah . . . I think

so too." Her heart sank, but she wouldn't cry. What good would it do anyway? Her husband's damaged brain was like a reprogrammed computer, not a file of information saved from his former life. She started the engine, put the gearstick in reverse, cruised out of the parking lot, and U-turned around the hospital complex to the gate exit.

"Well, we're home," Eva said, unbuckling her seatbelt. Andre was dumbstruck, looking at their two-story gray house with black shutters, centered on a small, grassy lawn. Evergreen shrubs were bunched on each side of the entrance. In front of the vehicle was a two-door garage with a half-circle window lodged above the doors.

Andre looked at the black roof and the puffy clouds behind it arrayed in yellow-orange sunrise. "Nice . . . big too."

Eva unclipped his seatbelt for him and stepped outside. She turned around to the trunk of her car and took out Andre's gym bag and a folded manual wheelchair. Having two floors in their home, Andre needed one to use after being ascended with the stairlift installed in the house. Eva opened her husband's passenger door again.

After Skye and Grandpa Ricardo guided Andre's electric wheelchair into the house, they helped him into his manual wheelchair. Taking her husband out of her car was easier than getting him in, as they handled it with ease.

"There you go, *nieto,*" Grandpa Ricardo said, removing the sling from under Andre's bottom.

"Thanks, Papa, Skye," Eva said. "I appreciate your help."

Grandpa Ricardo's thick mustache rose, grinning. "*De nada.* I'm always there for you and Andre." He looked at his grandson. "Maybe someday you come stay on the farm with me, eh? I have plenty of chores for you to do."

"I'd like to visit your farm," Skye chimed in.

Grandpa Ricardo's eyes lit up. "Would you, lad? Well, you're welcome any time." He slid Eva a guarded look. "Let me know how things go and be patient with him."

Eva smiled. "I will, Papa, and thanks again."

Grandpa Ricardo hugged Eva and kissed her cheek. "Guess my work here is done. *Adiós, Eva.*"

"*Adiós, Papa,*" Eva said.

Grandpa Ricardo walked away and glanced back at Andre one last time. "Goodbye, Andre."

"Bye," Andre muttered, staring down at his Air Jordans.

His grandpa sighed as if a weight fell on his heart. At that instant, Eva realized Andre's brain injury affected his grandfather who raised him too. He settled in his Ford pickup, cranked on the rattling engine, and drove out the smooth driveway, revving off Pasture Road onto East Boulevard.

Eva waved and watched as the green-and-white truck rode around a corner hidden by a crowd of red maple trees. It had been a while since she and Andre stopped by Grandpa Ricardo's farm. Maybe it would be a good idea to visit, especially for Andre.

Skye called for her attention.

She gathered her thoughts. "Oh, sorry. I guess we should go inside. Let me show you around the rest of our home so I can go to work." She held the handles of Andre's wheelchair and pushed him into the house, leading the way as Skye toted Andre's gym bag.

Skye struck up a conversation. "I never mentioned it until now, but I like how you coordinated the colors dark brown, teal, and tan in your living room. It makes the room pop and stand out."

Eva beamed, flattered. "Thank you. Interior Design is one of my hobbies, and probably the career I should've pursued instead of childcare. But, dealing with kids is also fun, and I have my good moments in that field too." She stepped backward and spread her arms in welcome, dropping them at her sides. "Well, you know this is the living room. Let me show y'all the kitchen."

She toured Skye and Andre to the kitchen where Mrs. Flowers greeted them "good morning." She was drinking a cup of hot coffee at the four-seat table. Andrew was in his highchair eating a bowl of banana oatmeal for breakfast.

"How is everyone?" Mrs. Flowers sipped from a mug.

"Fine, ma'am," Skye said, smiling.

Eva grinned and gestured a hand to the old woman. "Skye, this is Mrs. Flowers. She lives across the street and babysits Andy sometimes. If you ever need help with our house and I'm not here, she'll be able to help you. She's practically a member of our family."

Skye shook Mrs. Flowers' hand. "Good to meet you, ma'am."

"You too, sonny," Mrs. Flowers said.

Eva slapped her forehead, thinking of what to mention next. "Uhh . . . oh yeah, the utility room is right around the corner from the kitchen." She turned squarely and pointed at a glass door behind long white blinds. "Outside here is the patio and—" Eva turned another angle, facing an arched entrance— "the dining room is right through this walkway. Let me show you." She pushed Andre's wheelchair and toured the dining room. Making Skye and Andre comfortable in the house was important to Eva, but especially to her husband.

"All right, it's time we go to the second floor," Eva said, after exiting the guest bedroom on the first floor.

Skye helped Andre into the stairlift, which slowly ascended him to the top of the hardwood staircase. Then Skye toted the manual wheelchair upstairs and adjusted

Andre back into it again.

Just observing the caregiver lift and move Andre was making Eva tired, but Andre depended on them, and she and Skye had to do their best to cope with the process. She sighed and presented the rest of the house, including the master bedroom, Andrew's room, and the bathroom.

"And that's all the rooms," Eva said, after finishing her house tour. "Now, I've got to go to work with Andrew. I'll be back between three-thirty or four in the afternoon. Don't forget my cell number, work number, and Andre's daily schedule are on the refrigerator in the kitchen, and remember, you can ask Mrs. Flowers for help too."

"Super," Skye said.

"If Andre takes a long nap, he'll need to be rotated to prevent—"

"Pressure sores," Skye said, finishing her statement.

"Oh, and make sure he keeps up with—"

"His range of motion exercises," Skye said, completing her thought again. "I know what to do, Mrs. Lucas. You don't have to worry. I'll take good care of your husband. Everything will be fine."

"Sorry. I guess I was double-checking," Eva said. "I'll call home during my lunch break to check how the first day is going."

"Okay." Skye arched his eyebrow, wondering why Eva was still standing with Andrew in her arms. "Uh, you *are* going to work, aren't you?"

Eva shifted a worried gaze from Andre in his manual wheelchair to Skye. "Uh, yeah. I'll leave right now." She took a few steps and paused, looking over her shoulder. "Bye, Andre."

Andre sat with his elbows perched on the leather armrests of his wheelchair. He wouldn't look in her direction, much less say goodbye.

Eva blinked and forced a smile, but she knew Skye saw the sadness on her face. She turned and hustled downstairs. Although she wanted to avoid placing her husband on meds, she faced a challenging test of patience.

Getting Andre out of his depression would be tougher than she thought.

• CHAPTER 21 •

Eva

Same Day

"I feel like I'm his enemy," Eva told Louise during her lunch hour. "Andre wouldn't say goodbye when I left, and he barely said it to his grandfather. We're disconnected, and I don't know if it'll ever end. It's like he's *The Boy in the Plastic Bubble* and nobody's invited in." She shook her head and sighed. "What if I can't get him to open up to me? Maybe I shouldn't have stayed away for so long during his last weeks of therapy."

"He's probably scared," Louise said.

Eva frowned. "Scared of what?"

Louise shrugged. "I don't know. Maybe the fact you still feel like a stranger to him. Or he's afraid he'll be reliant on others forever, or he'll fail at being a husband and father. He's placed in an obligated position and recalls nothing of how his prior life was. He just knows you said you're his wife, Andy's his son, and you want his memory to come back again. Imagine the pressure he must feel, especially seeing you struggled to take control over everything yourself."

"Well, he can at least pay attention to me. It's rude not to speak to your wife when she talks to you." Eva ate a scoop of chicken noodle soup from her Styrofoam bowl.

"Do you have plans for Thanksgiving?"

Eva wiped her mouth with a napkin. "I've been so busy lately. I haven't given it much thought. Mrs. Flowers will invite us over with her family, but I doubt I'll be in the mood. It'll make me think of old times, and I want to love Andre for how he *is*, not how he *was* anymore." She scooted out her plastic chair from the center table in the classroom. "Can you monitor the kids alone a minute? I promised I'd call home."

"Sure." Louise drank from a can of Coca-Cola.

Eva tiptoed out of the room and shut the door. She exited and stood on the sidewalk in front of the stone daycare. Eva leaned against a giant, green crayon pillar of the entrance and dialed the home number on her iPhone.

"Hello?" Skye's voice cracked through the receiving end.

"Hi, Skye. It's Mrs. Lucas. How are things going?" Eva heard the television resounding in the background.

"Uh, everything's cool," Skye said, "Andre had lunch. He said he wanted beef stew, so I warmed a can for him with crackers. He's watching Animal Planet. After his episode, we're gonna review his vocab cards. I made him smile and laugh a little during breakfast. So, yeah, he's coming around, Mrs. Lucas."

Yeah, to you, Skye, but not me, Eva thought, biting her fingernail. She peered at the yellow-and-blue playground set in the distance behind the wooden fence. "Has he had a restroom break yet?"

"Uh-huh. His second break was about . . . fifteen minutes ago," Skye said.

Eva glanced at her watch. "Okay, I guess I'll catch you later. Tell Andre I said hi."

"All right, Mrs. Lucas."

"Bye, Skye." Eva hung up and shut off her phone. She was relieved Andre was safe and doing fine, but she was feeling like she had two babies instead of one. Nevertheless, though she wasn't Andre's mother, it was her job to ensure he was taken care of, even if someone else did it for her.

Eva returned to the classroom.

"How's everything at home?" Louise asked.

"Fine, Skye says. He's Andre's caregiver and seems to be doing a decent job." Eva plopped at the center table across from her co-worker.

"But?" Louise raised her brow, aware there was more on Eva's mind.

Eva nibbled her thumbnail and exhaled slowly. "But . . . I'm worried about tonight when I come home. Andre probably thinks Skye will be living-in, but I haven't told him *I'll* be caring for him overnight. I'm hoping Skye mentioned it already."

"Maybe he did," Louise said, "men have a way of discussing women sometimes."

"Perhaps," Eva replied, "I guess I'll find out after work, but that's the least of my concerns." She took a sip from her water bottle and screwed on the cap.

"What's your biggest concern?" Louise asked.

Eva wore a pathetic look. "It's . . . I mean I know I studied about his disabilities, Skye helped train me, and I know what to do, but I'm still scared."

Louise shrugged. "What's there to be afraid of? Andre's your husband and y'all have been married for seven years. It's not like it'll be the first time you . . . you know, see him naked and all."

"I know," Eva said, "but since his memory loss, it feels like it. I mean, he's a different person. I don't wanna mess up or make him feel bad."

"Don't worry," Louise said, smiling, "I'm sure you'll be fine. Just remember what you said Skye told you. The calmer you are, the calmer he'll be, and the more likely he'll trust you again. Besides, there's a chance he may already be smitten with you anyway, but being difficult and stubborn."

Eva pondered Louise's remark. Maybe it was true. The day he first awoke from his coma, she never forgot the stunned look in his eyes. It was as if he couldn't believe *she* was his wife. She didn't know whether it was because of her appearance or personality, but Eva didn't always find herself attractive.

During her teen years, she wasn't Esmeralda, that's for sure. But somehow, Andre still saw the beauty behind her average looks. It was one of the main things she loved and appreciated about him.

His kind heart.

Though her husband worked a lot and had problems managing his time—both inside and out—he always *truly* loved her.

Eva nosed the front end of her car to the garage and shut off the engine. She gripped her hands on her wheel and glimpsed in the rearview mirror. Andrew was asleep, slouched in his car seat like an old man in a recliner. She stepped out of her car, unclipped her son, and toted him into the house.

"Hi, everyone!" Her expression hardened, surveying the empty living room. *Where are they?* Loud footsteps approached her. She took a swift look at the staircase as Skye came downstairs to the living room. He stopped at the last step with his hand on the banister dome cap. "Hi, Mrs. Lucas."

Eva's smile faded a little. "Hi, Skye. Where's Andre?"

Skye jerked his thumb behind him. "He's taking a nap upstairs. It's been about two hours. I rotated him and came from using the bathroom. I hope you don't mind, Mrs. Lucas."

"No, it's okay," Eva replied, "thanks for everything. See you tomorrow morning."

Skye nodded. "Bye, Mrs. Lucas." He exited the door.

Eva walked upstairs and placed Andrew in his crib. She strode the narrow hall and pushed back the door of the master bedroom. Her husband was stretched out on the queen-sized bed, his chest rising and falling in soft breaths.

She tiptoed in and sat on her bedside. Eva untied her tennis shoes and slipped them off as Andre squirmed his head on his pillow. She looked over her shoulder at him.

His eyes fluttered open, staring at her.

"Hey, did you sleep well?" Eva said, smiling.

Andre readjusted his head on his pillow. His face fell, emotionless. "Where . . . Skye?"

"Let me explain something first." Eva laid beside him on the bed and crossed her ankles, propping her head in her hand. "Andre, Skye's a daytime caregiver. I should've told you earlier, but it worried me you wouldn't want to come home if I did. It means . . . he's here during the morning and afternoon, but I'll be caring for your needs tonight."

"No! Skye—stay . . . h-h-here," Andre faltered.

Eva pinched the bridge of her nose and sighed. Why did their marriage have to be this way? Something had to be done. Tension couldn't live between them forever. It was time to draw the line. She sat up. "Andre, I'm sorry, but he can't stay. Besides, caring for you myself at night will save money." She touched his right hand. "I promise I'll take good care of you."

Andre looked away from her.

Eva stood. "I'm about to start dinner. Do you wanna go back downstairs?"

Andre frowned and sighed wearily. "Yes, sure."

Eva rolled the manual wheelchair alongside the bed and placed the sliding board in the seat. She carefully rolled Andre on his left side and applied her pillow behind his back for support. Three other pillows she stacked on top of each other at the end of the bed. Eva slid Andre's legs down and lifted his upper body right side up, resting his head on the pillows.

"You okay?" Eva asked.

"Yeah," Andre said.

Eva took the gate belt off his nightstand and wrapped it around Andre's waist. "I'm about to transfer you. One .

. . two . . . three . . ." She enveloped her arms around him and clutched the gate belt, pulling him onto the slide board and into his manual wheelchair. She released a quick, whistling exhale. Her back ached a little, but not enough to complain about. She yanked the board from under her husband and adjusted his hands in his lap and his feet on the footrests of the wheelchair.

"How many times have you used the restroom?" Eva adjusted her husband back against the seat.

"Three," Andre said. "Skye took me . . . before left."

Eva nodded. "All right. I guess you can wait until later." She pushed Andre out of the master bedroom and down the hall to the stairlift. She operated the lever, lowering him down the flight of stairs.

At the end of the staircase, she sat him back in his electric wheelchair and turned on the television to keep him occupied while she cooked dinner. For Andre, she made baked tilapia with steamed green beans and brown rice with gravy, taking Dr. Brown's advice of providing him a healthy diet.

Along with his schedule, she had created an organized dietary chart to ensure he ate lots of protein and fiber to strengthen his muscles and ease his digestion. She made mashed potatoes with fish sticks for Andrew—and not being very hungry—heated a Marie Callender's frozen pasta meal for herself.

Eva sat in a chair in front of her husband and fed him

as much as he would eat before having her food. She tried to get Andre to chat with her about his first day with Skye, but he made little to no feedback. Andrew made most of the noise, babbling and drumming the tray of his highchair with his spoon.

Before bedtime, Eva bathed Andrew, dressed him in his PJs, and tucked him in for the night. Now, it was time to get her husband ready for bed. She knocked on the door of the master bedroom. "Hey, are you tired yet?"

"A little," Andre said.

Eva opened a left middle drawer of the dresser. "What do you want to wear tonight? You have lots of pajamas to choose from." Regardless, of his disabilities, she wanted her husband to have some independence. She held a pair of blue-striped pajamas. "Are these okay?"

Andre nodded. "Sure."

Eva flapped out the button shirt and pants and laid them across the manual wheelchair. She walked around and stood over him while he lay on the bed. As she slipped his arms out of his sweatshirt, his pupils were huge. She could tell he was nervous, so she smiled to help him relax.

A large birthmark blemished his left bicep. It was shaped like the continent of Africa, and about two shades darker than his cinnamon-brown skin. Eva hadn't seen him shirtless for so long, she forgot it was there. She pulled his shirt off over his head, grabbed his nightshirt, and buttoned it on him.

Afterward, she tugged off his sweatpants and put on his matching PJ pants for him.

"There you are. Nice and cozy." Eva tossed his dirty clothes in a straw hamper. She returned to his bedside and helped him sit up and transfer back to his wheelchair again.

"Uh, I'm taking you to brush your teeth." Eva rolled her eyes and drew a long breath, wheeling him to the bathroom. She would get to the real purpose for their departure, but she didn't want to ruin his calm mood.

Unsure she could assist him without making a mess on the bed, she didn't trust using the plastic urinal the hospital lent him. She flicked on the switch and picked up his toothpaste and red toothbrush from the sink holder. When she finished brushing his teeth, she gave him a chance to speak up for himself.

"Do you have spasms?" Eva spotted his grimaced face in the reflection of the medicine cabinet mirror.

"No." Andre smacked his lips as if he had a bad taste in his mouth.

Eva turned around to him with her hands behind her back, leaning against the sink counter. "Um . . . do you wanna go before bed?" She cast a sidelong glance from the toilet to Andre, and he quickly got her implication.

"Oh, no, I'm fine." Andre gulped.

Eva angled her head and sighed. "Andre, you haven't used it since 3:00 p.m. It's nine o'clock at night. I know you have to go again." She sat on the lid of the toilet in front of her husband's manual wheelchair and wove her hands. "Listen, I know you don't remember me, but you don't have to be embarrassed. I promise to be as gentle and careful as possible."

"I said . . . I'm fine." Andre frowned and pursed his lips, breathing heavily and looking away at their linen tower.

"You're supposed to cath at least four times a day to prevent kidney damage." Eva placed a hand on his knee. "I don't want anything worse to happen to you."

"O-kay," he muttered, reluctantly glancing at her.

Eva stood and raised the lid and seat of the toilet. "Now, let me wash my hands and gather your supplies." She pushed Andre in his wheelchair to the toilet bowl, folded the footrests, and repositioned his feet flat on the floor. "There, it'll be over in a jiffy."

She took a grocery bag of used catheters from under the sink cabinet and put the bag on the metal shelf above the toilet. Her husband never reused a catheter to avoid a urinary tract infection. Dr. Brown suggested they get disposed of in a bag and thrown out on trash day.

Eva washed her hands thoroughly with soap and hot water and dried them with a sheet from a paper towel holder. She exhaled to calm down her rapid heartbeat and unzipped Andre's gray carry pouch, taking out a new intermittent catheter, a lubricant packet, a Betty Hook to keep his clothes from getting wet, and two sanitary wipe packs. She placed these supplies aside on top of the sink counter and grabbed two latex-free gloves from a box on the metal shelf.

Snapping on the rubber gloves, she stole a glance at Andre and saw discomfort cloud his face. He was scared stiff, unusually ashamed for her to see his male anatomy. But she didn't blame him. If it were her who got in a car accident, had a brain injury, and no longer remembered her husband, she'd feel the same way.

Unease grew in the bathroom, but Andre wasn't nervous alone. Despite reading the directions in the brochure and getting tips from Skye, she feared hurting her husband. His daily routine required great care and cleanliness, and one wrong move could cause infection or damage him for life.

She braced herself, picked up the Betty Hook, and stood behind Andre's wheelchair. "You can close your eyes while I catheterize you if you want."

Andre drew a long breath. "Okay." He squeezed his eyes shut, his right thigh jittering slightly with a spasm.

Eva tucked the Betty Hook into Andre's pajama pants and underwear and fastened the long flat end under his wheelchair seat, exposing him. She took one of the sanitary samples, tore it open, and pulled out the wet wipe. After Eva cleaned him off, she tossed the used wipe in the bowl. She grabbed and opened the lubricant packet and intermittent catheter from the sink counter.

Still standing behind his wheelchair, she lubricated the thin, plastic tube, slipped her arms under Andre's armpits, and slowly inserted the catheter inch by inch. *Please, God, don't let me hurt him. I'll never forgive myself.*

Her heart drummed against her rib cage. *Oh, my gosh! How can he not feel this?* She thought she was going to faint or freak out and she wanted to cry for him.

"Are you okay?" she asked with concern.

"Yeah . . . put it in." Andre didn't sense it was already halfway inside him, and Eva realized just how paralyzed her husband was below his waist.

He felt absolutely nothing.

She exhaled to relax and proceeded with the insertion until urine poured from the funnel end of the catheter into the toilet bowl. *Phew. Thank goodness.* She sighed with relief. As the flow dwindled, she slid the catheter in one inch more to ensure his bladder was empty, releasing a short drizzle. "Okay. You're finished. I'm taking it out."

"Good," Andre said with a relieved exhale.

Eva chuckled at her husband's reaction. "How did I do, Mr. Lucas?" She carefully removed the catheter and put it in the plastic trash bag.

"Fine, I guess." Andre opened his eyes and wore a half-smile. "You're okay . . . woman . . . pretty."

Eva smiled. "Thank you." She cleaned him off with the other wipe and tugged up his pants for him. If she could get through to Andre during a sensitive procedure, they could mend their marriage too.

She flushed the toilet, took off the gloves, and washed her hands again. After many tense days, tonight was the start of rebuilding their relationship. But with Andre's fluctuating moods, she wondered whether it would continue improving.

• CHAPTER 22 •

Eva

Saturday, Nov. 18th

Happiness coursed through Eva as the postal worker stuck envelopes in their tan mailbox. The mailman whistled as he walked back to his delivery truck, climbed in, and zoomed to their next-door neighbor's house. She opened the front door and stepped outside in the chilly morning in her lilac robe and slippers.

Eva got the mail and sifted through the letters, searching for good news. Sixty days had almost passed, and she and her family needed those SSI benefits to make ends meet. She went inside and sat on the couch in the living room. Aside from fast food coupons and household bills, there didn't seem to be anything from Dr. Washburn or the Social Security Administration.

Eva bit her lip. *Come on. Where is it?* She flipped Burger King coupons behind the stack and found a letter from

Dr. Washburn. Her heart leaped. Eva grinned and ripped the envelope open like a child who found a hidden birthday present.

She unfolded and read the typed letter:

Dear Mrs. Lucas,

I'm writing to inform you your disability claim has been approved. After much deliberation and review of your husband's medical records, the SSA has agreed to supply you with financial assistance.

You and your family will begin receiving SSI and SSDI benefits on November 25th. If you have questions, please call, or email me.

Sincerely,

Dr. Barbara Washburn

Eva closed her eyes and placed the letter over her chest in gratitude. *Thank you, God.* She never thought she'd be so excited to get welfare, but that changed when she became the only working member of her household. She raced upstairs to the master bedroom. "Andre! Andre, the letter came! The letter came!"

"Good for you." Her husband clenched his jaw.

Eva's smile dropped. "No, Andre . . . it's good for all of us." She approached him and sat on the bed at his feet. "I don't understand. I thought you'd be happy. You can get more things you need to help you get better."

"Better?" Andre said, grinding his teeth. He narrowed his eyes with bitterness. "I'm—not—getting better!"

Startled by the angry tone of his voice, Eva flinched from the bed with a gasp. Tears shone in her eyes as she stared at her husband, pacing her breathing. "I'm sorry . . . I'm sorry for the circumstances you're faced with and your accident, but don't take it out on me! I'm . . . I'm trying to help you."

Andre avoided her gaze, ignoring her.

Every time Eva thought they were fine, darkness and pessimism spoiled their good relations. Her husband's mood swings were becoming harder to deal with. How much longer could she tolerate this? How can she keep offering love and support, only to receive anger and meanness from him?

Not once has Andre apologized for his bad attitude and spiteful behavior, and she got a hunch he was taking her empathy and compassion for granted.

"I'm going to the grocery store to buy a few things. You should come and get some fresh air," Eva said.

Her husband shook his head. "No, I'll . . . s-s-stay here."

"Andre, please," Eva said, tilting her head. "You hardly ever go outdoors anymore. You can't be a hermit for the rest of your life. It's time you—"

"I don't—want—people—seeing me!" He looked away from her, sniffling.

Eva swiped her eyes. "Fine. You can wait for Skye. He'll be here in a few minutes." She left and shut the door. Since the day Andre exited the hospital, her husband hid home, not wanting the public to see him in his condition, and especially with Andrew along.

Feeling unqualified as a mature parent, he left the responsibility of their son on Eva's shoulders. The shoes of fatherhood were too big for his feet, easily annoyed whenever his son was cranky, noisy, or misbehaved.

Eva pushed Andrew sitting in the front of her red shopping cart and checked her grocery list as she wheeled to the bread aisle of BI-LO's:

Grocery List

~~Chef Boyardee's Ravioli (microwavable cases)~~
~~Campbell's Tomato soup~~
2 Loaves of Sarah Lee's Wheat Bread
Quakers Oatmeal

Chicken Nuggets
Gala apples
Tilapia
Salmon
2 Heads of Broccoli
Pack of Huggies
Ivory body wash
Colgate Toothpaste
Orange Juice
Eggs
Milk

From her job to her hygiene, there was so much for her to keep track of, and she didn't want to forget anything. She looked and found a tiny, Caucasian woman with strawberry-blonde hair in the middle of the checkered aisle. The woman was pushing a cart piled with food with a cell phone pinned to her ear. Two children were trailing behind her, stepping on the red squares of the floor tiles and skipping the white ones.

One kid was a toddler-sized girl wearing a sparkly tiara and purple tutu. The other was a boy about eight dressed in a Little League baseball uniform. Based on the dirt stains on his knees and cleats, he had finished playing a ball game.

Eva grabbed two loaves of Sara Lee's wheat bread and

got a better look at the woman close to her.

She gaped. "Frankie?"

The reddish-blonde woman looked in her direction. "Eva?"

Both women grinned and laughed at their encounter.

Francine Nichols and Eva were close friends at Garden Ridge High School. Being four-foot-eleven, Francine was called 'shrimp' or 'shorty' a lot by her school peers, teased for her small stature. Together the girls endured the hardship of adolescence and the brunt of bullying for always getting good grades.

"Hey, it's been a long time," Francine said. "So, how are you?"

"I'm hanging in there. My husband . . . he had a car accident a couple of months ago."

Francine's smile faded, tilting her head. "Oh, Eva. I'm so sorry. How bad was it?"

"Well, he lost his memory," Eva said. "I showed him old photos and talked with him, but nothing works. He's been like a seesaw, and he's ashamed to be seen in public. It's so overwhelming and frustrating. Each day I feel like I'm losing him more, like a dark cloud is hovering over me. I'm drained and need some relief."

Francine studied her countenance, concerned. "You look tired. Maybe you should hire a caregiver."

"I already have," Eva said, "but daytime care is all I can afford. It's expensive paying a live-in caregiver these days. And besides, where would he stay if he lived with us? We only have three bedrooms, and my husband needs a bed to himself as a quadriplegic. As of now, he stays in the master room, and I sleep in the guestroom. There's been a strain in our marriage for several reasons."

"Wow. I'm sorry to hear that." Francine took a loaf of Wonder bread and placed it on top of a carton of eggs in her cart. She glimpsed back at her children and snapped her fingers, noticing them getting too far away from her. "Piper! David! Get back here. Now!"

"Yes, Mom!" David chirped. He and his little sister raced toward Francine's grocery cart.

"And no running!" Francine ordered, putting a hand on her hip. "Someone mopped the floor, and I don't want y'all to slip and fall."

David and Piper slowed to a steady walking pace the rest of the way back.

"Kids, they're a mess sometimes," Francine said.

"Tell me about it." Eva chuckled and glanced at her school friend's kids. "So, how old are they?"

"Four and nine. Their dad's name is Jake. He was a charmer, but also a jerk. After he lost his job, he drank late in the bar. We had plans to marry, but they went out of the window. We couldn't make it work." Francine cleared her throat and shoved her curly hair away from her face.

Eva frowned. "I'm sorry, Frankie, but maybe you'll

find the right man someday."

"Are you kidding me?" Francine widened her brown eyes. "I'm done with men. I'm fine living with my kids alone. You really have to know who and what you're standing at the altar with, and it's better to be safe than sorry later." A smile danced on her lips. "Who's the kid in your cart?"

"My son Andrew," Eva said. "He'll be two next April."

Francine chuckled. "He's a cutie-pie. I imagine he looks like his daddy."

"Yup," Eva replied, "just with more hair. Though, I do plan to have Andy's first haircut soon."

The two young women laughed again.

"I married Andre Lucas," Eva confessed shyly.

Francine pinned Eva with her eyes, her mouth hung open. "Andre Lucas? You mean scrawny, little Andre?" She chuckled, getting a kick out of the big news.

Eva giggled, amused by her friend's reaction. "He's not so *scrawny* anymore, Frankie. I have a picture of him." She opened her clutch purse, took out a photo from her wallet, and handed it to Francine.

"Wait, that's Andre? He's changed a lot. He looks so . . . *dreamy*." Francine wore a teasing smile. "I can see why you fell for him, but he always did have a crush on you too." She gave Eva her picture back. "And you . . . you've changed too. You look fabulous. Slender with a good height and everything."

"You're beautiful too, Frankie," Eva said.

"Me?" Francine curled her upper lip. "I look like I belong in the *Wizard of Oz*. All I need is clown makeup, a colorful puffy dress, and dwarf shoes, and I'm an official resident of Munchkin Land."

"Don't start talking about your height again," Eva said wearily. "You remember what I told you when we were in high school."

"Yeah," Francine said flatly, "small people can do big things."

"Well, they can," Eva said and giggled.

Francine's face lit up. "You know, our second class reunion is next week. Why don't you come?"

Eva wrinkled her nose, lifting a shoulder. "Hmm . . . I don't know."

"Come on, please, Eva. It'll be fun. We can pick up on old times. I missed you. I felt so out of place at the first one. The popular classmates bunched in their circles the same old way, and I was all alone."

"What about Alan Murphy? He always ate lunch at our table, remember?"

"Eva, Alan died two years ago before the first reunion," Francine replied.

Eva's heart stopped. "He did?"

"Mm-hmm," Francine said, nodding, "Nadine's the head sponsor of our class reunions. She said his wife told her he committed suicide. 'Everything seemed perfect,' his wife said, but then one afternoon, she found him dead in their bedroom. He shot himself."

Eva gasped and touched a hand over her heart. "Oh, no . . ." Alan was one of the funniest, brightest kids in school, but now he was buried six-feet under before his fortieth birthday. She had never forgotten the time two of the football players set a prank on him. They locked Alan in his locker when he had to use the restroom. He nearly wet himself after she solved his combination and helped him out. His frustration hurt her gut, kicking his locker before he walked to his class.

Because of her husband's depression and emotional problems, hearing about Alan's death made her fearful. Perhaps she should take Dr. Brown's offer and have him prescribe Andre an antidepressant. Maybe it'll recover his mood, but compromise with Andre was an impossible mission. Regardless, she hoped and prayed her husband never stoops as low as taking his own life.

"So, will you come?" Francine urged, snatching Eva out of her train of thought.

"Uh . . . I'll think about it," Eva said.

Francine smiled. "Thanks, Eva. You're the best friend ever."

Eva gave a crooked smile and rubbed her neck. She had seen none of her other classmates in many years and reuniting with them made her edgy. Her former crush, Caleb Williams, had moved away to New York with his dad after high school graduation. So, it was the girls who bullied her that worried Eva the most. On the other hand, she needed a breather from running like the energizer bunny. On the go for others all the time, she rarely had leisure time for herself.

Eva and Francine exchanged cell phone numbers.

"I'll catch you later, Eva," Francine said.

Eva waved timidly and watched her friend leave the aisle with her kids. "Uh, all right, sure."

"Hey, Mom. Can I have Cocoa Pebbles?" David asked, tagging alongside his mother with the cereal box in his hands.

"No, now put the box back," Francine said, pushing her cart away.

"But why?" David whined.

"Because I said so, and don't question me when I tell you something...." Francine turned off the aisle and the light chatter with her son faded in the store's commotion of country music from the ceiling speakers and other shoppers.

Eva laughed and pictured her and Andrew years later when her son's older. She looked at him in her shopping cart and poked his tummy, making him giggle. "You won't be bugging Mommy to buy you cereal, will you?"

"Nana . . . nana." Andrew moved his face close to his mother's and placed his hands on her cheeks, squishing them together.

Eva chuckled and kissed Andrew's nose. "Okay, okay. We'll get some bananas."

Andrew clapped and grinned. Eight little white teeth were in his mouth like shiny pearls in a clamshell, four at the top and four at the bottom. More would pop up soon, and Eva could already hear her son's hollering over sore pain and itchy gums. She rolled her pushcart from the bread aisle. After bagging a bundle of bananas, she went to the baby aisle and got a pack of Huggies for toddlers. She couldn't wait until Andrew was potty-trained to use the toilet himself.

It would save her the trouble of buying pull-ups every month. A single pack costs as much as her cell phone bill, and she could use the extra dollars to keep up with her payments. Eva checked out and loaded the groceries in the trunk of her car.

She buckled Andrew in his car seat, and studied the child for a moment, playing with Mookie in his lap. She marveled how two people from states over two thousand miles apart could meet, become friends, fall in love, and together create the beautiful life before her.

"Can Mommy have a lovie hug?"

"Lovie," Andrew said, stretching out his little arms.

Her eyes were glossy, encircling her arms around her son. "I love you so much, Andy, and no matter what, your daddy loves you too. He . . . he's just frustrated right now. But someday . . . someday he'll hug you, kiss you, and love you the way he used to. I promise." Eva swiped her hands over her damp cheeks, closed the back door, and sat in the driver's seat.

• CHAPTER 23 •

Eva

Skye helped bring the bags of groceries into the house and fill the kitchen cabinets and refrigerator. Visiting on the weekends, like Mrs. Flowers, the young man had become like a part of the Lucas family. Eva placed a can of Campbell's tomato soup in the cabinet above the stove hood and glanced at her son.

Andrew waddled over to Skye, hugging his pant leg like he was his big brother. It was the most adorable thing Eva had seen in a long time.

"Hey, Andy." Skye glanced down and smiled at her son.

Eva made a funny look with a hand on her hip. "Well, that was a surprise."

"Lovie . . . lovie." Andrew looked up at Skye and reached out his arms.

Skye looked at Eva like he wasn't sure what to do about the kid.

"He wants you to hug him," Eva hinted.

"Oh, okay." Skye smiled and lifted Andrew, embracing him. "Hi, Andy. Boy, he's heavy."

Eva grinned and watched the scene. She imagined Andre holding their son, standing tall, healthy, and in his right mind. It was a heartwarming moment—a dream which she wished would come true. An hour later, Skye left, and the rest of the day was like a prison sentence of seclusion. Once Andre performed his daily exercises and routines, there wasn't much he could do, but sit and stare at images moving across a television screen.

As time passed, Eva witnessed the nerve and willpower slowly dying out of him. It was in his droopy face, his shorter responses, and his dull, sad eyes. It was in his barely touched three courses of meals, and his distressful groans she overheard at night. Eva didn't know what took so long for Andre to walk again, or at least feed himself, but she strove to stay patient with him anyway.

Sunday before dawn, Eva came out of the guestroom in her robe and slippers and snuck in the kitchen for a late snack. She flicked on a lamp on a side table and curled up on the living room sofa with a small bucket of Edy's mint chocolate chip ice cream, her favorite flavor. She grabbed the family album on the center table and opened it in her lap, flipping through pictures of old memories. A tragedy had avalanched their marriage, burying the bricks that built the foundation of their relationship.

Now it was as if the pivotal chapters of their friendship never existed. They were strangers who shared a framed certificate nailed on the wall, and in heart-wrenching silenced lived in the same house. It was hard to laugh and connect like they used to—and getting harder to love one another. Whenever Eva saw Andre's stiff, motionless body in his wheelchair, the same old question echoed in her mind: *Why did this happen?*

She ate a scoop of ice cream and turned a page. Eva smiled faintly at a snapshot from their honeymoon. In the photo, they were sporting their tinted aviators in a side hug, standing on the peak of Copper Canyon on a sizzling August afternoon.

Eva remembered the sun's heat beating their backs as they climbed up the rocky ravine, following a Mexican tourist guide from a nearby village to the top. She flipped to a picture of Andre, laughing and playing airplane with Andrew when their son was two months old.

With a Christian, witty, loving man who would risk his life for her if he needed to, she had no reason to overthink anything. The second she said, "I do" to him, Eva felt a sense of relief. She turned to other photos of

Andre and her outside in their front yard on a winter day, playing in the snow. She looked down at a diagonal photo of them sharing a kiss on the bottom of one page.

From their different coats, hats, and gloves it was a picture of another winter season. Oddly enough, she didn't recall this one or who had taken it. Maybe it was Grandpa. Behind them was a red barn with a frosty roof hanging with icicles and a snowman they had built together.

Pain gripped Eva's chest, touching the picture. They hadn't kissed or been affectionate in months, but how could they? Andre had been so distrustful of her, and she had felt so awkward around him. The mere thought of touching intimately was like trespassing property.

Her throat thickened with sobs as she fought back tears. Was she falling out of love with Andre? Did she still love him? Why hadn't she told him while he was awake? Ever since dealing with his mood swings and coldness, she didn't know what or how she felt about him anymore.

Eva closed the photo book and placed it back on the table. She ate another spoonful of ice cream, musing over her present life. As her husband was a different man, she didn't feel like the same woman. No longer did her husband surprise her with pretty flowers with message cards, or tell her he loved her. No longer did he ask how she was feeling or about her workday. No longer did he take her out to dinner, carry her in his arms, or playfully chase her around the house. There wasn't a sign Andre was still in love with her. To him, she was nothing more than a kindhearted caregiver who was thoughtful enough not to leave him alone in a nursing home.

A tear coursed down Eva's chin, shuddering her out of a trance. She drew a gasping breath and dried her cheek, looking at the dinging grandmother clock beside the fireplace. Two hours passed, and she thought to rotate Andre again. Eva looked in her bucket of ice cream. She sat and moped for so long it had melted into a milkshake. She rose from the couch and put it back in the freezer in the kitchen.

Eva tiptoed upstairs to the master room where her husband slept and approached the bed. She always hated to wake him, but at least he was tolerant enough to accept the routine.

"Andre," she whispered, rubbing his shoulder. "Honey, it's time to wake up again. Last time."

He moaned in his sleep.

Eva pulled the blanket off Andre and positioned his right arm dangling off the bed. She turned his body onto his right side and tucked a pillow behind his back. In addition to the pillow under his head, a third pillow she placed between his legs with his top knee flexed. Lastly, she recovered him with the cool sheet and comforter.

"There . . . sleep tight, okay?" Eva said.

"Mm-hmmm," Andre replied drowsily.

She watched his body rise and fall as he drifted back out. Eva walked toward the door, but then stopped and returned to Andre's bedside. She stroked his smooth, freshly trimmed haircut and kissed his forehead.

"I love you," Eva said, longing for Andre's exchanged reply. But as usual, he said nothing again.

She wore a wistful smile and tiptoed out of the master bedroom, going back to bed alone.

• CHAPTER 24 •

Eva

Monday, Nov. 20th

"Mrs. Lucas, I'm afraid I can't work today," Skye said through her receiving end. Eva grimaced and adjusted the home phone in the lock of her shoulder. "What? Why not?" She peeled a banana and cut slices in Andrew's blue plastic bowl of oatmeal, hoping Skye wasn't quitting his job. "Is it money? I can pay you more."

Skye sighed over the phone line. "No, Mrs. Lucas. My grandma passed away in her sleep. Her burial service is today, and she wrote in her will to be put to rest in her hometown in Beaufort, South Carolina."

"Oh, I'm sorry, Skye. I send my prayers to you and your family," Eva said.

"Thank you. I'm sorry I didn't tell you sooner," Skye replied. "What will you do now?"

Eva puffed her cheeks and exhaled. "I guess I'll call my

director and ask to have today off. I mean, what else can I do? I can't leave Andre here alone."

"I feel terrible about this, Mrs. Lucas," Skye said.

"Well, don't, okay? It's not your fault your grandma died."

"I know," Skye said with a sigh, "but you do a lot during the week at your job. I know how much you need help. Is there anything I can do to make up for my absence?"

Eva recalled her class reunion and looked at the flyer she got in the mail on the kitchen counter, drumming her fingernails:

Garden Ridge High School

Welcome Back Class of 2002!

Join Us for Our 2nd year reunion.

When: Saturday, November 25th at 7:00 p.m.

Where: Garden Ridge High in the school cafeteria

Check on your old friends, classmates, and teachers.

Sing, dance, and have a blast from the past!

Refreshments will be served. Admission is free.

We can't wait to see you there!

The social gathering was in five more days, and she figured taking time out from her stressful, everyday life would do her body good. She inched up a smile. "Actually, there is. I reunited with an old classmate in the grocery store, and she wants me to attend our second class reunion. I thought it could be fun, a way to take my mind off my troubles at home."

"Good idea. When is your class reunion?"

"It's November twenty-fifth at seven o'clock, which is this Saturday coming. It would be great if you could sit in and watch Andre during this night for free," Eva said.

"Sure," Skye replied, "I'll come on the eighteenth to make up for today."

"Great! I'll have Mrs. Flowers come babysit Andy Saturday, so you don't have to worry about him too. I really appreciate this, Skye. Taking care of Andre has been difficult at times. You don't know how much I need this." Eva ran a hand through her hair.

"You're welcome," Skye said.

Eva poured cold milk from a jug in Andrew's bowl of oatmeal and stirred it with one of his easy-grip spoons. She walked to her son's highchair. "Okay. Goodbye, Skye, and take care."

"You too," Skye said.

Eva pressed the end-call button and looked at her son. "Well, Andy, it looks like we're staying home today."

"Oo-me! Oo-me!" Andrew babbled, drumming his small hands on his tray. She smiled and put the bowl of oatmeal in front of her demanding little man.

Eva caught another thought. "Mrs. Flowers will need

to be here. I can't be two places at once. But first, I need to call Mrs. Higgins and ask to call out." She dialed the number of the daycare and spoke to her director who allowed her the day off.

Afterward, she phoned Mrs. Flowers. As always, the elderly widow came over to keep a close eye on her son while Eva tended to her husband's needs. She had never spent an entire day with Andre, but for the sake of their marriage, maybe it would benefit them. She blew out a weary breath and glanced at Andre's schedule hanging on the refrigerator by a football magnet.

It was time to wake him up again.

Eva undressed Andre, strapped him in a full-body mesh sling, and attached the shoulder straps to the cradle of a patient lift machine. She pressed her foot on the push pad and carefully transported him into a soothing, warm bath. Eva sat on the sill of the white tub and lathered up a washcloth with a bar of unscented soap. "Can you close your eyes, please?" she said politely. "I don't wanna get soap in them."

Andre narrowed his brows and eyed her like a scared kitten. Today was the first time she was washing him, as Skye had always been the one to do this for him.

"It's all right. I won't hurt you." Eva reassured him with a smile, putting his sensitive mind at ease.

Andre gulped and closed his eyes.

"This will take a second." Eva gently wiped the cloth over his forehead, cheeks, and neck. She rinsed out the rag in a separate plastic basin of clear water and swiped the soapy suds off his face. "You can open your eyes now."

Her husband fluttered his eyelids. He tilted his head and studied her in awe, squinting from a beam of golden daylight piercing through the wood blinds of the window behind her.

Eva wondered what he was pondering about at that instant, but she was too distracted herself to ask. She gazed at him with a bashful smile, admiring his sculpted, well-built physique. Maybe he couldn't walk, but after combining his healthy diet with Skye's recent trips with him to the local city gym, he had gotten back into shape. Despite his ailments, outbursts, and muddled brain, he still took her breath away.

With a slight shake of her head, she got a hold of herself and looked at his angular face, remembering the first thing she loved about him. His sepia-colored irises were fierce and warm like red, desert sunsets, eclipses at the horizon of rolling sand hills. Eva sniffled and blinked repetitively, holding back her tears. Although disturbed and embarrassed by how she was feeling, she ached for her husband's thoughtful attention, combating the pain of unrequited love.

He drew a breath and relaxed his broad shoulders. "Hospital . . . put . . . put back . . ."

"What?" Eva frowned.

Andre sighed wearily, and she felt his hurt and dread of struggling to speak. Suffering from Broca's aphasia, he couldn't retrieve certain small words sometimes. He swallowed hard and attempted to talk again. "No more . . . no more b-b-burden. Must . . . d-d-divorce." He hung his head sadly.

Eva's heart ripped in half. She clamped her lips and angled her head. "Andre, look at me."

Her husband stared down at the sudsy water covering his lower body.

Eva lifted his chin and looked into his eyes. "Andre, you're not a burden, and we're not getting a divorce. I married you for keeps, and I meant it. We've had a rough time these past months, but we're gonna get through this together." She stared teary-eyed at her husband as he snatched his chin from her hand and looked away.

She needed to be careful about what she said around Andre and over the phone. Maybe he couldn't move his body, but he could hear and was aware it tired her to take care of him and almost everything herself. Originally, she considered admitting Andre into a nursing facility, but her compassion willed her to keep him with his family at home. Besides, Andrew needed his father whether or not he recovered his memory. Eva raised his left arm out of the tub and cleaned under and over it and across his bare chest.

When she finished giving his bath, she moved him with the patient lift to his shower chair. From head to toe, she rubbed and dabbed his body with a soft, clean towel. Andre took her gentle, loving care with ease and nearly fell asleep like a baby, watching her dry him off in silence.

"What do you want to wear? Your burgundy or navy sweater?" Eva asked, pulling a new pair if boxer briefs over his waist.

Andre blinked his drowsy eyes and hesitated to answer. "Uh . . . red one."

"Okay, burgundy it is." Eva smiled and dressed him in a white T-shirt, his V-neck burgundy sweater, and a pair of khaki pants.

"Good morning, Andre," Mrs. Flowers said, observing him buzz past her in his electric wheelchair and go into the kitchen.

Eva plopped beside the old woman on the chocolate-brown sofa and threaded a hand through her long, wavy, black hair.

"How'd the bath time go?" Mrs. Flowers asked.

Eva's eyes welled up, watching Andrew put a jumbo puzzle of colorful shapes together on the carpet floor. "It was a little tense, but okay, I guess."

Mrs. Flowers leaned forward and scrutinized Eva's hopeless expression. "You look worn down and troubled. Has Andre told you something?"

"Yeah—" Eva closed her eyes and whimpered— "he thinks he's a burden to me. He wants a divorce and for me to put him back in the hospital. I-I can't believe this."

"Well," Mrs. Flowers said, "he knows you've taken on a lot of responsibilities of him and Andrew."

"I know, but *divorce*?" Eva replied. "How could he ever suggest such a horrible thing?"

Mrs. Flowers shrugged. "Andre has his reasons. He's overwhelmed and confused. Remember, he still doesn't recall ever marrying you. It doesn't matter how kind you try to be to him; nothing will change that."

Eva threw Mrs. Flowers a furious look. "But does it mean we should get a divorce?"

"Of course not, honey," Mrs. Flowers said, "but you must understand where he's coming from . . . him seeing you take care of his needs above your own each night must bother him, especially since he knows you also have a child to take care of. Maybe he feels like he's taking time away from you spending it with Andrew."

"That's ludicrous," Eva said, crossing her arms, "and

not a good reason to split a marriage, even if I believed in divorce."

"Not to him," Mrs. Flowers said. "Personally, placing Andre in a nursing facility wouldn't mean you're a bad person, Eva. It would mean you're doing what he feels would best meet his and your needs. Because you've told him a lot about his former life, he probably feels terrible seeing you and Andrew suffer the losses of what he used to provide." She patted Eva's knee. "Perhaps you should let Andre be with people he remembers from rehab who understand him better."

A lump formed in Eva's throat. "No, I can't let him go. It's taking a while, but Andre *will* gain his strength and walk, and he *will* get his memory back."

"God willing," Mrs. Flowers muttered.

Eva knew God was sovereign, but she didn't want to hear the possibility of uncertainty. She rose and strutted into the kitchen. "What do you want for breakfast, Andre?" She turned around and waited for his response.

Her husband tilted his head with a long face, but said nothing.

Eva nibbled her lip and thought. Before Andre's car accident, he ate Cheerios with sliced strawberries every morning, and sometimes for an afternoon snack.

She took a deep breath and clasped her hands. "Okay, I'll give you cereal." She grabbed a bowl from the dish rack and the cardboard box on top of the refrigerator.

Eva poured some cereal into the bowl, the O-shaped oats clinking against the glass surface. She added milk and slices of strawberries in the cereal and brought the bowl with a silver spoon in it to the table.

"Will you say grace?" Eva said, strapping an adult bib on him.

Andre frowned. "Say grace?"

"Never mind. Just eat." Eva spooned Andre a scoop of cold cereal.

Milk dribbled down his chin. He frowned and chewed a few times, and with his eyes pinned into hers, let the food ooze out of his mouth. Mushy cereal fell onto the bib around his neck, losing a taste for it.

Flames of anger shot through Eva, gritting her teeth. She banged her fist on the kitchen table, making the salt and pepper shakers rattle and dance. "Now why'd you do that? If you didn't want cereal, all you had to do was say so! I pay your bills and work my tail off and this is —" She dropped the spoon in the glass bowl and smacked a hand over her mouth, regaining her bearings.

Eva closed her eyes and shook her head. "I'm sorry, Andre. I didn't mean that . . ." She sniffled and stood in front of Andre and held the leather armrests of his wheelchair, urging his response. "Andre, honey, are you hungry? Can you hear me?"

Her husband wore a straight face and avoided her gaze, dissociated in a stillness she didn't understand.

She removed the bib, tossed the yucky mouthful in the flip trashcan, and washed off the bib in the kitchen sink. "I'm gonna ask you one more time, Andre. *What do you want for breakfast?"*

Eva glanced over her shoulder at him, but he stared like a lifeless mannequin. She twisted off the faucet and turned around, gripping the marble counter behind her. Eva sobbed, pleading with him. "Andre, baby, please. Please, don't do this. If you're depressed, tell me. Talk! Don't shut me out!"

Stressed and frustrated, she buried her face in her hands and wept bitterly, not knowing what else to say. Despair dragged her down, and her high hopes vanished in thin air like rising vapor. The more Andre detached himself, the more she was getting convinced her husband would never get better.

If he couldn't accept and love himself for the man he'd become, how will he love her and their son again? With a negative mindset, he would remain stagnant in his misfortune, never sprouting to a renewal of mental and emotional recovery. They would forever remain enemies because of a stormy night that stole their happiness. If she could go back to their seventh anniversary, she would change their whole evening to a simple candlelit dinner at home.

But that wasn't possible.

Life and time wouldn't allow it, and there wasn't a doubt Andre's brain injury damaged more than his mind. It had also wounded his heart and spirit. Eva balled her fists and marched out of the kitchen like a soldier on a mission toward the living room, going to their master bedroom to pray for the man.

As she started upstairs, the doorbell dinged. She paused and shared a fishy look with Mrs. Flowers, both wondering who had come to the house.

Eva wiped her wet eyes and swung open the door, her heart skipping a beat.

Her mom had arrived.

• CHAPTER 25 •

Eva

Same Morning

"What are you doing here?" Eva gaped at her mother in the front doorway. She blinked in disbelief at the slim, fifty-one-year-old woman and thought she would faint from her unexpected visit. With her flawless, caramel brown skin and youthful face, Melanie Conway could pass for a woman twenty years younger, if it weren't for her gray pixie cut.

Her tan leather jacket and jean pencil skirt accentuated her curvy figure. She held a duffel bag in one hand and a vintage suitcase embellished with travel stickers of U.S states and foreign countries in the other.

"I'm homeless and lost my apartment, so I came here," Eva's mom said. "I was wondering if I can stay with you until I get back on my feet. I got stuck in bad traffic before I reached Seattle-Tacoma's airport. My flight was delayed because of a severe thunderstorm, so I stayed overnight and flew in this morning. I caught a ride from the airport and got dropped off here." Her mother darted her eyes, looking over her ruby, oval-framed glasses. "Are you gonna stand there like a popsicle or let me in?"

Eva clamped her lips with a hand on her hip. How could she reject her mom after the sacrifices she made for her? Although they had their squabbles, she was the backbone that inspired Eva to grow up into the strong-willed, assertive woman she had become. She sighed, dropping her shoulders. "All right, you can come in."

"Thank you," her mother said. "Can I get help with my bags?"

Eva took the duffel bag and stood back as her mom entered with her suitcase. She glanced heavenward as she shut the door. *God, please let things work for my good.* Ever since last year's Thanksgiving, she sensed her mother's jealousy over her close friendship with Mrs. Flowers. Who would've thought enjoying an old widow's sweet potato pie better than your mother's was a big deal?

Her mom wiped her leather, knee-length boots on the welcome mat and sized up the elderly woman on the sofa. Her voice dropped a notch, looking over her glasses. "Oh . . . hi, Mrs. Flowers."

"Hello, Melanie," Mrs. Flowers said.

Eva shifted a nervous glance from her mom to Mrs. Flowers and sensed tension lingering between them.

Her mother turned her attention to Andrew sitting in his playpen. She gasped. "Eva, honey, why is Andy surrounded by so many toys? What are you trying to do? Bury him alive?" She rushed over, placed down her suitcase, and picked up her grandson.

"No, Mom, Andy just gets—"

"There, there, munchkin. Are you okay?" her mother said, baby-talking him. She kissed Andrew's cheek.

Eva inched forward, cautious. "He gets bored and—"

"Oh, boy," her mother interrupted with a dramatic sigh, rubbing Andrew's back. "Where can I put my things?"

Eva gulped and her mind went blank, staring at her mother.

She gathered her thoughts to the current flow of their conversation. "Uhh . . . in the guestroom with me. Andre's staying in the master bedroom by himself."

Her mom's dark brown eyes went round, jerking back her head. "How come? Did y'all have a fight?" She placed her grandson back in his playpen.

"It's a long story. I'll explain it in the guestroom." Eva toted the duffel bag and led her mother to the guestroom. A twin-sized bed draped with a blue-rose comforter was on one side of the room, and beside the bed was a comfy blue chair. A pinewood dresser and nightstand set completed the guest bedroom.

Her mom placed her suitcase on the twin-sized bed.

She twisted her face and scanned the small, simply-furnished room as if she were looking for something. "Only one bed? Where will you sleep?"

Eva shrugged and put the bag on the floor. "No biggie. I'll sleep in the blue chair or on the couch. So, how long do you plan to stay?"

Her mom popped the silver latches of her suitcase and opened it. "I'm not sure, but I've got the time to spare." She eyed Eva with suspicion. "You aren't rushing to get rid of me, are you?"

A muscle twitched in Eva's jaw, rubbing her arms. She almost answered, "Yes," but bit her tongue to avoid a heated argument. "Uh, no . . . stay as long as you need. You can put your clothes in the middle drawers of the dresser."

"Thanks. Where's Andre?" Her mother took a stack of folded clothes out of her suitcase and placed them on the bed.

"He's in the kitchen. He's . . . depressed," Eva said. She informed her mom about Andre's car accident, his brain injury, his paralysis, and the emotional toll everything has been having on him.

Her mother frowned. "Oh, Eva. I'm sorry this happened. Why didn't you call me?"

Eva shrugged with downcast eyes, but she knew exactly why she didn't call her mother about her husband's incident. If she had, her mom surely would've boarded a plane and flown in the next day. Then she would've interfered in how *she* thinks her daughter should handle her husband's condition, instead of letting Eva figure it out for herself.

Her mom held her at arm's length. "Eva, sweetheart, you can talk to me about anything."

Anything? Eva chewed on her bottom lip, shifty-eyed. After being interrupted and ignored many times during arguments, Eva had her doubts, but she didn't bother retorting to her mother's kind remark.

"I don't want you to feel you can't express yourself." Her mom looked sideways and dropped her arms to her sides with a sigh. "If I had known about Andre, I wouldn't have bothered to come here. You know what . . . I'll check in a hotel." She loaded her stack of clothes back in her suitcase.

Eva felt the urge to speak up. "No, Mom! It's okay . . . you can stay. We can make adjustments."

Her mother faced her again, stunned. "Are you sure?"

"Yes," Eva said, "as long as you promise to respect my wishes."

"Which are?" Her mom arched her brow.

Eva sighed. "I want you to promise you'll let me make my own decisions without interfering in my personal affairs. And you'll keep your opinions about whatever I do to yourself unless I ask for your advice."

"Oh, all right . . . I promise," her mother said hesitantly.

"And that you'll respect my marriage and home," Eva added, cringing.

Her mom pursed her lips, wrapping her arms around herself like a pouting toddler. "Fine . . . it's your house."

Eva brightened with a smile. "Good. I'm going back to the kitchen. Would you like a cup of coffee?"

"Sure," her mother said, "I'll be out after I finish unpacking."

Eva stepped out of the guestroom.

"How's your mom?" Mrs. Flowers asked.

Eva closed the side door and sighed. "She's okay."

Mrs. Flowers' expression softened. "I hope she doesn't think I'm trying to take her place. I mean no harm to you and your mother's relationship, Eva."

"I know, Mrs. Flowers. You don't have to tell me that," Eva said.

Mrs. Flowers stood from the couch. "Well, maybe you know, but your mom's face was so green she could've turned into the Incredible Hulk."

"She'll get over it," Eva said, rolling her eyes. "I'll talk to her."

"Thanks," Mrs. Flowers said, chuckling, "and when you do, let her know a friend of mine would like her to paint a special portrait for her son's birthday. He's visiting home from the army for Thanksgiving. I don't know your mom's phone number, so I could never get a hold of her."

Eva grinned. "How nice! I'll ask her later." She let out a slow breath. "Well, let me talk with Andre. Hopefully, I'll get through to him." She returned to the kitchen and sat in front of her husband again. "Honey, are you hungry?"

"Yes," Andre said finally.

Relief spread over Eva's face, sighing. "Finally, we're getting somewhere." She chuckled and laced her hands on the table, looking at him. "Now, what do you want?"

"I want . . ." Andre lowered his eyes and thought a moment. "Eggs . . . cheese . . . uh, scrambled."

A corner of Eva's mouth lifted. Although Andre suffered from a speech impediment, sometimes she found his thinking facial expressions, stutters, and hesitations cute and likable.

"Okay, coming right up." She stood and whipped up a quick plate of scrambled eggs with cheese and switched on the coffee maker on the counter. Eva placed the plate of Andre's food on the table and strapped a new clean bib around his neck.

Andre blinked and watched her cut the eggs with a fork for him. "Sorry."

Eva stopped and studied him with his head hung in shame. She didn't know if he was saying it to her or to himself, but she accepted his apology anyway. She found a smile. "It's all right. Now, eat up." She stuck a morsel of eggs on the fork and attempted to feed him, but Andre continued talking.

Her husband's eyes danced with wonder, looking deeply in hers. "I wish . . . remember you a-a-and Andy . . . just don't."

"Shh, it's okay, Andre. Come on, eat," Eva said softly.

Andre took in the mouthful, chewed, and swallowed, but Eva couldn't get what he said to leave her mind. Despite his limitations, she realized he was curious about everything she and their son were to him, even though he didn't recall their past life. And for the first time, she believed maybe Mrs. Flowers was right.

The man she married was trapped inside.

The coffee maker finished brewing, and Eva filled two glass mugs, one for her and the other for her mom. She stirred in hazelnut creamer in each mug and joined her mother at the table. While they drank, they caught up on lost time and talked about what had been happening in their lives the past months.

After Eva recapped Andre's therapy in the hospital, her mother shared devastating news. One night someone burglarized her private studio and stole almost all her art equipment. Since then, she hasn't sold a single painting in weeks.

"I feel like a total failure," her mom said. "Nothing's been going right lately. Sometimes I think I should quit painting and do something else." She sipped from her mug.

Eva grimaced and placed her mug down. "Oh, no, Mom, you can't do that. You shouldn't give up on your painting because you suffered a big loss, or because everyone doesn't value your talent. And you're not a failure either."

"Thanks, hon, I needed that." Her mom sipped her mug again.

Eva traced the brim of her mug with her forefinger. "I hope you don't mind, but Mrs. Flowers said a friend of hers wants you to paint a portrait for her son's birthday. She said her friend told her he's coming home from the army to spend Thanksgiving with his family."

"Is that so?" Her mother raised her eyebrows.

Eva nodded. "Yeah. I mean, I know you do landscape paintings, but you've done a few good portraits of people before when I was a kid. It could be interesting."

Her mother curled her upper lip. "Humph, I don't think so."

"It's not because of Mrs. Flowers, is it?" Eva asked.

"Of course not," her mom said. "I just don't like painting people. It's too time-consuming. Too complex."

Eva snickered after sipping from her mug. "Complex? I always thought landscapes were harder. You have to add details to everything, including blades of grass."

"Well, with me, *portraits* are more difficult," her mom countered. "If you don't control my life, I won't control yours, deal?" She pursed her lips and rose from the table, taking her mug to the sink.

Eva zipped her lips and felt bad vibes, getting a cue there was no talking her mother into doing a nice favor for Mrs. Flowers' friend. "Fine, I'm sorry."

"Who takes care of Andre while you're at work?" Her mom's facial features slacked. "I know you don't leave him by himself, do you?"

"No, Skye Garrison watches him," Eva answered. "He's a nice, young man who also endured a brain injury when he was in his teens. Because he had to attend his grandma's burial in South Carolina, I had to stay home with Andre today. But he'll be here the rest of the week, including Saturday night. I'm going to my class reunion."

"Really?" Her mom sounded surprised. "Are you sure you should go? Won't Caleb Williams be there? You were kind of sweet on him."

Eva clamped her lips and leaned back. "Mom, Caleb moved away to New York with his dad after graduation. Besides, he's probably already married off to some model or movie star and I'm not attending for him anyway."

She beamed. "Last week, I came across Francine Nichols in the grocery store. You remember Frankie, don't you?"

"Uh-huh, tiny girl with reddish-blond curls, freckles and a bubbly personality," her mother said, examining the kitchen over. "Y'all had sleepovers every Saturday and always worked together for school projects. She was the smallest ninth grader I have ever seen. You almost needed a magnifying glass to see her."

Eva frowned and giggled. "Oh, Mom, she wasn't *that* little."

Her mom chuckled. "She was close. So, what inspired you to attend this year?" She grabbed the dishcloth and wiped a stain off the refrigerator handle.

"Frankie," Eva said, "she wants me to attend to keep her company during the occasion and for us to take a trip down memory lane. She might bring a yearbook. I never got one for many reasons. I wasn't the prettiest sight in twelfth grade and absolutely hated my picture."

Her mother sucked her teeth. "Please, Eva. You were a pretty girl back then."

That's not what Caleb Williams thought, Mom. Eva shook her head and finished her coffee. Some people changed over time, and she was one of them. But what about her other classmates? And most of all, who was still alive?

Hearing about Alan Murphy's suicide from her friend Francine, she still couldn't believe it was true. Aside from her class reunion, she also pondered whether she and her mother would get along the next couple of weeks. Eva trusted her mom would keep her promise, but grasping her envy toward Mrs. Flowers, she questioned if letting her stay was a big mistake.

• CHAPTER 26 •

Eva

Tuesday Afternoon

Eva walked and pushed Andrew in his stroller down the sidewalk of downtown after getting off from work. She paused at a big, square window of Macy's store and stuck her sunglasses in her hair, gawking at the most beautiful dress she's ever seen on a manikin doll. It was a long time since she's gotten a new outfit. With her class reunion around the corner, she wanted to look her best in the presence of everyone. She pulled back the swing door and entered with the stroller to check it out.

As soon as she surveyed the display of colorful clothing, hats, perfumes, and shoes, she felt herself coming alive as the woman she once was again. Easy-listening music played and welcomed her from the corner speakers of the store.

A short sales associate woman with cropped, platinum blonde hair smiled, arranging clothes on a metal rack. "Hello, ma'am. Welcome to Macy's."

"Thank you," Eva said, grinning. She walked around to the front window in which she looked at the orange, maple leaf-print dress. Eva glanced from the associate to the dangling price tag on the dress of the manikin doll.

Her eyes widened. *Two hundred and nineteen dollars?* It was steep for clothes on a dummy. She sighed dejectedly and released the tag from her hand. Having only a couple of bucks left in her purse, there was no way she could afford anything in the store. Besides, she needed to pick up a few more groceries and put gas in her car for her next work week. Of course, she can always charge it, right?

Eva opened her tote purse and slipped her credit card out of her wallet. She looked up and around at the name-brand clothing aisles again. Her mind spun with intriguing possibilities. Moisture blurred her vision as she pressed her card to her cheek, trying to decide what to do. *Why did I come in here? I'm so naïve.* Eva wiped her tearful eye and released a long, wistful exhale. She felt sick to her stomach. Facing difficult times, she thought like her mom—but under these conditions her mother was right.

Andrew prattled loudly and giggled, snatching her out of her wrestling thoughts. It hurt to walk away from a stylish dress or a pair of swanky heels, but her child's gut and her husband's disability supplies were more important than being a standout from the crowd. And like Mrs. Flowers said, she had an entire store in her bedroom closet. Truth is, she didn't need a new dress anyway. She needed her husband back. Maybe she should leave for her own good.

With Andre's financial support, she had become so accustomed to getting whatever she wanted it spoiled her. Something inside had driven her to spend a dollar—an intense high for approval and fashion. Maybe because she and her mother always used to pinch pennies, sacrificing desirable wants to meet essential needs.

Starving artists didn't live a luxury life.

I gotta get outta here. Eva put her credit card away and strode with the stroller out of the entrance. As much as she hated to admit it, sometimes what her mom said was what's best. Nonetheless, it wasn't a crime to touch and look at the dress, was it? A cool breeze washed her face. She brushed her wind-blown, dark hair behind her ears and continued walking back to her parked car along the sidewalk.

Although she was the money-maker, choosing priority was key for survival. It was the same thing Andre did when he managed all their finances himself. He always looked out for her and Andy's needs first before his own, having a few suits and ties on his side of the closet compared to her variety of clothes and shoes. That alone was selfless love—a man's unselfish act for the happiness of his family. She loved and admired him so much for it.

Now it was her turn.

• CHAPTER 27 •

Eva

Garden Ridge High School

Home of the Grizzlies

2nd Class Reunion – School Cafeteria

Saturday Evening

It was fifteen years since Eva stepped foot into Garden Ridge High, but everything looked the same. Built in 1942, the school was a strong, three-story structure of tan, sandy brick and concrete stone that survived the test of time. Eva entered and strode the gray linoleum hallway between two rows of evergreen lockers. She inhaled and smiled, smelling the same odor of polished wax from the hardwood floor of the basketball court in the gymnasium. She approached the double-end doors to the noisy cafeteria. Inside, the buzz of conversation and laughter mingled with American Idol alum Kelly Clarkson's, "A Moment Like This." Eva still remembered when Kelly Clarkson was crowned the winner. Three months after graduating, she watched the finale while eating junk food during a sleepover at Francine's house.

Eva gripped a cold handle and peeked in a rectangular window of one of the green doors. Many of her classmates were present in their fine or casual wear, huddled in social groups and wolfing down refreshments. Eva searched for Francine, but didn't see her.

Her heart shuddered in her chest. She felt like that shy, teenage girl who first enrolled at Garden Ridge High in ninth grade, afraid of what her teenage peers think of her. *Stay cool, Eva. It's just a class reunion.* She wiped her sweaty hands down her black maxi dress and stepped into the cafeteria. People eyed her with inquisitive and surprised faces like she had an extreme makeover.

Eva's face blushed as she observed the lunchroom. On the food service tables were party platters, deviled eggs, fruit kabobs, and two metal punch fountains. A gigantic cake with *Woo-hoo Class of 2002* written on top in green cursive icing was the centerpiece of one table. Green and white balloons and a sparkly banner reading '*2nd Reunion for Class of 2002*' hung above the announcement stage. Painted on the base of the stage was the school mascot—an angry, grizzly bear with green eyes and sharp teeth.

Eva looked at a front round table to her left, holding her leopard clutch purse underarm.

"Hey, Eva! Over here!" Francine waved a hand.

Eva fixed her eyes on another round table close to the fire exit. She grinned at her school friend.

Beside Francine was a plump woman in circle-framed glasses with rosy cheeks and dark gray hair in a side bun, dressed in a violet suede suit and two-inch heels. As soon as the woman waved, she raced over to them, her platform heels clacking across the checkered, green-and-white floor. It was Mrs. Chapman, her ninth-grade English teacher.

"Oh, my goodness, it's Eva Conway," Mrs. Chapman said in her Southern accent.

"Mrs. Chapman! Hey, I'm glad you're here." Eva giggled and embraced her.

Her English teacher was teary-eyed. "Honey, it's good to see you too. You and Francine were my favorite pupils. How are you?"

Now didn't feel like the time to talk about her husband, his car accident, or her strained marriage, so she left those things out of the conversation.

"I'm well, ma'am," Eva said. "Do you still teach here?"

Mrs. Chapman's bangs bounced as she nodded. "Yep, I'm still teaching ninth-grade English on the second floor in room one-twenty."

"Wow. That's great," Eva said.

Mrs. Chapman glanced from Francine back to Eva. "Y'all turned out to be two beautiful, young women. It's nice seeing you girls again. I'm going to the refreshment table."

"Okay," Eva said, smiling.

Mrs. Chapman walked off and greeted a tall, redhead woman in a light yellow, off-the-shoulder dress a few feet away.

Francine smiled. "We were looking at old pictures in my senior yearbook."

Eva drew near to her friend. She skimmed Francine's yearbook, flipped a page, and made a funny look as if surprised by her picture. "Haha! That's me!" She pointed at her student photo labeled with her name, her birthday, her school activities, and her likes and dislikes. "Eva Rose Conway . . . May 19th . . . Art and poetry club . . . favorite subject English . . . likes reading and making origami. Look at my glasses. I could see the craters on the moon with them." She chuckled and faced Francine. "Where are you?"

"I'm toward the end of the list . . . page sixty-five." Francine turned a couple of pages of the black-and-white student photos until she came to hers. "There I am!" She poked her forefinger to a picture of a small girl—who unlike her classmates—looked about fourteen. "Francine Nichols . . . February 6th . . . Girls soccer . . . favorite subject biology . . . likes candy and talking on the phone."

Eva and Francine laughed.

"That's right! You always carried bubblegum and Airheads in your pockets," Eva said, chuckling. "Mr. Bogart, our world history teacher, always caught you chewing during class."

Francine snickered. "I guess so, my parents ran a candy shop." She handed Eva a black sharpie pen. "Can you sign my yearbook? I never got your signature." She turned to the back of her yearbook where several other students had scribbled their names and little farewell messages.

"Sure, why not?" Eva took the pen from her friend and jotted her name and a quote of best wishes.

Francine angled her head as she wrote and smiled at Eva's signature and note. "You have the prettiest handwriting. Thanks for signing my book. I had bought my book late and searched for you and Andre on prom night, but I didn't see you guys."

Eva sighed. "That's because we weren't there. We stayed home."

"Why? It was *so* obvious Andre liked you," Francine said with a playful smile. "I thought he would've asked you out to the dance."

Eva held out her hands and shrugged. "He didn't see the need to go and thought us attending prom might've led to other things."

"Oh, I guess he had a point," Francine said. "I didn't do anything, but believe me, rumor has it some couples did things they shouldn't have that night." She pinned Eva with her eyes. "Need I say more?"

Eva shook her head and crossed her arms. "Uh-uh, I'm aware of what you mean. But you know, even though we weren't there, it still was a special time for Andre and me." She smiled, reminiscing. "It was when he said he loved me, which I was ignorant of since ninth grade. I hadn't ever felt the way I did the night he told me. It just happened so instantly. Suddenly, my perspective about him had completely changed."

Someone tapped on Eva's shoulder.

Eva spun around and studied the redhead woman who spoke with Mrs. Chapman. She placed a hand on her hip. "Let me guess, Nadine Sterling?"

"Correct." Nadine tilted her head. "Long time no see. I love your updo and dress. I didn't recognize you. How's it going, Eva?"

"I'm good," Eva answered. "What about yourself?"

Nadine snarled. "Meh, I guess I'm okay. I mean, I have a successful career as a district attorney, but relationship-wise, it hasn't gone well. Let's just say I haven't found my Mr. Right yet."

"How's Sammie Cooper?" Eva asked.

If anyone knew about Sammie, Nadine would. Sammie was voted 'Homecoming Queen' in their senior class, a blonde bombshell cheerleader. One of the most popular students in school, teenage boys flocked around her like flies on a horse's tail, but she never swatted at them. Sammie had liked to be the center of attention, which may have been because her parents gave her none at home.

They were divorced, and her mother was a cougar and party animal, dating lots of younger men. One day Eva found Sammie crying in the girls' restroom, telling her how lonely she felt. It was the first time they'd talked without Sammie teasing her. She and Nadine used to hang out with their other girlfriend Tasha Burke, the girl Caleb Williams had taken over Eva to their senior prom.

Nadine wore a sour look. "Sammie's . . . sick in the hospital. She has cervical cancer."

A pang shot Eva's chest. "That's terrible."

"Yeah," Nadine said, "but she's fighting, doing good with her treatments, and determined to get better. I visit her in the hospital a lot on the weekends." She cocked her head. "Hey, maybe you can come to visit her with me or we can chill and hang out."

"Okay, sounds . . . nice," Eva said, shifting her eyes, a bit surprised by Nadine's sudden interest in her.

"Great. Well, I gotta go. Excuse me, ladies," Nadine said.

Eva and her friend watched Nadine walk to the entrance and welcome two gentlemen wearing suits and ties to the class reunion.

"Poor Sammie." Eva frowned.

"Yeah, and poor Nadine too," Francine added. She closed her yearbook. "She told me she suffered three failed marriages. *Three*, can you believe that? None of them resulted in children."

"What happened?" Eva asked.

"Her first left her, her second cheated on her, and her third she found out didn't want children, so she broke up with him too," Francine said dryly. She sighed. "You're lucky you found someone compatible who truly loves you."

"Sure . . . I guess so," Eva said gingerly.

Francine twisted her face, confused. "What do you mean, guess?"

"He's not the same anymore." Eva sighed and rubbed her arms. "Since his accident, he doesn't remember our wedding day and everything we were together."

Her friend cupped her shoulder. "At least you have great memories. Everybody can't say that about their marriage. I'm gonna get a cup of pineapple punch. Want some?"

Eva allowed a smile. "Sure, thanks."

Francine trailed off to the refreshment tables.

Eva sat at the round table her friend left her yearbook on and flipped through the other pages of student photos toward the back.

Her eyes landed on a picture of an African American teenage boy grinning wide with a boxed, fade haircut. She skimmed the info beside his picture:

Caleb Williams

Birthday: Feb. 8th

Nickname: The CW

School activities: Boys basketball – Point guard

Likes: Girls, cars, chocolate, and seafood

Dislikes: Losing at anything, homework, and Brussels Sprouts

Eva's heart stopped. She shut the yearbook, looking at her school friend getting two glass cups of punch. Her former affection toward Caleb was childish feelings of the past, and she had no intentions of reliving them. She was a married woman with a lovable son. And though her marriage had turned upside down, as Francine said, she had made lots of happy memories with Andre.

As Francine returned with the cups of punch, Eva spotted a good-looking, black man in a brown vest outfit and blood-red bow tie stroll in the cafeteria. Her cheeks blushed, and she wanted to hide. It turned out the one she should've been most nervous to find at the class reunion was her high school crush, instead of her female bullies. The man joined a group of men who greeted him with handshakes and high-fives, other teammates of the boys' basketball team.

The group of men rooted with their hands in a circle.

"Gooo Grizzlies!" they said, raising their hands as they used to during Friday night games.

"Here you go, Eva." Francine handed her a cup.

"Thanks," Eva said, distracted.

Francine smiled and drank from her punch cup, eyeing the members of the basketball team. "Looks like Caleb Williams made it after all."

Caleb turned his attention from his friends and made a double-take in Eva and Francine's direction. His long gaze passed through Eva's whole being like laser beams, and though for once she wanted to remain unseen by him, *this* time he noticed her.

Francine waved. "Hey, it looks like he's coming our way!"

Oh, no, please, don't come here. Eva gulped and placed her punch down. "Listen, Frankie . . . maybe I shouldn't have come." She stood from the table, her knees wobbling.

"Don't tell me you're leaving." Disappointment contorted Francine's face.

Eva kept a nervous look-out at Caleb, grabbing her purse. "I'm sorry. I can't stay here, Frankie. I have to go." As Stevie Wonder's "Kiss, Lonely Goodbye" resounded from the speakers, she rushed out the fire exit before Caleb arrived at their table. Eva jogged in her heels to her car. She had her worries about coming to her class reunion, but her pride prevented her from taking heed of her mother's concern.

When she was a teenager, her mom always had to prove her wrong about everything, and she couldn't bear another moment of her interfering skepticism.

"Eva?" a man called behind her.

She stopped digging in her purse for her car keys and slowly faced him. Although a tad bit older, Caleb held the same charm. His smooth, dark brown skin and clothing made the thought of a Tootsie Roll come to Eva's mind. Over the years, his black, coiled hair had been trimmed to a short, low-cut style. He was about five-foot-nine—not as tall as her husband—but his robust arms close-fitting his white dress shirt showed he was as physically fit.

"Eva Conway?" Caleb blinked in disbelief.

"Hi . . .Caleb." Eva gave a shy smile and lifted a shoulder. Getting married hadn't stopped her attraction to other men, and she understood his surprised reaction to her changed looks. The last time he saw her she was a twelfth-grade teenager with a face speckled with pimples, metallic braces, and glasses as big as Petri dishes. There wasn't a wonder why a popular guy like him had chosen Tasha Burke over her to their senior prom.

"It's Eva Lucas now," Eva corrected.

Caleb inched forward and slipped his hands in his pants pockets. He arched his brow. "Where's your ring? You don't have one on your finger."

"Maybe not, but I have a certificate," Eva said with a smirk, tilting her head. "Wedding rings are a tradition.

They don't keep couples together."

A giggle slipped from Caleb, amused by her blunt statement. "I know, right?" He stroked his thin mustache above his upper lip, still baffled. "Wow, I can't believe it's you. I mean, you look so—"

"Different?" Eva interrupted before he complimented her. "I know. So does Andre."

"You've got to be kidding me. You married Andre Lucas?" Caleb said.

Eva nodded. "Yes. We have a son who's almost two. His name's Andrew." She slumped her shoulders. "But things have been hard lately." She hadn't told a soul of her graduating class about her husband. But somehow, seeing Caleb brought out what she'd been harboring inside. Of course, even though he showed little interest, she'd always told him things going on in her life before.

"A brain injury paralyzed him, but the doctor said it could be temporary. So far though there hasn't been a change," she said.

Caleb's forehead furrowed. "Oh, no. That's awful. I hope he gets well."

"Yeah, me too." Eva folded her arms. "So, when did you come back in town? I wasn't *exactly* expecting you." She rolled her eyes wittily with a smile.

Caleb chuckled. "I moved back to North Carolina two years ago. The city was fun and exciting, but too noisy and busy. I'm a real estate agent and interior designer.

What do you do for a living?"

"I'm a daycare provider for Sunrise Christian Daycare, but it was my mom's idea," Eva said. "Honestly sometimes I wish I pursued interior design myself."

"I figured you were a teacher," Caleb said. "You were always so smart. There's no doubt I would've never finished high school if you hadn't helped me study."

"So, are you married?" Eva asked.

"No," Caleb said, "I enjoy my freedom of the single life, but who knows? Maybe I'll settle down with the right woman someday."

Eva wore a wry smile. "I'm sure you'll find her."

"Perhaps I will." Caleb grinned. "You know, I have textbooks about interior design lying around my house collecting dust. I used them to study before I took and passed the NCIDQ exam myself. They might be helpful in getting you on track with pursuing the career too."

Eva twitched her mouth. "Um, thanks, but I'd be fooling myself into ever becoming an interior designer. Besides, my mom says it's a waste of time and money. She doesn't think I can make a sufficient living from it."

"It doesn't hurt to try," Caleb said. "I know from experience the process can be long, and the sooner you study, the better and sooner the results. It's up to you. I'm not pushing you into doing this, but there's no problem in wanting to do something different for a change."

Eva's mind reeled. She had been a daycare provider

for ten years, wiping runny noses, calming down tantrums, and singing so many kiddy songs she heard them in her sleep. She enjoyed her job and loved her kids, but she had felt like she was living a lie by denying her true passion for design. Maybe working toward her dream career was a good idea, a way to help build her, Andre, and Andrew a more promising future.

"You know what, why not?" Eva said.

"Awesome. I live on two-thirty Gold Street. You can pick up the books there, but if I'm not home, you can call me, and I'll come right over." Caleb dug in a side pocket, took out his wallet, and pulled a business card from it. "Here, just in case."

Eva smiled and took his card. "Thank you." She read the business title. "Coleman Housing . . . I've heard of it. It's the housing company Andre and I mortgaged our home from. I guess you've followed your father's footsteps in real estate, huh."

"Precisely," Caleb said. "It's a proud legacy. I gave up a basketball scholarship to keep it in our family. Like your mom, my dad had an influence on my future. He thought I needed a more *secure* profession, but in my case, I believe he was right. One injury can end an athlete's career forever."

"That's true," Eva agreed, "but you were a great ballplayer. I always liked watching you on the court during game nights." Her eyes sparkled with admiration.

Caleb smiled. "Thanks, I still play sometimes, but for fun." His smile faded. "Well, I suppose you'd like to go home. Nice talking to you."

"Yeah, good night." Eva turned to her car and took out her keys, but changed her mind. Because she and Caleb had talked and matters appeared to be innocent between them, there wasn't a need to leave anymore.

"Then again, I'll stay a little longer." She walked to the exit door to the cafeteria, which Caleb opened for her before she could herself.

"Um . . . thank you." Eva's skin flushed as his body stood behind hers.

"My pleasure." Caleb watched her enter the cafeteria and followed her inside.

• CHAPTER 28 •

Eva

Monday, Nov. 27th

Was it a crime to follow one's dream?

Getting more criticism and negativity than encouragement, her mom led her to believe it was illegal. Eva didn't know whether her mother's struggles as an artist had something to do with it, but she concluded to reach her goals she had better keep it a secret. Sharing with her mom about her studying to become an interior designer would split them further apart. Eva loved her mom, but she had to be what she wanted, and not what her mother thought was best for her.

Orange oak leaves swirled in the whistling wind into Caleb's front yard and fluttered onto the light brown roof of his peach, brick home. Eva locked the doors of her car parked along the sidewalk and marched up the pathway.

She took a deep breath and rang the doorbell, marveling over his luxurious house.

Caleb poked out his smiling face, hiding behind the opened door. "Hey, Eva! You can wait out here. Let me get the books for you."

"Okay," Eva said with a timid smile.

Caleb left the door ajar and slipped back inside for a moment.

Eva buried her face in her plaid scarf and rubbed her hands for warmth, trying to endure the chill in the air. Being thirty-six degrees outside, she hoped he wouldn't take too long , and especially with her son left in the back of her car.

About three minutes later, Caleb returned, opening the door. He held a stack of three thick textbooks. "You can read them as long as you want." He released the heavy books into Eva's gloved hands, and she nearly dropped them.

Eva grinned. "Phew, thank you."

"The red book is about *Design Elements and Principles*, the blue one is *Color and Lighting Theory*, and the yellow is *History of Interior Design*. All three subjects you must know to pass the NCIDQ exam," Caleb said. "But if you enroll in the Art Institute instead, you still should know and learn the same curriculum."

"Thanks, I appreciate this," Eva said. "I've wanted to get into interior design when I was younger, but I didn't know where to start besides choosing color palettes. Everything my mom said always felt right, but later I ended up regretting giving up on my dream."

"I'm sorry about your mom," Caleb said. "It's unfortunate she thinks you can't make a living being a designer. I think it's delightful to style and sell a lovely home for a family they can be proud of."

"Me too," Eva agreed.

"It's one of the best jobs ever," Caleb said, smiling. "I wish you the best of success, and I know you'll do well. You're a bright, young lady, Eva."

Eva wore a half-smile.

Since she was in grade school, she was always a little brainiac, her classmates asking her for help with their English papers or math homework. But for once, she wished Caleb would tell her how he felt about her in the past, instead of sparing her feelings.

When their senior prom came, Caleb told her last-minute he forgot he already asked to take Tasha Burke. But Eva knew it was an excuse to prevent him from keeping his promise of walking arm in arm with the "nerd girl" to the dance for her help with his final vocabulary test.

"Uh, how's your husband?" Caleb asked.

Eva shook her head and sighed. "He's still having a hard time. It's taking longer for Andre to walk than we expected. Sometimes he speaks to me, and other times he doesn't. I've tried to help him cope and talk him into taking an antidepressant, but he doesn't want one. I'm not sure what to do about him anymore."

"Oh, well, maybe Andre will come around soon." Caleb gave her a quick once-over. "I can tell you've stressed over him a lot. Take care of yourself."

Eva cradled the books and waved. "Yeah, you too. Bye." She strode to her vehicle as Caleb closed his door.

Her mother was painting barefoot in the living room when she entered the house, sitting in front of a bleached canvas on a wooden easel. Under the easel were sheets of old newspaper to protect the carpet if she spilled paint. On television she was watching an episode of *The Joy of Painting* with Bob Ross, attempting to copy his portrait of a forest.

Her mom added green paint from her palette to her thick bristle brush and dabbed fast strokes over the tree branches on her canvas, listening to Ross' gentle instructions to ensure she did them right.

"Looking good, Mom," Eva said, closing the door. As usual, Andrew was knocked out in her arms after coming home from working at the daycare.

Her mother smiled. "Thanks, hon."

"Where's Andre and Skye?" Eva asked, rubbing her son's back.

Andrew moaned in his sleep and turned his drowsy head on her shoulder.

Her mom rinsed her fan brush in a tin can of water. "They're in the kitchen. Skye's giving Andre an afternoon snack."

"All right, I'm going to put Andy in his crib." Eva started up the staircase.

"Where were you?" her mom said.

Eva stopped in her tracks and glanced back.

"It's four-thirty, and you said you'd be here a little after three this morning," her mom added.

Eva felt her defenses rising, but she kept her calm. If her mother distrusted her whereabouts, she wouldn't give her a reason to meddle in her business. "Traffic was busy on Garfield Drive," she answered. Garfield Drive was where her daycare was located, a narrow street next door to the Garden Ridge Police Department.

"Oh, all right," her mom said.

Eva turned her back and rolled her eyes upward. It wasn't a lie she told her mother, but she was thankful she wasn't thrown more questions. She walked upstairs to her son's bedroom and put him to bed to finish his afternoon nap. The textbooks she got from Caleb were still in the trunk of her car. At night, she would sneak outside to get the books, study, and hide them in the dresser. Eva pulled the blanket over her son, alarmed by a call from downstairs.

"Mrs. Lucas, Ms. Conway, hurry quick!" Skye said.

Eva frowned and hurled downstairs to the kitchen. She and her mother shared a gasp the minute they saw Andre. Her husband had a spoon in his right hand between his index and ring fingers, feeding himself his bowl of tomato soup. It was a small miracle, like watching Andrew stop eating with his hands again.

After months of her husband having everything done for him, he was fighting for his independence.

"Andre," Eva mouthed, her eyes filling with tears.

"I was about to feed him after I brought his drink to the table, but he tried to pick up his spoon. I realized he was attempting to feed himself. He was frustrated, but he kept trying until he could do it. His hand and arm exercises are working, Mrs. Lucas."

"That's terrific," Eva said.

Her mom smiled. "I saw utensil cuffs for paralyzed people to help with eating online." She faced Eva. "You should get a pair for Andre. It would make eating a lot simpler for him, and he can use them later to brush his teeth and hair too."

"Well," Eva said, "that depends on if Andre wants them." She sighed and folded her arms, looking at her husband again. His physical body was healing, but would his mind? If Andre never walked again, Eva wanted him to love and bond with her and their son Andrew above everything else. It didn't matter if Andre was stuck in a wheelchair the rest of his life, or if they never had another child. What mattered was them living happily and rebuilding their broken family household.

"Do you want the utensil cuffs, Andre?" Eva asked.

Her husband continued eating.

Skye frowned. "Hey, man, your wife's talking to you?"

Andre avoided eye contact with anybody surrounding him and slurped his soup.

Eva's mom was confused. "Andre?" She glanced from Skye to Eva. "What's wrong with him?"

"Andre . . ." Eva grimaced with her hands on the table and leaned forward in front of him. "Don't you dare ignore me?!"

Her husband remained silent, and a time of achievement had become another time of devastation.

Eva whimpered and fled from the kitchen, running back upstairs to the master bedroom. She slammed the door and cried on her pillow, tired of feeling invisible in her own house. Why did Andre treat her like this? Was it his brain injury? Or was it something else? Maybe he blamed her for his car accident.

No matter what, she was determined to follow her dreams. She would allow no one, not even her disabled husband to hinder her efforts. Besides, Caleb owed her his help in interior design after all she's done for him in school, and she was sure he knew this himself. But with her mother in the house, she had to be careful her mom doesn't find the books.

Knowing her mother, it would be a total disaster.

• CHAPTER 29 •

Eva

Monday Afternoon

Her mother knocked on the bedroom door. "Eva, can I come in?"

"Why not? I don't exist anyway." Eva rose from lying stomach-down and sat upright on the bed. She wiped her tears as her mom stepped inside and closed the door.

"What do you want?" Eva hoped her mother wasn't about to criticize how well she treats her husband. Ever since Andre was sent home, she'd done nothing except being loving and supportive toward him. Andre was the one who refused to keep their communication thriving and alive. He was the one that felt she was incompetent to care for him, and the one who suggested they divorce.

"I came to check on you," Eva's mom said. "Has Andre always been so quiet?"

Eva snickered. "He's doing it on purpose. Andre's been shunning me since he got out of the hospital. It's not every day, but he does from time to time. It feels like he's never gonna change his attitude. Part of me thinks he's testing how much I love him."

"Why would he do something so spiteful?" Eva's mom asked. "That's not the Andre I know."

Eva tilted her head and scowled. "Mom, Andre's not the same man I married on our wedding day. He has a different mind and personality . . . the Andre we knew is gone." Her expression softened, and she sighed, rounding her shoulders. "Of course, sometimes I feel like . . ."

"Like what?" Her mother perched a spot on the bed beside her.

Eva wore a wistful smile. "Like the old Andre is still there. Sometimes I look into his brown eyes and I think I see him, and he loves me and Andy so much, but he's . . . hurting so badly, and too ashamed to let it out." She bowed her head and wept.

Her mom wrapped an arm around her, rubbing her back. "Maybe he is. Andre was always a brave person, but I guess he had no choice. He's been through a lot as a child with his parents, and he wanted to be a better man than his father was."

"One day he said he wants a divorce," Eva confessed.

Her mom was stunned. "He did?"

Eva nodded. "Yeah, do you think he's right?" She raised her face to her mother. "Do you think we should divorce?"

"No way," Eva's mom said with a frown, "Andre's lost his memory. He doesn't know what he's saying, and I'm sure if he could remember his past with you and Andy, he'd never consider divorce. The love you and Andre had together is too precious to let go of, and it still is. Y'all are just going through a storm. But when the dark clouds pass away, the sun *will* shine again."

Eva covered her eyes. "I sure hope it's soon. This whole situation is wearing me out."

Her mother stood. "It'll pass. If Andre truly loves you, he'll change his behavior soon enough and be willing to recover your relationship." She walked to the door. "I'm gonna cook dinner. You can stay in here for a while. Andre seems to need more time alone to recuperate. Maybe you do too."

Eva gave a half-smile. "Thanks for your help, Mom."

"You're welcome, hon." Her mother exited the room.

Eva exhaled and relaxed her shoulders. It had been a long time since she felt the support of her mother, or was comfortable enough to open up about her feelings. Ever since Andre's condition, their mother-daughter relationship was slowly making progress. Maybe Eva was wrong, and she didn't have to hide her studying and ambition. Perhaps her mother would apologize for discouraging her in the past and allow her to choose her career for herself.

No, I can't risk it. Eva shook the hopeful thoughts from her head. She took off her tennis shoes, draped herself with the blanket and drifted asleep.

It was six o'clock when Eva awoke.

She left the master bedroom and entered Andrew's room to check on her son. Eva flicked on the light switch and found the white crib empty. She figured he was in the dining room having dinner with everyone else. Eva ambled down the staircase to the living room. The television showed a commercial on the flat screen. It was about a young, interior design female student who had recently finished high school and attends the Art Institute of Charlotte.

"Eva! Dinner's ready!" her mom called.

Eva glanced away. "I'll be right there!" She looked back at the TV until the commercial ended, inspired to enroll in the university's Interior Design Bachelor of Fine Arts program. She strode through the entryway to the dining room and sat at the six-chair dinette table across from her husband.

Her mom had made shepherd's pie with gravy and steamed broccoli with onions for dinner. Andrew was in his highchair eating a bowl of Spaghetti-O's with meatballs with a sippy cup of milk. Andre was in his manual wheelchair, struggling to use his left fist to place his fork in his right hand.

"Need help?" Eva grabbed a plate from the center stack.

Andre slipped her a guarded look. "No, I can do it myself."

Eva stared at her husband with surprise. Her spirits buoyed. It was the most words he said in weeks without hesitations or having to think clearly before he spoke. She was glad he responded to her, but she felt his bitterness in the tone of his voice.

"Andre," Eva said, "I know you aren't feeling too well, but it might help if you take some medication."

Her husband snarled and banged his fist on the table. "I told you I don't want an antidepressant! I don't need one!" He stared her down and paced his rapid breathing.

"I'm sorry," Eva said calmly. "I was just saying—nevermind, forget it." She faced her mother. "Can I have the broccoli, mom?"

Her mother passed her the bowl across the table.

"Thanks." Eva spooned a serving on her plate.

"Skye said you owe him a late check," her mother said.

Eva smacked her forehead. "Oh, no! I forgot. What'd you tell him?"

"I told him you weren't feeling too well, but you'll pay

him tomorrow," her mother answered.

"Nah, I'll call him after dinner." Eva cut a chunk of shepherd's pie from the dish and added it to her plate. Her husband already had his food on his plate, so she put the dish aside. She watched Andre feeding himself, using a side of his fork to cut his food in smaller pieces. From the time they ate dinner to the time Eva's mom brought out apple pie with whipped cream for dessert, she and Andre didn't speak to each other.

Her mother discussed the weather and made a list of corny jokes, trying to break the tension between them. Andrew was the only one who thought her jokes were amusing, making funny faces and giggling, but Eva appreciated what her mom was attempting to do. After dinner, she helped her mother put the food away and clean the dishes in the kitchen.

"Thanks for trying, Mom." Eva tucked a wet plate on the rack.

Her mom raised an eyebrow. "Trying what?"

"To get Andre and me to talk friendly with each other." Eva mocked a laugh and placed another plate on the dish rack. "And do you know what the funny thing is?"

Her mom pursed her lips. "What?"

"Regardless of Andre's attitude," Eva said, "he still needs to accept my help to use the restroom; at least, until Skye shows him how to do it himself. He said he'll teach Andre to self-cath when I called him on the phone. I'm hoping he'll listen to my advice and take advantage of the urinal the hospital gave him. It would save him the trouble of taking his wheelchair to the bathroom, but he's so stubborn."

"He's a man," her mother said, "most men have a dominant nature, but it's a good sign Andre's getting better."

Eva cocked her head. "How so?"

Her mom rinsed a soapy plate in the basin sink of water. "Well, because he's getting back more of his strength, maybe he'll stop feeling sorry for himself."

Eva sighed. "I hope so. I'm gonna check on him." She walked off and picked up Andrew from his playpen in the living room. "All right, little one. It's time for you to hit the sack." She frowned at Andre, who was focused on a Monday night NFL football game. "Thanks for *watching* him."

"You're welcome," Andre said, staring at the television.

"Pee-pee poo, Mommy," Andrew said and whined.

"Uh-oh." Eva felt his bottom and noticed his sweatpants were damp. "Come on, sweetie, you need a new pamper." She carried Andrew upstairs and changed him on the baby table in his bedroom. She tossed the dirty pamper in her son's diaper genie and switched Andrew into his Cookie Monster pajamas. Before Eva put her son to bed, she sat in his rocking chair with him in her lap and read him *Peekaboo Bedtime* by Rachel Isadora, one of his favorite stories. Then she laid him in his crib with his stuffed monkey and kissed him goodnight.

Their son was nineteen months old now, and she marveled at how much he developed in his mind, speech, and mannerisms. He could understand and say more words, he could build with his Lego blocks, and he was budding a sense of humor. It saddened her Andre was missing out on their son's growth process, but she prayed and believed someday he would escape his maze of depression and change his attitude soon.

Everyone was sleeping and the coast was clear.

After slipping into a pair of clothes, Eva tiptoed out of the guestroom into the living room. She snuck outside and brought the textbooks Caleb gave her into the house. Eva sat curled on the brown sofa, put on her glasses, and read the yellow book first: *The History of Interior Design*. She flipped through chapter one and used a neon green highlighter to mark keywords she'd need to know in her vocabulary. Eva studied many interior designs from the Renaissance era.

Turning ahead, she discovered the book also had text about other styles from Victorian age to Contemporary Modern. There was so much for her to learn and know, and Eva was so excited she read chapters two, three, and four, highlighting and jotting annotations on a yellow notepad.

When she finished reading the fourth chapter, she bookmarked chapter five and opened the red book next: *Design Elements and Principles*. She was more interested in this book, which was about basic elements to consider when designing rooms and creative ideas based on them.

By the time she read in the blue book *Color and Lighting Theory*, it was eleven o'clock and she had fallen asleep. One in the morning, Eva awoke, hid her textbooks under her clothes in the bottom drawer of the dresser, and climbed back on the couch. It wasn't until sunrise she realized she hadn't set her alarm clock on her iPhone. Eva lit up and peeked at her screen.

6:45 a.m.

She jumped from the couch to get her son and herself ready to leave for the daycare. Embarrassment seized her as she arrived late to work, but she apologized to Mrs. Higgins and promised her it would never happen again. Afterward, Eva got news from her director two more of her students were leaving the two-year-old class. One of them was Juan Diaz, and the other was Autumn McKee.

"Please, excuse me for my lateness. I had a long night," Eva said to Autumn's parents.

Greg looped an arm around his pregnant wife Amy, dressed in his lieutenant police uniform. At thirty, the tall and thin man was already going bald in the center of his jet-black hair. He nodded. "It's okay. We understand the pressure you've been under with your husband."

Eva thought to mention it had nothing to do with Andre, but she kept quiet. She glanced and smiled at Autumn, playing at a toy kitchen set with Chloe and Chelsea in the dramatic play area, twin sisters who were two of Eva's newest students. No one could say she wasn't Amy's daughter. They both had the same bright, reddish-brown hair.

Amy grinned. "I'll be seven months tomorrow. Greg and I've been working hard to keep our mortgaged home, but I need a serious vacation."

"I don't blame you," Eva said, "it's hard being pregnant and working at the same time. I've been there, and now, I'm pulling the weight again. I'll be praying everything works out for you and Greg and your delivery."

Amy smiled and placed a hand on her protruding belly bulging out her sweater. "Thanks, I'll continue praying for you and Andre. I know times have been tough on you, but we appreciated your caring for our daughter. You're a great teacher."

"Thank you, Amy." Eva felt a tug on her khaki skirt, causing her to look down.

"Mrs. Lucas, I'm gonna miss you." Autumn poked out her lip. She turned three last month and was transferred to Mrs. Drummond and Mrs. Timberlake's three-year-old classroom.

Eva brushed her hand over Autumn's hair and sighed. "I'm gonna miss you too, sweetie. But I'll visit you every chance I can get."

"You promise?" Autumn rubbed her eye and sniffled.

"I promise." Eva gave a smile and held the little girl in a side hug.

Greg shook Eva's free hand. "We'll never forget you and everything you've done."

Eva looked into his bluish-gray eyes. "I'll never forget y'all either. I can't thank you enough for finding Andre and calling in help after his accident. If you hadn't, he might've never had a chance."

"You're welcome again. Have a wonderful afternoon." Greg took hold of Autumn's hand and walked her out with his wife.

"You too, Mr. McKee." Eva waved as Autumn stared back at her. She would miss the friendly, little girl, and her innocent, blue eyes swelled her heart with remorse. Why in the world did she feel guilty?

• CHAPTER 30 •

Eva

One Year Later

Eva opened the refrigerator and shook her head at the Styrofoam tray and the slice of sweet potato pie wrapped in plastic. On Thanksgiving Day, this time Mrs. Flowers didn't invite Eva and her family over and instead gave leftovers from her family's annual gathering. But her mother hadn't eaten hers. She figured her mom thought Mrs. Flowers was trying to get on her good side. Eva clamped her lips and sighed. It would be a quiet ride to church, but at least Andre was coming today.

It was important for her husband to recover physically and mentally, but it was also critical for him to regain his spiritual strength too. Joy blossomed within her when he told her he wanted to go, and she expected it would be the start of Andre mending his troubled heart.

She took out a jug of orange juice and poured herself a cup. "When are you gonna eat your Thanksgiving dinner, on New Year's Day?"

Her mom was cooking breakfast at the electric stove. "Why don't you eat it? Mrs. Flowers gave the leftovers to you, not me."

Eva turned and sipped from her glass cup. "Mrs. Flowers gave each of us a plate, including Andrew. She was trying to be nice."

Her mother's expression hardened. "I don't need her kind gestures. I'm fine without her help, and that's what you need to learn to do too, young lady."

Anger thundered through Eva, banging her half-filled cup on the counter. "What is it with you? What do you have against Mrs. Flowers? What did she ever do to you?" She shook off the juice that splashed on her hand.

"Do *not* raise your voice to me!" her mom countered.

Eva stepped forward and glared at her mother. "Why don't you just say it? You're jealous I have a better relationship with her than my own mother!"

Her mom slapped her across her face.

Eva fought with her tears and ran out of the kitchen. Though she was hurting inside, she told her mother the truth that had been eating her up. It was the reason her mom was displeased with Mrs. Flowers' presence when she first entered the house.

It was why she didn't want to paint the portrait for Mrs. Flowers' friend, and why her Thanksgiving dinner from three days ago was still in the refrigerator. Eva went in the guestroom. She hated how her mother treated Mrs. Flowers, and especially a widow who lost her husband. If her mother placed herself in Mrs. Flowers' shoes, she'd realize the woman who she thought was trying to take her place was simply a lonely old woman.

Eva dried her eyes and opened the bottom drawer of her dresser. She laid out her amethyst and white floral dress on the bed to wear for church. Then she bathed and dressed Andrew. After Eva took her son in the kitchen to have breakfast, she entered the master bedroom to check on Andre. He was in his manual wheelchair, adjusting on a sky blue, long-sleeve dress shirt.

Eva's spirits buoyed.

Her husband needed help with small objects and a few tangible doings, but he was getting much better with his speech and daily tasks for himself. She was grateful she had less to do than when he first came home a year ago.

Andre looked at her reflection behind him in the oval mirror of their cherry wood dresser. "Can button shirt . . . fix collar, please?"

"Sure." Eva walked to his wheelchair and fastened each button. "You look handsome."

"Thanks," Andre said with a weak smile. He tilted

his head and frowned. "Uh, you . . . okay? What happened . . . mother?"

Eva rolled her eyes and closed the last button of his dress shirt. "She's got issues. It's something about being jealous of my relationship with Mrs. Flowers. We get along so well, that's all. She feels like the grandmother I wanted, but never had in my life."

"Oh," Andre said lowly.

Eva pulled down his neck collar. "Do you think you can fix your tie?"

Andre twitched his mouth and shook his head.

"Okay, I'll do it then." Eva put his silky blue necktie on for him and tied it in a knot. "Perfect. You're all done. There's breakfast downstairs if you want."

"Not hungry. Going . . . brush my teeth." Andre wheeled himself out of the bedroom to the bathroom.

Eva sighed pensively at him and sagged her shoulders. Where was God? Sometimes she felt like He wasn't listening to a word she said. Praying for Andre's depressed mood over the past year became a worn-out routine, and she didn't know him too well anymore. But after all his days of seclusion, she realized the only way he would allow love to reenter his heart was if he wanted it himself.

"Praise the Lord, church! Can I get an amen in the house?" Pastor Tyson gripped the pulpit and bounced with a spring in his step, teetering his bald head from side to side.

"Amen," the congregation said.

"I said, can I get an amen in the house?" the pastor emphasized.

"Amen!" the congregation repeated louder.

"It doesn't matter how you feel, or what you're going through. You can always depend on the Lord Jesus," Pastor Tyson proclaimed through his pulpit microphone. "Please, turn with me in your bibles to the book of first Samuel chapter seventeen . . ."

Eva glanced at her husband sitting beside the front row of the men's side of pews. He didn't look happy, which worried her. Her mind drifted off with concerns for him. She had paid little attention to the pastor, but somehow his sermon swerved from the triumph of David against Goliath to his downfall of lust and sin. After King David remained in Jerusalem, he saw a beautiful woman named Bathsheba bathing, and temptation led to a heap of trouble and scarlet sins.

One evening also affected Eva's life, and she got a hunch the pastor's message was a warning to herself. At first, she saw their conversation and her visit as purely innocent. But sometimes, how she felt around him the night of her class reunion reared its ugly head.

Should she have gone to Caleb's house? Was getting the textbooks a good suggestion? Or was it an avenue for temptation? Of course, she didn't mean to destroy her marriage, but what about Caleb? Although he was never interested in her when they were teenagers, he was also a single man known for playing the field.

Eva gulped and listened as the paster expounded David's tragic experience. He taught how one mistake can lead to another and advised to always be honest and ask for forgiveness for one's sins. She leaned forward and cast a sidelong look at her husband again, who had his head hung low.

As Pastor Tyson read in First Corinthians chapter seven verse eleven, Eva was absorbed into a daydream, remembering how Andre used to be. Sometimes he read bible verses to Andrew in his lap, telling their son how Jesus loves him more than he can himself. Andre *loved* God and had taught her to do the same at the end of their senior year. If it wasn't for him, she would've never gone to church. But many things had changed. It felt strange he didn't know about God's love anymore, the sacrifice of Jesus' death on the cross, salvation from sin, or eternal peace in Heaven.

Nonetheless, building a relationship with Jesus Christ

guided her to make wiser choices. It also allowed her to find the strength to love not only others boldly, but also herself. From a child to a woman, Eva wondered why none of her grandparents bothered to visit her, and why they couldn't accept and love her. Maybe her parents had her out of wedlock, but it wasn't her fault. She was a harmless child, who wanted to spend time with her grandmas and grandpas like other normal children.

As a little girl and teenager, Eva suffered from great depression for struggling to fit in, feeling ugly, and never having a boyfriend. But it appeared saving her heart for a worthy man paid off. In high school, she had wanted to be popular with the coolest trendy clothes, but after attending her class reunion, it seemed the simple life was better.

Not all, but many of her classmates she talked to were divorced or had fatherless children. Despite his changed lifestyle, she was grateful Andre had worked to make her and their son's lives sufficient.

On the night of the senior prom, Eva accepted Jesus Christ, her heart filled with remorse. Disgusted by her excessive covetousness and her low self-esteem, she desired God's love more than anything. In her bedroom, she cried and asked God to forgive all her wrongdoings. She also prayed for God to help her save herself for a good man who loved and respected Him and her. Later, Pastor Tyson baptized her for the remission of her sins and she had striven to serve the Lord ever since. Now musing over her adult life, she realized her prayer had been answered, regardless of the present decline in her marriage.

"Sister Lucas . . . Sister Lucas, the pastor called you to the front," a fellow woman beside her said, pulling her out of her reverie.

Eva wore a dazed look. "Huh?"

"Pastor Tyson asked you to come forth," the church sister whispered. "He has a special presentation for you and Andre."

"Oh?" Eva found Andre in his manual wheelchair beside the pastor. She rose from her pew with Andy and strode the aisle. "What's this about?"

Pastor Tyson smiled. "The church and I know of you and your husband's financial struggles, and we couldn't help but offer a helping hand. Therefore, we've raised a donation of two thousand dollars to be presented to the Lucas family."

Eva wore a sad frown. "Oh, no, you didn't have to—"

"We wanted to," Pastor Tyson interrupted. "Please, say you'll accept our donation. It's the least we can do."

Eva faced the congregation seated on the church pews and tried to smile. "Uh, thank you. Thank you so much."

"Yeah . . . thanks," Andre added.

The congregation clapped and cheered for them, but Eva darted her eyes with uncertainty. Would the church's generous offer conflict with the financial benefits they were already receiving? There was one way to find out, and it would be from their latest letter from the Social Security Administration.

• CHAPTER 31 •

Eva

Saturday

The first day of December rolled in, but no check arrived from social services.

Eva pulled her Volkswagen Golf into the driveway of the house. Her wipers swished off the flurries sprinkling from the gray, cloudy heavens on her windshield. Today marked the first snowfall of the year. She switched off the engine and sat in her driver seat with her head leaned against the neck rest. Her heartbeat pounded in her chest as she massaged her brow, trying to organize her cluttered mind of her husband's mental health, her son, her job, and more.

She needed an outlet or breather—a way to escape her laundry list of obligations. Stress burdened her like it never had before. Although the church meant well, she hadn't spent most of their donation in time, and the SSA counted their contribution for her monthly payment. And if matters weren't bad enough, her mother was still in her home, struggling to piece her life back together again.

Eva peeked in the rearview mirror at Andrew.

A smile tugged at her lips. She liked to watch her little boy sleeping, bundled up in his winter toboggan, red-and-black plaid coat, red mittens, and black boots. To her, he looked like a tiny lumberjack. He was so precious and endearing. She couldn't believe Andre hadn't tried to know their son more. Of course, he'd been so mentally consumed in his own thoughts and problems, he forgot others were emotionally suffering too.

But Andrew still loved his daddy and wanted to play with him. It was in his smile and alert eyes when Andre rolled around in his wheelchair, his firm grip whenever he crawled over and touched Andre's leg or foot. Maybe she ought to be thankful Andre smiled at the child, but since gaining use of his hands and arms, he never tried to hold him. Having little hand dexterity, he was scared he'd drop Andrew and cause him to get hurt. But there were other ways he could show affection toward Andrew besides giving a hug.

Eva unbuckled her seatbelt and snatched her key out of the ignition. She never thought she would be, but she appreciated her mother's visit to town. Even with their differences over Mrs. Flowers, it allowed her to focus on her studies of interior design and prepare for the spring semester. Last Sunday's quarrel had stuck in her mind her entire workweek. Her mom had never slapped her before, and neither had she apologized for hitting her.

After church service, Eva didn't eat lunch or dinner that she prepared and went to bed early to wake later to study at night. Mrs. Flowers was coming to the house less out of fear she was ripping Eva and her mother apart. And with no change in her husband through prayer, she felt like nobody cared about her pain and loneliness.

Eva climbed out of her car and unfastened Andrew from his booster seat. Carrying her son, she unlocked the door and entered the warm house. Andre was in his manual wheelchair, playing UNO with Skye while watching a dog show on the Animal Planet channel.

"Hi, fellows," Eva said, closing the door.

Her mom walked into the living room, kneading a dishtowel. "Eva, can I talk with you, please?"

Eva's heart felt light. "Sure, let me put Andy upstairs." She turned her back and let out a relieved breath, glancing upward. For the past seven days, her mother had given her the silent treatment, as she had many times in her past. She reckoned she was finally ready for them to move forward. Eva trudged up the staircase to her son's bedroom and laid him down, placing Mookie under his arm.

Then she returned downstairs again, awaiting her mother.

"She's in the guestroom." Skye tossed a card on the middle pile of a coffee table. "Change the color to . . . yellow."

Andre inspected his playing hand and slammed his cards. "Gah!" He huffed and puffed with frustration.

Eva studied him with concern, stepped into the guest bedroom, and closed the door. She wove her hands and smirked. "I accept your apology."

Her mom peered at her as if she were an alien from Mars. "Apology? What apology?"

"For Sunday about Mrs. Flowers." Eva's countenance fell. "Isn't that what this is about?"

Her mother cackled. "If you think I'm giving an apology, you've got another thing coming, honey."

Eva's stomach knotted. *Oh, God. Here we go again.* She squeezed her arms around herself as if trying to contain the burst of rage she felt fueling inside of her.

Her mother walked over to the dresser, opened the bottom drawer, and pulled out the three textbooks Caleb gave her.

Eva's chest tightened so much she couldn't feel her heart beating. She closed her eyes a split second and a sense of vertigo passed over her.

"The Art Institute of Charlotte called about their spring semester program, and while I did the laundry, I discovered your little secret. What are you doing hiding these books?" Her mom was stone-faced, glaring at her. "And where did you get them?"

Eva's chin bobbed. "I knew you'd try to talk me out of going back to college to become an interior designer, just like you did when I was younger. And the books . . . I got them from an old classmate."

Her mother crossed her arms. "Who?"

Eva gulped and straightened. "I got them from Caleb Williams. He's an interior designer and real estate agent. He allowed me to use them to study."

Her mom raised her eyebrow. "Have you considered he may be using you?"

"Using me? I don't know what you're talking about, Mom." Terror crossed Eva's face.

"Don't act ignorant with me, Eva. I'm talking about being generous and kind to . . . womanize you," her mother said, "either that or to make someone else he's interested in jealous."

Eva grimaced and shook her head. "Caleb wouldn't do that to me."

"How do you know? When he was a teenager, he didn't exactly have a good reputation." Her mother tossed the books on the twin-sized bed beside clean, folded towels and studied her reaction.

Eva glanced from the bed to her mom again. "Maybe not, but he's always been kind to me, too nice to admit he wasn't interested in me when we were kids."

"Who says he's not interested in you now?"

Eva gagged at her mother's startling question, trying to catch her breath. "Why do you keep making accusations? You're just trying to prevent me from pursuing interior design." Fury ignited her as she gathered the books on the bed in her arms. "You know, I've got all this pressure on me! I'm always doing something for someone—"

"You're always doing something? What about me?" her mother countered, interpreting. "Who's the one always cleaning and cooking around here?"

"Well, why are you complaining? You never liked Mrs. Flowers doing it. I've let you stay in our house, and helping with chores is the least you can do to pay me back." Eva turned her back and marched from the guestroom, her mother trailing her from behind.

Skye and Andre were in shock with their mouths open, observing the intense argument.

"Eva, come back here!" Her mother pulled her arm, yanking her toward her. "Eva, listen!"

Eva gave her mom a dirty look. "No, you listen, Mom! You made a promise to keep your critical opinions to yourself! You're my mother and I thought to take your word and let you stay in our home, but I guess you were lying the whole time." Her eyes swam with tears, shaking her head. "You never think I can do it, do you? The least you can do is encourage me, instead of criticizing what I'm doing!"

Her mom frowned. "Where are you going?"

"I don't know, but I can't stand another second of your insolence!" Eva exited and slammed the front door.

Now it seemed like only one person understood her—Caleb Williams.

• CHAPTER 32 •

Eva

Saturday Evening

"Eva? What are you doing here?" Caleb said, holding his doorknob.

Eva held his three books with tear-streaked cheeks. "I came to return your books. I think I shouldn't go back to college, but mostly because of Andre and my son." She sighed. "They need me more than they ever did before, and I imagine it'll be harder to continue with my studies after my mother heads back to Seattle."

Caleb waved a hand. "Nonsense, you can keep them. When things simmer down, you can pick up on your studies again."

"Are you sure?" Eva asked.

Caleb nodded. "Sure. I don't use them anyway." He studied her disturbed expression. "Are you okay?"

"It's my mom." Eva hung her head.

"Do you wanna come in and talk about it? Maybe I can relate to it about my dad. I'm a good listener."

Eva sucked her teeth. "It's not a good idea. Besides, I don't wanna bother you."

"Nothing you say will bother me, Eva. We're friends."

Eva arched a brow. "We are?"

"Well, sure we are," Caleb said. "Now, come out of the cold and sit down."

Eva gave a half-smile. "Well, all right."

Soothing warmth embraced her the second she entered his house. She sat on a Chesterfield brown leather sofa in front of a brown-and-black marble table. Her eyes scanned across her environment in the living room.

Blue flames danced on artificial logs in an electric fireplace. Tribal masks hung on the walls, and knick-knacks of elephants, giraffes, and lions decorated the TV stand, bookshelf, and wine chest. Looking around, Eva felt like she had left North Carolina and stepped into an African Safari.

Caleb joined her on the couch and closed his HP laptop on the table. "Excuse me, I was skimming through house listings in the area when you arrived." He grabbed a dish filled with gold-wrapped Ferrero Rocher chocolates and offered it to Eva. "Would you like one? They're delicious."

Eva shook her head shyly. "Oh, no, thank you." She placed the books on the table and looked around again.

"You have a beautiful home. It has a woman's touch."

"I'm pleased you like it." Caleb put the candy dish back on the table. "So, what's going on between you and your mother?"

Eva puffed out a breath and leaned back against the smooth curves of the sofa. "We don't get along well. She's always interfering in my business. She's been homeless over a year, and I allowed her to stay in my house if she respected my boundaries. Of course, she butted in like she always does."

She emphasized her next statement, hitting one hand in the other. "I mean, I was clear, assertive, and everything, but she still broke her promise." She licked her lips, thinking deeply. "It's like she believes she's entitled to because I'm her daughter and she raised me. Sometimes I think it's because she's unhappy, and she assumes whatever I work to achieve will lead to heartache, like what happened with my father."

Eva hung her head. "My parents broke up because my mom wasn't welcomed in my father's Italian family."

"So, you're half Italian?" Caleb said, rubbing his chin. "I always wondered what your heritage was. I mean, I knew you were mixed with something." He clenched his teeth, afraid of offending her. "Sorry, I didn't mean to phrase it like you're a dog breed or—"

Eva chuckled and glanced at him. "Don't worry, I get your point." She sighed. "My father's from Rome, Italy.

He was a handsome and talented landscape artist, Mom said. It's all I know about him. I gave my son his name Andrew when he was born."

"That's nice. I'd love to meet your son someday," Caleb replied, smiling. "I'm sure he's cute as a button."

Eva giggled. "He is, and he likes to make me laugh."

"I bet he got his looks from you," Caleb remarked.

Eva crinkled her nose. "Perhaps a little." She stared ahead with a dreamy smile. "I think he mostly got them from his father."

"It's been years since I've seen Andre," Caleb said. "Maybe I could visit him sometime if he'll be willing to see me."

Eva smiled and placed her shoulder-length, wavy hair behind her ears. "Sure, I think he'd like that."

Caleb stood and grabbed two shot glasses from the rustic mantel above the fireplace. He perched back on the couch and put the glasses on the table. "Care to have a drink?" He handled a bottle of Calvados beside his laptop and filled one cup to the brim, casting a sidelong glance at her.

"Oh, no thanks. I don't drink." Eva clasped her hands in her lap.

Caleb cocked his head with a playful grin. "Aw, come on. A little drink can't hurt. Besides, it's practically fruit juice. I don't drink heavy, nasty stuff like hard liquor."

"What is it?" Eva said.

"It's called Calvados, a French fruit brandy made from pears and apples. I had my first drink when I was nineteen at one of my father's business meetings. It's my favorite. I'm sure you'll like it too." He held the glass of brandy. "Here, smell it."

Eva took a cautious sniff and bit her lip. A Christian woman and teetotaler, she had never consumed anything stronger than a can of ginger ale. Her mother would be furious if she found out she drank alcohol. "Well, it smells good, but it wouldn't be safe. I have to drive home and—in fact, I should get going now." She jumped to her feet and flinched backward.

"What's the rush?" Caleb gave her a disapproved look. "Ever since you were a teenager, you've always been uptight and afraid to try new things. You hardly ever let yourself have fun. You've let your mother dictate your whole life. You know, parents aren't always right."

Eva thought about what Caleb said and found some truth. She was always a goody-two-shoes, always playing it safe and sticking her nose in books, the main reasons she didn't have many friends growing up as a kid.

"You're right." She plopped back down. "I'm a boring person."

"I don't think so," Caleb said, staring at her. "You're . . . just afraid, but you don't have to be. You can trust me. Chill out, it's only one drink." He handed her the shot glass.

Eva took the glass from Caleb and glanced at him with a nervous smile. She knew she shouldn't drink, but it felt good to make a rash decision without her mother talking her out of it. She gulped the brandy and giggled, already feeling the alcohol work its way through her system. "That *was* good. It tastes kind of like apple cider."

"I told you," Caleb said, grinning. "You want another one?"

"Hey, why not?" Eva said in a carefree tone.

Caleb refilled her glass and poured in the other for himself. "How about we propose a toast?" He held up his shot glass. "For the times you helped me pass my vocabulary and geometry tests."

"Cheers!" Eva laughed and tapped her glass to Caleb's. They drank from their glasses together, but two simple drinks had become two others for Eva.

Caleb reclined with an arm around the sofa, crossing one foot over his thigh.

"I was expecting Tasha Burke at our class reunion last year," Eva said. "You and she were close. What happened between you two? I thought maybe y'all got married."

Caleb shrugged and swiped the residue from the brim of his glass with his thumb. "Tasha, she became a fashion model and lives in New York. We went out a few times, but later I left to avoid seeing her with another man."

"Oh, I'm sorry. I shouldn't have asked." Eva cringed inwardly.

Caleb chuckled and scratched his temple. "No, it's okay. I like how my life is. Things wouldn't have worked out between us anyway. We're not the teenagers we used to be, and things changed."

There was a moment of silence, and then Caleb spoke again, "Eva?"

She faced him and placed her shot glass on the table. "Yes?"

"I know you won't believe this, but I think you're so beautiful. Andre's a lucky man. You've changed so much, and it makes me ashamed of how I treated you in the past. I knew you had a crush on me. I'm sorry. I should've told you the truth, but I was too embarrassed."

"The truth about what?" Eva asked with suspicion.

Caleb sighed. "You know, how I felt about you back then?"

"Oh, that." Eva moved her hair to one shoulder and lowered her head.

"I liked you, Eva," Caleb added unexpectedly.

Eva raised her head and studied his eyes in awe. "You did?"

"Yeah . . . a lot," Caleb whispered and scooted closer to her on the couch.

Eva gulped and sprung from the sofa, nearly losing her balance.

Caleb grimaced. "What's the matter?"

“I need to go home. It’s . . . late,” Eva said and smiled timidly.

Caleb smiled but didn’t pressure her to stay longer. “Okay, we can chat another time. I’ll show you out.”

“Thanks.” Eva strode to the door and stepped outside in the frigid night.

“Don’t forget the books,” Caleb mentioned. “I said you can have them.” Holding the textbooks before her, he lifted his brow with a wry smile.

“Oh, yeah. I forgot.” Eva blushed and plastered a timid grin, taking the books from his strong, ebony hands. Her stomach throbbed with a warm, fuzzy feeling.

Caleb looked concerned. “Uh, do you think you can drive?”

“Yeah, I’ll be fine,” Eva said, clutching the books to her chest. “Good night, and thanks again.”

“No, problem.” Caleb watched her leave and shut the door.

Eva drove away, but she would go to a convenience store before returning home.

“That’ll be three dollars and nine cents,” the cashier lady in a red T-shirt said.

Eva fished the total out of her clutch purse. All she had left was change. Her expression winced, and she giggled.

"Sorry . . ." She placed a handful of quarters, nickels, and dimes on the checkout counter and sifted through them with her forefinger. "There's one dollar . . . two dollars . . . three dollars . . . and ten."

The cashier scraped three rows of quarters and a dime off the counter and wore an amused smile. "Thank you, ma'am." She popped open her drawer, dropped the coins in their proper slots, took out a penny, and ripped the paper receipt. "Here you go. One cent is your change."

"Thank you." Eva took the penny and her receipt. She snatched the pack of spearmint Icebreakers she bought from the counter and exited the swing door.

Eva settled in her car under the well-lit gas station and gazed inside the Circle K store. *Am I crazy? God forgive me.* She must've been out of her mind to drink and drive, and especially after arguing with her mom. But maybe what she needed was a little booze to ease her stress load. One thing for sure, she felt better than she had in days.

Spending time with Caleb was nerve-racking, but also comforting at the same time. He understood how she was and what she was feeling. She didn't know whether he told her the truth, but as silly as it was, it thrilled her a little he said he liked her when they were teenagers.

Eva opened the pack of mints and tossed two in her mouth. Her mother had a nose like a bloodhound. But perhaps if her breath smelt fresh, her mom wouldn't be able to tell she drank brandy. She cranked her engine when her cellphone rang. She picked it up from the passenger seat and answered the call, confused. "Hello?"

"Hey, Eva, it's Nadine."

"Nadine?" Eva frowned and shifted her eyes. "How did you get my number?"

"Sorry, I got it from the class reunion. The sign-up sheet, remember?"

Eva thought back for a second and massaged her forehead. She rubbed her hand down her face and winced, feeling a migraine coming on. "Oh, yeah, I remember. So, what's up?"

"I was just calling to ask you to visit Sammie in the hospital with me. She said she wants to see you and I thought later we could hang out and have lunch at a new vegan restaurant afterward. Maybe next Saturday?"

Eva blinked in disbelief, puzzled by Nadine's friendly invitation. From the look of it, she was the answer to one of her prayers—a much-needed outlet from her busy life. Eva smiled. "Uh, sure, I'll try to fit it in my schedule."

Excitement filled Nadine's voice over the phone line. "Awesome! I'll see you next Saturday around noon."

"Okay, great. Bye." Eva hung up and mused over her weekend with Nadine. First, it was Caleb, and then it was her female rivals. She never expected to spend time with the same girls who bullied her when she was in high school, and certainly not in a pleasant and relaxing way. Things were different now, and she couldn't help being suspicious of everyone's motives.

Of course, she was curious and concerned about Sammie too. She was a pretty, glamorous cheerleader with long blonde hair, so the thought of seeing her sick with cancer was hard for her to fathom. She shifted her gear into drive, pulled from under the gas station, and careened down the street. The ride back wasn't long, and Eva was grateful. She swerved a little on the road, but she managed to safely pulled into the driveway in one piece.

Knowing her mother was probably waiting for her in the living room, she dumped four more mints into her mouth. She figured her best bet was going through the patio door. Maybe she can sneak through without being noticed. Eva got out of her car and snuck behind the house in the backyard.

It was either that or burn in humiliation.

Luckily, the patio door was unlocked. Eva slipped her thin frame through the door opening into the pitch-black kitchen, rattling the long, shading blinds. Either someone forgot to lock it, or she was falling into her mother's trap. Eva slid the door shut and fastened the latch.

Like a teenager who passed her curfew, she tiptoed toward the arched entryway to the living room. The light switched on in the kitchen before she made it mid-way. Eva turned around and saw her irritated mother in her soft white robe and slippers.

Her mother pursed her lips and crossed her arms over

her chest, tapping her foot.

"Mom, before you hound me, don't forget I'm a grown woman responsible for making *my* own decisions and you're in *my* house," Eva stated.

Her mom smirked. "Then why'd you come through the patio door?" She made a mocking snigger and scuffed a couple of steps forward in her slippers, her fists on her hips. "I'm not gonna ask where you've been, Eva." She sniffed her daughter's breath and frowned. "Spearmint?"

Eva darted her eyes and nodded. "Uh, yeah. I came from the store."

Her mother gave her a once-over. "I tucked *your son* Andy in bed, and Skye came over briefly to help with Andre. I'm going to sleep. You won't have to put up with me too much longer. I'll be gone soon. Good night." She strode past Eva and paused, adding another remark. "Oh, there's aspirin in the medicine cabinet, in case you'll need it."

Eva cringed with embarrassment as her mother strutted out of the kitchen. Though she was thankful her mom didn't nitpick her as much, guilt consumed her from within. Drinking wasn't something she was accustomed to doing, and part of her wished Caleb hadn't influenced her to take a swig. The other half of her was contrary to what her mind knew was wrong, as temptation and morality battled within her.

She wanted to visit Caleb again.

• CHAPTER 33 •

Eva

Next Saturday

Visiting Sammie Cooper was as hard for Eva as the time she first saw Andre lying in his hospital bed. Her memory of how Sammie looked from high school had disappeared the minute she stepped inside her treatment room. She was a completely different person. Her curly, blonde hair had been shaven as her chemotherapy was making it fall off her head. She was wearing a Pittsburgh Steelers ball cap to cover her baldness, a thin hospital gown, and an IV tube was taped on one of her hands.

Her peaches-and-cream complexion had faded to a dull gray that made her appear older than she was, and crow's feet creased her aquamarine eyes.

Eva's mouth was buttoned shut. She didn't know what to say other than a casual "Hi," and a nervous "How are you?" Nadine eased the silent tension, starting a conversation of old memories from high school, and Eva was almost glad that she did—*almost.* While listening to her former bullies talk, she felt like they were making her a laughingstock until they apologized for all the pranks they did.

"We were bad girls, Eva," Sammie said. "But trust me, it was only because we envied you for being smart. It had nothing to do with how you looked." She reclined on the pillows behind her back.

"I'm sorry about your cancer," Eva said finally.

Sammie shrugged. "Yeah, well, if I recover out of this nightmare, I'll take it for a lesson not to mess around so much anymore." Sorrow clouded her baggy eyes. "You don't know how well you've got it, Eva. I wish I were in your shoes right now."

Compassion pricked Eva's heart. She stood from the edge of the hospital bed and embraced Sammie. "I'll be praying for you. Be strong, girl, okay? You're a fighter. I know that better than anyone." She smiled and closed her eyes as a tear fell down her cheek.

Sammie chuckled and sniffled, hugging her. "Mm-hmm, thanks, Eva."

"We'd better go," Nadine said, glancing at her watch. "I have a meeting with a client at two."

"All right, but don't you forget about me," Sammie replied, pouting like a child.

"I won't." Nadine laughed, walked over, and likewise gave Sammie a goodbye hug.

Then Eva and Nadine waved and left.

The teenage, African American waitress brought over two plastic cups of green goo to their table and walked off in her orange apron to the side food bar. Most people looking at Eva's thin, petite frame would assume she's a vegan, but she had never eaten in this type of restaurant before.

She stared disturbingly at her cup of lime, kiwi, and spinach smoothie and picked it up, examining the drink over as if it were a chemistry beaker. Nadine had ordered Eva one of her favorite drinks to try out for herself.

Her redhead classmate giggled. "Will you stop looking it over like it's a witch's evil potion? It's good and healthy for you." She shook her head and slurped from the straw of her cup.

Eva tittered and blushed. "Sorry." She took a careful sip and smacked her lips.

Nadine inclined her head, raising a brow. "Well?"

"Well, I guess it's okay," Eva said and sipped from her straw again. "But I'm not a fan of kiwi."

"What? You've got to be kidding me."

Eva twitched her mouth. "No, I'm not. I don't like the

little black seeds in them— how they're kind of grainy in your mouth."

"Oh, well, that's unfortunate," Nadine said. "So, how'd you like our last class reunion?"

"It was okay," Eva replied. "A bit noisy with the music playing, but it was fun and nice seeing everyone."

The teenage waitress dropped off their serving baskets of veggie wraps with sweet potato fries. "Here's your food. I hope y'all enjoy."

"Thank you, ma'am. We will," Nadine said.

The waitress left to take another group of customers' orders at a round table.

"I bet you weren't expecting Caleb Williams," Nadine said and snickered.

Eva pressed her lips and fiddled with the straw in her cup. "You're right, I wasn't."

"You two talked and seemed to hit it off," Nadine said.

"Actually, it was kind of him talking to me," Eva corrected. She cocked her head. "I was a little nervous and didn't know too much of what to say to him."

"Absence makes the heart grow fonder," Nadine said, smiling.

"Well, I don't know about that," Eva replied, "but we're still friends."

Nadine nibbled on a fry, studying Eva. "You could seriously be a Miss America or supermodel. It's amazing how people change. You look so much prettier. I mean, not that you weren't beautiful back then, but—"

"I get your point, Nadine," Eva said, rolling her eyes. "I've made a couple of changes for the better. It was hard growing up on welfare with my mom, but things improved after marriage; at least, for a time." She sighed wearily. "But then I went back to square one again."

"Oh, so, you're married?" Nadine enlarged her green eyes and wiped mayonnaise from a corner of her mouth.

"Yeah. I'm married to Andre Lucas. Frankie, didn't tell you?"

"No," Nadine said, "I thought you were still single. So, how's married life treated you over the years?"

"Ups and downs," Eva said and grabbed a fry from her basket. "More ups than downs though."

"Humph, that's funny," Nadine said casually, "for me it's been more downs than ups." She let out a slow exhale, looped her red, chin-length hair behind her ears, and crossed her arms on the table. She peered at Eva with wonder. "Have you ever wished you could rewind time and start over again?"

Eva cocked her head. "Sure, I know the feeling. Why do you ask?"

"Just wondering." Nadine perked up and changed the subject. "Hey, let's go to the mall after lunch. Today they have special sales going on at a lot of the clothing stores."

Eva cringed. "Oh, no, I shouldn't—"

"Come on, Eva," Nadine interrupted. "You've got to live it up. You don't always have to study or read books all the time. Have fun and get some fresh air. Give yourself a break," Nadine said.

"Well, okay," Eva said shyly, "but only to look around, not to buy anything."

"Don't worry, Eva," Nadine said, "anything you want, it's all on me." She touched Eva's wrist and giggled, shaking her. "We're gonna have *so* much fun!"

Eva tittered and wore a weak smile. She knew how she was in a clothing store, and she wasn't confident she could restrain herself after being deprived from shopping as she pleased for so long.

"Hey, Eva, look at these sunglasses They're *so* cute!" Nadine shouted across the store.

Eva looked away from a rack of coats and walked over to Nadine at a display shelf of chic sunglasses.

"This pair totally looks like you." Nadine grinned and handed her a pair of dark shades.

Eva tried them and checked herself in the mirror, fingering her long, dark hair down her shoulder. "They're nice, but why buy them in the winter?" She smiled and slipped them off.

"Are you kidding? I buy summer clothes year-round,

especially during discount sales." Nadine put on a pair of red sunglasses and smiled. "What do you think? Are they me?"

Eva wore an uncertain look and shrugged, unenthusiastic. "Uh, sure, I guess so."

Nadine pulled down the shades to her nose and looked at her. "Honestly, Eva. You need to get out more."

"That's hard to do sometimes," Eva said, "especially when you have a disabled husband and a toddler to take care of."

Nadine took off the sunglasses and placed them back on the rack. "Disabled husband? What happened to him?"

"Andre suffered a car accident and had a brain injury the night of our anniversary last year," Eva said.

Nadine gasped and frowned. "Oh, no. I'm so sorry, Eva. How's he been doing?"

"Well, he's gradually recovering physically," Eva said, "but mentally, he's been dealing with amnesia and some depression. I phoned his grandfather and asked him to keep Andre on his farm for a couple of days with his caregiver Skye. Maybe being around the farm animals will help him feel better."

"Yeah, hopefully." Nadine sighed. "So, did you see anything you want? I promise I'll get it for you."

"No, I'm good," Eva replied.

Nadine picked up a pile of dresses and T-shirts on hangers she found for herself and tossed them over her other arm. "All right, I'll cash out and then we can go."

Eva watched her redhead classmate as she strode toward the checkout lane, getting the sense something about her wasn't quite right. Nadine was struggling desperately to fill her undeniable void with the fads and pleasures of the world. She was a fun, outgoing, and exciting person, but was dealing with a problem, a relatable situation Eva knew all too well.

A broken heart.

• CHAPTER 34 •

Andre

Andre was falling.

He hollered and swung his arms, hoping for something to break his fall. He landed and opened his eyes.

It was dark. Very dark.

Gray smoke arrayed the blackness.

A woman's scream echoed. Her voice was familiar. He heard it before, but he couldn't place from whom it belonged. He struggled to his feet and peered in the distance.

There was a scorching lake—orange, steamy, glowing lava mixed with cakes of ash.

Stepping stones rowed across it to a large, rocky cliff.

A young woman in white was at the peak. Her wrists tied; her slender body chained to a chair. He couldn't see her face, as it was veiled by her hair. She called for help again, fighting to break loose.

Not a soul was in sight—but Andre.

He had to save her.

Andre coughed from the smoke and stepped on the first stone. It sank. He panicked and leaped to another stone and another as they sank, trying not to lose his balance. He made it halfway to her and smiled.

Hold on! I'm coming! His voice echoed, and the beast heard him.

It knew he would come for her.

The ground shook when Andre reached the last stone.

He widened his eyes at the horrific sight before him. He could barely breathe, and he couldn't move.

A gigantic king cobra burst up from the cliff like a jack-in-the-box, wrapping its tail around the woman's chair, hindering him from saving her. It was multicolored with red, glowing eyes. It turned its hooded head and looked down at him, licking its split tongue.

Then it struck down to bite him.

He cried and blocked his face with his arms, his voice fading in the darkness.

Andre yelled from his sleep and stared at the dark ceiling. Breathing rapidly, he gulped and tugged his sweaty, white sleeveless undershirt from his chest, recalling his whereabouts. He frowned and tried to piece together his nightmare. Although he loved many kinds of animals, he despised snakes. Unable to interpret the meaning of the dream, he shut his eyes and released a long sigh, falling back into sleep.

Sunrise came, and Skye knocked and entered the master bedroom. "Good morning, Andre." He flicked on a bedside lamp.

"Ugh . . ." Andre squinted at the bright light and held his right hand over his eyes. His paralysis disability was a conjoined twin that followed him everywhere and his life had become the same routine. He was tired of feeling worthless. What was the point in being alive? He saw no purpose anymore, nothing to make him feel useful.

"Come on, man. It's time to get up," Skye said, pulling the blanket off Andre. "You've got a big day ahead of you. Eva called your grandpa. You'll be staying with him a few days."

Andre sat up in bed, supporting himself with his arms behind his back. Unless he looked down, he wouldn't know his legs were there. He hated having to use a wheelchair to help him get around. He wanted to stand on his two feet and walk like most anyone else. His leg exercises kept him from getting stiff, but he still hadn't regained a hundred percent mobility—complete freedom to get around as he pleased.

He screwed up his face. "What?"

"You're going over to Grandpa Ricardo's farm," Skye said. "Your wife phoned him. She thinks if you stay busy it'll cheer you up." He rolled Andre's wheelchair close to the bed and locked the brakes. "For starters, you can transfer yourself this time. I'll stay if you need me."

Andre wore a weak look. "But . . . I can't."

"You won't know unless you try, man. Here, using this will help." Skye placed the wooden slide board on the bed. "You have most of your upper body strength from doing your core and arm exercises, Andre. Just remember what I taught you. You can do it."

Andre puffed up his cheeks and exhaled slowly. He gripped the slide board and positioned it under his buttocks and partly in his wheelchair. He bit his lower lip and tucked his flimsy hands under his long legs, adjusting them along the bedside. Andre scooted his bottom across the board inch by inch until he got into the wheelchair and yanked the board out from under him.

"You did it!" Skye grinned.

Andre pursed his lips and rolled his eyes with attitude. "Maybe, but it took almost forever."

"You know your weekly schedule," Skye said. "We'll begin your warm-up exercises after you shower and get dressed."

"All right." Andre grabbed his Velcro-strapped portable urinal from the nightstand and attached it to his chair in his lap. Then he took his gray supplies pouch, unzipped it, and placed it on the bed.

Skye wore a wry smile. "Looks like you're a trained pro. I'll give you your privacy. Call me if you need help." Skye exited and closed the door.

Andre yawned and sighed. Emptying in a plastic container made him feel awkward. He remembered being uncomfortable as the bedside nurses catheterized him in the hospital. Now, having more liberty for himself, he didn't take the small things he could do for granted, but losing sight of what he couldn't do was still a hard test.

"I'm done!" Andre called.

Skye cracked open the door and peeked inside.

Andre leaned forward and pulled up the back waistline of his pajama pants.

"Okay." Skye took the filled container to the bathroom. Meanwhile, Andre gathered his clothes for the day from a bottom dresser, choosing what to wear. Someone knocked, and he checked behind him who it was.

Eva gave a smile, looking in from behind the door. "Good morning."

"Morning," Andre replied.

"Did Skye tell you about Grandpa Ricardo?" Eva asked.

Andre nodded. "Yes, he told me."

"You'll need to pack clothes in a suitcase." Eva entered and opened the large, side closet, taking out a navy-blue suitcase with wheels. She laid the bag on the bed and unzipped it.

Hope sprung in Andre's heart as he observed her. He had longed for this day to come, overwhelmed of being a burden to Eva and her constant looking after him and his needs. With his departure from home, did he accomplish his goal? Had he finally gotten Eva to give up on him? He needed to find out.

"You want . . . to get rid of me?" Andre said.

Eva paused and frowned. "Of course not. This is a get-away vacation to help keep your mind off your troubles, and maybe improve your memory."

Andre went poker-faced. "Oh, okay."

"I'm about to go to work," Eva said. "I'll take you over at Grandpa Ricardo's farm this afternoon. If you want, you can pack before I get home."

Andre placed his long-sleeve gray shirt, underwear, and jeans in his lap and rolled himself in his wheelchair. "I'm taking a shower." He sighed and left the bedroom. What else can he do? Nothing seemed to convince Eva to call the stress of her life quits. Both highly impressed and deeply frustrated, one thing was left to lessen her work-load and relieve her of him.

Killing himself.

As they passed the dead, golden stalks of cornfields, Andre stared out the passenger window of Eva's car. He looked to his right at an old wooden house with a collapsed roof. His eyes didn't want to leave it the farther it got in the distance as a moment of déjà vu came over him. Had he seen it before? Andre turned his attention to a white farmhouse and red barn as Eva cruised into a wide, healthy-green pasture, enclosed by a barbed-wire fence.

She shifted the gear into park and turned off the engine. "Look familiar?"

"No. Just from the pictures you showed me." Andre blinked and rummaged through his hazy thoughts again.

A flock of chickens behind a wired coop beside the farmhouse pecked in the dirt and flapped their wings. Grandpa Ricardo stood inside the cage, feeding them grain from a tin bucket.

"*Hola! ¡Buenas tares, Papa!*" Eva climbed out of her car.

Grandpa Ricardo put down his bucket and waved. "*Hola, Eva!*"

Eva ran over and hugged Andre's grandfather.

Andre observed them discussing matters, but they were too far away to hear what they were saying. They walked over to Eva's car in a side hug. Grandpa Ricardo helped Andre into his manual wheelchair, and Eva took Andre's luggage from the trunk.

A ramp for Andre to wheel himself into the house was built on the side of the porch. Like his own home, it would take time before he got used to living on a farm. But when he inhaled the earthy air, he became comforted by the great outdoors.

"Welcome back, *nieto*. Guess you'll be living with me a few days, eh?" Grandpa Ricardo grinned.

Andre cocked his head, shading the radiant sun from his face. "Can you . . . tell me my parents, please?"

Grandpa Ricardo tilted his cowboy hat back a tad and slipped a handkerchief from a pocket of his striped shirt. "Your parents lived in Philadelphia. Their names were Derek and Marie, my daughter. They fought and did bad things. I took you in when you were five and raised you on my farm." He wiped his dirty forehead. "Perhaps you'll feel useful here. There's a lot to do."

"Maybe," Andre said with a half-shrug.

Eva let out a slow exhale, dissipating her tears. "Well, I better go before Andy has a fit. Skye will come over to the farm tomorrow morning to help with Andre's daily exercises and speech therapy." She started to leave, but turned around and hugged Andre. She hadn't embraced him in weeks, afraid of invading his space.

Andre hesitantly wrapped his arms around her and closed his eyes. For once, out of nowhere, he felt a strong connection with Eva and wanted to stay in her arms, his hurt feelings rising to the surface. Although he couldn't recall marrying her, he was drawn to her beauty since he arose from his coma, and her compassion and generosity made him admire her. But with his angry outbursts and ailments, he didn't feel he deserved her affection.

"Goodbye, Andre. I'll miss you," Eva said, looking into his eyes.

Andre gulped a hard knot. *Go ahead, Andre. Tell her . . . tell her how you feel.* His heart grieved and called out to him, but he restrained his emotions. "Yeah, uh . . . bye, Eva."

His wife waved and left from the porch.

After she sped down the country highway, Grandpa Ricardo introduced Andre to Carlos and Hank, his hired hands. The two men worked for his grandpa's corn farm and were clearing the dead stalks for the new crop season. His grandpa also showed him the farm animals in the barn, teaching him their Spanish names. There were two spotted cows or *vacas* named Wilma and Thelma, and two pigs or *cerdas* named Prissy and Twinkle. But Andre's favorite part was when he met the four horses or *caballos* as his grandfather called them.

Grandpa Ricardo named them unique names according to their colors. Two of the horses were male and the other two were female. Black Thunder or *Trueno Negro* was an American Quarter with a silky, dark mane and tail that sparkled in the sun. He was the top dog of the pack, the one his grandfather said Andre went horseback riding with in the pasture when he was a teenager.

Gold Star or *Estrella de Oro* was a Colonial Spanish Mustang and a sweetheart with her tan coat and brown mane and tail. His grandfather told him she was the horse Eva liked to ride when she came by to visit. Gray Cloud or *Nube Gris*, a gray thoroughbred, was stubborn, compared to his other four-legged companions. But he was big, strong, and dependable. Last, there was Brown Sunset or *Puesta de sol marrón*. She was an Arabian filly and the youngest of the group, always prancing around when out of her stable and searching for adventure. With his grandfather, Andre helped groom the horses, learning how to brush them and clean their hooves.

Later, his grandfather made Mexican black bean soup and buttered biscuits for dinner. While listening to his grandpa share stories from his youth, Andre had two bowls and two biscuits. Ever since he received some use of his hands, his appetite increased, or maybe he was trying to suffocate the grief and shame he felt inside.

He was thankful his grandfather and the other men noticed nothing off about him. He didn't want anyone to worry. He wanted everyone to be happy, especially Eva. His first day on the farm went better than he expected, nearly forgetting about fulfilling his secret plan.

But going away was what he concluded he had to do—what he thought was best for his family. It would be for Eva's peace and happiness and the chance for her to find a mentally stable man to give Andrew a better father. As smart and graceful as she was, he was confident she would attract another man and manage without him. When he came home, he felt like he was experiencing the world for the first time. Life and its most basic needs and concepts were hard to understand. Not knowing how to love, he didn't have the proper skills to be a husband and father anymore. Besides, what can he do for them anyway? What can he give? And how can he improve and benefit their lives?

These questions troubled him as he thought of the years ahead and the probable fate he would never walk or remember them. He lay in bed and aimlessly stared at the moonlight on the ceiling, his mind consumed with hideous thoughts and methods of death and dying.

It had to be simple and quick—something he could do without having to stand. Once his solution materialized, he closed his eyes, premediating the execution of his actions. Hours upon hours later, Andre tossed and turned, haunted in his sleep by the cobra snake.

The nightmare began again.

• CHAPTER 35 •

Andre

Wednesday, Dec. 19th

Grandpa Ricardo knocked on the door and stuck his head with his gray cowboy hat on in Andre's bedroom. He twitched his thick mustache and smiled. "*¡Buenos Dias, nieto!* How did you sleep?"

Andre looked over his bare shoulder at him. "Just fine. The bed was okay."

His grandfather made a snorting laugh. "A bit too short for your legs, eh? I'm sorry, *nieto*. I promise I'll get a bigger one put in for you the next time you visit me. I'm going to the fruit stand down the road to get some fresh produce. Do you want to come with me?"

Andre raised his head and glanced at his grandpa's reflection in the doorway behind him. *Perfect timing. I'll do it today.* "Uh, no, you go on. I'll . . . be fine here alone."

Grandpa Ricardo frowned. "Are you sure?"

"Yeah," Andre said with a little smile. "Skye . . . he'll be over soon anyway."

"All right," Grandpa Ricardo said. "I'll be back in a few minutes. See you later."

"Yeah, bye." Andre took a gray, V-neck sweater and a clean white undershirt from his suitcase.

His grandfather smiled and closed the door.

Andre's smile faded as he gravely stared back at the young, shirtless man in the reflection of the dresser mirror. He looked so tired around his reddish-brown eyes. Maybe the bed was comfortable, but he hadn't slept well last night. Misery kept him company, trapped in a dark pit of self-loathing he struggled to climb out of.

He wanted to let his tears flow, but he couldn't seem to break. Why couldn't he cry? Maybe he was in denial and thought his accident was a dream. He wasn't certain, and he wasn't about to find out. Andre didn't care about that. All he cared about was setting himself free of his and others' pain, fulfilling his private mission.

Andre slipped his sleeveless undershirt over his head and tugged it down. He put on his sweater and looked at his suitcase again. *Do it, Andre. Go on. There's nothing to live for. Just do it.* His teeth chattered and his heart thumped in his chest. He lifted the top of his suitcase and unzipped the interior pouch of it, taking out his belt.

It was now or never.

Andre held the belt in his trembling hands and looked at himself in the mirror again. He contorted his face in disgust and looped the leather belt around his neck. Andre pulled one end through the gold bucket and tightened the belt against his skin, cutting off his airway.

A car drove up outside to the house.

Andre peeked through the curtain and saw Skye walking toward the house from his Jeep Wrangler. Annoyed, he yanked the curtain closed, squeezed his eyes shut, and resumed the lethal suffocation, clinging to the belt. The pigment of his skin darkened from maroon to a deep purple. Pressure built in his eye sockets, cheeks, and neck, making him gag. His heart pounded and his brain felt as if it would explode.

It was nearly done—almost over.

"WHAT ARE YOU DOING?" Skye hollered, barging through the door. "ANDRE, STOP! STOP, MAN! STOP!" He rushed over and pulled at Andre's stubborn hands, fighting to loosen his grip. "ANDRE, LET GO!"

For a split moment, Andre growled and refused, but quickly moving toward his last breath, a burst of petrifying fear made him give up. He removed his hands and fluttered his eyelids, coughing uncontrollably as Skye unraveled the belt from his neck.

"WHAT'S WRONG WITH YOU? ARE YOU CRAZY?" Skye said.

A dead silence lingered as Andre rested his head on the

back of his wheelchair, wheezing and gasping for air.

"You regain use of your hands, and you try to kill yourself!" Skye said. He grimaced and tossed the belt aside on the bed. "What's gotten into you, Andre? Why did you do this?"

Andre closed his eyes and turned his head from side to side, still catching his breath. His thoughts were like a pile of scattered puzzle pieces, all over the place without making sense. He moaned in his emotional pain. "I . . . I don't know. I-I thought . . . I just thought . . . I don't know. I guess . . . I wasn't thinking." He hung his head.

"That's the problem," Skye scolded. "I can't believe you tried to kill yourself. That's the most selfish thing anyone can ever do—try to take the easy way out of life. I mean, seriously, man! Do you think my brain injury recovery was easy? Everybody's got problems. It's not just about you all the time."

"I know, and I'm sorry!" Andre lowered his volume to a calm whisper. "I'm sorry . . ."

"Don't tell me you're sorry," Skye said, "you tell your wife and son who love you."

Andre's body calmed back to normal as the pressure vanished from his face and head. He sheepishly glanced at Skye as if he were a little child. "What . . . what is love?" He fluttered his eyelids and studied Skye, waiting for his caretaker's answer. The question nearly made him cry, feeling ignorant of one of the most basic needs in life.

Skye relaxed his shoulders with his hands on his hips and blew out a long breath. "There are all kinds of love, man." He thought and spoke on. "I haven't had much experience; at least, not with romantic love, but I can tell you one thing, love isn't this. It's not trying to kill yourself or purposefully neglecting your family. Love is patient and kind. It's selfless and being there for someone not to obtain something, but just because you care."

Unshed tears pooled in Skye's blue eyes. "It's being loyal in times of distress and heartache, showing kindness even when others don't reciprocate it. But it should never be taken for granted. You're loved, Andre. It's why we help you out and look after you. I love you, Eva loves you, your grandpa loves you, and Andy loves you too."

Skye glanced at the belt and back at Andre. "Never do anything this stupid again. I mean it." He started to exit the room, but paused and took the belt with him through the doorframe.

"Can you tell Eva . . . what I did?" Andre asked, looking at Skye's reflection in the dresser mirror.

Skye shook his head. "No, man. You tell her yourself." He looked down and closed the door.

Andre bit his lower lip and shut his eyes, sniffling in his shame. How could he face his wife now? And why would she love him anymore?

She will be so disappointed in him.

• CHAPTER 36 •

Eva

Wednesday Afternoon

"What color is this triangle?" Eva said, holding up a construction paper shape. She and Louise had gathered their daycare kids around the alphabet circle rug. They were reviewing shapes, colors, and numbers one through ten with their new students. All the toddlers watched them and their instructions, eager to shout out the answers.

Even Andrew was excited about learning. When he first moved into the two-year-old's room, he clung to Eva like a leech, stressing over the fact he had to share his mommy's attention. But now Andrew made friends and was becoming a sociable little boy.

"Yellow!" the kids said.

Eva clapped and smiled. "Great job, everyone!"

Louise raised another paper shape. "What color is this square?"

"Red!" the kids answered.

The phone in their classroom rang.

"I'll get it." Louise took the call as Eva continued talking among the class.

"Okay, kids, I've got one more. What color is the circle?" She held the round shape and grinned.

"Green!" the kids answered in unison again.

Louise glanced at Eva with her hand over the receiver. "Eva, it's for you. A man wants to speak with you."

"Oh, okay." Eva took the phone from Louise.

"Hi, Eva," the man said.

Eva knitted her brows and processed the man's tone of voice. "Caleb?"

"Yeah, it's me," he said, "I'd like to apologize for the other night in my home. I knew you didn't want to drink, and I shouldn't have forced you. It was impolite of me."

Eva was taken aback. "Oh . . . uh, thank you. I accept your apology."

"I couldn't help it." Caleb sighed. "I don't want to ruin our friendship. I let it happen once in the past, and I'm not gonna do it again."

Eva bit her upper lip. "Well, thanks, I appreciate that." She glanced at Louise and her two-year-old class. "Listen, I'm in the middle of teaching my lesson plan, so I have to go right now." She removed the phone from her ear, but

Caleb spoke over the line again.

"Wait up!"

Eva cradled the phone to her ear. "Yes?"

"Mr. Coleman, my boss, is having a dinner for his real estate agents at the Redfish Grill tonight. He allowed us to invite one friend or family member. I'd be more than happy if you come."

Eva thought about the invitation. She loved to eat at the Redfish Grill, but she hadn't gone there since her husband's accident. She was scared it would evoke memories of the incident that occurred on that dreadful night. But Eva knew she shouldn't allow one disaster to prevent her from enjoying her life, and she figured it was a good time to face her fears.

Her company with Caleb helped her cope with her present situation. He was always willing to hear whatever she had to say without judging her, and she liked that about him. Eva shifted her eyes around the classroom, trying to decide. The last time she spent an evening with him, she drank alcohol, something she thought she'd never do.

Her mind wrestled with conflicting thoughts. *Forget about it, Eva. Think about your husband. Caleb's underhanded. You know what happened last time.* She closed her eyes and sighed, biting harder on her lip. *No way. You're just having dinner. What harm can come from this? Besides, your husband will never know about it anyway.*

Eva gritted her teeth. She felt like she had an angel on her right shoulder and a devil on her left.

"Hello? Eva, are you there?" Caleb said.

She shook her head and focused back on the phone call, fidgeting with an ink pen on the teacher's desk. "Oh, sorry. I blanked out for a minute. Uh, sure. What time?"

"How about nine o'clock?"

Eva darted her eyes, unsure of herself. "Uh . . . that's fine."

"Perfect! Nine it is," Caleb said.

"All right, goodbye." Eva hung the phone on the hook and stared into space out a side window.

Louise walked over. "Everything okay?"

Eva spun around with a startled look. "Yeah . . . I'm fine. Just fine." She allowed a smile. "Thanks for answering the call." She returned to the circle rug and sat down, but her mind was restless with worry, wondering if she made the wrong choice. Caleb's attention and friendship eased the pain of forgotten love, and his invitation flattered her.

Undoubtedly, her mother wouldn't like her spending time with another man, but it was a friendly night out, right? Other people with their loved ones and close friends would be present. Wouldn't it make it a different atmosphere compared to a romantic encounter? Eva thought so, but she would find out tonight.

All the lights were off. Stillness captured the house as Eva tiptoed downstairs, dressed in a canary yellow, floral print maxi dress and off-white pump heels Nadine had bought and given to her. She touched the cold knob of the front door, but as she expected, her mother caught her in action, flicking on a lamp in the living room.

"Where are you going, Eva?" her mother said.

Eva faced her mom, who was sitting cross-legged on the sofa, wrapped in her robe with her slippers again.

Her mother lifted her brow with suspicion.

"I'm going for a drive." Eva inhaled and craned her neck, displaying to her mother she's a capable, responsible adult.

"Where?" Her mother's jaw tightened.

"Just *out* . . . I need some fresh air," Eva said.

Her mom pressed her lips together, eyeing her new clothing. "I hope that's all. You're pretty dressed up for going for a simple drive."

"Is it wrong to look presentable?" Eva said.

Her mother jammed her hands in the pockets of her robe. "No, I just don't remember Andre buying you that dress or those heels. Where'd you get them?"

"Nadine Sterling," Eva said, "she bought them yesterday and thought they would look nice on me."

Her mom flattened her mouth again. "Have a good night. I'll listen in for *my grandson* Andy." She stood from the couch and strutted around the corner into the guestroom.

Shame corroded Eva's insides. She couldn't believe it. Her mother thought she was having a secret love affair, but even if she was, it was her personal business. She was an adult woman who could make her own decisions, and her mom needed to accept she wasn't her shy, little girl anymore.

Eva swung open the door and exited the house. While driving to the restaurant, she felt a million butterflies fluttering in her stomach. As a teenager, she had longed to have leisure time with Caleb. Though she saw tonight as an innocent, social meeting, she couldn't deny her former crush still existed.

Caleb was the first boy she liked, and not being too eye-catching to other teenage boys, the only popular guy who smiled and spoke to her in school. His wide, ivory-white grin and wink used to make her heart throb. She remembered how amazed she was watching him play basketball in the gymnasium after the cheerleaders' pep rallies. He never missed a shot and passed and dribbled like nobody's business. Many girls were crazy about him, but back then Eva was equal to his shadow, tagging along behind him and hardly noticed for her doting actions. Eva parked in a lot and entered the five-star restaurant, welcomed by an upbeat piano jazz melody playing from the wall speakers.

She surveyed the dining area and spotted Caleb outside a large window. He was standing at an outdoor table near the shoreline of Horseshoe Beach, waving his hand. Businesspeople in formal suits and dresses sat in the rows of chairs at the table across from a relative or close friend they had invited for dinner. Caleb had told her the truth as she expected, and there were no more worries.

Eva laughed and passed through the glass door to the outdoor dining tables. "Hi! I wasn't expecting everyone to sit out here."

"Hey," Caleb said, "Mr. Coleman thought it'll make a pleasant view if we dine outside." He placed a hand on her shoulder, introducing her to his group of comrades. "Everyone! This is Eva Lucas, an old classmate and friend of mine. If it wasn't for her, I would've never passed my twelfth-grade English and Geometry classes."

Two African American women and two Caucasian men greeted her with smiles and waves.

"Eva, this is Rachel, Paige, Vance, and Lou," Caleb said, pointing to each of the real estate agents.

"Hello, Mrs. Lucas," Rachel said, smiling. "Caleb's told us a lot about you and your interest in interior design. Please, take a seat and join us."

Caleb pulled out a wrought-iron chair for Eva.

"Thank you." She sat and placed her clutch purse aside on the table.

Caleb grinned and took his seat across from hers. "I'm glad you made it."

"Me too." Eva smiled. A breeze washed over her face and shoulder-length hair as she gazed at the peaceful sandy beach. "It's lovely out here."

Caleb joined her in the view as roaring, foamy waves tossed and broke from the shoreline, serenely ebbing away. "It sure is."

Eva opened her menu. "So, what's your favorite meal here?"

Caleb faced her and was about to answer when Mr. Tony Coleman—the real estate broker—returned to the table and made a whistle for attention.

"Welcome associates, family, and friends!" Mr. Coleman said. "I'm happy y'all made it and brought someone with you." He looked down and raised his eyebrows at Eva. "Mrs. Lucas, I'm surprised you're here."

"Hello, Mr. Coleman," Eva said. "Your associate Caleb Williams invited me. We attended the same high school together."

"Well, what do you know! How are you and Andre enjoying your home?" Mr. Coleman said.

Eva straightened. "Fine, sir. We've been in it a little over a year."

"Wonderful!" Mr. Coleman regained his train of thought. "Excuse me, everyone. Where was I? Oh, yes . . . I'm glad so many faces are here tonight. Coleman Housing is a great real estate business committed to ensuring clients have the best homes and sales on the market. But it wouldn't be what it is today without reliable agents, which is why I've arranged this dinner celebration. Let's give them a hand." He and all the guests clapped for the group of agents.

"And," Mr. Coleman added, "I'm also increasing their shares of the profit from forty percent to an even fifty per agent."

"Woohoo!" Paige cheered and clapped.

"Well, somebody's happy," Lou murmured in a flat voice and laughed.

Eva and Caleb chuckled.

"That's all I have to say. Everyone enjoy!" Mr. Coleman unbuttoned his gray suit jacket and sat in an end chair.

The applause died down, and the agents communed with each other and their invited guests, deciding what they wanted to order.

"Steamed lobster with butter dip and fresh tomato pasta salad," Caleb said, folding his hands on top of his menu.

Eva frowned. "Pardon me?"

"You asked me what my favorite meal was, remember?" Caleb said.

Eva moved her dark hair onto one shoulder. "Oh, of course."

"What's yours? The shrimp scampi linguini with garlic bread?" Caleb said, reading from his menu.

Eva shook her head. "I like it, but no. It's the grilled salmon with broccoli slaw. I order it a lot when I come here. Andre and I used to eat out at the Redfish Grill a lot, so he always knew what I wanted." Her eyes moistened a little, but she snickered and smiled away her sorrow.

"You mean, for your anniversary?"

"No," Eva said, "before then. We first started coming at the Redfish Grill while we were in college, but that was before Andre arrived late." She sighed and dropped her shoulders, scrutinizing the tiny print on her menu.

Caleb giggled and simpered. "Do you need those old Coke-bottle glasses you had in high school?"

Eva blushed and chuckled. "Apparently, I do." She looked at him over her menu. "I misplaced my reading glasses while studying. I tried to put my contacts in, but my hands were trembling, so I couldn't get them in before I came tonight. I was nervous about having dinner with you."

"How come?" Caleb inclined his head.

A chill rose up Eva's spine. "Well, I guess because getting married hadn't made you ugly to me."

Caleb tilted his head back and laughed. "Some things never change, but you . . . you're different. You look good without glasses. I could hardly recognize you at our class reunion."

"I know," Eva replied, widening her eyes for emphasis. "You looked like you'd seen a ghost."

Caleb sighed and leaned back. "I didn't mean to be so shocked, it's just you're a remarkable person. Like I said, your husband's fortunate to have you as his wife."

"Yeah," Eva said plainly. With Andre's changed attitude, she wasn't too convinced he felt that way anymore.

An African American waiter with gray, receding hair strode to the outdoor table and stood beside Mr. Coleman's chair. He asked each person's order around the table and jotted it on his notepad. Caleb told the waiter he wanted his favorite meal of lobster with pasta salad and then ordered his drink.

"I'll have lemonade," he said, "but make sure there's no ice."

"Gotcha." The waiter wrote and flipped a page. "And for you, ma'am?"

Eva squinted under the entrees label. "I'll have . . . the fried tilapia with scalloped potatoes."

"Okay, and to drink?" The waiter scribbled Eva's main course.

"Just iced water," Eva said, leaving out her lemon slice.

"All right, I'll be right back with everyone's orders." The waiter traveled to another empty table and gathered dirty dishes left from missing customers. He left through the swing door to the main dining area and traveled to the kitchen.

"Didn't you want your salmon?" Caleb looked puzzled.

Eva shrugged. "No. I wanted to try something different."

Caleb stared at her and played a grin on his lips. He glanced at the Atlantic Ocean and took an inhale of the salty air. "Have you tried a dessert here?"

"Yeah," Eva said, "their brownie parfait. It's *so* delicious."

"I've had their key lime pie with whipped cream, but I didn't like it." Caleb grimaced. "Too sweet for my taste buds."

Eva crinkled her nose. "I don't like key lime pie either, or lemon meringue pie. I'm not a fan of citrus-based desserts."

"I bet you like apple pie," Caleb said.

Eva chuckled and raised a shoulder. "Well, sure, it's an American symbol. Doesn't everybody?"

Caleb laughed at her engaging wit and character. He angled his head and gazed at her a short moment. "You know, I wish I had known you better earlier. You're a fascinating woman."

"Thanks." Eva smiled shyly, struggling to contain the delightful thrills flowing in her. Tonight was one of the finest nights of her life in a long time, and Caleb's sweet witty remarks topped it off.

After Caleb paid for their meals, he walked Eva back to the parking lot. Without her contacts or glasses, there was no way she'd find her vehicle in the pack with her blurry vision. They stood under a streetlight beside her car. Eva turned off her honking car alarm. She chuckled. "Thanks for *steering* me to my car."

Caleb laughed and slipped his hands in his dress pants pockets. "You're welcome. I enjoyed myself with you and the others. I had a great time."

"Me too. Ever since Andre's accident and depression, sometimes . . . I feel so lonely. Thanks for paying for my check, but it wasn't necessary." Eva clenched her purse.

"Oh, no need to thank me," Caleb said. "For you, I'd do it again."

Eva raised her head and studied him in awe. "Well . . . good night."

"Good night." Caleb gazed into her eyes with a wistful smile. "I'm sorry things have been difficult for you, Eva. Someone like you . . . deserves the best." He caressed her cheek with the back of his hand.

Desire bottled up inside Eva, comforted from getting a man's attention. But if she stood there a minute longer, she'd do something she'd regret. She closed her eyes, her thoughts wandering in the past of her and Andre reclining in beach chairs and holding hands around the swimming pool outside their hotel in Chihuahua, Mexico. Surrender whispered through her, imagining herself with her husband. Eva drew closer, attempting to kiss him. Then she saw his face—it was Caleb. Turned off, she fought the urge and shook the vain folly from her mind, catching herself in motion. *Wait a minute. What am I doing? I'm a married woman.*

When she opened her eyes, Caleb's lips were inches away from hers, but she turned her face last minute, making it land on her cheek. Something about his lips on her skin didn't sit right with her, cringing away.

Caleb blinked and sighed heavily. "Sorry, I shouldn't have done that."

"No, it was my fault," Eva said, embarrassed. "I lost it a minute there."

He gulped and stroked his mustache. "Look, let's just forget about it and go home."

"You're right. I'm sorry. Good night, Caleb." Eva fidgeted her key in her car door as Caleb walked off and sat in her driver's seat. She pressed her hands over her eyes, choking on sobs.

Guilt pinched her heart. How could she have let something like this happen? Temptation and loneliness were getting the best of her, and she needed to bring Andre home as soon as possible. She was in danger, tied in a mixed-up, confusing situation that was a tangle of lust and love.

Her crush was blossoming.

• CHAPTER 37 •

Eva

Wednesday Night

"It's about time you got home," her mother said after she came into the house.

Eva's annoyance flared as she turned and faced her mother. "Mom, I'm a grown woman! I'm not a child anymore! So, can you please stop treating me like one?"

Her mother raised her hands in a prayer pose under her chin, approaching her with caution. "I'm sorry, but I was worried about you. Were you with someone?"

"That's none of your business," Eva said. "You know, ever since you found out about me going back to college you've been hounding me."

"That's what mothers do," her mom said.

"They also trust their children will make the right choices," Eva retorted. "But instead, you butt in, deciding solutions based on what you think is best." She grimaced and jabbed a finger on herself. "You don't care about what I want! All you care about is your happiness!"

Her mother frowned. "That's not true!"

"Yes, it is!" Eva said. "You don't respect my boundaries, you make little snooty remarks like I'm a terrible mom, and you always break your promises. Honestly, sometimes I wish you'd leave me alone!"

Her mother bit her lip, on the verge of crying. "Fine! I'll take the first flight to Seattle tomorrow. If you think I'm a *pest,* I'll leave, but don't call me if you need help." She stormed off into the guestroom.

Eva massaged her forehead. She never intended to be so harsh, but a frenzy of emotions overwhelmed her. She rolled her eyes and raked a hand through her hair. The night was well-spent, and she was mentally drained. Her mother's help had been valued, but with Andre recuperating, she didn't need as much support anymore.

And no matter what, she could always depend on Mrs. Flowers for anything. But having her mom leave on bad terms wasn't an option. Despite their disagreements and arguments, she loved her mom, and she refused for them to remain enemies. Maybe Andre's accident happened for a reason, an opportunity for her and her mom to resolve matters and make things right.

She entered the guestroom and found her mother folding her clothes and stacking them in her suitcase and duffle bag. She slumped her shoulders. “Mom, you don’t have to leave yet.”

Her mom continued packing. “I’ve already made my decision.”

Eva drew nearer and held out her hands. “But where will you go?”

“I’ll stay in a hotel suite until I can get another apartment elsewhere,” her mother said. “I’ve contacted the director of the educational department of an art museum back in Seattle. I’m planning to do a workshop. Maybe it’ll help me start a landscape painting exhibition. Besides, I’m sure you’ll be glad to have me gone anyway.” She shut the middle drawer of the dresser.

“Please, don’t leave like this,” Eva said wearily. “Can’t we talk calmly?”

“What’s the use?” Her mom faced her. “You and I are like oil and water. I’ve overstayed my welcome, and it’s time I go home, wherever that is.” She took Eva’s oval-framed glasses from on top of the dresser and handed them over. “Here, I found them between the couch cushions.”

“Oh, thanks.” Eva slipped on her glasses. “I must’ve fallen asleep with them on one night while studying.”

Her mom opened the closet and took out her wooden easel. “You should be more careful with your glasses. You don’t want them to break.”

Eva peered at half of a velvet frame buried under the

clothes in her mother's suitcase. She walked over, pulled it out, and studied the colored photograph. Shock paralyzed her, looking at the handsome Italian man smiling in the photo. He stood in front of the Colosseum with a palette in one hand and a paintbrush in the other. On his left was a landscape portrait on an easel, a replica of the gigantic stone structure.

His raven-black, curly haircut and coffee brown eyes reflected the light of the sunny day. Through his heart-shaped face, dark eyebrows, and olive skin, Eva found the resemblance of herself and her son. She imagined it was how Andy would look years later. The sleeves of his half-unbuttoned, baby blue dress shirt were rolled up to his elbows and gray paint was smeared on one thigh of his khaki shorts. On his bare feet was a pair of leather buckle flip-flops.

Eva looked below at the date scribbled in ink on a corner of the photo: *August 29th, 1983*. Her jaw went slack. *Oh, my gosh. Could it be him?* She stared at her mother, holding the picture. "Is this who I think it is?"

Her mom turned and froze with her tan leather jacket over her arm. She glanced at the framed picture in Eva's hand and sighed dejectedly. "Yes . . . he's your father."

Eva's knees weakened. She plopped on the twin-sized bed and held a hand over her mouth. Waterfalls ran down her cheeks. Since childhood, Eva never met or saw her birth father. Mixed emotions from surprise to heartache swelled in her, as she couldn't believe her mother never showed her his photograph before.

"I'm sorry, honey." Her mom sat beside her and sighed again. "I wanted to show you his picture when you were little, but I was dealing with some things. The mere sight of your father made the pain of our breakup and bad memories come back again."

Eva sniffled, raising her head. "What about the good ones?"

"They came too," her mother said, "but we had few of them, Eva. We got to know each other for only a couple of weeks. When he found out I was leaving back to the States, he proposed and I accepted, but you know what happened afterward. Your father, Andrew, couldn't bear disappointing his parents, and especially his mother. He was a part of an Italian family that held strong ties and traditions."

Eva removed her glasses and wiped beneath her eyes. "Did he . . . did he know about me?"

"No," her mother said, "not until you were one. I kept my pregnancy a secret when I left Italy. I guess it was an act of retaliation after what Andrew and his family had done to me. But then, I felt guilty and wrote to him. We exchanged letters for a while until one day he stopped mailing them to me."

Eva frowned. "Why did he stop writing to you?"

Sadness clouded her mom's features. "He told me . . .

he got married in his last letter. After that, I never heard from him again."

"Who did he marry?"

Her mom sighed and swiped her wet cheek. "Silvia De Vecchi. She's a gorgeous Italian nude art model he met in a café downtown, but he wasn't happy. He admitted it himself. Aside from his mother and sisters, Andrew Martello loved no other woman but me."

"You still love him, don't you?" Eva said.

Her mom buttoned her lips and nodded, too hurt to speak.

"What did he say about me?"

Her mother drew a breath and exhaled. "He said he was sorry for not being there for you, and he hoped y'all would find each other someday in Rome." She brushed Eva's dark hair with a weak smile. "Whenever I look in your eyes, I see your father. I couldn't control the past with Andrew and his family, or with my parents disowning me. Then, you fell in love with a man and got married too . . . and I felt like I lost your father all over again."

"Oh, Mom . . ." Eva's face contorted as she embraced her mother, sobbing on her shoulder with her glasses in one hand.

Her mom rubbed her back. "I'm sorry for being pushy, Eva. And I'm sorry for slapping you and being so cruel. You were right. I was jealous of your friendship with Mrs. Flowers, but it's only because I wanted us to be closer. I'll make amends with Mrs. Flowers tomorrow." She held Eva at arm's length. "From now on, I'll respect your marriage and home. I could tell my coming unannounced used to bother Andre, but he's a good, patient man who kept his peace."

Her mother held her hands. "I'm sorry for discouraging your passion for interior design too. Thinking about how my career has gone, I realize how I made you feel. It hurts when you're hindered from doing what you love." She found a smile. "I should've known better. Your father and I are artists. Regardless of what kind it is, creating art . . . it's in your blood. I love you, honey. Just please be careful. I don't want you and Andre's marriage to fall apart. Lately, I've been concerned about y'all so much."

After what happened with Caleb tonight, Eva thought to say her mother had good reason to worry, but she was too ashamed. Feeling vulnerable and unsettled about her marriage, she needed her mother's comfort and support more than ever.

"I love you, Mom, and I'm sorry too." Eva hugged her mother again. Her shoulders bobbed as her mom held her tighter, but she wasn't crying only because of her relationship with her mother. She was also crying because of the threat Caleb posed and her fondness toward him that never died. Most of all, she cried for her hopeless longing for Andre to become the devoted husband and father she believed he could be. Somewhere deep inside

Andre's broken heart, he had to want to stay in her and Andrew's lives, and for one main reason.

She felt it when they said goodbye.

• CHAPTER 38 •

Eva

Friday, Dec.21st

"I'll pray for you and your flight," Eva said to her mother in the Piedmont Triad International Airport. She gave her mother a side hug, holding Andrew on her hip. Garden Ridge had no airport, so she drove her mom to the closest one in the city of Greensboro, North Carolina.

Her mother smiled and squeezed her. "Thank you, sweetheart." She tickled her grandson's tummy, making him giggle. "Oh, I'm gonna miss you, little munchkin."

Eva handed her son to her mother. Her eyes watered as her mom cuddled him in her arms, cherishing the heartwarming moment. She thanked God her and her mother started rebuilding their mother-daughter relationship. If they could forgive and move toward a better future, she and Andre could do the same, right?

Her mom looked over her ruby eyeglasses at Andrew. "Now, you be a good boy, you hear?" She kissed his cheek and gave him back to Eva.

"I'll let you know when we have his third birthday," Eva said, adjusting her son back in her arms.

"I'll look forward to it," her mother replied. "Sesame Street, right?"

Eva grinned and nodded. "Yes, ma'am."

With a playful smile, her mother cast a glance from Andrew to her, pondering what present to get her grandson. "Hmm . . . I'll see what I can do for Andy." Her mom winked at her.

"Cookie Monster is his favorite," Eva noted.

Her mother chuckled. "All right, I'll remember when I go shopping. Bye, Eva."

"Goodbye, Mom. Best wishes with your workshop." Eva shared another hug with her mother. "I hope you get an exhibition at the Seattle Art Museum."

"Bye, Andy." Her mother pinched Andrew's pudgy cheek and walked off with her luggage.

"Grammie, bye-bye," Andrew said, waving his hand.

Eva watched her mother pass through the crowd of passengers in the airport terminal, tossing her suitcase and duffle bag in a drop-off queue. Next, her mom got in the airport security line where two security guards were waiting. She handed one guard her driver's license and passed through a full-body scanner.

"You're good, ma'am," a security guard said, giving her mom a thumb's up.

Her mother blew her and Andrew a goodbye kiss and waved for the last time before proceeding to her designated boarding gate.

Eva smiled and waved her son's hand.

Her heart shuddered as her mom left, anxious without her mother's intuition. Her mom had interfered in her life, but her apprehension and concern had also been out of love. She was her mother's only child, and as a single parent, her mom strove to keep her from harm. Eva got a pack of Goldfish cheese crackers from a vending machine and waited on a leather chair for the flight departure.

Some minutes after she and her son finished sharing their snack, a flight attendant announced the flight name and time from an intercom.

Her mother's plane was preparing for lift-off.

Eva walked to a large window and looked outside at the Delta Airlines aircraft. The plane wheeled down the tarmac runway and glided off the road into the gloomy sunrise. It looked like it would rain again. Eva touched the pane and closed her eyes. A tear trickled down her cheek. *Please, God. Give Mom safe travels.* She watched the plane until it disappeared behind the thick, foggy clouds.

Maybe she should've told she almost kissed another man, but their bond was headed in the right direction, and she wanted nothing to spoil it. Even so, her mother's assumption about Caleb was true. Suddenly, he found her attractive and was interested in her more than he ever was when they were teenagers.

An uproar of cheers and applause caught Eva's attention. She beheld a group of people near a pizza side food bar, having an impromptu celebration. Among them was a redhead man with a buzz haircut in a camouflage Army uniform and chunky boots. Unfamiliar with the soldier, Eva frowned with wonder, but then it occurred to her.

Neal Witherspoon had finally come home.

He marched to his blonde wife and children, toting a hefty backpack, and carrying a bouquet of red roses in his hand. He gave his wife the flowers and accepted her kiss and tight embrace as their two kids screamed and grappled his waist and leg during the commotion.

Envy ached Eva's heart, snuggling her son. Her eyes glistened with tears as she observed the excitement and joy of the Witherspoon family. She never thought she'd know how it felt to be a soldier's wife. But since Andre's accident, she endured a long wait for the man she loved to return too: a desperate need for him to be a hero and rescue her from a battle against sin.

Eva sniffled and slipped into a nearby elevator that opened its automatic doors. She pressed the first-floor button and waited as she and her son descended to the parking garage. During her drive back from Greensboro, she thought about Andre again. If he didn't find it in his heart to come home today, she didn't know what she would do.

Bringing her husband home was the best decision she could make for herself and their marriage. Eva got out of her car and walked up the rickety porch steps of Grandpa Ricardo's white farmhouse. A red cardinal chirped on a branch of the bare oak tree in the front lawn. She daintily sneezed from the scents of wet earth and freshly mowed grass. Eva knocked and waited for an answer.

Grandpa Ricardo opened the front door, talking behind the mesh screen. "*Hola, Eva!* I was making breakfast burritos. Want some?"

Eva smiled and chuckled. "No, Papa, but thanks. So, how's Andre?"

Grandpa Ricardo grinned. "He's doing good. I've been keeping him busy doing chores and his appetite has also gotten bigger too."

Eva brightened. "That's great. I came to take Andre back with me."

"Take him home?" Grandpa Ricardo's unruly eyebrows rose.

"Yes," Eva said, "I mean, it's been almost two weeks since he left home. I thought he'd be ready to start fresh . . . maybe we can finally work things out?"

Grandpa Ricardo sighed and twitched his thick mustache. "Well, you can try. He's been all right here the past few days, much brighter and cheerful."

Eva tilted her head, inquisitive. "Where is he?"

"He's in the red barn. He likes grooming the horses."

"Thanks, Papa," Eva said. "Can you listen in for Andy? He's sleeping in his car seat."

"Sure thing," Grandpa Ricardo said.

Eva walked down the steps of the porch and passed the chicken coop beside the farmhouse. She strode in the barn to her husband's wheelchair with her hands in her coat pockets, the dirt ground crunching under her knee-length boots. Her nose tingled from the pungent odor of chicken manure.

Wilma and Thelma mooed and chomped, eating their plastic pails of hay. Prissy and Twinkle squealed and oinked at each other like two friends holding a conversation. Black Thunder and Brown Sunset were quiet and chilled behind their fenced stables. But when Gold Star spotted Eva, she neighed and bobbed her head as if greeting her hello.

Eva walked to Gold Star's stable and brushed her hand over the horse's brown mane. She grinned. "Hey, girl. I missed you too." She patted a side of the horse's back.

Andre was brushing Gray Cloud. Dust particles spread from the horse's gray coat and dissolved in the cool, gentle wind.

"Hi, Andre." Eva sat on prickling haystacks aside of Gray Cloud's stable with her keys in her lap.

Andre paused and hung his head. "Hi." He cleaned the dandy brush in his hand with a plastic currycomb in his other.

Eva fidgeted with the penny keychain hooked to her keys, hesitantly asking him what she wondered about for the past twelve days. "How . . . how are you?"

"I'm fine." Andre continued brushing Gray Cloud's long neck in short, flicking movements.

"Andy and I miss you being home," Eva said. "My mom flew back to Seattle today. I'm sorry for the clashes we had over at the house, but we're doing much better."

"Glad . . . t-to hear that," Andre stuttered. He coughed from the dust and placed the dandy brush and currycomb in his lap. "My arms . . . back tired." Andre grimaced and kneaded his right arm with his left hand.

"Hey, let me help you." Eva placed her keys aside and hopped off the haystacks.

Andre's expression tensed, nervous. "Oh, no, it's all right. You don't have to. I'm—"

Eva stood behind him and massaged his arms, working her way further to his shoulders. From his sigh of relief, she knew he couldn't help giving in to relaxation. She peeked at him with his eyes closed and smirked, kneading his shoulders. "Feel better?"

"Yes. Uh, thanks." Andre cleared his throat and moved

one of her hands from his shoulder with a weak look as if uncomfortable by her closeness and touch. Just that quickly, like a mole hiding underground, he withdrew himself from her again.

Eva's smile faded. "Oh, okay . . . sorry." She sat and watched her husband again. "Gray Cloud looks white. You're doing a good job with him." She gulped and figured it was about time she speaks about the reason she came to see him. "Andre, you've been here over a week. Your appetite's increased, and you appear to be doing well, and—I guess what I'm trying to say is . . . I'd like you to come home."

Andre paused and frowned. "I wanna stay here."

"What about your exercises at the gym?" Eva asked.

"I quit! Leg exercises . . . not working anyway," Andre replied. "I'm not getting better."

"But . . . you can't," Eva said, dismayed. "You can't stay here forever. Please, come home with Andy and me. We need you."

Andre glared at her. "What do you need me for, huh? To stare at when you're bored?"

Eva crumbled inside. His sharp words were a knife to her heart. She had brought Andre to his childhood home to help him cope with his situation and move on in life with her and their son. Instead, it gave the impression of making matters worse. Will she and her husband ever get on good terms?

"Andre! That was uncalled for," Grandpa Ricardo said with a frown, walking in on his grandson's rude comment.

Eva balled her fists and leaped from the haystacks. She threw up her hands and backed away from Andre. "No, Papa! You heard him. Let him waddle around in his pathetic pity! Let him do whatever he wants!" She kicked a clump of dirt and stomped to her car.

"Eva, wait! Don't go!" Grandpa Ricardo placed down a bucket of grain and raced after her.

Eva slammed her car door and revved her engine. She zoomed out of the front yard as Grandpa Ricardo chased her vehicle, pleading in Spanish and English for her to not drive away. But what was the point in staying? What was the purpose of showing unconditional love while constantly suffering emotional neglect? When it came to emotional and mental support, her husband was the only one reaping the benefits—she earned nothing.

Besides, Andre said he didn't want to come home, and talking to him wouldn't change his stubborn mind. Eva understood Andre suffered a lot, but for once she wished he showed more empathy instead of always pondering over his own misfortunes. Why couldn't he grow up?

Her husband turned into a selfish brat, and having a class of daycare kids, she already had enough tantrums to deal with. What happened to the emotionally mature gentleman she married on their wedding day? Every time he retaliated, her hope for Andre was dying out more and more. If he continued behaving the same way, their relationship would never get resolved. But if it didn't, Eva wanted Andre to at least make a greater effort to be a part of their son's life. Did Andrew matter to him?

Depression submerged his being so deeply all he focused on was not being able to walk and function like he used to. Eva rode to their house, laid Andrew in his crib, and fled in the master bedroom. She cried on her pillow and swaddled herself in the comforter. Her cell phone vibrated on the nightstand.

Eva sandwiched her head in her pillow and stirred from the sight of her phone.

It vibrated two more times.

Please, shut up! Eva filtered a breath through clenched teeth and turned over on the bed. She snatched the phone and saw a Messenger notification in a corner of her iPhone's screen. Eva frowned and swiped it down with her thumb.

A circle profile photo of Caleb's dark brown, grinning face was beside the text message.

Caleb? Shivers ran through Eva's chest. Not having given him her cell number, he must've searched up her Facebook account to get in direct contact with her. Some of his message was hidden with ellipsis dots. She sat up and tapped his message to read all he sent: *Hi, Eva. Sorry to intrude. I'm feeling low and haven't been truthful to u. Need someone I can trust to talk to. You're the only one I feel will understand. Please, meet me 3:00 p.m. @ Starbucks on Olive St. so we can talk.*

Eva nibbled her lip and hesitated on what to do. She took a deep breath and typed him a quick reply: *Feeling low too. I'll be there shortly.* She called Mrs. Flowers over to listen out for Andrew and left the house to meet with Caleb. She wasn't fully aware of what he wanted to say, but he at least convinced her of one thing.

Unlike Andre, he cared about her feelings.

• CHAPTER 39 •

Eva

Friday Afternoon

On the way over, Eva received a phone call from Nadine who asked to hang out again. Feeling like there was nothing left to lose, Eva agreed to join her next Saturday for lunch and a shopping spree get-together. She stepped into Starbucks and found Caleb at a booth, staring in a porcelain mug. Her face fell as she paused and observed him. She had never seen him so unhappy before. From what she recalled, he was always grinning and parading himself, showing off his perfect, wide smile. He knew he was fine-looking, and being a lauded basketball player, he was always popular and admired by others.

Now he was a successful real estate agent who made big bucks, had a refined red Jaguar XF car, and lived in a fancy, two-story home. What did he have to mope about?

She walked to the table and sat on the long seat in front of him. "Hey, I got your message. It kinda creeped me out."

Caleb gave a little smile. "Sorry, I didn't mean to scare you." He cupped his hands on his mug.

"What's wrong?" Eva frowned and angled her head. "Are you sad?"

Caleb sipped his coffee.

"You said you weren't truthful. What did you mean?" Eva wove her hands.

He perched his elbows on the table and hunched his shoulders. "I told you I liked the single life, but it wasn't true. Yes, I was a player, but I've changed. All those casual dates of making out with girls from my teenage years ended shortly after graduation. I've wanted to settle down for some time." He sighed and glanced at Eva. "Truth is, I've suffered three broken engagements with other women."

Eva's jaw dropped, blinking in disbelief.

"I know," Caleb said and winced. "I understand you're shocked. I would've mentioned it at our class reunion, but I didn't want you to feel sorry for me." He shook his head and leaned backward with defeat. "What am I doing wrong? I'm confident and take responsibility for my actions." He studied the tiled floor. "I thought women valued men like that."

Eva chewed her upper lip, thinking, "Well, they do

but many women also want to be treated as equals. Most women like relationships with men who can trust them and treat them like people instead of things."

Caleb's forehead creased. "What's wrong with being protective?"

"It depends on what your definition of that is." Eva darted her eyes, and based on his shifted body language, she knew she struck a nerve.

Caleb pressed his fist against his cheek. "I can't help it if my definition of *protective* doesn't suit some women. I like to make sure nobody's trying to take her away from me, that's all."

"You can't be insecure, Caleb," Eva said. "If you want a solid relationship with a woman, you're gonna have to learn to not be possessive, give her space, and trust her."

Caleb snickered. "That's not what my dad said. He always said, 'To keep a woman, you gotta stay on your toes.' My mom keeps nagging me I need to find a wife. Since my father passed from heart disease, she gets lonely, and she wants me to give her grandkids to fill her big, empty house." He glanced at her again. "Eva, I know you're married with a son, but the other night in the parking lot made me realize how much I'd love to have a woman like you."

Eva gulped and hung her head. "Caleb, I—"

"Please, listen a minute," Caleb interrupted, "Eva, if Andre isn't willing to be there for you anymore, maybe it's time you consider moving on. You should be with somebody who will make you happy."

Eva knitted her eyebrows. "Andre makes me happy!"

"How? By leaving you alone?" Caleb grimaced and leaned back. "If he loved you, he wouldn't allow one incident to ruin his whole marriage, but he would fight for it. He would stay committed to you, and he would do his best to care for you and your son."

Numbness infused Eva's body. She couldn't help but agreed with Caleb. He had spoken the thoughts which had swirled around in her mind for the past year. And as much as she didn't want to admit, lately she found more comfort in another man than her own husband.

"I'm repairing a house property on Lime Street," Caleb said, changing the subject. "I'm going over to paint the porch and do other minor fixes today. Would you like to help? With you interested in interior design, it might be a fun learning experience."

Eva hesitated. "Uh . . . sure, I'll come."

Caleb grinned and sighed. "Great, and Eva . . .thanks for the advice. I'm thin-skinned when it comes to criticism, but you told me right. I guess I've screwed up, but I promise I'll do better. Trust me, we're *just* friends. Don't take what I said out of context; but as a friend, I'm saying maybe think about it?"

Eva nodded slightly. "All right." She wore a timid smile and relaxed her shoulders.

Moving on and forgetting about Andre wouldn't be easy-peasy, but it was obvious her hopes were vain, and her husband wanted nothing to do with her and their son. As Caleb said, they deserved the best, and after Andre's frequent rejection, he persuaded her this wasn't coming from her husband again.

"You've got a smooth stroke for a daycare teacher," Caleb said, observing how Eva handled her paintbrush.

Eva giggled. "Thanks. My mom's an artist, so maybe that's where I get it from. Or perhaps it's from watching my students do arts and crafts." She dipped her brush in the white paint can and continued stroking the middle stair of the porch steps while Caleb finished the first one.

"I appreciate you being here," Caleb said. "I didn't think you'd come after what happened the other night in the parking lot. I'm sorry for embarrassing you after dinner. I should've thought twice."

"I forgive you," Eva said. "Besides, I led you on a little."

Caleb paused with his brush in his hand. "Eva, I hope I'm not meddling, but how long have you and Andre been married?"

Angry tears brewed in Eva's eyes, blurring her vision. She froze and rubbed her denim jacket sleeve over her face. "Eight years now. Sadly, our wedding anniversary has become like any other day. We didn't celebrate this year. Of course, Andre also doesn't remember marrying me."

Her strokes became faster and harder. "We had a spat before I met you in Starbucks. I was attempting to take Andre home after he stayed over his grandfather's farm, but he thinks he's a burden." She sighed. "Because of this, he's given up on our relationship, and worse, he doesn't bond with our son as he should be. I mean, how can he not love this kid?"

Eva took her iPhone out of her jacket's pocket, unlocked her pattern code, and showed her home screen wallpaper photo of Andrew to Caleb.

Caleb smiled. "Oh, wow. He's a heartthrob."

"Exactly," Eva agreed with enthusiasm.

"How old was he in that picture?" Caleb asked.

"Andy was nine months. He had just learned to crawl. That's why he's so happy in it." Eva put her cell away and finished painting the middle stair.

"Who's watching him now?" Caleb said.

"Mrs. Flowers, our neighbor," Eva answered. "She babysits Andy sometimes. Her husband died, and our son helps keep her company. Her adult children only visit her during Thanksgiving."

Caleb frowned. "That's a crying shame. Your son must be special. Maybe we can have a picnic and I could meet him."

"Okay . . . Andy would like that." Eva wore a half-smile. "He likes giving hugs and it doesn't take him too long to warm up to new people." Satisfaction consoled her from within. Wanting strong male influences who accomplished high goals in Andrew's life, it pleased her Caleb wanted to know her son, and she couldn't wait to introduce him.

A low, chugging engine approached behind them.

Eva looked back as a 1994 white Ford F-150 pickup rode up and parked beside her car. A scruffy, Caucasian man in gray coveralls climbed out of the truck. He grabbed a toolbox from the flatbed and walked toward them.

"Morning," he said in a deep, husky voice.

Eva scrunched up her nose at the stench of cigarette smoke from his clothes. "Good morning."

"Hey, you're right on time," Caleb said, "but you'll have to go through the back door. The porch is still wet."

"Gotcha." The man toted his toolbox around the back of the house.

Eva frowned. "Who was that?"

"That was Max, my plumber."

"What's wrong with the plumbing in the house?" Eva asked.

Caleb ground his jaw. "During my inspection with the previous owner, I discovered the sinks in the kitchen and bathroom don't drain. The pipes are clogged."

Eva made a short laugh. "Unbelievable."

"Yeah," Caleb said, "the owner didn't want to contribute to making repairs, but she expected me to set a high asking price. Nobody would buy this little old house for what she was requesting. I had to negotiate with her until finally, she lowered the cost."

"Have you gotten buying clients?" Eva said.

Caleb exhaled a mist of fog. "Nope, but I'm sure once the place is completely renovated the house will sell before Simon Says, "Hold your nose."

They exchanged smiles and continued painting.

Eva stole another glance at Caleb, her smile fading. The smell of the fresh paint made her reflect on another cold, foggy afternoon. After a tech had identified from a sonogram they would have a baby boy, Andre was so excited he wanted to get an early start on preparing their son's bedroom.

Neither of them could agree on what design to choose. She wanted a circus theme, but her husband thought a train theme was better. Trying to find a common ground, they hilariously fought over their differences like forever, until they agreed with Mrs. Flowers' sailor boy design. Often, Andre peeked in the vacant, finished room, expecting their unborn son.

Some nights they talked in bed, whispering loving messages to the baby, and marveling over kicking moments he showed sign. She missed those times, but now they were nothing more than a closed album of snapshots and photographs. Her eyes teared up, but she exhaled a sharp breath to keep her composure, stroking her brush on the rail of the porch.

Ignoring a strong love was hard. And Caleb's prior relationships with women made her fearful there was something fishy about his friendship, and a question she was too scared to ask arose: what were his true intentions toward her?

• CHAPTER 40 •

Andre

Friday, Dec. 28th

Night fell and Andre sat in his wheelchair on the porch of his grandfather's farmhouse. He blinked and studied the waxing crescent moon hanging in the black velvet sky. *Who am I, God? Please, tell me. Just tell me.* Listening to the chirping crickets and droning locusts from the backyard woods, he felt a sense of loss, regret, and indecision. He had accomplished his mission and what he wanted, but he still wasn't satisfied. *Why aren't I happy?*

Even despite his memory loss and granted isolation, he missed his supposed wife. How can this be? Maybe he'd spent a short time with her, but for the longest, she and their son had felt like total strangers. Being homesick was something he never expected of himself. It didn't make sense to him, and he felt silly and confused.

Maybe he'd gotten accustomed to their house, but that would never return his normal personality. Seeing old photographs wasn't enough for him to identify what kind of man he was. He wanted to step in the shoes of the man smiling and looking back at him in the unfamiliar pictures. It would mean the world to him to recover at least a pint of what he had forgotten. He had wondered why Eva was constantly nice to him, but it wasn't until after his talk with Skye he realized why.

If it were him, he didn't know if he could do for himself all Eva had done. She was always kind and supportive since the time he first beheld her, maybe before then. Andre knew the bad news he had to confess, but he was afraid for the chance of a broken heart.

Truth is, he was getting sweet on her.

Fear of vulnerability, his disabilities, and the shame of his suicide attempt were the main reasons he wanted to stay away from her. Nonetheless, Andre hated himself for his misbehavior. He didn't remember marrying this beautiful, caring woman, but she had well-proven she loved him unconditionally. He couldn't deny she tried her best to fulfill her role as a wife and working mother. He frustrated, offended, and upset her many times, but she still wanted him to live with her.

Andre didn't understand what she wanted with him, but pondering everything he did prior; remorse pricked his heart. *How could I have acted mean toward her? Why was*

I so rude and spiteful? He needed to get help and control his mood swings. Eva was a good, strong-willed person, who he had taken for granted and pushed away.

Last Saturday, Eva had told him she called Dr. Brown. She tried to convince him one last time to take an antidepressant prescribed for his clinical depression, but Andre refused again. Now she had gone about a week ago, and she hadn't come back for him.

Every passing day, Andre wrestled with his unstable feelings, his misery of being only part of the man he was. Having hardship in his marriage, it appeared he suffered a loss. He wished he could dive into the cogs of his brain and repair whatever dysfunctions caused him to act and speak the aggressive ways he did.

But overcoming himself like this wasn't possible.

Grandpa Ricardo peeked out the squeaky, screen door into the chilly evening. "Supper's ready, *nieto*."

"Not hungry." Andre stared at the glowing moon.

"What's wrong, Andre? Are you thinking about Eva?"

Andre bowed his head and sighed downheartedly. He was always thinking about her—pondering the love and patience she showed him, trying to understand himself better, and wishing he could remember his past life.

Grandpa Ricardo walked onto the porch and stood beside him. He patted Andre's shoulder and pointed across the country road from them. "Look, there over yonder."

Andre lifted his head and peered in the direction.

"That's Old Thomas family's place. It caught fire some time back." His grandfather wore a smile and faced him. "The house is like you. Its roof had collapsed." He peered back at the shack in the distance. "But one wonders . . . how it still stands after *all* these years." His grandfather took a deep inhale of the cold air. "Focus on what you can do, Andre, not on what you can't do. Your inability to walk and speak normally doesn't make you more or less of a man."

"It's hard . . . I c-c-can't provide . . . family," Andre faltered and bit his lip.

Grandpa Ricardo turned toward Andre. "Who says you can't? You can get paid right here on the farm. Your only hindrance is yourself." He wore a stern expression. "Cherish your good qualities. Learn and strive to improve your bad qualities. Be thankful for who you are. No matter what, you're a survivor, *nieto*. Never forget that." He patted Andre's shoulder again.

Andre thought about what his grandfather said. He didn't know what a paralyzed man could do on a twenty-acre farm besides tending to the livestock animals, but he grew weary of watching Eva struggle to handle almost everything herself.

Grandpa Ricardo held back the screen door for him as he wheeled himself inside. Without dinner, Andre entered his room and transferred into bed, musing over his repetitive thoughts about Eva and himself. Several hours passed, and the same dreadful dream had invaded his sleep:

Andre was falling again.

He hollered and tumbled down a passage of nothingness, hoping for a ledge or branch to break his fall. He landed face down on his chest and stomach, the impact throbbing through his body. He fluttered and opened his eyes.

It was dark. Very dark.

Wisps of gray smoke arrayed the surrounding blackness. A woman's scream echoed. Her voice was familiar. He knew who she was. He struggled to his feet and peered in the distance.

There was a scorching lake. Orange, steamy, glowing lava with cakes of ash.

Stepping stones across it led to a large, rocky cliff.

A young woman adorned in a white silky dress was at the peak. Her wrists were tied, her slender body chained to a chair. He couldn't see her face, but he knew she was there.

Andre, help me! she called, fighting to break loose.

Not a soul was in sight—but him.

He had to protect and save her.

Hold on! I'm coming! Andre coughed from the smoke. He stepped on the first stone. It sank. He panicked and leaped to another stone and another as they sank, trying not to lose his balance.

Don't worry! I'm almost there! His voice echoed, and the beast heard him. It knew he would come for her. It knew he loved her. An earthquake shook the ground when Andre reached the last stone. His eyes widened at the massive creature before him. He gasped and he couldn't move a muscle.

A gigantic king cobra barged through the cliff, blocking Andre from saving her. It was multicolored with fiery, piercing eyes and sharp fangs. It lowered its hooded head, its face transforming to the shape of a man's. He looked at Andre, viciously licking his split tongue.

Then he struck down to bite her.

The woman screamed and looked away, her black, wavy hair covering her face.

"Eva!" Andre sat up in bed and stretched out a hand before him. Cold sweat trickled down his neck and chest. He raised his comforter and groped his boxers and the clammy sheet beneath him, thinking maybe he made an accident.

Nothing but sweat.

Phew. Andre sighed with relief and rubbed his hand down his face. He winced with confusion, having a horrible migraine. It was the third time he had the same nightmare, but this time was a little different. He couldn't place his finger on it, but somehow, he knew Eva was in danger. He could sense it—feel it in the air. Static crackled in his ears. He shut his eyes tightly and clutched his head.

One after another, snippets of evocative images came flashing back and pieced together in his mind: *A colorful flower bouquet tied with a blue ribbon. An orange tabby kitten.*

A tire swing on a peach tree. A ticking wall clock. A vase of white roses. A navy-blue ship helm engraved with Andrew's name. A stuffed plush monkey. His hand dripping with blood. A deer in headlights. A penny keychain sparkling in the sunlight . . .

Great emotion engulfed Andre. He opened his eyes as a spark of intellect shocked him. Everything he had been told for days, weeks, and months was true. He didn't remember his car accident in complete detail, and neither did he know all he's ever done with Eva and Andrew. But now, he was fully aware they were his wife and son. It wasn't because of the old pictures or anyone telling him anymore, but it was because he *remembered* and adored them.

"Dear God, oh, dear god . . . Eva . . . Andy . . .," Andre said, his voice cracking with regret. He pressed his shaky hands over his eyes and hung his head. Andre switched on the lamp on the nightstand. A framed photo beside the digital clock caught his attention.

He grabbed it and studied the center image of his teenaged self, wearing a riding helmet, a western dress shirt, and jeans, mounted on a young, black colt—Black Thunder. Andre turned his head and paced his breathing, surveying his whereabouts as if he were seeing them for the first time. It was then he realized he wasn't just in any bedroom—he was in the room he grew up in as a kid.

His old bedroom.

Golden little equestrian trophies lined the top shelf of a short, green bookcase next to the closet. On the middle shelf was a collection of books about many animals from domestic farm to the Sahara Desert. Toy dinosaurs and horses were rowed on the last shelf. Beside the bookcase was a small writing desk where he always did his homework after school.

Andre's vision clouded with tears as he placed the picture back down on the stand, gawking at the items and traces of his childhood.

Grandpa Ricardo barged into the bedroom dressed in his striped pajamas and nightcap. He caught his breath. "*¿Qué te pasa, nieto?* What happened? Are you okay?"

Andre looked over at the old Mexican man with silvery hair and a thick mustache, trapped in awe. "*Mi . . . mi abuelo?*"

"*Si, Andre.* I'm your grandfather." Grandpa Ricardo grinned and exploded with laughter. "*Gracias a Dios! Tu recuerdas!*" He knelt near the bedside and hugged him tightly, crying with joy. Until recently, Andre hadn't spoken a word of Spanish, and the fact he said something without being taught, showed he regained a part of his memory.

They held each other with outstretched arms.

Andre remembered his troublesome nightmare. His mouth went dry as he panicked, feeling like he was going crazy. "Where 's Eva? I gotta find her . . . go home."

Grandpa Ricardo frowned, gripping Andre at arm's length. "I've tried calling, but she won't pick up. When I visited, Mrs. Flowers said she wasn't home." He looked down and sucked his teeth. "Something was off last I saw her."

Andre's heart thudded in his throat, pacing his rapid breathing. "I'm scared, Grandpa. I don't w-wanna lose her—I can't lose her!"

"Relax, *nieto*. You won't," Grandpa Ricardo said. "She loves you. You'll go home tomorrow. Rest yourself now, okay?"

Andre gulped and calmed down. "Tomorrow. Yes . . . tomorrow." He lay back in bed, pulling his blanket over him.

Grandpa Ricardo turned off the lamp and left his bedroom.

Thinking of Eva, Andre wiped his sweaty forehead and struggled to fall back to sleep.

He hoped he wasn't too late.

Andre observed the hoary head of their two-story house as his grandpa pushed his wheelchair up the brick pathway. Snow blanketed the black shingled roof and the evergreen shrubs and front lawn. Another December was ending, and in the short time that whizzed by, it felt like years since he'd been home.

It disappointed Andre his wife stopped visiting him on his grandpa's farm, but he didn't blame her. He had been a crabby man and made their marriage more complicated—a marriage which though he couldn't recall the start of, he wouldn't change for the world.

Grandpa Ricardo knocked a gloved hand on the front door.

Eva answered, but her stunned expression showed she wasn't expecting either of them. She clamped her lips and crossed her arms.

"*Hola, Eva*. Andre wanted to come home." Grandpa Ricardo blinked and wore a lopsided grin.

Eva averted her eyes from Andre to Grandpa Ricardo. She flared her nostrils and sighed. "All right, he can come in. I'll call Skye and ask him to come here. I'm about to go to work."

Grandpa Ricardo lifted Andre's wheelchair over the steps and let Andre push himself inside the toasty-warm living room.

Andre looked over his shoulder and eavesdropped as his grandfather whispered with Eva.

"Do you want to talk?" Grandpa Ricardo arched a brow and set Andre's suitcase with wheels inside next to the coat rack.

Eva sighed with her arms still folded, impatiently tapping her tennis shoe. "No, Papa. We'll be fine."

"Okay," Grandpa Ricardo said," but I'm here if you need some advice."

Eva nodded. "I know you are, and thanks." She closed the door.

"Hey," Andre said.

Eva turned around and faced him, leaning her back against the door while holding the knob. "Hi."

Andre gazed at her as if ensuring he never forgot her again. Warmth spread in his chest, and his heart danced from her presence. He pulled off his toboggan hat and winter gloves and set them in his lap, inching up a smile. "Sorry . . . I missed you . . . Andy a lot too."

Eva turned her back to him, rubbing her arms. "Really? Then, what took you so long coming back?" She hissed with contempt and rushed upstairs to the second floor, leaving him to sit alone in silence.

Andre blew out a long breath and threaded a hand through his curly haircut. He would've told his wife he remembered her and their son, but none of that mattered at the moment.

He had to prove he loved them first.

• CHAPTER 41 •

Andre

Later in the afternoon, Andre peeked through the blinds of their bedroom window and viewed below him. Outside, Eva was laughing and talking to a somewhat tall, black man leaning against a red car. Suspicion gripped him as she held the man's hands, kissed his cheek, and took their son from the back seat of the man's car. Apparently, he wasn't only someone Eva knew, but the man had taken her to work and drove her home. Another man added to the equation, his hope for reconciliation was crushed the minute he saw her kiss him.

Andre blinked and glanced away. *Eva loves him. I know she does.* After all, why else did she hang around him? He looked back out of the window at them. As Eva carried Andrew, she led the man to come into their house.

Andre's heart quaked with worry as he processed the unexpected man's invasion. Their separation had flowed like a river between them and formed gaps of loneliness and resentment. For the past few weeks, he had no clue what happened with Eva or their son, and neither could he recall this strange intruder.

"Hey, Andre! Eva's home!" Skye called from downstairs.

"I know!" Andre stared at the tire tracks imprinted in the snow on the driveway. Heavy steps came up to the second floor and someone knocked outside the bedroom.

"Come in." Andre stared at the closed door.

Eva stepped into their room, holding Andrew. "Hi, Andre. Uh, how are you doing?"

Andre shrugged. "Fine, I guess."

Andrew moaned and brushed his forehead against Eva's chest.

"Andy's sick," she said with a sour look. "He caught a cold from a kid at the daycare." Eva exhaled a long breath, swaying to comfort their son. "Listen, there's someone I'd like you to meet. He's an old classmate of ours and he wanted to say hello."

"Okay." Andre rolled himself from the master bedroom, following Eva down the hall to the top of the stairs. At the base of the staircase, the man from outside stood with his hands in the pockets of his tan trench coat. His long, rectangular face portrayed a smile meant to be friendly, but one Andre didn't trust.

"Hi, Andre," the man said.

Eva introduced the man to him. "Andre, this is Caleb Williams. He played basketball at Garden Ridge High where you and I graduated."

"Hi," Andre said.

Eva shifted her eyes between the two men, nibbling her upper lip. "Well, y'all can get acquainted while I tend to Andy." She walked their whining little boy down the hallway into the bathroom.

Andre and Caleb studied each other as if they were in a staring contest.

"Goodbye, Andre," Skye called as he left the house.

Andre blinked but didn't look away from Caleb. "Bye, Skye. Have a good night."

Caleb cleared his throat. "I'm sorry about what happened. Being in your condition must be miserable."

Andre smirked and wove his hands. "It's not t-too bad. I have . . . own vehicle wherever I go."

Caleb laughed. "I never thought about that." He raised his eyebrow. "But I heard you've been depressed. I can understand you wanting a divorce."

Andre's expression hardened. "What? I don't want a divorce."

"That's not what Eva said," Caleb remarked.

Andre breathed heavily, wondering how he could've ever wanted to do such a thing. But being in an emotional and mentally confused state, he wouldn't deny he hadn't requested it for a time.

"She also told me you've felt like a burden to her," Caleb added. "Frankly, I don't blame you for feeling that way. It must suck . . . seeing *your wife* do everything you can't." He pinned his eyes at Andre as if urging him to blurt an angry outburst.

Andre gritted his teeth but made no comment.

"Maybe you came home, but you won't win back Eva's heart after how you've treated her," Caleb said. "Yelling at her, ignoring her when she speaks to you, refusing to be with her and your son . . .you're better off killing yourself and being done with it."

Andre curled his hands and wanted to jump out of his wheelchair and attack Caleb. After recently surviving a suicide attempt, his rude remark wasn't the most appropriate thing to say to him, and his cunning expression made him believe Caleb knew exactly what he had tried to do. He was an evil man, clearly full of himself. How did Eva get so close to someone like this?

Caleb inched forward to the last step, glaring up at him from below. "Eva doesn't want you anymore, Andre. You're too late. I haven't asked her to marry me, but when I do, I'm sure she'll say yes. And she, I, and Andy will live happily together, and you . . . you'll be dead or in a nursing home."

Andre's blood boiled. Was Caleb telling him the truth?

Had Eva given up on him? Why else would she want him to get familiar with this other man? He closed his eyes and dropped his head, ashamed.

"Eva's gonna be mine," Caleb whispered deviously. "I assure you I'll take *great care* of your wife for you."

A flash of the cobra passed through Andre's mind. With terror, he looked into Caleb's eyes. Maybe he was paralyzed with impaired speech and emotional problems, but he was smart enough to understand who this man was. He was the serpent from his nightmare—the man hindering him and Eva from making amends and threatening to break apart their marriage.

"While you were away, we've spent much time together. Uh, I hope you don't mind." Caleb licked his lips and sneered, rubbing his hands together.

Andre gulped and hung his jaw. His heart shattered into a million pieces. Had Eva cheated on him? Or was Caleb trying to manipulate his fragile mind?

"Andy's resting peacefully," Eva said, coming back to the staircase. "I gave him some medicine. I'm sure he'll get better soon." She smiled from Andre to Caleb, ignorant of what they said out of her presence. "So, how did everything go?"

"Everything went fine, *right*, Caleb?" Andre pursed his lips.

Caleb grinned and lifted his chin. "Right. I'll be leaving now. Goodbye, Eva, Andre." He exited the house.

Eva released a relieved sigh. "Phew, I'm glad things went so well."

"Are you kidding me?" Andre glowered and wheeled away from her.

"What? Andre, wait a minute . . ." Eva frowned and followed him into the master bedroom.

Andre peeked outside the window and watched Caleb speed off in his car.

"What do you mean? What happened?" Eva said.

Rage swept over him, throwing a glare at her. "What do you care? You told him . . . everything that—happened—between us!" He exhaled rapid breaths and clutched his head, his brain exploding with fury.

"I needed someone to talk to!" Eva shouted, on the verge of tears.

Andre's lips drew back in a snarl. He banged his right hand on the armrest of his wheelchair. "What about your mother? Or . . . Grandpa? Or Pastor Tyson?" He shook his head. "You didn't have to talk to Caleb." He glanced down and raised his hand with a scowl. "Tell me, what's going on with you two? Why'd you spend t-t-time with him?"

Eva looked startled. "We have a lot in common. Caleb gave me textbooks. I've been studying interior design, and plan to enroll back in college soon. He's just a friend! He's a real estate agent and designer. He's been helping me get hands-on experience with some of his projects for clients."

She sighed and brushed her hair on one shoulder. "I wanted you to realize our friendship has strictly been about house design, so I asked him to tell you what's been going on between us for himself. He said he would. I thought he told you those things."

"Well," Andre said, "he didn't. He told me you told him I wanted a divorce." He slumped his shoulders, folded his hands in his lap, and exhaled a slow breath. "Maybe I did once, but I don't anymore." He rolled closer to his wife and gave a weak look. "Eva, you gotta listen to me. Caleb's no good. He said m-m-many *harsh* things."

Devastated, Eva was taken aback and plopped on an edge of the queen-sized bed. "I can't believe this. Caleb's always been understanding toward me."

"It could've been a cover-up," Andre said. "He was pretty wretched . . . upset, to say the least. I'm worried about you."

"Andre, I'll be fine. Believe me, I've been a little skeptical of Caleb's friendship and his interest in me too, so I'll consider your warning."

Eva started to walk off.

"Wait," he said, holding her hand, "I'd just like to say . . . I'm sorry about how I acted and . . . I'm here to stay. Just please . . . don't leave me."

Eva's throat thickened with sobs, looking away. "I'm sorry, but . . . I can't promise that. I need time to think. I don't know how to feel about you right now."

She slipped her hand free and turned her back.

"I understand. You can have the master bedroom. "I'll take the guestroom." Andre looked down and rolled his wheelchair out of their bedroom. Maybe Caleb was right about him never having a chance with Eva again. One thing for certain, Andre felt bad distrusting his wife and her integrity. But if she was only studying for college and getting experience with design, why had she kept it a secret from him?

• CHAPTER 42 •

Eva

Wednesday, Jan 2nd

Eva browsed the LED sign beside a fenced-in baseball field on Wilbur Street, waiting at an intersection. Bright, digital, golden lights reading *Happy New Year* blinked twice, froze, and scrolled across the blackboard. Then an animated image of a baseball player struck a ball with a bat. The ball flew up and filled the center of the screen, the new year in large, dark numbers on the gold baseball: *2019*.

She tapped her forefinger on her steering wheel and mused over her weekend with Nadine and the past week. Last Saturday was a little unusual. As much as Nadine enjoyed shopping, Eva found her sitting on the edge of the wishing well in the mall. Her arms were folded in her lap and her head was down on her knees, drowning in sorrow.

Eva wasn't sure it was Nadine until she looked up at her. Nadine sniffled and wiped beneath her green eyes with a crumpled tissue. She played off her sadness with a smile and talked about going to Burlington for a new winter coat, but Eva wasn't convinced she was okay. Eventually, they talked about Nadine's first husband named Glenn and her being a shopaholic, a habit she'd inherited from her friends in high school.

As it turned out, Nadine and Glenn were a perfect match who met in college and shared similar interests in law and politics. But then their bills got out of control due to Nadine's frequent spending. Two years ago, Glenn had reached his limit, packed his things, and left Nadine to start a law practice in Washington D.C.

The couple had remained separated since then, and although Nadine had married two other men, she had confessed she still loved Glenn. Eva brought up her past of never having enough while growing up on welfare, and how she learned life was bigger than getting a new dress or other worldly gains.

While talking with her classmate, she felt like she was counseling herself aware of her failures and mistakes. After her spat with Andre on his grandpa's farm, she had shopped recklessly for clothes she doesn't normally wear and had gotten acquainted with Caleb in the heat of the moment. Their friendly little gatherings made her feel a mixture of fear and adoration. He arrived at her house and drove her to work the past few days, but after Andre came home, guilt prevented her from riding with him again. Caleb said he understood, but apparently, he was offended.

Regardless, she still had fun with Caleb. Together they painted houses, shopped at Lowes and Home Depot, arranged furniture, and welcomed clients in their new homes. Their camaraderie reminded her how well her marriage used to be. She wanted to forget her husband and strove to get beyond their past love.

Remembering their former life was too painful with everything changed, but Caleb had made her feel special again. He sent her flowers, took her out to dinner, and encouraged her pursuit of interior design. Enjoying his company, she was gradually falling for him. Aside from kisses on the cheek, they hadn't gotten sexually involved, but she was approaching in that direction.

Mostly, because she'd felt she owed him for stringing him along. The script had flipped, and now she was the one admired. At their class reunion, she'd held Caleb's attention, which was unexpected of him. Of course, her appearance also improved and was a lot different than before. Her braces were removed after high school, and she had gotten eye contacts during college.

Skin acne treatments accentuated the natural beauty of her olive skin, which according to Andre had always existed. Looking in Caleb's eager mahogany brown eyes, the more she hung around him, the more she was aware he was attracted to her physical looks and cared very little about anything else. But strangely enough, she didn't care either. What happened to her self-esteem? Where was the love of God she showed toward Andre? Pride and unforgiveness decayed her dignity, and when she stood in the mirror, lately she didn't feel so exquisite anymore. Her mom warned her there was a difference between love and lust, and Eva had learned the difference the moment Andre knelt and proposed to her on his grandpa's farm.

During an August sunset, Eva sat on the tire swing tied to a peach tree in the farmhouse's backyard. Holding his hands, she followed his gaze and listened to his words like music floating in the breeze. When Andre ended his nervous blabbering, her heart skittered, and she nodded and whispered yes, flinging her arms around his neck.

Eva wanted to kiss him, but he placed his fingers over her lips and shook his head. Fearing it may lead to an unlawful sin, he advised they wait until their wedding day. Instead, they hiked to the mountains where they watched the clouds and talked about their future hopes and dreams for each other. Being so young at the time, most folks thought they had puppy love and would break up before long, and especially without an engagement ring on her finger.

But they proved everyone wrong.

Their promises and mature behavioral conduct were enough to sustain their devoted love and friendship. And when the ceremony and their honeymoon arrived, Eva understood the reason for their long delay. As they came together, there was a pure virtue—the realization their relationship wasn't a matter of trial-and-error.

But they forever belonged to each other.

A tear trickled down Eva's left cheek. She swiped it with her thumb and drew back to the present, smiling at her son in the rear-view mirror. "Hey there, baby."

"Hi, Mommy . . ." Andrew grinned, framing his cheeks in his red, gloved hands. About a week ago, she had taken him to the barber again. Though he cried and screamed at his first haircut, now at thirty-three months old, he handled the buzzing razor like a pro. With his curly, black hair smooth-shaven he was like a mini version of his daddy before Andre's hair grew back.

Eva focused back on the road and hit her gas pedal when the light flashed green. It was amazing how life repeated itself. Like she and Andre had been with their parents, Andrew was in the middle of their broken relationship. Whatever future decisions she made, she had to consider not only herself and her husband, but also their son.

A chill ran through her as she checked her side-view mirror for cars. She couldn't get over the strange feeling she was being watched. Caleb found her in more places than mere coincidence, grinning and waving at her in retail stores and the public library. Every day her iPhone dinged off and rang nonstop. It turned out messaging with Caleb and giving him her number were bad ideas. She was getting creeped out and figured his compulsive and possessive behaviors were the main reasons for his previous breakups with women. He impressed her about his achievements in real estate, but other times she found his bragging annoying.

From what she could tell, he liked Andrew a lot the afternoon they had a picnic at the town park. But he had changed her views on Andre, and now she didn't know how she felt about him nor her husband. Eva had the urge to read her bible for direction, something she hadn't done for some time, being engrossed in her studies.

She would read it after she got off from work.

Louise tilted her head. "How are things with Andre? I know you're glad he's home." She smiled tenderly at Eva, snapping open a can of Coca-Cola.

"Maybe," Eva said and sighed. "I'm so confused."

Louise made a funny look. "What's so confusing? You love Andre and he loves you."

"I'm not sure, Louise," Eva said. "He has a new mind, a new character, which I struggle to understand. He's a little better than before. His speech has improved, and he bonds with Andrew more than he used to, but he's still detached and withdrawn. I should've had the doctor prescribe him medication a long time ago, but I wanted to respect his wishes. After all, it's his body and he's the one who would be taking it, not me."

"It takes time to adjust to physical changes," Louise said, "but Andre's also always been one to have fire in his belly. I have faith things will work out between you two."

"I don't," Eva said bluntly. "Last I heard he quit his leg exercises and he and Skye mentioned nothing about him going back to the gym. Whenever I ask, they both give a shrug and a plain "I don't know" hum and it's driving me nuts. Sitting in his wheelchair for hours stiffens his body. He needs to practice steps again." She sucked her teeth. "It hurts he's given up. He could walk if he tried harder. And yet, he's not my main issue."

Louise bit a cucumber. "What's your main problem?"

"I've spent time with another man," Eva confessed, "but mostly for business purposes. His name is Caleb Williams. He's an old classmate I encountered at my class reunion, and he's unusually attracted to me." She bit her lip. "He was my high school crush, and I wanted him to like me a lot. Now that he does, I've started falling for him." Eva lowered her head, picking her nails.

Louise raised her brow and placed her long, skinny braids down her shoulder. "Does Andre know?"

"Not entirely." Eva's eyes pooled, looking up at her co-worker. "But he suspects something is going on. Caleb treated me better than I've been treated in months, but he has another side to him. Recently, I noticed him being present almost everywhere I go. It's a miracle he's not in our classroom. Because he once drove me, sometimes I think he might follow me to work and home."

Louise contorted her face. “Sounds like a stalker. You should call the police.”

“I know,” Eva said, “but Caleb’s been so kind, and I’m afraid of what might happen. For months, I’ve wanted Andre to show he loves me as Caleb did . . . the way he used to. Since I heard of his accident, I was there for him through thick and thin, but when will he be there for me?”

She laid her hand to her heart. “I mean, I’m thankful he’s home and does nice gestures, but I want him to be willing to get medical help, so we can get along better. If he cared about our love enough, he’d try harder to recover his clinical depression and mobility and take the chance to improve the function of our marriage.”

Louise leaned back. “I’m sure he didn’t mean to be selfish and uncaring. Imagine if it were you that had a car accident and suffered from memory loss.”

Eva sipped from a Styrofoam cup of iced water. “I’d feel lost . . . lost and fearful.”

“Andre probably does too,” Louise said.

“But what about me? Aren’t I entitled to happiness?” Eva said. “I’ve been doing for others and haven’t gotten the chance to fulfill my desires. Caleb’s been helping me hone my skills in interior design. It’s a dream come true.”

“Of course, you have the right to be happy,” Louise responded. “I just believe there are other ways to achieve your goals, ways that wouldn’t put your marriage at risk.”

“My marriage is already at risk.” Eva glanced from the rows of sleeping toddlers to Louise. Tears spilled on her cheeks. "I don't know how to put it back together again."

Louise sighed and placed her hand over Eva's.

Eva's heartache over her marriage had followed her into the new year, and she was exhausted over the whole situation. Andre told her he was a burden, and although she said he wasn't, his self-indulgent pity sometimes made her feel like he was.

Eva had no intentions of jumping the broom with Caleb, but maybe Andre would be better living without her in the house. Maybe he'd be happier, as her presence had been an irritation to him than anything else the past year. It was the perfect solution. Andrew could always visit his daddy, but it was time now.

They had to go their separate ways.

• CHAPTER 43 •

Andre

Wednesday Afternoon

Andre clenched his teeth and watched Skye count his number of reps, working up a sweat from a handicap lat pulldown machine at the Body Shop Fitness Center. He inhaled with each pull of the cable handles and exhaled when he released, building up his chest muscles, biceps, and mid-back. The metal weights slid and clanked faster as he sped up his pace, releasing bursts of grit and frustration. Contemplating his nightmare and everything he endured from his car accident to his therapy, a soup of emotions stirred within him.

Somehow, he had to prove to his wife he wasn't a sourpuss or helpless weakling. Dealing with his depression for him had been like a stubborn rash he couldn't cure, but ever since he came home, he reached the rebirth of his manhood. On the first morning he saw Eva again, he admitted to himself he couldn't let her slip away. Like Dylan, his physical therapist said, with hard work, one day he believed he'll get out of his wheelchair and walk again. But if he doesn't, he'll do whatever he could to help take care of his family. Having paralysis and low testosterone levels, he thought he was fooling himself, but maybe someday they'll have another baby.

Since he had no spinal cord injury, he had hoped for a second child, but he also had his doubts and insecurities. It was obvious the process would be a little more difficult, and maybe Eva wasn't physically attracted to him anymore. But regardless of their differences or preferences, their marriage could still get back on track.

Besides, there was no way he'd allow another man to steal his wife and son. After his awareness of Eva and Andrew and who they were, he felt an emotional connection to them and realized how much they meant to him. They weren't strangers as he had thought or aliens from Mars.

They were his family.

Being freed from a shell of confusion and loneliness, he needed and wanted them in his life. Yesterday, he and Skye along with his grandpa snuck to the hospital for him to have a brief follow-up with his critical care physician. Dr. Brown was intrigued with Andre's ability to retrieve some information about himself, his loved ones, and specific events of his former life. When the observation was over, the doctor explained certain distinctive objects he encountered became cues to evoke some of his memories, a medical phenomenon he referred to as *selective memory*.

Andre didn't know Eva's plans toward Caleb, but her commitment during his muddled state of mind showed she wanted them to stay together. Keeping his memory miracle and motivated recovery a secret, he asked Skye, his grandpa, Pastor Tyson, Dr. Brown, and Mrs. Flowers not to say a word.

He felt a tad wrong for testing her, but if Eva was truly in love with him, she would forget about Caleb and accept him whether or not he remembered her.

"Hey, take it easy, man," Skye said. "Your muscles look like they're about to explode."

The kilogram plate weights clanked loudly as Andre lowered them with a deep exhale.

Skye unstrapped Andre's wrists from the cable handles.

Andre licked his sweaty upper lip, grabbed a white towel Skye handed him, and wiped his face and neck. Wet spots soaked his royal blue T-shirt over his chest and his underarms.

Skye wrinkled his nose. "Are you feeling, okay?"

A drop of perspiration trickled down Andre's left temple. "Yeah . . . I feel great." He dabbed the towel at his sideburn and plastered a smile.

"Are you sure? You look like something's bothering you.

What is it?" Skye said.

Andre wrapped his towel around his neck and rolled his wheelchair from under the lat pulldown machine. He looked down and sighed, blinking and contemplating. "I don't know, man. I keep having this bad dream."

Skye frowned and sat on the leather seat of a bench press. "What's it about?"

"I'm falling down in darkness . . . and I land in this dark, smoky place."

Skye peered and inclined his head. "Then what happens?"

Andre knitted his brows. "I hear a dark-haired woman . . . screaming. Her hands bound . . . someone tied her to a chair. There's a lava lake . . . I go across these stepping stones and try to rescue her, but every time I try . . . a king cobra comes." He squeezed his eyes, his chin quivering. "It . . . it bites her, and she dies." He gulped a hard lump. "I know she's Eva, and Caleb's the snake."

"Have you told your wife?" Skye said.

Andre shook his head. "No, she'll think it's silly."

"How do you know?" Skye asked. "Eva's always cared about your thoughts. It might be a warning. Maybe she'll take it seriously. You told me she accepted your warning about Caleb before, right?"

"Yeah," Andre said, "but I think she still hangs out with him sometimes. So far, she hasn't cared much about anything nice I've done for her. I mean, she thanks me, but it's more like an indifferent type of thanks."

Skye chewed his bottom lip. "I've talked with Eva, and she's been dealing with a couple of problems too. Both of you should talk privately and stop all this crazy secrecy."

"I'm giving her some space as she did me," Andre said, shrugging. "She said she needed to think things over."

Skye crossed his arms. "Maybe so, but you should be careful and make sure it isn't an excuse because you still feel like a burden to her. You know what happened before on your grandpa's farm. Honestly, you should tell her the truth of what's been going on, and especially that you remember her and Andy again."

"Not yet," Andre said, "I don't want her to stay with me because I remember her, Skye. I want her to stay because she loves me."

"If you keep pushing her away, you're gonna lose her," Skye admonished.

Andre sighed. "I know . . . but it's complicated." He blushed and glanced behind Skye at three men talking, laughing, and running on electric treadmills, working up their cardio.

"What's so hard about bonding with your wife?" Skye arched his back and cupped his knees.

Andre drank from a bottle of dragon fruit Vitamin water, and then screwed on the cap. "You're too young to understand." He placed his drink in a holder strapped to his wheelchair.

Skye straightened and rounded his mouth in an O, getting the picture from Andre's discreet response. "Oh, you're afraid you can't get . . ."

Embarrassment consumed Andre, feeling as if the whole world knew his personal concern of whether he suffered from impotence. He bit his lower lip and wore a timid, blushing look, gripping his neck towel tighter.

"Well—" Skye twisted his mouth— "if you're worried about that, you don't know how much Eva loves you." He stood from the bench press seat and slapped Andre's toned left bicep. "Come on, it's time to work your quads." He winked and walked past to a leg extension machine.

Andre growled, tilting his head back. It hurt exercising his legs, but he knew it had to be done if he would ever move around on his own again. He pushed his wheelchair to the machine.

Skye aided him out of his chair and onto the leather seat, placing his legs between the two roll pads. Next, he set an easy weight, making sure Andre doesn't injure himself. When Andre was well-positioned, Skye knelt in front of him and smiled.

"Okay," his caregiver said, "we're gonna take it slow. Ten leg curls at twenty kilograms. You ready?"

Andre puffed his cheeks and released a slow breath. "Yeah."

"I'm gonna do the same thing as before. I'll operate the lever," Skye added.

"All right, but nice and easy, okay? I can already feel the burn with my legs stretched out." Andre reclined on the leather backrest and released a series of heavy breaths.

Skye chuckled and nodded. "Just chill. I told you I would, didn't I?" He gripped Andre's ankles and carefully pushed down so Andre's legs bent over and ascended the metal weights. He slowly raised it up and continued the process, picking up on counting the reps. "Two . . . three . . . four . . . five . . . six . . . seven . . . eight . . . nine . . . ten. Are you all right?"

Andre's legs quivered. "You mean besides my muscle spasms?"

Skye wore a half-grin and cocked his head. "They'll ease up and stop soon."

"Get me back in my chair, will you?" Andre grimaced. With the pains in his legs, he imagined Eva thought he didn't exercise like he was supposed to. But constantly working out his legs, his muscle spasms hurt terribly and weren't so funny anymore. He wished he had kept up with his exercises instead of taking a short break.

Skye pushed Andre's wheelchair closer and helped him back into it again.

"Thanks," Andre said, adjusting his feet on the footplates.

"You know we'll be back tomorrow, right?" Skye reminded him, arching his brow. "You need to rebuild your leg muscles, as they've worn down over time."

"I know." Andre gave a smile, gripping the rubber tires of his chair. "And I can't wait. I don't wanna stay in a wheelchair forever. God be my helper, I will walk . . . for Eva, Andy, and myself."

"That's the spirit!" Skye gave Andre a high five. "Come on, it's time you practice standing again." He and Andre left from the gym and went to his grandpa's farm.

Without Eva knowing, Grandpa Ricardo built wooden makeshift parallel bars in the backyard shed. Monday of the week, Andre began practicing standing and taking steps again.

Andre took a long breath and rolled his wheelchair between the two parallel boards. He nodded at Skye in front of him, his expression serious and determined. "Let's do this."

Skye grinned and strapped Andre with a gate belt around his waist. He clutched the belt and counted, preparing Andre to stand up. "Ready? One, two, three." He tugged Andre out of his chair, which Grandpa Ricardo pulled away from behind him.

Andre straightened his back with a growl and gripped his fingerless-gloved hands on the rough, sandy boards. He was a few inches taller than Skye. He inhaled deeply.

It always felt good to be on his feet instead of restrained in his wheelchair.

A tender smile curved his lips as he closed his eyes. He

imagined himself walking toward Eva on a sunny, spring day: *He saw the blissful smile on her pretty face as he stepped to her in the open green pasture, her raven hair dancing in the wind. He made it to her, and she embraced him in her arms. They gazed in each other's eyes and exchanged smiles, approaching a kiss . . .*

"Looking good, *nieto*," Grandpa Ricardo said, interrupting his romantic fantasy. "How long you standing this time?"

Andre sighed with longing and snapped out of his muse. He glanced over his shoulder at his grandfather. "Two minutes, Grandpa."

His grandfather held a stopwatch and clicked the start button. "All right, it's counting."

"Okay." Andre exhaled slow, pacing breaths, holding his standing position with Skye's help. Each day he felt a little tingling in his toes and feet and an ounce of strength building to his legs.

"Time!" Grandpa Ricardo said, pressing the stop button.

"You can sit down now." Skye held the gate belt and eased Andre back into his wheelchair. "Great job, man! That's the longest you stood yet. You ready to try steps?"

"Give me a minute." Andre licked his lips and leaned back his head. He glanced at the wooden ceiling and relaxed his speedy heart rate. "Okay, I'm ready."

Skye held the gate belt and counted again, lifting Andre back out of his chair. He stood farther at the end of the boards and observed as Andre dragged his numb, flimsy legs across the dirt ground, taking small steps.

Andre's eyes watered, fighting shooting pains in his legs, but he refused to quit and give up. He had to get out of his comfort zone of lies and hopelessness, and regaining his mobility and taking his medication were two ways in which he could do this.

Now his marriage and family were worth more to him than holding his adamant opinion. It wasn't easy learning everything over, but in the year and four months since his car accident, he had made a miraculous recovery.

Earlier in the morning, Andre found a Sony camera in the master bedroom closet and turned it on out of curiosity. He swiped through the video footage and watched several clips from his and Eva's honeymoon vacation in Mexico to his rehab therapy. All the smiles and laughs from their past made him nostalgic and realize how much Eva credited him for the progress he made, sticking by his side during his therapy sessions.

She was always behind-the-scenes—always with him.

Remembering some days more than others, his memories were like a few found words in a search puzzle of scattered letters. Nonetheless, he had come a long way from where he was. Eva couldn't grasp how it felt to be a self-reliant, strong man, and then become helpless as a child. Or how it was to fall in a chamber of despair so deep he had to look up to see the bottom. But Andre wouldn't hold it against her though.

He loved her too much to hold a grudge.

• CHAPTER 44 •

Eva

Same Day

Eva sat in the driver's seat and took her Holy Bible out of the glove compartment of her car. She closed her eyes and held it across her forehead, pleading with God. *Guide me, Lord. Show me what to do*. She stuck her thumb in the gold-edged pages, flipped open to where she had bookmarked in (1 Corinthians 7:11), and whispered the verse to herself: *"But and if she depart, let her remain unmarried or be reconciled to her husband: and let not the husband put away his wife."* She lifted her head and glimpsed outside her windshield as Louise waved and buckled her baby girl, Kenya, in the back of her white Nissan Pathfinder.

Recollection settled within her mind. Pastor Tyson read the same verse during one of his sermons one Sunday ago, but she had paid little attention. Marriage was an institution arranged by God since the day He presented Eve to Adam in the Garden of Eden. Eva nodded in accordance with what she read. As a virtuous woman who held her integrity, she couldn't forsake the law of God to please her flesh, even if she wanted to. Aside from separation and living alone, resolving her marriage with Andre was her only option.

Divorce was the law of the land constructed by man, which allowed married couples to sever their ties, particularly for another. However, Eva was determined to be in a committed relationship with her husband, and that they'd work out their differences.

But with a brain injury involved, it was extremely difficult. Andre's stonewalling wouldn't get her anywhere, but neither would her spending time with another man. Both tested each other's love and vows of commitment. They were in the wrong, and she wanted it to stop.

Eva closed her bible and switched on her engine. She needed to talk to the pastor and consult him in her final decision. She couldn't say she wasn't attracted to Caleb. If she did, she would be lying through her teeth. Her heart was overwhelmed with conflicting desires, not knowing whether to stick with Andre or back away.

Regardless, for the sake of their son, she wanted Andrew to keep his father in his life, a privilege which Eva hadn't been able to have as a child. There were too many fatherless children, too many women trying to fill the shoes of mother and father in their children's lives.

Eva pulled out of the parking lot of the daycare and drove to the church. One elder was outside mowing the church lawn. She smiled and rolled down the passenger window. "Hello, is Pastor Tyson here?"

"Yes, ma'am. He arrived about five minutes ago," the old brother said.

"Thank you." Eva got out of her car and took Andrew from his booster seat. She entered the church and walked down the carpet aisle with her son by the hand. Pastor Tyson was talking with someone in his office as Eva was about to knock. She hesitated and waited on a front pew.

About ten minutes later, the office's door opened and a pregnant, teenage girl and a woman who Eva assumed was the girl's mother exited with tear-streaked faces.

"Hi," Eva said meekly.

"Hello," the woman replied, holding an arm around the girl's shoulders as they walked by in the middle of the aisle.

Eva closed her eyes and inhaled a deep breath in her lungs. She stood and tapped on the ajar door of the pastor's office. "Pastor Tyson?"

Pastor Tyson looked up from an open bible on his desk and grinned. "Sister, Lucas, how are you doing?"

"I wanted to talk with you." Eva's eyes swam with tears.

Pastor Tyson stood and directed a hand to the chairs

in front of his large desk. "Sure, come right in, sister."

Eva entered the office with Andrew and sat in a chair, adjusting her son in her lap.

The pastor closed the door and took his seat in his chair. "What's the problem? Is it Andre again?" He wove his hands on top his bible and studied her attentively.

Eva's shoulders' sagged. "Pastor Tyson, I have sinned. I haven't done right by myself or my husband, and now I'm paying the price for my actions."

The pastor frowned. "What happened? What have you done?"

Eva hung her head and sniffled. She told Pastor Tyson she spent leisure time with another man who she liked during high school, and he appears to be attracted to her. "I think he . . . he expects me to have a love affair with him, but I don't want to. I mean, I find him attractive, but I never meant for our relationship to be more than friendship. Many things fell out of control, and I retaliated out of anger."

"Have you talked with Andre?" Pastor Tyson said.

Eva shook her head. "Sort of. He knows about Caleb, but not about me spending time in his house and going to dinner with him. It's been impossible to discuss matters with Andre without him having a fit. It's bad enough he quit his exercises. I don't think he's doing much to better his condition. He's been getting more pains in his legs lately. Whenever I come home, I find him sitting in his wheelchair and watching television in the living room." She sighed. "We hardly talk, and we sleep in separate bedrooms. At first, it was because of Andre's quadriplegia, but he can move around a lot more than he used to. So, there are no more excuses for us sleeping apart now."

Pastor Tyson gripped a sharpened pencil in his hands. "So, what's the reason you came here?"

"I'm thinking of separating from Andre," Eva blurted, "I know what the scriptures say, but I guess I was wondering what you suppose I should do."

The pastor rubbed his chin. "I see. Well, I'm afraid my opinion doesn't matter, sister. I can only give you what's written in the Good Book. You're the one who must decide whether to live with Andre." He angled his head. "I mean, you've always been a gracious person, and you and your husband have been in love since high school. Do you want to be alone?"

"Well, no," Eva answered, "but I can't deal with his inattention. So many times, he's been mean or aloof toward me, but he's more distant than anything."

"Maybe Andre should be on meds," Pastor Tyson suggested.

Eva wiped her nose with a tissue. "I've tried to get him to take some, but he refuses. He doesn't think it'll help him."

"Perhaps he's changed his mind." A twinkle sparkled

in the pastor's eye, inching up a smile as if he knew something she didn't. "Go to him, Eva. Talk with him."

"But he—"

"Go to your husband," Pastor Tyson interrupted, "and try talking to him. See if you can't get matters resolved, all right?"

Eva exhaled and massaged her brow. "Okay, but if he doesn't respond or listen to me—"

"Don't expect the worst," Pastor Tyson said. "Hope for the best. Remember, Andre came back home to you after weeks of being away. He might listen to your perspective this time if you're ready to talk with him."

Eva stood with her son and swiped her eyes. "Okay, I'll try, but if he doesn't listen, I see no other solution than us splitting up. Goodbye, pastor."

"Bye, sister. I'll be praying for you two," the pastor said.

Eva left and rode home. Thick gray clouds coated the sky as sundown drew near. She unbuckled her seatbelt and stared at their house. *Please, God, let things work out. Let us be in unity*. She sighed and dragged herself out of her car and took Andrew from the back seat.

Eva strode up the walkway, her heart pounding with the click-clack of her leather winter boots.

Fresh lavender scent met her as she entered through the door. Eva gaped and scanned the entire living room. Everything was clean and organized. A cozy fire burned in the brick fireplace, and the flatscreen TV was off. She closed the door with a suspicious look, wondering what Andre and Skye were up to tonight.

She placed Andrew upstairs in his crib and returned down to check things out. As she got closer to the kitchen, the aromas of meaty sauce, herbal spices, garlic bread, and cheeses mingled in a delicious fragrance that wafted through the air.

Her stomach growled.

Italian lasagna was her favorite pasta meal, and Eva couldn't wait to get a slice. She found Andre and Skye in the kitchen gathering dishes and silverware.

Eva crinkled her nose with a half-smile and jerked her thumb behind her. "What's going on here?" She darted her eyes to Andre's caregiver and giggled. "And Skye, why are you wearing my apron?"

The color drained from Skye's face, gawking at her. He fidgeted off the flower-print, full-body apron tied on him and tossed it on the counter. "Don't mind me. I make a mess when I cook, and I didn't want to get my clothes dirty."

Eva chuckled. "What are you guys doing?"

Andre pushed his wheelchair to her and smiled. "We made dinner for you."

Eva glanced from him to Skye. "Well, thank you both."

"Don't thank me, Mrs. Lucas," Skye said with a goofy

look, "the whole thing was Andre's idea. I was his cooking assistant."

Eva marveled at her husband and his bright, healthy, countenance. She smelt a fresh whiff of his dusky cologne and his dark, curly haircut was gelled and neatly trimmed. He looked as handsome as he did on their wedding day. Something was immensely different about him. She'd been suspicious and known it for some time, but she hadn't believed his sincerity until today. Maybe she could talk personally with him after all.

Since they married, Andre had *never* cooked dinner, and especially not her favorite pasta dish. Figuring out his changed behavior was like trying to crack a secret code, but then she remembered her prayer after visiting him in Acute Care.

Her beloved husband, who for the longest had been down in the dumps, was finally reflecting the selfless love she had shown him for the past year and one month. They struggled through many valleys and climbed over many hills to reach their turning point, and she thanked God for this pleasant evening.

No matter what fun, exciting times she had with Caleb hanging out and designing homes, she could never pluck Andre out of her heart. Everywhere she went with Caleb, something or someone reminded her of a special time *they* had spent together. And though her husband had been a workaholic, it showed he was a loving, giving person.

Eva's spirits buoyed. "Um, thanks for dinner. It smells amazing." She tilted her head with a flirty smile, placing a hand on her hip. "It was very considerate of you, Mr. Lucas. I didn't know you could make baked lasagna."

"I couldn't," Andre said and snickered. "I Googled an online recipe."

"Oh, well, I guess that explains it," Eva said, rolling her eyes.

They shared a lighthearted laugh.

Andre gripped the wheels of his chair. "It'll be ready in a couple minutes."

"Splendid. Andy's upstairs sleeping." Eva smoothed her hands down her khaki skirt. She thought about her talk with the pastor and cleared her throat. "Uh, Andre, can we talk—" she glanced from Skye to her husband—"privately please?"

"Okay." Andre followed her in his wheelchair through the entryway to the living room. "What do you want to talk about?"

Eva sat on the couch and placed her hands together to her chin as if praying for the right words to say. "Andre, I've been trying to build up the courage to speak with you, so please, try not to get upset, okay?"

"I'll try," Andre said.

Eva sighed and looked at him. "I have a confession to

make." She gulped loudly. "Caleb and I . . . we've spent time together, besides about our interest in interior design."

Andre wore a disturbed expression but continued listening.

She cleared the air before he could assume the worst. "Nothing too serious happened between us. We've just gone out to dinner, and I talked and had a few drinks of brandy over at his house. Since you came home, I haven't spent time with him, but he's been stalking me."

Andre's eyebrows rose. "Stalking you? That's terrible! Why didn't you tell me? We should report him to the police."

"No," Eva said and shook her head.

"What do you mean, no?" Andre frowned. "Eva, stalkers are dangerous. I don't want you to get hurt."

Eva folded her forearms on her knees. "I know, but I wanna give him a chance before we get the police involved. If I talk with him and explain how I feel, maybe he'll leave me alone."

Andre screwed up his face. "What is it with you and Caleb? Why can't you let him be and move on?"

"Because I—"

"I'll tell you why," Andre interrupted. "It's because you love him, isn't it?"

Eva pursed her lips and stared at him in silence, annoyed by his hot temper.

"Isn't it?" Andre urged.

"No, I don't!" Eva's cell phone vibrated against her hip, most likely Caleb.

Looking at her husband's irritated face, she fought to ignore the call, but her exasperation pulled her aside. She glanced at the face of her iPhone and wilted her shoulders with dread. "Someone's calling me. Don't worry, I promise I'll be back for dinner, okay?"

"Uh, sure." Andre's expression softened, but she knew he was still distrustful of her involvement with Caleb.

Eva stood and ran up the staircase. She went to the master bedroom and answered the call to stop her phone from buzzing again. "Hello?"

"Hey, Eva. It's Caleb. Listen, I've been trying to reach you, but you've always gotten away. Can you meet me in the town park tomorrow? I have something important to discuss with you."

Eva searched her eyes around the room and licked her lips. "Oh, um . . . I don't think I can make it."

"Come on, please. It'll only take a couple of minutes. I really need you to come," Caleb said.

Eva sighed and gritted her teeth. Her mother always told her if she didn't want a certain man and his advances to either ignore him or tell him. Pretending she didn't notice Caleb around her hadn't worked. So, it was time for plan B. By meeting with him face-to-face, she could explain she appreciated his help with her college studies, but intends to stay with her husband and no longer wants to hang around him.

"Okay," Eva said with a tired exhale, scratching her brow. "I'll meet you after work."

"Excellent! I'll see you then."

"Bye, Caleb." Eva ended the call and released a long breath. Her stomach was queasy, uncertain she'd be able to eat tonight. What Caleb wanted to talk about was her least bit of concern.

She was too worried she made the wrong choice again.

• CHAPTER 45 •

Andre

Wednesday Night

Having dinner with Eva tonight was sociable and worked out well, but Andre was concerned about her; not to mention, he still had to think of how to break the heavy news of his confession. Telling your wife you tried to kill yourself wasn't the easiest thing to do. But he knew he had to get around to it if they were to rebuild a mutually honest relationship. He wanted to tell her while they were eating, but he struggled to escape the words from his mouth.

Instead, Andre ignored himself and focused on her problem with Caleb. He advised her to change her cell number and deactivate her social media accounts for the time being. Eva agreed and then talked about her passion for interior design. Afterward, she discussed her Interior

Design program at the Art Institute of Charlotte. Lastly, she expressed her desire someday to start a home decor business like the one and only Martha Stewart.

Andre loved her animated mannerisms and enthusiasm over the subjects. Her cocoa brown eyes lit up as she mentioned her course schedule, her college professors, and the time her spring classes will begin Friday night. He volunteered to help Eva study whenever she needed to, and she smiled and thanked him.

When dinner was over, he prepared himself for bed in the guestroom. His mind echoed with thoughts as he fastened on his burgundy nightshirt with his button hook tool, urging him to speak on his matter. *Tell her, Andre. Just tell her what you did.*

He sighed deeply and looked at his reflection in the mirror of the guest dresser. Why couldn't he say it? What was holding him back? Maybe it was anxiety or shame. He had detached himself from his emotions so long, he thought his heart would burst like a water balloon if he released them.

What would Eva think of him? He didn't know how she would take it, but as long as it was since the incident, it was obvious Skye hadn't and wouldn't say a word about it for him. He fixed his collar and closed his eyes. *Come on, Andre. Be a man and just tell her.*

Andre rolled his manual wheelchair out of the guestroom, surprised by the lighting in the living room. A lamp on a side table was still on and his wife was asleep on the couch with her books around her legs on the snowflake fleece blanket draped over her. On the center table was her pink, Mother's Day mug from when he had made hot coffee for her earlier.

He smiled, shook his head, and wheeled over to her. As he expected, she had her reading glasses on again. He fingered some of her hair away from her forehead and slipped off and folded her glasses, putting them on the living room table.

Andre inched up a little smile and cocked his head, admiring her. He *loved* this woman and liked to watch her. She looked so pretty and calm, like a sleeping beauty. If confessing the truth makes her depart and look at him differently, it'll crush his heart.

He kissed on her forehead. "I'm sorry. Good night." He sighed and was about to leave, but stopped his wheelchair at the edge of the couch. Beside her feet on top of one of her textbooks was her Bible. He grabbed it and opened it to where she had bookmarked in his lap.

She was reading in Hebrews 4. His eyes dropped to the last two verses of the chapter: *For we have not an high priest which cannot be touched with the feeling of our infirmities; but was in all points tempted like as we are, yet without sin.*

Andre raised his head and meditated on the verse for a moment. Having Skye by his side was encouraging, but despite their similarities with brain injury, there was a part of Andre the kind, funny guy would never understand.

His soul and spirit.

But Jesus Christ, the Lord and Savior—He knew everything without him saying a word. He ran his forefinger across the last verse, whispering it to himself: *Let us therefore come boldly unto the throne of grace, that we may obtain mercy, and find grace to help in time of need.* He closed the Bible and lifted his head again. A lot had happened to him. He'd lost touch with God through his sickness, but he wanted to redeem His love and grace.

Andre hung his head. *Please, help me, Lord. Help me . . .* He stared at Eva again. It was late and he didn't want to interrupt her sleep, but it was time for him to let go of everything that had been hurting inside him.

He would tell her tomorrow.

• CHAPTER 46 •

Andre

Thursday, Jan. 3rd

Andre yawned and rose from the bed in the guestroom, overhearing his wife and Mrs. Flowers chattering about their son. Andrew was cranky from growing new teeth and under the weather with a low-grade fever, so the elderly woman had come over to babysit today. Eva spoke her usual, perky goodbye, headed off to work, and shut the door, but he worried for her safety and life.

Based on her hesitant behavior, he knew it was Caleb who called on her phone yesterday. He could've grilled her again, but he didn't want to ruin the friendly relations budding between them. Trust was the foundation of any relationship. As hard as it was, he had to believe Eva would be wise and make the right decision for herself and their marriage and son.

But that didn't mean he wasn't afraid for her.

Andre rubbed his hand down his drowsy face and checked the time on the digital clock.

6:20 a.m.

He grimaced and swallowed a gulp of warm saliva. A metallic taste filled his mouth, and his lower back pulsated with a throbbing muscle spasm. By now, he knew what he needed to do. He looked at the nightstand and saw his gray carry tote, but his plastic urinal was missing. He widened his eyes and dread plunged in his gut. *Crap! It's in the bathroom sink cabinet.* He had gotten sick of looking at it and hid it away from time to time.

Andre dragged his wheelchair closer to the bedside and tucked the wooden slide board under his buttocks. He flared his nostrils and tightened his lips as he gradually transferred from the bed into his wheelchair. The struggle of moving his one-hundred-and-eighty-pound weight took a good five minutes before he got seated.

It always annoyed him how long it took, but it wasn't the time to get upset. He leaned to the side and pulled the board from under him. Then he set his gray tote in his lap. Feeling dampness on the crotch of his burgundy pajamas, he realized he suffered minor leakage in his sleep.

Andre rolled his eyes and sighed. *You idiot! I'm such a loser.* He hated having to use a catheter, but it was the only way he could safely empty his bladder due to his problem with retention. He looked around desperately for another container to use.

Nothing.

Andre wheeled himself out of the guestroom, careful not to scuff the off-white drywall in the hallway.

Skye entered through the front door right on time.

Andre brightened. "Good morning."

Skye grinned. "Morning, Andre."

"Hey, my urinal's in the bathroom upstairs," Andre muttered glumly. "Can you get it for me, please?"

"Sure." Skye raced up the staircase.

Andre cupped his hands around his mouth, shouting with urgency. "And make it quick!" He thought he would die from his embarrassment. He rubbed his forehead, trying to keep from stressing so much. He wished there was more than one bathroom in the house. Maybe it was a renovation he and Eva ought to consider for the future.

Holding his water too long was a health risk to his system, and as Eva warned, the last thing he needed was another medical problem. He overhead Skye excuse himself from Mrs. Flowers who was giving Andrew his bath.

"I got it!" Skye hurled downstairs with the clear plastic container and handed it to Andre.

"Thanks." Andre took it from Skye and pushed himself back in the guestroom, slamming the door. He wheeled himself close to the dresser, placed his gray tote on top of it, and fidgeted out his supplies from the bag. His heart hammered in his chest, springing another leak. *Rats!*

Sometimes he felt like his bladder had a mind of its own, choosing to signal whenever it was inconvenient.

"Are you okay, man?" Skye asked outside the door. "You need help?"

Andre hesitated. His eyes moistened as he rubbed on hand sanitizer. He attached his Velcro-strapped urinal on his chair between his inner thighs and clipped the Betty Hook to hold down his pajamas and boxers.

"I'm good!" Andre answered over his shoulder, though he wasn't sure he'd make it without wetting his wheelchair. He cleaned himself, quickly lubricated a sterile catheter, and inserted it in. When he finally relieved himself, he thought the flow wouldn't stop. He must've drunk a little too much iced tea during dinner last night.

Andre closed his eyes and felt a tear slip down his cheek. *Why do I have to be like this? It's not fair.* One night had ruined his life forever. Was he cursed? Was God punishing him for his workaholic mindset? Was he afflicted to spend more time with his wife? If this was why he suffered so, he was sorry from the depth of his soul.

As his bladder emptied, his back spasm throbbed less and less. He sighed with relief, fluttering open his eyes. Why hadn't he listened to Eva's advice? She told him to keep his urinal close to him, but he was hardheaded, preferring to use the toilet like normal men whenever Skye was on duty. From now on, he would guard it with his life, or one day he may completely wet himself or suffer from kidney malfunction.

He sniffled and dried his cheek with the knuckle of his forefinger. These times were always uncomfortable to him, despite not being able to feel it. He slid out the catheter, cleaned himself, put the used wipe in the torn plastic packet, and pulled up his pants. He rubbed more sanitizer on his hands and paused, studying his reflection of the dresser mirror.

Since his brain injury, he'd completely lost interest in being intimate, and in his present condition, he wasn't confident he could anymore. It was one of the main reasons he worried about losing his wife. If he couldn't satisfy her physical needs in their relationship would Eva cut out on him? He knew she was lonely during his depressed state, and after his withdrawn nature and her late returns from the library, he feared she and Caleb were having a secret affair.

Remorse collapsed on him. He buried his face in his hands and sobbed, recalling his past mistakes. *Please, forgive me, God.* They wanted another baby, but he always made excuses and prevented them from ever trying to do so. After the critical birth of their son, out of fear and doubt, he couldn't take a hopeful chance and go through with it. Now he faced possibly never being able to have another child with his wife again.

Skye knocked on the door, startling him. "Hey, Andre, are you finished?"

"Oh, yes! I'm done!" Andre swiped a fist over his teary eyes, rolled his wheelchair over, and opened the door.

"Feeling better?" Skye wore a silly grin.

Andre tittered and handed over his urinal. "Yeah, relieved."

"I hope you've learned your lesson, *Mr. Lucas,*" Skye said, arching his brow. "Let me dump it out. I'll be right back." He took the container upstairs to the bathroom.

Andre facepalmed and sighed. *I'm so sorry, Eva. I love you so much.*

It was three-thirty in the afternoon.

Andre held the bridge of his nose and blinked faintly. He and Skye were playing a game of checkers on a side table. Mrs. Flowers was knitting socks and watching the news. On the television, the weatherman was reporting a severe thunderstorm expected to bring ice pellets tonight. Andre watched as Skye double-jumped a black chip on the checkered board, stealing his last red chip.

"Booyah! I win again." Skye's smile faded, looking at Andre. "Hey, dude, you look tired."

Andre nodded and fluttered his eyelids. "Uh, yeah . . . I guess I am."

"It's probably from your exercising," Skye said. "Do you want me to help you upstairs for a nap?"

"Yes, please," Andre replied, but he doubted he'd be able to sleep without having a nightmare again. He pushed his wheelchair to the staircase and lowered his footrests. Skye helped him into the seat of the stairlift and operated the lever. Andre rose over the flight of stairs. After he reached the top, Skye carried Andre's manual wheelchair upstairs and helped him into it.

"Thanks, Skye," Andre said. "I've got it from here."

Being accustomed to using his slide board, he could get in and out of bed himself. As Skye went downstairs, Andre wheeled to Andrew's bedroom and stopped himself. He pushed back the door and turned inside to the white crib. It was the first time he entered his son's room after returning home. His fatherhood hit him as he surveyed the childlike environment, and he desired to be the best dad he could be with his new life.

He looked through the safety rail bars, checking on his son. The little boy was resting with his stuffed monkey under his arm, snuggled in his Cookie Monster fleece blanket. His small body rose and fell peacefully, taking an afternoon nap after whining and crying all day. An hour ago, he held and rocked his son in his tan recliner in the living room, putting him to sleep.

Mrs. Flowers had tried to shush and calm him, but he wanted his daddy's touch this time. Holding Andrew was magical and brought joy to his soul. He wished he could stop the pain of his son's teething, but it was a part of him growing up. Andrew's baby years were fading away. Eva had already begun potty-training their son and Andre longed for the months he lost bonding with him.

He would *never* get them back.

Spring around the corner, he and Eva made plans for their son's third birthday party last night, deciding on a Sesame Street theme.

Andrew was a special gift.

Even in his dazed state, the kid's contagious smile had moved his heart. But he didn't feel qualified to be a father then, especially since he had lost mindfulness of what a father was. Now aware, he wanted to stay involved in his son's life. He wanted to play catch with him on hot, summer days, and have snowball fights on cold, winter evenings. He wanted to read him bedtime stories, send him on his first day of kindergarten, and one day watch him marry the woman of his dreams.

Andre reached between the safety bars and held Andrew's hand, stroking his thumb over his son's fingers. Unshed tears shimmered in his eyes. Thinking of another man taking his wife and raising his son disturbed his spirit. He licked a tear that fell on his lips and whispered, "I'm sorry, Andy. Daddy's been missing for some time, but I want you to know . . . I love you. I promise . . . nobody will take you from me."

"Nobody," he whispered with more vigor. He narrowed his eyes and tightened his mouth. As he studied his son, a strong sensation of worry swept over him. He released his son's hand and pondered his apprehension.

A still voice spoke to him in the silence. *Pray for Eva. Pray for your wife now.*

Andre's breaths quickened. He hadn't prayed for the longest, but he believed God enough to know it was Him who strengthened and spared one's life. He bowed his head. *Okay, Lord. I'll pray.* He clasped his hands and exhaled a breath. "Dear God, please help my wife. Let her stand her ground and protect her from the attack of the enemy. Please . . . don't let her leave me."

He sniffled repetitively, contorting his face. "Forgive me for not being there for Eva like I should have. Renew her love for the man I am . . . not for the man I was. Help restore my strength . . . and get me on my feet again. I pray in Jesus Christ's name . . . amen."

Andre opened his eyes and inhaled sharply. He sighed and wiped his runny nose. Eva was off from work, but he got a hunch she had other plans besides visiting the college or public library before coming home.

She was going to see Caleb.

• CHAPTER 47 •

Eva

Thursday Afternoon

"Have a good evening, Louise!" Eva smiled and waved at her co-worker in the jam-packed parking lot behind the daycare building. She settled in her car, buckled her seatbelt, and cranked the engine. Within seconds, the bridge of CeCe Winans' song "Never Have to Be Alone" blasted through her car speakers, startling her.

Eva decreased the volume and listened to the song's ending. She held her steering wheel and lowered her head in meditation. The lyrics were counsel to her heart and soul, both about her relationship with God and her husband. If she remained patient and relied on the Lord for comfort through her difficult times, she wouldn't have gotten in an emotional mess. And though she was fond of Caleb and impressed by his success, since they were teenagers, Andre had always been her main man, making her laugh and cheering her up after Caleb's disappointing lies and drawbacks. Talking with Nadine and witnessing her sadness reminded her of something significant. She didn't need the latest trend or fashion to build her confidence. She already had everything that mattered most to her.

She had God—the Supreme Father and counselor who had always been there and supplied her needs. Her son Andrew—the little clown and miracle who had filled her days with joy and laughter. And her husband Andre—an inspiring man who had been her earthly confidant and guiding light during some of the darkest times of her life.

Eva lost hope there was anything left of her husband, but yesterday proved Mrs. Flowers was right about him making a comeback and showing up someday. Andre was her soulmate who had led her to the love of God and cherished her before she was aware.

Suffering from memory loss, it amazed her he cooked Italian lasagna, her favorite pasta. She wondered if her husband remembered her, but considering he couldn't recall the old photos she showed him, she thought it was a coincidence.

A female radio announcer stated Fred Hammond's "I Will Trust" as the next song for the gospel station, but Eva turned off the radio. She sighed, turned her gearshift into drive, and cruised out of the sloped entrance of the daycare. Her mind spun with anxious thoughts as she rode to meet Caleb at the town park. He had called her while she was at work in the middle of her lesson plan with her class again, asking if she was still meeting him. She told him she was, and his joyous reaction made her more nervous about her bad news. He was totally unaware of her purpose for coming to speak with him, but he was about to learn the truth.

Eva regretted the camaraderie she built with him over the months. It made ending their company more challenging. She prayed he'd be able to take another woman's rejection. Eva pulled along the sidewalk a little distance away from the town park.

Caleb was sitting on a wood bench in his tan trench coat and black gloves, resting an arm on top the seat. He looked at her with his wide grin and waved.

A shiver ran up Eva's spine. She exhaled and parked her car. Turning away from Caleb was the right thing to do. Besides, having another man in her heart, she would never be satisfied with him, even if she wanted to swap into a brand-new relationship. She got out of her car and stepped on the sidewalk caked with ice.

She took a deep breath and daringly walked toward Caleb, her suede boots clacking on the wet pavement. The park was a winter wonderland. Icicles dangled from bare oak trees and the center pond and water fountain were crystallized with sugary frost. Piles of snow tainted by exhaust surrounded the open field and naked grassy patches had discolored to a dried, crisp brown.

But the park still tugged Eva's heartstrings—for she and Andre had their wedding in this same place roughly ten years ago. She pictured the decorations, the guests, and the sounds from the event: *the rows of black folding chairs in the lawn, the white rose altar where Andre and the pastor stood, the mossy trail sprinkled with rose petals, and the soft piano music playing "Canon in D" as she walked the aisle.* There were special memories all around her. How can she ever forget them?

Eva perched on the park bench.

"Hey, I'm glad you're here," Caleb said finally.

She gave a weak smile. "Hey."

Caleb sat squarely, facing her. "Eva, I have to tell you something, and I need you to really listen to me."

Eva nibbled her upper lip. "Before you speak, I have something to say too."

"All right, fine," Caleb said, "but can I go first? It was my request for us to meet here."

She made a slight nod. "Okay . . . what is it?"

"Eva . . . we've spent much time together," Caleb began, "and I know it may be sudden, but we've also known each other for a long time. We grew up together." He dug in a coat pocket and took out a small velvet box.

Eva's heart shuddered. For a man who had been a player in the past, she knew where his conversation was drifting—a marriage proposal.

"I know you're skeptical of these, but maybe it'll show how much you mean to me." Caleb opened the tiny box.

A ring lodged in the black interior velvet sparkled in the afternoon sun.

Caleb met her eyes. "Eva, I know what I said before about us being friends, but the truth is, I love you. I think about you every second of the day. I'll be honored if you become my wife. We have much in common with design. Andrew's gotten used to me, and I promise I'll treat him as my son. I'll take care of you two, and we can be happy together. Will you marry me?"

Like a whisper, Mrs. Flowers' words spoke to her: *True love never dies*. For a while, she tried to discard her love for Andre and replace it with the thrill of fashion and her attention from Caleb, but neither one of them had worked.

It hadn't resolved the question embedded in the back of her mind since the downfall began of Andre's health and outlook on life. How could she divorce her husband when his brain injury and the emotional strain it caused on their marriage were neither of their faults?

Eva's mouth hung open, glancing from the diamond, fourteen-carat gold ring to Caleb's face again. She had to admit the ring was beautiful, but she couldn't dishonor her husband and agree with the proposal. "I'm sorry, but I can't accept your ring or marry you." She stood on her feet, her heart pounding.

Caleb frowned. "Why not? You enjoyed the times we spent together."

"Not entirely," Eva confessed and wrapped her arms around herself.

"What are you talking about?" Caleb stood.

Eva sighed and shook her head. "I gotta be honest here . . . I wanted to forget Andre the way he had done me and our son, but whenever I hung out with you, I thought about the life we had and our memories." She turned her face away. "And it doesn't make sense why you're so interested in me either. You never paid attention to me in school, except if you needed help with your homework."

"I wanted to, Eva. Believe me," Caleb said with a sobered expression.

Eva gave him a stern look. "Then why didn't you? Was it because I wasn't pretty enough then?"

"No," Caleb said and angled his head. "I just had . . . a reputation. I was the point guard of the boys' basketball team. You know how that goes in high school."

Eva grimaced and hissed. "Yeah, the *popular* kids ignore all the outcasts." She crossed her arms and inched backward. "I wanted to give you the benefit of the doubt, but now thinking about it, I believe it's true. Andre told me you said cruel things to him."

"That's a dead lie!" Caleb shouted.

"Is it?" Eva retorted. "Before his accident, Andre never lied to me. He always told me the truth, even if it hurts."

She raised her hands and spoke openly. "Look, I appreciate your encouragement with interior design, but deep down I never wanted to be more than friends. I should've told you sooner instead of stringing you along, but I guess I was fascinated by your attraction, especially since I wasn't expecting it."

Eva gulped and continued. "Since Andre's amnesia, it had been a long time I've felt special and wanted, and your attention helped me cope with my unfortunate situation, but it's time for it to end." She inhaled a breath and looked him in the eye. "I'm sorry, Caleb, but I won't be seeing you anymore."

She sighed and angled her head. "I wish you well and I hope you meet another woman right for you. I'd appreciate it if you stop following me around. I don't want the police involved in this. I'd rather we go our separate ways in peace."

Caleb pursed his lips and held out his arms like a gangster. "Fine! Stay with your stupid, crippled husband!"

"Don't call him that!" Eva's eyes widened and flooded with tears. "Maybe he can't walk and sometimes stutters, but he's more of a man than you'll ever be!"

Caleb's expression hardened as he squinted his eyes at her, running his tongue across his upper lip. He gave her a piercing gaze from head to toe as if looking through her clothes. "We'll see about that, won't we?" He gave a chin jut.

Eva wore a haunted look and slowly backed from him as he tucked the ring box in his coat pocket, frightened of his next moves. Witnessing his switch over from a saint to a savage, a mask of portrayal had been pulled off Caleb, exposing his rotten character to her. As she left down the sidewalk, he cupped his hands over his mouth and yelled a boastful remark.

"I'm gonna getcha, Eva! 'The CW' always *steals* what he wants!" he said and chortled. He trailed behind her like a possessed zombie, harassing her with vain fantasies and obscene remarks. "You're gonna be mine, Eva! All mine! I own you! Do you hear me? I own you!"

Fear snagged her like a tight noose around her neck, too afraid to look back. "Get lost and leave me alone!" Her heart raced in her chest, trotting as fast as she could to her car. As she cranked on her engine, Caleb startled her with a knock on her driver's side window. "Hey, Eva! You know you want some of me! Andre can't feel down below! He can't do nothing! Girl, I'm gonna rock your world! You wait and see. . . we'll make a perfect team!"

Eva glanced at him and swiftly looked away from his foolishness with embarrassment as he smooched on her window and laughed, teasing her.

"Go away!" Her throat clenched and her heart burst with remorse, wishing she'd taken Andre's advice. Caleb was super obsessive. He was as dangerous as a ticking time bomb, and she should've reported him earlier to the police. She needed to go home and apologize for nearly allowing temptation to overpower her.

Andre was her husband, and regardless of his brain injury, memory loss, and his below-average attitude at times, she was still in love with him. His willingness to spend quality time with their son and his kind favors toward her lately showed he was trying to make amends. No, their marriage won't be the same, but she believed they could reconcile and make new, good memories with their son in the future.

After all, Eva always wanted this from the start.

• CHAPTER 48 •

Eva

Same Day

Eva jogged in the windy weather toward the house and barged through the front door. Humiliation fell on her countenance. Her shoulders sagged as she calmed her rapid breathing. She looked to the couch and found Mrs. Flowers and Skye in the living room, watching the latest update on the approaching ice storm. She shivered from the freezing coldness in the air and hitched her breath. "Where's Andre?"

Skye's brows puckered, holding the remote. He stared speechlessly at her drained presence. "He's . . . upstairs."

"How is he?" Eva asked with a concerned look.

"Not too good," Mrs. Flowers said, focused on knitting her stitches. "He's been pretty quiet and hasn't talked much to anyone since this morning."

Skye nodded and added, "Yeah. He skipped breakfast and lunch today. He hasn't been down since he took a nap this afternoon."

Mrs. Flowers frowned at her. "You don't look too well either, Eva. Something wrong?"

"No, ma'am, I'll be all right." Eva ran up the staircase to the second floor and peeked into Andrew's bedroom, calling her husband's name. Andre wasn't in there, but their son was still asleep in his crib.

She sniveled and bit her nails, calling for him down the narrow hallway and checking the bathroom and then the master bedroom. Her husband was in the master room in his manual wheelchair. He was looking outside the curtained window behind the bed at the cloudy sky. Since daylight savings began, it already started getting dark by the time she came home from work.

"Andre?"

Her husband turned his head and eyed her with a shamefaced expression.

Guilt dropped in her heart from his unhappy face. She scurried over and knelt before him. Her vision clouded with new tears, holding her husband's hands.

Eva gulped and studied his eyes. "Andre, I'm *so* sorry. I'm sorry for spending time with Caleb behind your back. I thought my crush on him was over, but temptation had a hold on me. I almost . . . I . . ." Eva rested her forehead on Andre's knees and closed her eyes. Her slim shoulders shook and bobbed from stifled sobs. "Please, forgive me." She felt Andre stroke his hand over her long hair.

"I forgive you," Andre said, "and I'm sorry too. Everything wasn't your fault. You were trying to help me, but I made things harder than they had to be. I was trying to get you to give up. I didn't think you deserved a burden like me."

Eva raised her head and frowned. "Andre Miguel Lucas, how many times have I told you? You're not a burden, and I know you'll get better as time progresses."

Andre's chin quivered. "I'm sorry I'm like this, Eva. I'm sorry . . . I'm half a man."

"Oh, Andre, you're not half a man," Eva said. "You're whole and complete." She placed her hand over his chest. "You have a good heart." Her face contorted with sorrow as her husband broke down.

She placed a hand to her mouth and stifled a sob. She always hated seeing him cry, but it was a breaking point he needed to make—a release of the pain and grief he had caged inside for a life he no longer had. Before his accident, he had always kept a stiff upper lip and strove to be strong for her and their son. She cradled his bowed head and planted affectionate kisses over his haircut.

Andre lifted his face to hers and held her hands, stroking his thumbs over her knuckles. "I'm sorry. I-I wasn't there for you. I wasn't supportive of your pain or feelings. All I cared about w-was myself."

"Shh, it's okay." Eva stood and hugged him. "We can work things out. I understand you've been distressed and scared about the medicine, but maybe—"

Andre nodded and wrapped his arms around her. "It's all right. I'd rather take meds than lose you." He whispered in her ear, "I love you . . . Eva Rose."

"I love you—wait." Eva sat on his lap and linked her arms around his shoulders. She searched his eyes with wonder. "Rose . . . you said Rose. How did you know my middle name?" Her breaths quickened and her heart sped up, flabbergasted. "Andre?"

Her husband gulped and looked down. "My memory . . . partially returned. I don't remember everything, but just who my loved ones are and little significant things about them. It's how I knew lasagna was your favorite pasta." Andre took a quick breath and explained how Dr. Brown said certain objects evoked some of his memories.

"Recently, I've been taking an antidepressant he prescribed me, and it's been working," he added, "I didn't realize how much I needed help until—"

"Until what?" Eva inclined her head.

Ashamed of himself, her husband squeezed his eyes tightly and turned his face, sniffling as if he were a little child.

"It's okay, Andre," Eva whispered. "Go on, tell me what's the matter."

Andre glanced hesitantly up at her, and then kept his head down. "On my Grandpa Ricardo's farm, I . . . I tried to kill myself. I waited until my grandpa left and I was alone. Then I put my leather belt around my neck . . . I nearly choked myself to death. If Skye hadn't come, I would've been dead. I'm *so* sorry, Eva."

"Why didn't you tell me about this?" Tears ran down Eva's cheeks.

Andre licked his lips and sniffled. "I was afraid you'd l-l-leave me and too ashamed of what I'd done, and due to your company with Caleb, I wanted to make sure you stay because you love me. I also wanted to surprise you about my memory changes and going back to the gym. Skye and everyone else knew about it. I asked them not to say anything. Do you . . . do you forgive me?"

Eva smiled tenderly. "Of course, I forgive you."

"You don't think I'm a nutcase?" Andre said, arching his brow.

Eva shook her head, inching up a smile. "No, Andre. You're not crazy. We've been going through a storm, but it'll pass."

Her husband wore a lopsided grin. He framed her face in his hand and dried a tear on her cheek with his thumb. "Thank you for being my wife and friend, and staying by my side . . . even when I didn't want you to." He swallowed and his chin trembled again. "I felt lost, confused, and alone for so long. I can't believe I forgot who you and

Andy were. I pray I never forget y'all again. I love you so much, Eva."

"I love you too, Andre," Eva said, closing in on him.

They leaned their foreheads against each other and exchanged smiles, gazing in each other's eyes. For a split moment, they were shy and hesitant to approach like on their wedding day.

But after being distant for over a year in their house, they surrendered to love and shared a slow, gentle kiss, their fears and hard feelings, overcome by compassion. Everything good, warm, and pleasant Eva had felt for Andre in the past all came pouring back to her in an instant, flowing through her heart like an oasis in a desert.

As their lips touched, she opened her eyes and saw Skye stroll in on them from her peripheral vision. Embarrassed, she gasped and leaped from Andre's lap, turning her attention to him.

"Oops, sorry. I guess I should've knocked." Skye held out his hands and shrugged.

Eva swiped moisture beneath her eyes and gave a wry smile. "That would've been polite of you, but since the door was open, I don't blame you for coming straight in. What is it, Skye?"

"It's my payday. Every two weeks, remember?" Skye flexed his brows and gave a dopey grin that showed his chipped front tooth.

"Oh, sorry." Eva chuckled, took her checkbook out of

her purse on the dresser, and wrote Skye a check for his weekly wages. She ripped the check strip off and handed it to him. "Here, I forgot again."

"Yeah," Skye joked," I can see why." He swung a teasing glance from Andre to her.

Eva giggled and blushed, while Andre shyly smiled and looked away, rubbing his nose with his forefinger.

"Well, thanks for the check," Skye said, holding and flapping the paycheck between his thumbs and index fingers. "*Ciao.* Good night, lovebirds." He hunched his thin shoulders and snickered, walking out of their room.

Eva put her checkbook in her clutch wallet and clipped it, standing in front of Andre. "Um, well, I guess I'll go tend to Andy." She backed away from her husband as if it pained her to leave him, bumping into the chest at the end of the bed.

"Okay," Andre said and chuckled. He watched her and gave another smile.

Eva walked out of the bedroom and entered back in Andrew's room. The little boy whined from his nap and squirmed under his blanket as she reached his white crib. "Hey, baby. Mommy's home. You feel all right?" She lifted him in her arms and felt his forehead with the back of her hand.

Andrew whined and leaned his head against her.

He was still running a fever.

Eva frowned. "Uh-oh. You're burning up."

Andrew moaned and rubbed his left eye with his small fist.

"Mrs. Flowers! Are you still here?" Eva called.

"Coming, honey girl!"

Eva listened as Mrs. Flowers came upstairs and into Andrew's bedroom. "Has he had medicine today?" She rubbed and patted her son's back.

"Mm-hmm, around eleven," Mrs. Flowers answered. "About an hour after lunch, Andre rocked him in the recliner, and he's been asleep for a good while until you came home."

"Hmm, that was four hours ago." Eva looked at Andrew. "Come on, honey. Let me get you more medicine." She took Mookie from the crib, gave the stuffed monkey to her son, and toted him out of his room to the bathroom. She grabbed a bottle of Children's Tylenol from the medicine cabinet.

Eva put the lid of the toilet down, sat on the top with Andrew on her lap, and poured an amount of medicine into the plastic cup. "Here you go, Andy. Maybe more medicine will help bring your fever down." She put the cup to her son's mouth and helped him drink. Luckily, Andrew liked the taste of the medicine and swallowed it like juice.

Eva smiled and placed the cup on the sink counter.

"Well, I'm going home now," Mrs. Flowers said and waved.

Eva rocked Andrew. "Okay. Thanks for babysitting."

"You're welcome, honey girl." Mrs. Flowers smiled at the little boy in Eva's arms. "Bye, Andy. Hopefully, you feel better tomorrow."

"I'm sure he will." Eva put a hand on Andrew's chin and opened his mouth, peeking inside. "His lower second molars are almost in, especially the right one."

Mrs. Flowers hummed and waved a rejoicing hand. "Hallelujah! Little Andy's growing up!"

"He sure is." Eva chuckled at the old woman's carrying-on and grinned.

"Well, I'll see y'all later, but let me know if you need anything," Mrs. Flowers said. "I'm a knock or phone call away."

"Okay, thanks," Eva said.

Mrs. Flowers tapped on the doorframe and waddled down the hallway, saying goodbye to Andre.

"Bye, Mrs. Flowers!" Andre replied from the master bedroom.

Eva stood and adjusted Andrew on her hip. "Come on, baby. Let's get you some chicken noodle soup." She ambled out of the bathroom and trotted downstairs to the kitchen. After Andrew was fed, changed into his PJs, and put to bed, Eva and Andre ate leftover lasagna for dinner in the dining room and talked about their day. Andre told about his close accident on himself in the morning. Eva sighed and placed her fork on her plate, but didn't bother hounding him too much about it.

When he finished, she discussed her hectic shift in the daycare. A new boy named Rodney had colored the walls with crayons and yanked a handful of his brown hair off his head. As she shared the hilarious story about her workday, Andre snorted a laugh, and she couldn't resist laughing too. But the funny atmosphere changed when she talked about Caleb and what happened at the park.

Fear chilled her soul, worrying about what Caleb had in mind. Discovering she spent the months with a man who was a liar and compulsive jerk made her skin crawl. It turned out the attractive, star basketball player she secretly admired wasn't as charming as she thought.

He was a monster in disguise.

• CHAPTER 49 •

Andre

Thursday Night

Andre pulled off his San Francisco 49ers sweatshirt over his head as Eva leaned against the doorframe of the guestroom in her robe, arriving from taking a shower.

"Hey, I have room for two. Do you wanna sleep on the queen bed with me?" she said.

Andre slipped his left, birthmarked arm in a sleeve of a satin, green pajama shirt and shyly glanced at her. Heat tiptoed up his spine from her fixed look. He gulped and put his other arm in his shirt, adjusting the collar. "I'm fine in here."

"Can I join you?" Eva asked and drew nearer.

Andre wore an uneasy expression, fastening his shirt with his buttoning tool. He sighed and slumped his broad shoulders, frustrated with his low hand dexterity.

"You don't have to," he said with a half-shrug. His nerves bothered him from her unexpected presence. Spending the night in the same bed with her felt like a corny joke. With his knobby knees, flimsy legs, and limp wrists, he didn't feel too attractive.

Andre lowered his head, fidgeting with his nightshirt. Some things were still challenging for him, and he dreaded having anyone watch him struggling with simple tasks. Andre looked up with shock as Eva stepped in and closed the guestroom door.

She untied her robe and as soon as she slipped it off, his cheeks flushed, and his heartbeat raced in his chest. She was adorned in a dark gray, silk-and-lace lingerie nightgown that accentuated her smooth, olive skin and graceful figure. She hung her robe on a hook behind the door and undid her side bun to let her wavy, black hair fall down her shoulders.

Andre stared dumbfounded at her as she walked to him. He wasn't quite ready for physical relations, but he fought to look away from her.

Eva climbed onto the small bed and sat on his left side close against the plain white wall. She pulled back the blue-rose comforter and tucked herself underneath beside him.

"W-what are you doing?" Andre stuttered and blinked in disbelief. "What—"

His wife cradled his face in her hands and planted a

long, tender kiss on his lips.

Andre closed his eyes and melted in her affection, all his lingering thoughts of doubt whether she loved him vanishing away. He looked in her tearful eyes as their lips broke, mesmerized by her.

Eva mustered a smile and followed his gaze. "If you're staying in here, I am too. From now on, we're sharing the same bedroom. I love you so much, Andre. I'm gonna keep saying it until you get it through your thick head." She knocked her knuckles on a side of Andre's noggin, making him chuckle.

She looked down and dug her forefinger nail in the stitching of their blanket, contemplating. "I was furious the time I tried to take you home from the farm and bought a lot of expensive clothes I don't usually wear."

"I know," Andre said, yawning, "I found them in the closet."

Eva giggled. "Actually, *you* bought all of those, Andre."

Andre played a frown. "I did?" He blinked and thought for a moment, confused. "Oh, I forgot."

His wife sighed and tugged up the blanket from her waist to just below her breasts. "I returned back all the clothes I got from the store. I don't need them anyway. They weren't me." She tilted her head. "I missed you . . . *so* much."

Andre wore a wry grin. "I missed you too. I just didn't know it."

Eva laughed at his witty joke. "Let's get some sleep, okay?"

"Okay," Andre whispered lovingly. A corner of his mouth lifted as he flicked off the lamp on the nightstand and rested his head on his pillow.

Eva cuddled her slender, petite body closer to him and laid her head on his chest, wrapping an arm around his waist. She sighed and looked up, studying him as if disturbed by the thought, *I almost lost this man*. "It's been so long since we've been close and together, like a whole century. Hold me, Andre. Just hold me."

Andre encircled his arm around his wife, hearing the sadness in her voice. He kissed her forehead and ran his fingers through the waves of her hair. "Eva?"

"Mm-hmm," she answered drowsily, approaching sleep.

He swallowed hard. "Uh, if I can't . . . if I can't, you know, perform, will you still love me?"

Eva stirred and sat up, looking over him in the dimly lit room. "Of course, Andre. Our love goes far beyond physical intimacy."

Andre sighed with relief and then recalled how things were before. "But we had plans for another baby. What if I can't—?"

"Shh . . ." His wife placed her forefinger over his lips. "Don't worry about it. No matter what happens, I'll always love you. Now, let's take things slowly and get some rest, okay?" She smiled, laid her head back on his chest, and embraced his waist again.

"But I had this dream—"

"Andre," Eva interrupted, "please, go to sleep." She kissed his cheek.

Andre chuckled. "Okay, sorry. Sweet dreams, Eva." From her light breaths and feeling the rise and fall of her body against his, he knew she fell asleep. He held her close and sighed, thankful for the new bridge they built in their marriage and to know how much Eva loved him.

Crying wasn't easy for him, but he felt better after finally letting out his feelings. Maybe he'd never recall everything of his past life, but there were some things he would remember. He would remember how wonderful his wife looked in her pretty nightwear, the passionate kiss she'd given him, and how great it felt to hold Mrs. Eva Rose Lucas under his arm.

• CHAPTER 50 •

Eva

A Few Hours Later

Thunder crashed and ice pellets tapped the roof of their house.

Eva awoke from her sleep to Andrew crying in his bedroom. He was terrified of thunder, and his teething and fever added to it was a disastrous combination. She arose in the guestroom with a gasp, and Andre jerked out of his sleep, feeling her presence leave him.

She studied his face, seeing the alarming look of fear in his stretched wide eyes. His forehead was slightly slick with sweat.

"Andy's up. I'll be right back," Eva said. "I'm gonna go check on him. You can go back to sleep." She climbed out of bed, but her husband grasped her arm, stopping her from departure.

He rose to a sitting position. "No. I'll wait up for you

in my wheelchair." Lightning flashed and cast shadows of the dresser and blue reading chair on the white wall.

"Okay." Eva smiled and caressed his jaw. She grabbed her robe from the door, slipped it on, and tied the waist belt. "I'll be right back," she said again, trying to reassure him. She opened the door and glanced back with another smile. A flash of lightning struck, her petite silhouette gliding across the wall beside the bed as she exited the room. Booms of thunder followed her as she tiptoed down the dark hall.

Eva entered her son's bedroom and found the little boy standing in his crib, gripping the bar railing.

"Shh, calm down, baby," Eva whispered. She picked up Andrew and rubbed his back. She felt his forehead, which was still warm to the touch. "The storm will be over soon. Now you be a big boy, okay? I'm gonna get you some juice to help cool your fever."

Eva kissed her son's forehead, sat him in his crib, and placed his plush, brown monkey in his arms for comfort. "Keep Mookie with you. Mommy will be right back." In the refrigerator she filled Andrew's sippy cups with apple and grape juice, making sure he had plenty of fluids for his fever to drink. She left her son's bedroom and traveled the rest of the way to the staircase.

Outside, freezing rain pitter-pattered and whistling wind crackled the branches of the tree in the driveway.

Eva crept downstairs to the living room. She couldn't wait to go back in the safety of her husband's arms.

Darkness surrounded her like a prowling beast following her steps, and she was too afraid what or who she'd see if she flicked on the light. She groped the marble counter and realized she made it to the kitchen. *Thank God.*

Eva grabbed a sippy cup of apple juice from the fridge and turned around, bumping into someone. She gasped and dropped her son's cup on the floor.

"Hey, Eva," Caleb slurred, standing in front of her in the unlit kitchen. A burst of light flickered and revealed him dressed in black. He wore a silly grin spread across his face.

"What are you doing here?" Eva shrank back against the cool refrigerator.

"What else? I came fur you." Caleb gazed into her eyes. "You're the most . . . gorgejist woman I've ever sheen. I hadn't forgotten de feel of your lips on my sheek. I'll believing soon, but I had to she you again."

Eva took a deep, nervous breath. "Caleb, you're drunk. You need to go." She called for her husband. "Andre!"

"Why're ya so cold now?" Caleb glared at her. "We're friends, Eva. Good friends..." He held the "s" of friends longer than he should.

Eva's defenses rose. "Not anymore. I want you outta here now!"

"C'mon, don't be like dat. Gimme a kiss, Eva. Please, jest one." Caleb leaned his body close against hers and she smelt the fruit brandy from his breath. "Y'know ya want me," he whispered in her ear, running his fingers through her raven-black hair.

Her heart drummed in her chest, squirming to escape him. "No, I don't! Andre, hel—"

Caleb snatched her face in his hands and forced a harsh kiss on her.

Eva whimpered and slapped his face, and his strong hands clutched her slender neck quicker than she could blink, making her gag and cutting off her airway.

"Oh, Eva . . . why'd ya do dat? I waz tryin' be nice. If I cain't have you . . . nobody will. I'm gonna havetokillya, and den . . . your baby." Frustration eclipsed Caleb. His eyes pooled, gritting his teeth and squeezing her neck as hard as he could. "I gave my harp . . . and ya broke it to pieces."

Adrenaline pumped through Eva's body, clawing his hands for air. Her body shuddered with each second as her oxygen became shallower.

More lightning flashed, and she felt her life slip out of her. She thought about her husband Andre, the time she'd wasted, and the truth in her heart she'd known all along. She thought about her precious son Andrew, and his innocent life being stolen after she was gone. How could Caleb do such a horrible thing?

She accepted the mistake she made, but killing her wouldn't make matters better. Her mind reflected on her mother who'd flown away after they'd finally gotten on good terms. For the next Mother's Day, they made plans to eat out and go to the hair salon and spa together, but in a no-win situation, it was nothing more than a wish.

Eva stared into Caleb's fierce eyes, convinced of the fate of her demise. What can her husband or son do? Andre was paralyzed, and Andrew was cranky and too young to fight. Having the odds against her one possible outcome remained in her mind.

This was the way she would die.

• CHAPTER 51 •

Andre

"I'm coming, Eva!" Andre said, rolling down the narrow hallway in his manual wheelchair. He had messed up too often with not being there when his wife needed him, but God be his helper, he wouldn't do it again. His heart kicked and his palms sweat, panicking over Eva's muffled scream. She was in danger. He'd known it would happen. His nightmare was a warning of an event to come, and now it was happening for real.

He was the only one who could save her.

Earsplitting thunder exploded, and lightning flashed twice. Andre pushed himself through the darkness of the living room and arrived at the kitchen. Two dark forms were standing by the refrigerator. He heard Eva's dying gasps and Caleb's slurred speech.

Lightning flickered, and he witnessed his wife pressed

against the refrigerator, a tall man in black clothes strangling her to death. He widened his eyes and wanted to yell or flick on the light switch, but he figured it would've blown his cover. Besides, he didn't know if the man had a gun or other weapon. He lowered the footrests of his wheelchair and placed his hands on the leather armrests.

Andre lifted his head skyward. *God, give me strength.* He pushed himself from his wheelchair and fought the burning pain of his legs. Supported by the counter, he stood, but walking was the tricky part. He took a step and felt his legs get weak. He gripped the counter and leaned forward against it, taking a long breath. *Come on, Andre. You gotta do it.* Andre straightened his back and limped over, sneaking behind Caleb's back.

"I hatetokillya, Eva, but you're too beaudefoe," Caleb slurred.

Andre growled and tugged on the man's shirt, but Caleb pushed him on the floor and continued choking Eva.

"Let her go!" Andre demanded, struggling to get back on his feet.

Caleb smirked and released his wife a few seconds after, confident she was already dead.

Unconscious, Eva slid down the refrigerator and collapsed on the linoleum floor like a broken doll.

Andre's heart broke at the sight of his wife. *No. Please, God, no . . .*

"You're too late, Andre," Caleb slurred and laughed.

Andre roared and watched as the man in black strode toward the patio door. With every fiber of his being, he pushed himself up from the floor and charged into Caleb like an angry bull at a rodeo, knocking him face down. More thunder crackled as the two men rolled and tussled in a wrestling match, each trying to win the upper hand.

Caleb dragged Andre to his feet, trapped in a standing rear choke. He grasped hold of Andre's arm, squatted, and threw him over to break free. Then he kicked Andre in his face and chest. As Andre turned over with a groan and held his side, Caleb drew a butcher knife from a wooden block on the counter. He yelled and rushed to stab Andre in his back, but somebody walloped him, and he and the knife dropped to the floor.

The vibrating sound of metal dissolved, and the light switched on in the kitchen.

Kneeling, Andre looked over his shoulder. Behind him stood an elderly woman dressed in a clear raincoat over a butterfly-print housecoat with rubber boots. Her gray hair was set in pink curlers, and she held a cast iron frying pan.

"Thank you, Mrs. Flowers," Andre said with an arm around his waist, wincing in pain.

"Any time." Mrs. Flowers raised her chin and nodded with spunk. "I saw the fool break in from next door and called 9-1-1."

"Police!" a duo of officers called and knocked.

"I'll get it." The elderly woman glanced from her skillet to Caleb. "Y'all safe now. He'll be out for a little while. This pan is the best iron skillet one can have." She nodded and added with a grin, "Fries chicken quick in it too."

Andre gave the old woman a hint of a smile.

"Let me get the front door." Mrs. Flowers left.

"Eva?" Andre dragged himself over to his wife, crawling up to her with his arm. *Please, God, let her be all right.* He sniffled and his chin quivered as unshed tears stung his eyes.

The skin color of her face drained to a faded purple and her eyelids were dark, closed. Finger marks streaked her neck from Caleb's violent hold, and he thought he'd lost her.

Andre's heart sank, repentant. He had attempted to strangle himself, and now his delicate wife lay hurt and unresponsive before him, a curse of his sin. Why had he ever tried to kill himself? He hung his head and whimpered, brushing her hair back with his hand.

Like his nightmare, Eva had gotten bitten by a snake. He looked up as a sergeant policeman and Lt. Greg McKee walked into the kitchen with Mrs. Flowers.

"Officers, there's the man . . . the one in the black." Mrs. Flowers grimaced and pointed at Caleb as he was waking from her hit, rubbing the knot forming on his head.

"All right, get up!" The sergeant cuffed Caleb with his hands behind him and pulled him up on his feet. Then he read Caleb his rights, leading him outside to the squad car.

"I'll get Andy." Mrs. Flowers walked from the kitchen and headed upstairs.

"My wife . . . please, help her," Andre said weakly.

Greg knelt at Eva and checked for signs of life as Andre fearfully watched them. He rested her head and tilted her chin to open her airway.

The lieutenant met his eyes and offered a smile. "She's breathing, but barely."

Thank, God. Andre sighed with relief.

"Keep her still. I'll call in an ambulance." Greg placed Eva in a recovery position, laying her on her side.

Andre nodded. "Thank you, sir." He leaned his head against the refrigerator and sat beside his wife, grateful to be loved and alive.

. EPILOGUE .

Three Months Later

"It was my fault," Eva said, shading the warm sun from her eyes. She peered at Mrs. Flowers in their backyard, who was pushing Andrew on his Little Tikes swing set. After testifying and Caleb was convicted, she hadn't spoken about her strangulation, but she completed her first semester and was on her way to becoming a certified interior designer.

Andre placed an armful of Sesame Street-theme gifts on the umbrella picnic table on the patio and limped over to her. By mid-March, he was walking nicely again. Yesterday he donated his wheelchairs to his co-worker Karen whose son suffered a spinal cord injury after being struck by a drunk driver.

Grandpa Ricardo had passed away, but his legacy of fresh sweet corn lived on as Andre and his hired hands continued working on the farm.

Her husband hugged her from behind. "Eva, you can't blame yourself for a man trying to force his affection on you. Maybe it was late, but you told Caleb how you felt. Honestly, I'm proud of you for speaking up as you did. It took a lot of courage, but he just couldn't take your rejection. It wasn't your fault." He kissed her cheek.

Eva loosened his arms from her waist and turned to face him. "Yes, it was—" she glanced at her wedge sandals— "if I didn't go to my class reunion, Caleb would've never seen me, and it would've never happened." She leaned her forehead against her husband's chest, fidgeting with a clear button of his orange-and-blue Hawaiian shirt. "I don't deserve your love."

Her husband raised her chin with a crooked finger. "Grandpa Ricardo once said, 'Love isn't something one should have to earn to get.' It's free."

A tiny butterfly fluttered past them.

Eva found a smile and felt her eyes get wet. She didn't know which Andre she loved better—the before or the after. She thanked God for this young man, the wisdom he had acquired from his grandpa, and having not only *who* she wanted, but also *what* she wanted in a husband.

"We can't change what already happened, or predict what's ahead. All we can do is move forward, one day at a time," Andre added.

Eva embraced him and sighed. "I know, but I'm still scared. I'm afraid he'll come back."

Using a crowbar, Caleb had easily broken into their old patio door, according to the crime investigation of their home. She glanced at the new Innotech terrace swing door a specialist installed for them back in February.

"There's no need to be. God can protect us," Andre said and wrapped his arms around her again. "Besides, he'll be in jail for a long while."

This was true.

Caleb was sentenced to fifteen years and denied parole. But Eva wasn't the only one responsible for him being behind bars. Tasha Burke and two other women also testified about Caleb's aggressive behavior and verbal abuse while they were engaged with him. Apparently, he had a record for aggravated assault and had fled from city to city to avoid trouble with the police.

He'd thought coming to his small hometown would be his safest bet. Through tears, Caleb had confessed he was raised in an abusive household and saw his father beat and control his mother many times after school. "It was the norm," he said at the trial.

After his former breakups, he had reached an all-time low. Eva was his last resort, and he was highly impressed with her beauty and changed appearance. Being rejected by an attractive woman who used to be infatuated with him caused Caleb to lose his mind.

Eva apologized to him in court as the bailiff led him away, but maybe he was reaping what he sewed for all the times he made false promises to date her in exchange for help with his homework.

Ironically, now he was the one with a crush, only his developed into an obsession. His term in the Mount Road Correctional Institute would be a miserable reflection of bad choices, which started in childhood. Eva was grateful she hadn't brought Andrew downstairs with her. Things could've been a lot worse. She prayed Caleb would find redemption through the Lord during his sentence.

As the breeze blew, Andre swayed with her in his arms and whispered in her ear, "I won't let him hurt you."

Eva looked up and squeezed his waist. She smiled. "Thanks, for looking out for me. I'm gonna put the candle in Andy's cake."

"All right, I'll get the hotdogs for the grill," Andre said.

Eva gave her husband a smooch, and he returned the gesture with his charming, lopsided grin. They cuddled and giggled. It had taken a lot of time and patience, but the spark of romance had ignited back in their marriage.

Their hardship had benefited them and bloomed a positive effect on their relationship. She was grateful for how much closer they had become. Still holding each other, they looked toward the patio door as Skye stepped outside on the brick courtyard.

He wore lime-green star sunglasses and a party hat with sparkly blue fringed foil at the top cocked on his head. Skye blew a party horn. "Happy Birthday, Andy!" He played a German oom-pah song on the iPod clipped to his denim shorts and performed the Chicken Dance.

Eva and Andre laughed as Skye made chicken beaks with his hands, flapped his bent elbows, shook his hips, and clapped to the polka, accordion music.

Eva chuckled. "Skye, you're too funny."

"Hey," Skye said and shrugged, turning off his iPod. "What can I say? I love birthdays." He removed his geeky sunglasses and hung them on the collar of his gray polo T-shirt.

"Well, I guess you wouldn't mind helping me with the grill," Andre said and winked at Eva.

A flush crept in Skye's face. "The grill?"

"That's right." Andre studied Skye's nervous expression. "Don't worry. I'm handling the cooking myself. You can clean the grill when I'm finished."

Skye grinned. "Okay. Sweet!"

Andre slid back the patio door and walked into the house as Eva's mother came outside.

"Is the party still on, or am I too late?" Her mom held a blue gift-wrapped present.

Eva took the gift from her mother and hugged her. "Hi, Mom. It's just beginning."

She added her mom's present with Andy's other gifts. They squinted out at the backyard surrounded by a white picket fence. Mrs. Flowers was walking Andrew over by the hand across the grassy lawn to the umbrella table.

Her mother swatted at a buzzing bee and marveled at her grandson. "You know, I can't believe he's three. I still remember when you sent me the picture of him after he first learned to roll over."

"Me too." Eva beamed at her mom. "Time flies fast, doesn't it?" She stuck a number three candle in the Cookie Monster cake displayed on the picnic table. It was a chocolate cake made with blue fondant coating and fluffy blue frosting for the fur. The cake decorator added chocolate chip cookies in the blue monster's mouth for a special finishing touch.

Eva lit the candle with a lighter.

"Okay, everyone! It's time to sing 'Happy Birthday' to Andy," she announced.

As everybody gathered around, Andre walked through the patio door with two packs of ballpark hotdogs. He placed them on the steel counter of the barbecue grill and snuck a spot in the group beside Eva, singing with the others. After the song ended, everyone clapped for the three-year-old guest of honor.

Eva stood Andrew on the bench and looked at him in playful wonder, pointing. "Can you blow out the candle, Andy? Go ahead, blow it out."

Andrew puffed his cheeks and blew, but the flame wavered and straightened.

Some giggled.

"Try again, honey. Come on, you can do it," Eva said with a smile.

Andrew inhaled deeply and blew again. A wisp of smoke vanished in the light wind. Everyone cheered and clapped for him again.

Eva and her husband laughed and exchanged smiles, and she knew in her heart this was the life she was meant to have. Together they had gone through stormy days, but as her mother said, the sun had shined again.

Their marriage hadn't been perfect, but there was a perfect God who had enough grace and forgiveness for their imperfections. However long He let them live, they would have, hold, and love each other for the rest of their lives.

Forever.

Acknowledgements

Firstly, I'd like to thank my Lord and Savior Jesus Christ for allowing me to write this novel and use my interest in writing to be an inspiration and encouragement to others. Publishing my own book has been a dream I've had since I was a little girl; and honestly, many times I thought I was fooling myself and it would never come true.

Secondly, I'd like to thank my first readers of my debut novel when it was originally called *With You Forever* on Inkitt who added this story to their reading lists and thought to give it a read. Getting feedback means a lot to us writers as sometimes we can feel like nobody cares about the stories we write, except ourselves.

Thirdly, I'd like to thank different members of the writing community for their pep talks and helpful tips of the craft of writing. Though I don't know y'all personally, I appreciate your encouragement from your videos and online posts.

I'd also like to give a special thanks to Regina Boger for handcrafting the anniversary keychain of my characters and sending me pictures to use for my book cover design. It brought my story much more to life, and it's a memento I can always keep as a reminder of this novel.

I'd also like to thank myself for pressing through, not giving up on this story, and working toward making it better.

Being a writer has its risks and challenges. Writing a book is a tough and sometimes daunting task that takes a lot of time and effort, but I worked hard and believed in myself to make my dream a reality. Lastly, I'd like to thank my family, and especially my mom for listening to my moments of story inspiration and being supportive of my writing endeavors.

Author's Note

It all started in March of 2016 while I was moving from Goldsboro, North Carolina. I silently looked around in my nearly empty bedroom when the story idea came to mind of a young wife whose husband gets in a terrible car accident and suffers a brain injury. I didn't have a clear picture then as to how the accident happened or what kind of brain injury the husband had.

Character names or where the story takes place were also uncertain. However, I knew I wanted it to be not a retelling, but a symbolic representation of the biblical story of Adam and Eve in the Garden of Eden. Why? Because the theme of the story was about commitment and standing against divorce through adversity, and I haven't read in the Holy Scriptures where Adam and Eve ever divorced.

I also haven't read where either of them wore a wedding ring, which let's be honest, is a Roman tradition that doesn't guarantee faithfulness in relationships. Anyway, when I first wrote this story, the original title was *With You Forever*, which was published back in October of 2019. Although a good story, the quality of my book wasn't up to standards as I wanted it to be. Therefore, I decided to redo the book with a different less common title of *Eva's Promise*. The title *With You Forever* was just too frequent among other authors' books, even though some of them rearranged the wording in different orders.

As a result, my debut novel got lost in the forest over time. But *Eva's Promise* stands out more and revolves around the main female character and concept of my story: a young wife striving to keep her wedding vows to her disabled husband. Divorce rates are steadily growing in our society, and based on magazine tabloids displayed on the checkout lanes of grocery stores, among some celebrities in Hollywood.

Among brain injury couples, these rates are also high as the tragedy can be an emotionally draining and overwhelming experience. After brain injury, a spouse or loved one can become withdrawn, or even verbally or physically violent, behaviors that never existed in him or her pre-injury.

Eva's Promise is a novel that represents the meaning of true love and how God intended marriage principles to be from the beginning. It is also a story that shows the beauty of abstinence before marriage, which is often frowned upon in our modern world. Many teenage girls and women feel like outcasts because of being inexperience, which results in many cases of unwed mothers having to take care of their children themselves. Years ago, girls and women were ashamed of having a child out of wedlock. But now, it's like most people don't make it a big deal. I mean, they even make reality TV shows promoting this unlawful act. Older women are also looked at strangely who have pursued a college education and kept to themselves, which I think is wrong. This is how our society has evolved over time.

Eva's Promise wasn't an easy project as I had to do a lot of medical research. As serious as brain injury is, I wanted to make Andre's medical diagnosis, his therapy, his paralysis, and his disabilities believable and other things, such as Eva's studies of Interior Design and Caleb's career in Real Estate.

If I were asked by someone why I wrote this story, one of the only answers I could give was because I wanted to write a novel that expresses the truth of what I've been taught by my pastor and other ministering brethren about the laws of marriage according to the Word of God, something which is often ignored, despite the common said wedding vows, "til death do us part."

I also wanted to write a different story about a woman who faces temptation but works out things with her husband instead of getting into a new relationship with another man, which is quite common among some Christian Romance novels.

As mentioned in my story, marriage is an institution designed by God, and so often people forget that they've made vows not only to the person whom they married but also in the eyes of God too. He holds us accountable for the words we utter, including during marriage vows. For this reason and others, it's imperative that one be *extra* careful as Francine said in my story before they say those two little words, "I do."

Some people go into marriage for the wrong reasons, and then they regret who or what they married after its already been done. Love has been abused, misinterpreted through the media, and camouflaged as sex, money, or wealth for years. We see it every day, but true love has nothing to do with these things. True love comes from God, at least to me it does. Have you ever met someone having everything materialistic they could ever want, but they're still dissatisfied? It's because there is a void only God can fill.

For members at my church attendance (First Church of our Lord Jesus Christ) interested in marrying, my pastor (Pastor Gino Jennings) and ministering brethren often emphasize the importance of making sure whomever he or she is interested in that they're the *who* and the *what,* and especially to the women. I'm so glad that I'm under a wise leader who teaches not only about God's love and Jesus dying on the cross but also how to survive in this crazy, wonderful world we all live in and cope in life with different types of people and situations.

My hope is *Eva's Promise* will inform and inspire readers. Maybe the book will prevent some teenage girls from being more statistics of teen pregnancy. Or maybe it will encourage someone whose spouse or other relative has recently suffered a brain injury. I don't know, but I pray this novel blesses all those who read it and is a reminder no matter what hardship one goes through as Melanie said, "The sun will shine again."

Peace be unto you,
M. L. Bull

Monroe, North Carolina
August 09, 2021

P.S. If you're interested and want to join a true church that immensely follows God's Word in the scriptures, you can find out more about my church attendance at the website: **www.truthofgod.com** or visit the **First Church Truth of God Broadcast** on YouTube.

Discussion Questions

1. What does Andre's birthmark represent about the origin of humanity from the days of Adam & Eve?

2. What perennial violet plant does Mrs. Flowers symbolize? And what comparisons are there to her as a widow?

3. Organ donation is a difficult and painful decision for families to make of their loved ones. Did Eva make the right choice concerning her husband's organs?

4. What is the meaning of Mrs. Flowers' quote, "True love never dies"? Why can't it ever end?

5. Toxic parent relationships can affect children later in their adulthood. Why did Eva feel guilty about pursuing a career of Interior Design?

6. What does the snowman in Eva and Andre's winter photo represent? Why was she so emotional about this picture?

7. How does the appearance of the vase of white roses and the town park relate to Eva and Andre's marriage over time?

8. What is true beauty?

9. After her own experience with Eva's father, why did Melanie worry about her daughter so much?

10. How are the changes of the seasons significant to the moods of the story?

11. Why do you think Eva ordered something different when she went out to dinner with Caleb?

12. Why did Andre first dream the snake in his nightmare attacked him?

13. How did Andre's nightmare make you feel? And what do the lava and stepping stones represent?

14. If Eva had suffered a car accident and brain injury, what do you think Andre would've done?

15. How do Andre and Caleb differ as men?

16. During a wedding, the priest usually says he's joining the couple in holy matrimony. What is a holy marriage?

17. What do Andre and his brain injury and the Old Thomas family shack have in common?

18. What similarities do Andy's child development and Andre's recovery process share?

19. What significant lesson did Andre learn about love after his brain injury? What actions of Eva caused him to come to this understanding?

20. People change over time. What's ironic about Eva's love life compared to Caleb and some of her classmates?

CONTACT THE AUTHOR

Follow the newsletter & sign up to the Risen Halo Book Club monthly email list!

For new releases, free giveaways, book trailers, discounts, and other special offers and info from the author:

Visit the author's website at **www.mlbull.com &** sign up under the "Join My Book Club" page.

Or follow the publishing company: at **www.risenhalopublishing.com**

ABOUT THE AUTHOR

Michaela L. Bull aka "M.L. Bull" lives in Monroe, North Carolina, but is from Salisbury, Maryland on the Eastern shore where she was born and raised. She is the youngest of three daughters. Her passion for writing started during fifth grade in elementary school, and she has enjoyed it since then.

Presently, she writes Christian and women's fiction novels and stories based on characters who make changes in their lives through faith and determination, which she prays will create a positive influence and encourage and inspire readers to never lose hope through the adversities of life. She is also an occasional blogger who writes about former and present authors and poets of American Literature, commending writers for their talented abilities and great accomplishments in the literary world. Her writing motto is: *Touching Hearts One Story at a Time.*

Aside from writing, she likes playing piano, drawing, arts and crafts, watching classic TV shows, and creating her own book trailers for her stories.

Eva's Promise is her debut novel.

FOLLOW M.L. BULL & RISEN HALO ON SOCIAL MEDIA:

M. L. Bull:
Twitter: @mlbull_writes
YouTube: Journey of a Christian Writer series

Risen Halo Publishing:
Twitter: @halo_risen
YouTube: Risen Halo Publishing

THANK YOU FOR READING!

Please send an honest review on Amazon, Barnes & Noble, or other book retailers of my novel and let me know what you thought! If you enjoyed this story, don't forget to suggest it to your friends and family. It would be very helpful and appreciated. Thanks, and God bless!

www.ingramcontent.com/pod-product-compliance
Lightning Source LLC
Chambersburg PA
CBHW030523310726
48979CB00010B/1785/J

* 9 7 8 1 7 3 3 3 2 4 8 3 0 *